Learning to Walk Again

Other Books by S. L. Kassidy

Please Baby

Scarred Series
Scarred for Life - Book 1
New Cuts, Old Wounds – Book 2
Bandages – Book 3
First Degree Burns - Book 4

Learning to Walk Again

S.L. Kassity

Desert Palm Press

Learning to Walk Again
by S.L. Kassidy

copyright© 2018 S.L. Kassidy

ISBN (book): 9781942976844
ISBN (epub): 9781942976851
ISBN (pdf): 9781942976868

Desert Palm Press
1961 Main Street, Suite 220
Watsonville, California 95076
www.desertpalmpress.com

Editor: Kellie Doherty (http://editreviseperfect.weebly.com)
Cover Design: Jamani Hawkins-El (http://www.maddrandom.com)

Printed in the United States of America
First Edition June 2018

Dedication

This book is dedicated to my family, who supported my writing long before I thought it was worth anything, and to my friends, who helped me believe in myself and allowed themselves to be conscripted into betareading stories, whether they wanted to or not. Thank you all.

Chapter One

FOR THE FIRST TIME, Dane Wolfe found herself looking forward to Christmas. It felt like a holiday to her. In the past, it had been just another day of the week. She'd never gotten gifts, except last year when Nicole Cardell, her remarkable girlfriend, had broken the streak. Last year had also been the first time she purchased gifts. She felt the Christmas spirit this year, all light and happy.

December in general had been promising, and she kind of wanted to push it a bit, do something special to celebrate this jovial month. She'd have to run the idea by Nicole. She wasn't sure if Nicole would want to do much considering she had schoolwork to finish up and finals, but it never hurt to try.

"Hey." Crow snapped her pale fingers in front of Dane's face, pulling Dane from her thoughts.

Dane blinked and shook her head. The bustling mall came back into focus as a person hustled by, squeezing between her and Crow. Her senses were flooded with flashing, colorful lights, cinnamon and apple spice scents, shiny tinsel, wreaths, mistletoe, trees covered in shimmering baubles, and green and red colors. Carols played low as people rushed by each other, hunting for their perfect bounty. Elves and reindeer littered the place, with fake snow in windows, bait to lure people inside.

This was a first for her—serious Christmas shopping for more than one person. She had always thought she'd go through life as a loner, and she was damned glad to be wrong. Having people, having family, was an amazing thing, and she wouldn't trade it for anything.

"Sorry," Dane replied, looking to her friend. Crow was dressed for Christmas as much as the next person, adding crimsons and emerald shades to her usual black attire. Her onyx corset had red bands going through it, and a bright green belt looped through her pants. It was a bit funny to see Christmas Goth-style, but Dane loved the creativity.

Dane picked at her pants, which she was forced to wear due to

1

weather conditions. Her clothes had never been artistic or expressive, just functional. *I think I wanna change that.* She wouldn't know where to begin, but trying never hurt.

Crow studied her, squinting eyes the color of emeralds today thanks to her contacts. "What's up?"

Taking a deep breath, Dane shrugged. "I was just thinking about doing other stuff. I want to really get into the Christmas spirit." The mall definitely was there. The sounds of bells chimed, as Santas asked for charity. They had passed a 'North Pole' village populated by elves, who manned a long line of giddy children eager to see Santa and make requests.

Crow laughed. "You're feeling real good, huh?"

With a smile, Dane shoved her hands into her pockets. It was a snug fit in her right pocket, as her wallet lived there and her pants never seemed to have the same room her shorts had. "It's been a really good few months."

Despite her camping trip with Nicole's family that didn't go as planned, everything else had been good since then. She reconnected with the couple who raised her for the first eight years of her life and she was building a relationship with them and with their kids. Hopefully, they'd become family again.

"I can't call you a liar on that. So, who do you have to get?" Crow put her hands in the pockets of her tight black pants for a moment and then took them out.

"Tons of people." Well, tons to her. "Nicole, obviously. I got you already."

Crow blinked. "You got me?" She pointed to herself.

Dane gave her a sidelong glance. "Yeah. Should I not have done that?"

Crow got her presents when the occasion called for it. It was time for her to start doing the same. *Maybe I did this wrong, though.* It was entirely possible since friendship in general was new to her. She felt like a baby bird, pushed out of the nest, but she was determined to fly.

Crow rubbed the top of her head, mussing her short black hair. "No, it's...well, I didn't expect anything."

Dane frowned and shook her head. "I know, which is bad. Trying to be a better friend here, okay?" She held her hands up in surrender, needing to appease Crow, even though she didn't seem upset.

Crow smiled and rubbed Dane's bicep. "Okay."

Dane felt a little sting in her chest, and it took a lot of willpower to not massage the space over her heart. Crow didn't expect a Christmas gift from her? She thought she had gotten better at this friend thing, but apparently, she was still terrible. At least she didn't ignore Crow like she used to, but she wanted Crow to not be surprised when she did regular friend things. *I need to make sure I get her a birthday gift, and I need to stop feeling proud I know when her birthday is.*

"I still have to get things for damn near everybody." Dane sighed as they dodged some people standing by the window of an electronics store, watching a Christmas show. "Have I started too late?"

Crow laughed. "Nah. Late's Christmas Eve. Don't be that guy. Ever."

Dane balked. *Who in their right mind tried to buy gifts on Christmas Eve?* Just the thought of avoiding all the people and hoping to find anything worthwhile made her stomach twist into knots. She couldn't imagine the pressure of that sort of last minute shopping. It had to be like wandering in the desert during a sand storm, hoping to find water.

"No intentions of being that guy. I made a list." Digging into her pants, Dane pulled out a sheet of folded paper. Thirteen people and too many ideas that didn't grab her in quite the right way.

Crow gawked at the list. "Wow. You're surprisingly organized when you're sober and dating a lawyer."

Dane ran her hand through her short hair as she felt a blush flare up on her cheeks. "I wasn't sure if I'd remember stuff I wanted to get once I got out, so a list made sense. I don't usually come to the mall. You do, so I figured you'd be able to help me."

Smiling, Crow patted her on the shoulder. "That's what I'm here for, if you tell me what you got me for Christmas."

Dane laughed. "You'll find out on Christmas."

Letting out a loud, dramatic breath, Crow dropped her shoulders and gave an exaggerated pout. "Well, after Christmas. I go to my folks for Christmas and don't make my way back here for a few days."

Dane nodded. *I gotta remember that.* "Well, you can take it with you. Just stop by the house before you leave. You know I'm always there."

A huge smile graced Crow's painted black lips as she nodded. "It's good you get to spend Christmas with family, Dane."

"Thanks."

"So, let's get some gifts to knock them for a loop, too." Crow clapped her hands together, a brilliant shine in her eyes.

Dane grinned. Joy boiled inside of her, making her feel like she could float off on blissful steam, matching Crow's emotions. She looked forward to this long list of things she had to get.

Her nephews were pretty easy. She got Luke a karaoke machine. It was a simple thing, something a child could operate without much help. He could perform with it, which would be more than good enough for him. Thomas got an electronic drum kit. He already had one, but it wasn't great. The sound was off, almost hollow in certain spots, and didn't work at all in other areas, just tapping plastic with a drum stick. Dane tested out the one she bought him and thought he'd get some good sound out of it. Plus, it had a feature to teach him songs.

"I want to get Nicole's parents something special. Mine, too," Dane said as she crossed her nephews off the list.

Crow arched an eyebrow while her mouth twisted up a little as they dodged more shoppers. "Your parents?"

"Well, you know, I kinda consider them my parents." A half-smile worked its way onto Dane's face as she rubbed the middle of her forehead. She had been in contact with Lynn and Henry Briarmoor for several months now and they had raised her for eight years. They cared more about her than her biological father and possibly more than her biological mother. They were happy she was in their lives again, and she felt the same. Why not consider them parents?

"I wonder about them. You know, the people who raised the goddess of rock around here. Did they put that first guitar in your hand?" Crow asked.

I wish. She'd probably have been even better had they bestowed her favorite instrument on her, as they would've been attentive about her playing. They'd have come to more of her recitals. How many instruments would she have played if they were the ones caring for her?

Dane sighed. "They had a hand in it, but Christine gets that honor. Henry heard me playing a song on my violin one day and said I really needed a guitar. When I went to my lessons, I mentioned it to my tutor and started playing. He told Christine I damn sure needed a guitar. The next day, I had one."

An elegant, ebony eyebrow arched on Crow's pale face. "Dare I even ask what the hell you were playing on your violin?"

Dane gave her friend a smirk as someone pushed through them. She looked back at the rude person for a second, but Christmas crowds seemed to be an excuse for such behavior. She ignored it. She wouldn't let someone else spoil her day for even a moment.

"Maybe one day I'll play it for you." The song on her violin would be a part of Crow's birthday gift. Crow would love it and understand how special it was.

Crow stuck her tongue out. "You're no fun. Come on, what's next? Have you gotten Terri?"

Dane blew out a breath and rolled her eyes. "Terri's too easy."

Crow's eyes went mockingly wide. "Oh, you got her a girlfriend then?"

"As an ex-god, I no longer have that power." Dane gave Crow a playful shove. Terri was a gamer through and through, so she picked her up a popular video game. She scratched her head. "I want to buy Mina some writing supplies. Apparently, she's one of the few people on Earth who doesn't store everything on her phone or on a tablet. A nice pen and journal, I guess."

Crow punched her fist into her palm. "I know just the place."

"Your job?" Dane guessed.

Crow blew a raspberry. "Not for high-end stuff and I know you want to make an impression on your princess' best friend. I know a classy place that sells what you're looking for, but it's expensive."

Dane shook her head. "Doesn't matter. I just want to make sure it's nice." She'd been saving for Christmas all year. Money wasn't a problem for once.

"Oh, it'll be nice. Who else?"

Dane glanced down at her list, zeroing in on the one name that lacked suggestions under it. "I'm not entirely sure what I want to get Clara. She's mostly interested in her son and the stuff he's doing, but I don't want to get her something that's actually for him."

Crow nodded. "My mother always liked a day away from us as a gift."

A laugh burst from Dane. "I can imagine. Other than them, I have to get Ben and Allison. I might get for Nicole's cousins, too. Maybe I should get her grandparents. They're always nice to me and try to include me. Her grandfather would probably like any football stuff and her grandmother likes to bake."

Crow looked at her with wide eyes and rubbed her forehead. Then she laughed, throwing an arm around Dane's shoulder and pulling her close. "You do have a lot of people to shop for."

"I'm lucky and I want people to know I feel that way," Dane said, grinning.

"Well, then, let's go get you some stuff to knock everyone's socks off." Crow threw her hand in the air, not caring that she almost hit someone in the face, earning looks from several people. Of course, folks tended to stare at Crow anyway. Dressing in all black tended to attracted attention, especially when one of the accessories was a black leather corset in winter.

***

Nicole sighed as she entered the house and heard the hurried padded footsteps of Haydn, their white shepherd pup. She had just enough time to put her briefcase down before the dog rubbed his head in her stomach, almost pushing her over and getting white dog fur on her long, wool coat. *Why do I bother wearing black with him around?* He hadn't realized he was a full-sized dog yet, which she knew was partially her and Danny's fault.

Nicole rubbed his head and muzzle before leaning down to give him a kiss. She drew back just in time to avoid being licked in the face. While she loved him with all her heart, she wasn't a fan of doggy kisses or slobber. "Hey, boy. You been a good young man?"

He barked, and dashed off into the kitchen, and she smiled. *I swear he speaks English.* Nicole took off her coat and followed. Danny was on her almost as quickly as Haydn, embracing her and giving her a kiss. Stress of the day melted away at the feel of Danny's soft, full lips. Haydn moved from his spot near the counter that housed his treats and danced around them, wanting attention he wouldn't get at the moment.

Nicole smiled as they pulled away to stare at each other. "Hey, baby. How was your day?"

"Good. I did some Christmas shopping. I'm almost done with dinner. Go get out of your clothes and everything. Relax, for soon we feast!" Danny grinned to the point her grey eyes sparkled, which got a laugh out of Nicole.

Nicole nodded and inhaled, getting a good smell of dinner. Her stomach rumbled as an aroma of toasted bread invaded her senses. Danny pressed her open palm to Nicole's abdomen. Nicole's cheeks burned, but Danny gave her another kiss.

Danny smiled. "I'm guessing you worked up an appetite today, huh, angel?"

Nicole nodded and went to do as suggested. It had been a long day, as it always was when class was involved. *Class.* It was almost over, and there was just one more semester to go. Her stomach bubbled as her guts tied themselves in knots. What would she do when it was all over?

She never thought she'd get this far and the idea of crossing the finish line could be mind-blowing and overwhelming if she dwelled on it.

"You're not there yet. Focus on the now. You've still got class and you're still in school. Beyond that, you have a wonderful woman downstairs cooking your dinner and willing to cuddle. Life is good," Nicole muttered to herself.

Taking a breath, Nicole changed into comfortable clothing of beige cotton leggings and one of Danny's t-shirts, feeling her anxiety slip away as the worn fibers touched her skin. She returned to the kitchen as Danny set their plates on the table. She eased into the nook and Danny sat across from her.

"You sent our boy to his room?" Nicole asked, noticing Haydn's absence.

"It's the only way to eat meatballs without him shoving his nose in everything." Danny motioned to the spaghetti and meatballs with marinara sauce in front of them. A small basket of buttered bread rested between them.

Nicole laughed. "Don't I know it!" The first time Haydn snatched a meatball from the table it had been from her plate right under her hand. She was thankful he hadn't taken her fingers with it.

"How was class?" Danny asked before shoving a forkful of spaghetti in her mouth.

With a sigh, Nicole shook her head. "I'll be so happy when this semester is over." She was tired. It was a good tired, though. It was an accomplishment and a dream almost coming true. It was hard work paying off. It was living her life for herself for once. Her mind spun, but Danny's voice brought her back to reality before she got dizzy.

"One to go. So proud of you." This simple response lifted Nicole's spirits quite a bit rather than bringing back the anxiety. Danny reached over and ran a finger over Nicole's free hand. "Glad you followed your dream, Chem."

"Thank you for pushing me, baby." Nicole took Danny's hand and let her fingers do the caressing now, stroking the outside of Danny's hand. With the other hand, Nicole sampled some of Danny's fine spaghetti. It was tricky, but worth it.

Danny held Nicole's hand firmly, which settled her into the here and now, and allowed her to enjoy their time together. "Just made a suggestion. You made it happen. You've done a great thing, and you're about to see it all the way through. That takes great strength."

Nicole felt like her face might split open as she smiled. After the spring term, she'd officially have a master's degree in chemistry. Organic chemistry to be exact. She wasn't sure what she would do after that. She planned to leave the firm, so she'd have to start looking for a new job. *Can I make it at a new job?* Her heart sped up for a moment.

Her entire life had been about following her parents, or they were heavily involved in whatever she was doing. *I can forge a new path.* She could hold herself up. Her parents had raised her to do so. They just rarely allowed it. She took a breath and decided to focus on Danny instead. They ate a little before Nicole checked in.

"How was your Christmas shopping? Your leg feel okay?" Nicole was exhausted, but she'd massage Danny's knee and leg if she needed it.

Danny's eyes shined. "It's a lot better. I wore the brace."

She had surgery on her knee not too long after their ill-fated camping trip. She still had the limp, but her leg was getting stronger. She didn't put up a fight over physical therapy anymore. She liked talking about one day taking a short hike with Nicole whenever they went camping again.

"Very good. I didn't even have to yell at you." Nicole had been proud of Danny when she elected to have the surgery. Danny seemed intent on taking the best of care of herself now.

A blush stained Danny's cheeks and she glanced away. "Not that bad," she grumbled, twisting her mouth up cutely. She shoved some food in her mouth, as if that'd cover up her bashfulness.

"Anymore." She had to get on Danny's case often early on about the knee brace. Less so after the surgery since the doctor stressed how much it would help Danny's leg heal, but still, she had to make sure Danny put it on almost every day.

"Anyway, I was thinking while I was out shopping," Danny said, changing the subject.

"Still not sure what to get everyone? I can help." Nicole had offered before, but Danny was insistent on doing her own shopping. She wasn't sure why Danny wanted to do it by herself, but she had backed off.

Danny shook her head and waved the whole idea off. "No, no, no. I want to do some other stuff for Christmas. I'm just...I dunno." She shrugged. "I feel really good and I wanna...maybe catch up on Christmas stuff? Does that make sense?" Her eyebrows knitted together as her eyes drifted to her plate, and she ate some more.

Nicole smiled. "Perfect sense."

"Anyway, I got us some tickets to a show." Danny released Nicole's hand in order to run her hand through her hair.

Nicole furrowed her eyebrows. "What's wrong? You know I love a good show and school's almost done, so I don't mind." In fact, she wanted to see more shows with Danny.

Danny looked away. "Yeah, it's not that kinda show. It's actually like a kiddie thing called *Christmas Time*. There's music and retelling of Christmas stories or something."

Nicole scratched her chin and then ate some more as she tried to think of the proper question. "Is this because you didn't go to Christmas shows as a child?"

Danny shook her head and glanced at Nicole. "No, actually, I just want to take all the kids in our lives and do something with them. I figure they might like it. Well, maybe not Allison. I mean, she's kinda old, so this might not be cool."

Nicole chuckled. "No, but she thinks you're cool, so she'll want to go." It was marvelous to her to see how Allison looked up to Danny, even though they had only known each other for a few months. For Allison, Danny seemed to be the big sister she always wanted and Danny never wanted to let her down, never wanted to let the Briarmoors down.

Danny nibbled her lower lip. "You think Lynn and Henry will let them go?"

"Oh, baby." Nicole reached across the table, taking Danny's hand in hers once more. "Lynn and Henry aren't Sharon. I'm sure they'll love that you want to spend time with Allison and Ben, and they get the day to themselves. It'll be fine."

Danny smiled, but it looked forced. There was a tension in her face and lines under her eyes. "Yeah? I got tickets for Luke and Thomas, too. Hopefully, Adam'll be cool about things because the show's at six."

"I'm sure he'll be fine, but we'll talk to him together." If anyone would give them trouble over going to a show, it would be Danny's brother. Nicole still couldn't figure out Danny's biological family. Adam didn't seem to have a problem with Danny being around his kids, but Sharon, his wife, did and he never seemed interested in arguing with Sharon. Nicole and Danny had taken Luke and Thomas plenty of places with Adam's permission. She didn't see why this should be any different.

"I got tickets for Sabrina and Eddie, too." Danny scrunched up her face.

Nicole let out a long breath as her nerves trembled at the thought.

She sat back in her seat, releasing Danny's hand. Okay, six kids and just them. Were they ready to do such a thing? Well, all the children were well behaved, and Allison wasn't even really a child. She was about to be a teenager. It shouldn't be too difficult to take five children and a preteen out on their own to a show.

"Well, we'll call everyone's parents tomorrow and let them know about the show."

Danny's face brightened. "Yeah?" It was like she hadn't expected Nicole agree.

"Yeah." Nicole took Danny's hand again and gave it a gentle squeeze. "I'm looking forward to it."

It really shouldn't be too hard. *Am I trying to convince myself?* It would explain why her belly flipped and it felt like sparks danced over her skin. It was good Danny wanted to spend time with all the children in their lives. She just hoped none of the kids decided to have a bad day.

"Was that it?" Nicole asked, turning her attention back to her food. She needed to eat more, but she needed to wait for her stomach to settle down.

"Well, no. I was out with Crow and she was talking about how she spent Christmas with her family and all. Now, I already know we're going to your grandparents' house on Christmas, which is cool, but I was wondering if you'd be up to hosting a party here, like a week before Christmas or something like that."

"Oh, baby." Nicole couldn't help cooing and she felt a warm quiver in her chest. Danny wanted to have their own family gathering for Christmas. "I'd love to."

Grey eyes blinking hard, Danny leaned forward, worry lines marring her caramel colored forehead. "You sure? I mean, this is a lot. You've got finals and papers and experiments and stuff. Now, a show and a party to plan?"

"Baby, it'll be fine." Nicole smiled. She'd do her best to make sure it was fine for her love. "When's the show?"

"The tenth."

"Okay. I should have almost everything done by then. We'll plan the party after that."

Nicole's heart fluttered when Danny grinned at her, eyes glinting like mercury. It'd be tight pulling all of this off before Christmas, but she'd do anything for Danny, especially when Danny looked so damned happy. This would be a great Christmas.

***

Dane washed the dishes while Nicole dried. Once that was done, they walked Haydn together. When the weather was nice, they liked to savor the walk, taking Haydn to the park and letting him roam. In the cold, they begged him to go. He glanced at them, tail wagging, and kept walking.

"It's like he's teasing us," Nicole said.

"More like freezing us. Come on, boy," Dane said.

Nicole giggled, grabbing Dane's hand and swinging it. Nicole had on gloves, though. Skin contact would warm Dane up. Dane laughed, too, and moved closer to Nicole. Haydn barked.

"Yes, your moms are in love. Now, can you please go?" Nicole asked. Haydn yelped and skipped, as best a big dog could skip.

"We should know better than to ask," Dane replied with a sigh, dropping her shoulders.

"He gets this from you," Nicole said, burrowing deeper into her wool coat.

"What? You're the stubborn one. Wouldn't even let me finish the dishes. You should be studying for finals."

"I'll do that when we get back in. You cooked. In a fair and just world, I'd have done the dishes and you'd have liked it."

Dane scoffed, seeing her breath in front of her. "I'm the housewife around here. I handle the chores and we all know that. Come on, boy. You have to be cold...and embarrassed. You have on a sweater for crying out loud."

Nicole gave her a little shove. "Hey, I got him that sweater. He looks dashing, just like you do."

Haydn gave them a bark and then did his business. Back home, in the beautiful warmth, they curled onto the couch. Dane turned to a movie, but Nicole was busy with schoolwork, rereading notes to study for finals. Haydn was content at their feet. Dane leaned down to scratch his head every now and then, keeping him calm, happy, and quiet. She stayed quiet, not wanting to interrupt Nicole's study time.

"Are you watching this movie again?" Nicole groaned as she closed her book. She set it on the coffee table.

"You weren't paying attention and I love it," Dane replied.

"What? The storyline doesn't even make sense," Nicole said.

"Uh, pretty sure it being a cartoon, it's allowed to not make sense." Dane stuck out her tongue.

"Promises, promises."

Dane leaned in, kissing Nicole's neck. "Yeah, promises. What do you wanna do about it?"

"Pack my bag, so Haydn doesn't eat my book."

Dane cracked up, pulling away. "Go ahead."

Nicole packed away her things while Dane hustled Haydn to the music room. He went to his pet bed, tucked in the corner out of the way of her instruments. Glancing over at her new guitar, she cut her eyes from it. She made sure there was water for him in a bowl by his bed and then climbed the stairs to a promise.

Nicole was on the bed, now only in Dane's t-shirt. It was like looking at a dream. Nicole beckoned her with a crooked finger. Dane didn't have to be told twice. They met at the lips, kissing like the action would keep them alive. Eager fingers found the hem of Nicole's shirt and off it went.

"Oh, look at that. No bra." Dane grinned, hands weighing ample breasts.

"While you will have a sleeveless tee under this tee and a bra under that," Nicole said.

"Layering, my only weakness!" Dane put the back of her hand to her forehead.

"Really? Not these?" Nicole pressed her breasts together.

Dane's mouth fell open and licked her bottom lip to prevent drooling. "Gifts from God."

"Then, stop talking and do something."

Dane chuckled, and Nicole grabbed the bottom of Dane's t-shirt to rid her of it, as well as the shirt under it and the bra. Once she was shirtless, kissing resumed and Dane crawled onto the bed. Her right hand went to Nicole's luscious breast, thumbing the plump nipple. Nicole moaned into her mouth and Dane swallowed the noise, wanting more. Nicole pressed forward, directing Dane to the pillows.

"What are you doing, angel?" Dane asked as if she didn't know while Nicole's lips drifted from her mouth to her jaw to her neck.

"I must be doing it wrong if you're asking," Nicole replied, a smile in her voice and her lips in between Dane's breasts.

Dane's response got stuck in her throat and turned to a coo as Nicole's tongue flicked her nipple and her hand kneaded the other swell. Pleasure jolted through Dane and she bucked against Nicole, needing friction. The movement earned her Nicole's teeth, grazing her nipple. Dane moaned.

"I'd like to eat you," Nicole said before she bit Dane.

Dane groaned, and her hips moved. "Please, do," she breathed. She enjoyed the nips, the drag of teeth, and bites. She loved when Nicole marked her.

"If you insist." Nicole sank her teeth in and stars danced in front of Dane's eyes.

Dane needed something to anchor herself and grabbed Nicole, pulling her close. Nicole moaned as soon as their skin touched. Dane's hand found Nicole's nipple and gave it a gentle tug. Nicole let out a little noise, urging Dane on. Dane moved enough for her mouth to reach Nicole's shoulder and she peppered the area with wet kisses, needing more soft sounds. Nicole moved back, staring Dane down.

"Let's get you out of these," Nicole said, tugging at Dane's shorts. Dane nodded. "Yes, please."

Nicole wasted no time yanking the shorts off, along with Dane's boxer briefs. Dane took the moment to sit up and come in for a new kiss. Nicole yelped against her lips while Dane went to remove Nicole's underwear. Nicole kicked them off as soon as she was able.

"Down, girl," Nicole said with a cheeky wink.

"Not when I have you right where I want you," Dane replied. Her hands went to Nicole's breasts and she sighed while Nicole's breath hitched. Few things felt as good as holding Nicole in her hands, kneading, caressing, loving her.

"No fair. I had you first." Nicole's breathing increased.

"And I have you now." She kissed Nicole's throat. "But, I'll give you a treat."

Nicole made a curious noise and then Dane fell back to the pillows. She wiggled until she was in the right position. Nicole paused until Dane stroked her thighs and then she got the idea if the devilish, clouded look in her eyes meant anything. She made her way up, settling nicely right over Dane's mouth. Dane licked and Nicole bucked, moving away.

"Come on, baby. Let me taste your secrets," Dane said, hands gripping Nicole's fabulous ass. She guided Nicole to her and Nicole cooed as soon as Dane's tongue made contact.

Dane groaned, finding herself at peace in ways she never thought possible. Nicole moved her hips, chasing exactly what Dane desired to give her. Tongue and lips kept time with Nicole, tasting precious nectar. Nicole's legs muffled Dane's ability to hear, but she could just make out Nicole's cries. Nicole's hips picked up, her hand tangled in Dane's hair. Dane pressed on.

Finally, Nicole shuddered, legs clamping around Dane's head. Dane massaged strong thighs, kissing every inch of pulsing skin. Nicole purred and sighed as she eased down Dane's body, curling up against Dane as if she was boneless. She kissed Dane as soon as she could, touching her forehead, cheeks, ear. Eventually, their lips met, but Nicole continued down.

"My turn now," Nicole said before running her tongue along Dane's throat.

"Do you worst because when you're done, I've got so many wicked ideas."

"Promises, promises."

Dane laughed. "Yeah, you said that before, and we saw what happened. You're asking for it."

Nicole smirked. "I hope so."

Dane settled in. Nicole could have her way all she wanted. Dane would have the last laugh, and Nicole would have the last orgasm.

Chapter Two

NICOLE SAT ON THE couch and Haydn rested his head in her lap. They both watched Danny pace the living room, her limp quite obvious, even with her knee brace on. Danny clutched the phone in her hand, speaking with Lynn, explaining about the Christmas show and how she wanted to take Allison and Ben. Nicole couldn't help smiling. Danny was nervous she ran her hand through her hair every few seconds. She had even worked up a light glow, sweating more than anyone should over a phone call. She might need a shower when all was said and done

"I understand if you don't want us to take them," Danny said.

"Danny, I'm not saying no," Lynn assured her through the speakerphone.

Nicole guessed Danny had it on speaker in case she wanted to jump in. Nicole didn't see a reason to do so yet. Lynn had been polite and hadn't turned Danny down, even though her slumped shoulders suggested otherwise.

Danny scratched the back of her head as she sighed in defeat. "I know it's last minute."

Lynn chuckled. "It's not, Dane. I just need to check with them. They're not on break yet, and it's a school night."

Danny frowned. "Okay." Her shoulders dropped even more.

"You said the show ends at eight, right?"

"Yeah."

"You'll feed them, right?"

Danny glanced at Nicole, who nodded. If necessary, why wouldn't they feed the kids? It was such a silly question. Lynn was probably as nervous as Danny. *Why?* Maybe she wanted things to go perfectly between her children and Danny or maybe she wasn't used to other people taking her children out.

"Of course. We're not going to starve them. We want them to have a good time," Danny replied.

Lynn laughed, sounding a little awkward. "I'll have to make sure

15

they do any homework they might need to do."

"Is it too much of a hassle?" Danny asked, a pout settling on her face.

Danny really wanted a relationship with the Briarmoors, as a whole and individually. She was always scared she might mess it up somehow, and Nicole felt for her. She knew Danny would never be able to truly accept that the Briarmoors accepted her. She'd always tread cautiously with them, fearing they'd throw her away again. Added to that, whenever she tried to do something with the children, Nicole knew she'd always be nervous about being shut down thanks to her sister-in-law.

"Dane, it's all right. Allison just came in from her writing group. Allison, Dane wants to invite you and Ben to a show. You up for it?"

"Dane?" Allison's voice was an enthused chirp. There was a shuffling sound. "A show? About what?" Allison's voice came through the phone now, low but eager.

"A Christmas show. I dunno what it is really. I mean, I think it's a retelling of Christmas stories. It's just called *Christmas Time*." Danny rubbed the end of her nose.

Allison hummed a little. "It might be nice."

Nicole kissed the top of Haydn's head and hugged him close, feeling tickled. Allison was delightfully shy, but she liked being around Danny. It was cute to see them together. They were both awkward with each other, but it was a loving awkward.

"I hope you like it. You have to get your homework done, though. Okay?" Danny rubbed the back of her neck and looked like she ate something sour.

"Yeah, I will."

"And make sure Ben gets his work done, too."

"I will."

"Good. Put your mom back on, okay?"

Another shuffling noise and then Lynn was back on the line. "She looks really happy, Dane. I'm glad you want to spend time with her and Ben."

"They're cool and I like them." A blush rushed onto Danny's cheeks. "Speaking of spending time together, Nick and I wanna do this Christmas party thing. Not on Christmas or anything like that! Like, a week before Christmas or something. Just to have our families kinda get together and meet." Danny groaned, eyes falling to the floor. She scratched her head again.

Nicole had never seen Danny so flustered before. It was downright adorable. Nicole already vowed to make sure everything went perfect during the night of the show, just so Danny felt comfortable taking Allison and Ben out like she did with Luke and Thomas. She made the same silent promise regarding their Christmas party. *Danny deserves this.*

"That sounds wonderful," Lynn said.

"Then, you'll come?" Danny looked up and her eyes sparkled. She bounced with childlike joy, like it was already Christmas morning.

"Of course. Just call when you have a solid date and we'll be there."

Danny grinned. "Okay." She let out a long breath. "I'll see you when we come to get Allison and Ben."

"I look forward to it."

"Me, too."

"Goodbye then."

"Bye." Danny let loose another long sigh as she disconnected the call. She turned to Nicole and looked like she had run a marathon. She actually had to wipe sweat from her shining forehead.

"You're okay, baby. Maybe take another breath," Nicole suggested while patting Haydn to get him to move. He looked at her, unwilling to surrender his space to Danny.

With a laugh, Danny followed Nicole's advice. Flopping down on the sofa, she curled up against Nicole, forcing Haydn to move over, even though he was on Nicole's opposite side. He whined a little, but was pacified when Danny caressed his head.

Nicole wasted no time wrapping her arms around Danny. She could feel Danny breathing heavy. This was more of an ordeal than she thought it was. Holding Danny tightly, she kissed her cheek with the hope of calming her down. Haydn even moved enough to touch Danny with his nose. Danny rubbed his muzzle and he licked her fingers.

"I didn't think she'd let us take them," Danny whispered. There was awe in her voice.

"Not everyone is like Sharon. People see you, see how good you are, and see how good you are with kids. Look, let's call my aunt next." Nicole plucked the phone from Danny's hand and dialed Katrina.

"Yes, my darling niece," Katrina greeted her.

"Hey, auntie. I was calling to find out if it would be all right for me and Danny to take Eddie and Sabrina to a Christmas show on the tenth. I know its school night and all, but the show will be over at eight," Nicole said.

"If you think you can handle both of them, feel free. I'm glad you didn't jump the gun and try to take Wayne, too."

Danny winced. "I thought he'd be too little."

Nicole waved her off. "I think we know we're not equipped to handle a cranky toddler and his older siblings. I'm sure he won't mind."

"No, I doubt he will. He'll probably be happy to watch his cartoons and have me all to himself. What time is the show?" Katrina asked.

"It's at six. If you want, we'll feed them beforehand." Nicole winked at Danny.

"I'll handle that. I'm happy you want to take them out. They'll love it. They're both doing Christmas stories in school right now, so this is right up their alley."

"Okay, then we have a date. Oh, also Danny and I want to have a Christmas party here. Not on Christmas, but close to Christmas. Do you think you'd be able to attend?"

"Probably. The only other parties I have to worry about before the family one are all work related. I can easily wiggle out of at least one of those. Eduardo lies to get out of office parties all the time."

Nicole chuckled. "What? Why?"

"He hates all of his coworkers. He'll be glad for a real excuse to not go somewhere. I'll call Kimber and let her know, too, okay?"

"Yes, thank you. See you on the tenth."

"All right." They disconnected the call, and Nicole chortled.

"No fair. You got the easy one." Danny pretended to grumble, puffing out her cheeks and curling her eyebrows up.

Nicole laughed even more. "Yes, but now we both get to do the hard one." She could only imagine how difficult it'd be to convince Adam to let them take the boys out on a school night.

"Maybe we should take a break before that phone call." Danny rubbed her palms together.

"No, let's just get it over with. I'll make the call and you can just listen if you want." Nicole knew dealing with Adam was one of Danny's least favorite things, especially when there was a chance he'd deny them. *He's not my favorite person either, but I definitely have more patience for him than she does.* Of course, he hadn't stood idly by while she was abused as he did with Danny, so it was easy to have more patience for him.

Danny shook her head. "No, we're a team. Let's make this call together and then hang out for a while. Maybe let Haydn play in the backyard for a couple of minutes." Haydn picked his head up at the mention of his name, and Danny cupped his face with both hands, making kissy noises at him.

Nicole scowled. "No, no, no. He's not going outside. It's freezing." They didn't have time to deal with a sick pup. Besides, she didn't want to explain to his vet how he got sick. They'd look like irresponsible parents, allowing their dog to play outside when the degrees hovered in the teens.

Danny had the nerve to smile at her. "He can wear his sweater."

"No. It's too cold," Nicole said.

Danny snorted. She was serious about letting Haydn out and Nicole was serious about him staying inside. There was no reason to risk Haydn catching a cold to play outside when he could easily play in the house. Danny seemed to believe Haydn should get time outside every day, no matter the circumstances. They'd have to talk about that later.

"Hey, Adam. How are you?" Nicole made sure to sound bright and polite.

"I'm fine. How are you?" Adam sounded quite pleasant himself. *Of course, that doesn't mean this won't be hard.*

"I'm fine, as well. We have tickets for a Christmas show on the tenth and were hoping you'd let us take the boys," Nicole said.

"It's from six to eight," Danny added.

Adam made a humming noise. "Six to eight? Isn't that a Thursday?"

"They were the only tickets left," Danny said. Yesterday, she admitted to not thinking the whole thing through when she bought the tickets because they were the only ones left. "That's a school night, Dane. I don't want them out late," Adam said.

"They'll be back by nine," Nicole replied. They would drop Luke and Thomas off first.

"They're usually in bed by nine."

Danny scowled and glared hard enough to burn a hole through the phone. "Okay, so this one day they'll be in bed by 9:30." Her voice was clipped. It was a good thing her brother couldn't see her expression, or he'd probably deny them taking the boys ever again.

"That's late," Adam said.

"That's a thirty-minute difference!" Danny huffed, slapping her hands against her legs.

Nicole put her hand on Danny's thigh to help calm her down. Danny growled and pulled at her hair. Nicole turned her attention back to the phone.

"Adam, I understand your concern and we respect that the boys have a bedtime, but the tickets have already been purchased and we were looking forward to seeing the show with Luke and Thomas. The show is supposed to be good." Nicole had no idea how the show was supposed to be, but figured if it sold out then it had to be something.

"That may be, but they still have a bedtime."

Nicole took a deep breath. She'd have to break out the big guns. "I understand that, but Danny's looking forward to going with them. This is her first Christmas show, and she wants to share that experience with the boys. I'm sure they'll be disappointed when they find out Danny went to her first Christmas show with other kids and they got left out."

"You are evil," Danny mouthed to her and Nicole smiled.

Adam grunted. "You'd tell them they missed it?"

"I wouldn't, but I know my little cousins would tell them all about it when they saw each other, and they see each other every now and then. Maybe at the Christmas party Danny and I are having. I mean, I'm sure you wouldn't keep the boys away from two Christmas events with their aunt." Nicole hated doing this, but she wasn't in the mood for Adam's cowardice. He'd either have to put his foot down and say the boys couldn't go or he'd have to handle the boys knowing he stood in their way of sharing a moment with Danny.

Adam growled. "You're trying to force my hand."

"I'm not forcing anything. We want to take the boys out. You can let us or not. But, you should be aware they'll eventually find out about the show. They'll be upset, and it won't be at us." Maybe Adam was willing to face the wrath of the boys. Sharon probably would, but Nicole wasn't sure if either of them would be able to take the pain they'd put the boys through. It was one thing to deal with upset children, but a completely different issue to deal with hurt children.

"I'll call you back about it."

"Okay. We'll let you know details about the party later." Nicole hung up. Sighing, she ran her hand over her mouth for a second.

"Wow. I don't think I've ever seen you so tough on him," Danny said.

"Yes, well, I know how much this means to you." Usually, Nicole would have to scold Danny for being cross with Adam, but sometimes a firm hand was necessary.

Danny grinned. "It does." Danny kissed her on the cheek.

***

Dane was certain she had suffered from insanity when she purchased tickets to take six kids out. In fact, she'd plead it in court if she could. Who knew it was so hard to keep track of so many kids? And why didn't she think about how they all wouldn't fit in Nicole's car? They had to borrow Terri's SUV. Thankfully, Terri was cool about it.

"Guys, keep together," Dane called, her breath visible in the winter chill, as they stood in line to get into the show. For some reason, Ben kept following the people ahead of them in the line outside of the theater.

"Make sure you have your buddy," Nicole said. The buddy system had been her idea. Dane hadn't known what the hell it was until the kids partnered up. That didn't stop Ben from moving with a family of three almost ten feet away.

"Ben, that's not us," Dane said. He turned around, made eye contact, and then stayed where the hell he was. Was he trying to get lost? Her heart felt like it had a million jagged icicles in it every time she lost sight of that kid, and it had nothing to do with the below freezing temperature. It didn't help he was basically a hat and a puffy coat in a sea of hats and coats.

Allison was kind enough to wrangle her young brother while standing close to Danny and making sure to stay buried deep in her long bubble coat. She emerged every couple of minutes to take a breath they could all see and then she'd duck back in, leaving only her green eyes and glasses visible. Blonde locks poked out of ski cap that matched her coat.

"We still have everybody?" Nicole checked around. Dane did a head count and nodded. Nicole smiled, which managed to highlight the lines under her eyes and they hadn't even seen the show yet. Feeding the crew had been as perilous as waiting in line with them.

Nicole had cleaned off Sabrina and Thomas after their early dinner, wiping their faces, coats, and mittens. Both of them managed to get ketchup everywhere, including the back of the car. The surprising thing was they hadn't eaten in the car and they hadn't handled the ketchup when they did eat. Thankfully, Nicole carried wipes with her, but she was about to run out. Chicken fingers shouldn't be so messy.

"Dane, I'm cold," Thomas said for at least the millionth time for the five minutes they had been in line.

"I know, buddy. We're almost inside," Dane replied, pulling him closer to her to share her body heat. He leaned so close he almost knocked her over. "Hey, where's your brother?" The line moved up.

Thomas shrugged. "He was just here." *Well, that doesn't help at all.*

"Luke?" Dane looked around as she handed the ticket-taker their tickets. She couldn't see Luke anywhere. "Luke?" Her heart sped up, and her chest hurt. It was impossible to breathe. *Please, don't do this! Oh, god, the last thing I need to do is lose Adam's kid.* Adam would never let her hear the end of it and she'd never forgive herself if something happened. "Luke!"

"Here!" Luke popped up at her side, adjusting his blue winter hat with both hands. It seemed hard to get right with his gloved hands.

Dane breathed a sigh of relief, but her heart still beat a mile a minute. *These kids are gonna be the death of me.* "I need you to stay with us. We're going to our seats now." She decided to hold his hand, even though he insisted he was too big for that. He didn't argue this time, taking in the crowd and probably sensing how easily he could be swallowed up by all these people and never seen again.

"My, this thing really is popular," Nicole said as they worked their way through the lobby, flooded with people, flowing with all the control of a rapid river. She had Sabrina's and Eddie's hands. Allison still had Ben and was practically glued to Dane's side as they went through a pair of wooden French doors into the audience proper. Dane made sure to hold onto Thomas and Luke.

They settled in their seats, putting the younger children in between them. Allison chose to sit by Dane, but away from the other kids.

"You think this is all right?" Nicole motioned to the five children between them. It was a lot of space in between, but probably made the most sense.

Dane studied their setup. "You think you should move one, so we don't have as many between us, but we're still next to everyone?" She'd feel more comfortable if they'd be able to lean over and reach any of the kids.

Nicole tried, but everyone was happy with where they were. Dane and Nicole didn't argue, and the lights dimmed. The crowd applauded as the first story began.

Dane tried to pay attention throughout the show, even though it seemed like every five minutes she had to get up and escort at least one child to the restroom. Several of the stories presented she didn't know, which was troubling. She thought she was rather well read.

"What the heck is with these elves? Is that guy Santa?" Dane muttered.

Allison turned to her. "No. That's the shoemaker."

Dane squinted. "The shoemaker?" What did shoes have to do with Christmas?

"Yeah, you know. The elves help him make shoes because he couldn't do it by himself."

Dane shook her head. She didn't know that one. Allison directed her attention to the elves and talked her through the basics of the tale. Allison's hands moved with each explanation and her excitement made Dane smile. Dane let Allison give her details on all the stories, even the ones she knew.

"What do you think of the music?" Allison asked.

Dane sighed. "It's okay. You like it?"

"The piano sounds good, right?"

Dane nodded. "It does."

"I'll sound that good one day, right?"

Before Dane could answer, a hiss to her right caught her attention. Ben dropped nachos all over himself. Dane sighed and brushed him off, but took him out into the lobby for light to make sure she got him totally clean. As they returned to their seats, Nicole stood, about to take Sabrina and Thomas to the bathroom for the umpteenth time.

"I never knew kids had to pee so much," Dane said. "I got it." She took the two and hoped it was her last bathroom run of the night. Of course, that wasn't the case.

***

"Oh, my god, I'm exhausted!" Nicole collapsed onto the bed, making a slight thumping noise when she impacted the mattress. It was like running a marathon with weights on her back and then having to scrub the entire house on her hands and knees. She hadn't even put on pajamas, just grabbed one of Danny's t-shirts to sleep in. The room was dark already, night holding them gently as they settled in for sleep.

Danny made a noise, which could've been words, but she was face down in her fluffy pillow already. She looked like she had fallen out of the sky. Nicole snuggled in close enough for Danny to turn her head and be nose to nose. Danny gave Nicole a tired smile.

"I can't believe that was so hard!" Danny groaned. She closed her eyes tight.

"Proving that sometimes it is quantity over quality." None of the children had been particularly horrible, but keeping up with each child's want or need was overwhelming. Keeping track of each child was nerve-wracking, and she still shook thinking about whenever they lost sight of someone. The bathroom runs alone were tiresome. Making sure each one walked away with a souvenir was murder on their wallets, too, even though they had spending money, just not enough for everything they wanted. And how hard was it for food to make it into a mouth?

"The drop offs were unbelievable. Adam and his damn bedtime. I mean, we practically had to come home to drop the boys off and go to the other side of town to drop your cousins off." Danny curled her upper lip and groaned.

Nicole stretched out, throwing an arm over Danny. "That was annoying, but it kept Adam calm, so we'll be able to see the boys for the Christmas party hopefully."

"That's true."

"Everyone else was understanding about the time. We know Adam wouldn't have been."

Danny moved some of Nicole's hair out of her face. "Which just makes him suck more."

Nicole snickered through her nose. "That he does."

Danny tried to hold in a yawn, but it escaped through her nose. "What did you think of the show?"

A lighthearted scoff came from Nicole. "I barely saw the show. I saw a lot of the bathroom and I'm beyond grateful it was mostly clean. I've seen enough kiddie Christmas shows to get the gist of it. What did you think? Allison was so shocked it was your first one." All of Allison's conversation post-show had to do with Danny not knowing many of the stories and she could not get over Danny confessing it was her first Christmas show.

Danny sighed. "I hope that doesn't make her look at her parents different."

"No, but I do wonder. I mean, Allison and Ben have had experiences. Why not you?" Over the months they had gotten to know the Briarmoors, they weren't slouches in the parenting department. Their kids went places and did things, so why not Danny?

Danny shrugged. "The world may never know."

Nicole frowned. No, they'd eventually know. Danny was afraid to ask those sorts of questions, but Nicole doubted the answers were as bad as Danny feared they were. Lynn and Henry were good people. Something had to have happened.

"Did you enjoy yourself?" With a struggle, she moved a hand to the small of Danny's back.

Danny nodded. "I liked hanging out with the kids. But, the show itself..." she trailed off.

Nicole squinted, studying Danny's face, and trying to figure out if she was disappointed. "What about the show?"

"It was really generic. I mean, the dancing was fine. But, I'd have done something different. Like, maybe a jazz version of 'Dance of the Sugar Plum Fairies.' I definitely would've done a hip-hop version of that 'Swan Lake' thing. I'd have had Santa sing the blues."

"What? You can't make Santa sing the blues!" Nicole shook her head as much as her tired neck would allow.

Danny chuckled. "Okay, maybe not, and I understand you're retelling these Christmas stories, but I'd have done it different. It sold out, so obviously kids liked it."

"It reminded me of Christmas shows I saw as a kid, but now I kind of want to see your show." The vision Danny had seemed interesting and her music would be beyond magnificent.

"I'd put on one hell of a show if I knew you'd be in the audience."

Nicole smiled. "You're too sweet. I'm glad you knew the stories, too."

Danny slid her hand to Nicole's neck and massaged it. "Yeah, not all of 'em, but enough. I might not have gotten to watch Christmas stuff when I was little, but I read a lot of things in high school."

"Ah, this is where all your trivia knowledge comes from?" Nicole had been curious about that. Danny had a wealth of knowledge for someone who acted like she almost didn't graduate high school.

Danny gave a short nod. "Yeah. The teacher who cared about me getting out of school—Mr. Preston—said art helps influence art. He knew music was my thing, but made sure I was well versed in other arts. I read the classics and poetry. He kept trying to take me to museums, but I didn't have the time. I didn't think it was that important."

Nicole nodded. "Do you think it was important now?"

"Definitely. Reading all of the poetry alone was worth it. My lyrics got better by leaps and bounds. I believe him about art influencing art. It gives you a starting point. Of course, once you have that, I don't necessarily think you need to stay on course."

Nicole chortled. "And we're back to the show. You're an art snob."

Danny laughed a little and pulled Nicole closer, enough to give her a kiss. "I had a good time with the kids, even though I'm dead on my feet."

Nicole puffed out a laugh. "You're not even on your feet."

"I'm so tired I didn't even notice. You sure you still want to have a party?"

Nicole yawned. The party would be as exhausting as this expedition. Hell, they'd have to prepare the house and then clean up after. The work ahead would probably make Cinderella weep. But, she remembered Danny's smile when they came in after dropping all the kids off. Danny looked like the heavens had blessed her. The concept of family had seeped into Danny and taken root, blooming and opening her up. How could Nicole ever deny her that, especially when that was what she wanted for her?

"We'll handle everything for the party as soon as I'm done with finals. It'll be great," Nicole promised.

Danny's fingers caressed Nicole's back, and Nicole sighed from the comforting touch. She fell asleep with thoughts of their Christmas party still lingering in her mind.

Chapter Three

PLANNING THEIR CHRISTMAS PARTY wasn't as hard as Nicole expected. It was mostly cooking, which she and Danny handled together. She also made sure everyone knew the date and stayed on their cases to RSVP. Danny found background music to play, all revolving around the holiday season, but not in an annoying way. Nicole set out board games and a deck of cards, in case the children were bored during the party and needed something to do.

The house was already decorated. Nicole didn't usually buy a tree, but got one this year for Danny. Christmas trees always seemed to suggest happy home and family to her. After all, her family always had one, and her grandparents as well. There were lots of happy memories wrapped up in Christmas trees, and Nicole hoped Danny would one day feel the same. They started off right, decorating the tree and Danny smiled the entire time.

"Do you think we made too many cookies?" Danny asked as they plated the last batch of treats. The sugar cookies smelled heavenly and wafted through the whole house.

While closing the oven, Nicole scoffed. "You know you're asking the wrong person. There's no such thing as too many cookies as far as I'm concerned." She'd definitely eat whatever was left behind.

Danny laughed. "Can't call you a liar there."

They put the rest of the snacks and drinks out on the coffee table and the table by the stairs. Thankfully, they were already dressed for the party. Nicole decided to wear a Christmas sweater for the event, knowing she wouldn't be alone, as her friends and family were bound to do the same. Danny had on a red shirt with a green sweater vest over it and black shorts. Danny claimed her outfit was just as festive as anyone's "ugly sweater." Nicole couldn't even argue her sweater wasn't ugly. It was like the designer went out of the way to knit in the singing elves to be something out of a horror movie, even making their skin an odd pale purple, but it was comfortable and sure to win her a prize at the firm's "ugly sweater" contest at their holiday party.

A knock at the door turned out to be Mina and her husband Shawn. Shawn grinned broadly as he stepped into the house right behind Mina. He was the same height as her, so she almost hid him, but his shoulders were too broad to fit behind her.

"It's been a while," Shawn said, brown eyes scanning the place as if to refresh his memory.

"Yeah, I'd say. The housewarming party was more than a while ago." Mina smirked as Shawn helped her out of her coat, revealing her own Christmas sweater covered in frolicking reindeer. Her chocolate features had a hint of red to them from the cold outside. Nicole was thankful to not have to venture out. It had to be chilly for cheeks to flush from the driveway to the door.

Nicole hugged them both, and they squeezed her tight, as if they had not seen her in years rather than days. Danny hugged Mina while Shawn got a handshake, taking their coats from him, too.

Shawn took a deep breath. His chest covered in a cheesy sweater with dancing snowmen in the middle of snowy field expanded. "It smells good in here."

"You know there has to be tons of sweets at any party thrown by Nicole," Mina said, rightly guessing the sweet smell in the air was from cookies, cakes, and brownies all decorated for the occasion.

"Hey, there'll be children here, too," Nicole said.

"Just don't fight them to the death over the last cookie," Mina replied with a teasing smile.

Nicole chortled. "I make no promises."

"I didn't expect to see you, Shawn, especially since I know you've been letting your time be consumed by your little pup," Danny said.

Shawn laughed, throwing his head back dramatically, making his thick, short dreadlocks fly, and then he smiled. If this were a commercial his teeth would've sparkled. It was this made-for-TV smile that got Mina to fall for him back in college.

"You're just mad that Night is cuter than Haydn," Shawn replied.

At the sound of his name, Haydn barked and rammed the gate keeping him in the music room. Nicole hoped he didn't try jumping it again, as he had hurt himself twice doing that already. He missed the first time and tripped the second. Danny was kind enough to free him, and he charged both Mina and Shawn, lapping up their attention.

"Who names a white shepherd 'Night'?" Nicole stuck her tongue out at Mina.

"It's called irony, like your ability to keep me as a friend," Mina replied with a smug look.

"I think you mean that the other way around," Nicole said.

Danny hung up their coats in the closet while Mina and Shawn made their way to the living room. Haydn followed them, whining a little. He expected a treat, but Nicole doubted they had any. The couple gave Haydn more attention, which was good enough for him.

Minutes later, Clara arrived with her son. Little Paulo was bundled up so tightly it took Nicole and Clara together almost a minute to unwrap him. As soon as he was free, he wrapped Nicole in a scorching hot hug then ran off to play with the dog.

"Thanks for coming, Clara." Nicole hugged her friend.

"Anytime, especially if he gets to play with other children," Clara replied. "Besides, I know you'll throw one hell of a party."

A blush ignited on her face. She went to hang up their coats while they greeted Mina and Shawn. Not too long after, more guests arrived.

Soon, the party was in full swing with soft Christmas music playing in the background. Well, it was Christmas music according to Danny, but Nicole couldn't place many of the tunes. It was a nice holiday variety, though. Snacks were eaten, and everyone mingled. The only ones missing were Luke and Thomas. Nicole hoped Adam hadn't decided to get revenge for the show.

Nicole chatted everyone up, doing her best to play the good hostess, though she didn't really have to do much since almost everyone knew each other. Terri and Crow took care of themselves as far as making their own introductions and starting their own conversations. Nicole paused when she saw her parents speaking with Lynn and Henry.

It was wrong to eavesdrop, but Nicole was curious. She eased her way over to her parents toward the sliding doors leading to the backyard while acting like she was trying to get Haydn away from the tree. Of course, Haydn was playing with her toddler cousin Wayne and not even close to disturbing the tree. Wayne lived in a house with a dog and Haydn knew to be gentle with kids, so she wasn't worried about them.

"Here, boy," Nicole said softly, knowing Haydn wouldn't respond to such a whisper while he was over-stimulated thanks to all the people.

"You actually raised Danny?" her mother asked as if it was an impossible concept to grasp. Her wide-eyed expression didn't help.

"I don't know if I'd call it that. We only had her until she was eight,"

Henry said modestly. He swallowed hard after and covered it with a sniff. For a moment, he picked at something on his blue oxford shirt, eyes focused on that. He and Lynn had come dressed almost like this was a job interview, like they needed to impress all these people in Danny's life, which Nicole thought spoke volumes. *Has Danny noticed their effort? The nervousness?*

"Why didn't you just keep her? It doesn't seem like her father wanted her in the first place. You could've gone to court," her father said.

Henry scoffed as a frown conquered his face, hardening his typically genial visage. "And lost. We're not totally without means, but that bastard has more connections in the legal system than a jacked-up computer. Plus, we didn't have a leg to stand on. She wasn't related to us at all."

Lynn backed her husband up with a slight glisten to her teal eyes. "We've experienced his power and how far it reaches. Believe me, nothing we did would've worked."

"For all of his connections, you could've found someone who hates him enough to take him to court, if only to make his life difficult for a while," her mother said. Nicole had no doubt her mother would've loved the opportunity.

Lynn shook her head. "We couldn't put Dane at risk like that."

Nicole sighed and eased away. She didn't want to hear any more of the horror and agony these people or Danny went through thanks to Danny's father being a bastard. What would Danny's father have done to her if the Briarmoors fought him for her? She couldn't even imagine, and her parents probably couldn't either, but the Briarmoors probably had nightmares over it.

***

The party was awesome, but Dane felt a twinge every time she heard a child giggle and knew it wasn't Luke or Thomas. Allison stuck close and took her mind off it a bit. This was definitely too much of a crowd for the poor kid. For the moment, they were in the music room, away from everyone. Allison breathed easy for the first time and busied herself by looking at Dane's equipment, her fingers tapping at Dane's keyboard.

The room held a bit of a smell, thanks to Haydn spending so much time in it, but Dane tried her best to keep it spring fresh in there. The windows were opened, cracked in the winter months. A plug-in air freshener helped. Now, if she could get Haydn to stop drooling, she was certain the room would smell even better.

Dane also did her best to keep order to her things, even though Haydn liked touching more than a dog should. She could only wonder what he would do if he had an opposable thumb. Allison didn't seem to mind.

"You should get a newer computer," Allison said, standing in front of her laptop on top of a speaker.

Dane shrugged. She was lucky to have that. It survived from her other life. She lost files on it, but she wasn't sure how. She didn't use it much, but Nicole had taken it in to make sure it didn't have viruses or anything. Allison moved on.

Dane watched Allison tentatively touch the few pieces of equipment she managed to collect. Allison tucked a curled, blonde lock of hair behind her ear as she inspected a guitar, hidden away in the corner. It appeared brand new, but was far from that in terms of age. Allison ran a finger along a string, but didn't linger. Dane was about that interested in the instrument.

Allison paused at the keyboard again, eyes locked on it and long fingers posed above the keys. She didn't play, instead going into the pocket of her below the knee-length, red and white plaid skirt. She pulled out her cell phone.

"This is the keyboard I was trying to talk Mom and Dad into getting." Allison held up her phone for Dane to see.

Dane blinked as soon as she saw the price. "You don't need something that top of the line yet. We just started lessons." They were barely ten lessons in. Besides, high price didn't always mean it was the best. Allison needed to learn that.

Allison gave her these sad eyes that tugged at all of Dane's heartstrings. "But, I'll get better. You said I was good for a beginner. I don't want to have to get another one when I do get better. Isn't that more of a waste?"

Dane couldn't argue that. In fact, she often found it hard to argue with Allison, which was how Dane ended up teaching her the piano in the first place. Dane had tried to get Allison to go to someone with two good hands, but Allison wouldn't hear of it. She wanted Dane to do it. Dane wasn't sure if it was to bond, because of Allison's shyness, or something else. It was nice, though.

"We'll talk to Henry and Lynn about this," Dane replied, distracted as the doorbell chimed. "Lemme get that."

Dane moved toward the door, half expecting Allison to follow her. Instead, Allison made her way over to Nicole, which made Dane smile. Dane opened the door and was tackled around the waist by her nephews.

"Merry Christmas!" They cheered in stereo.

"Merry Christmas to you guys! So glad you could make it." Dane gave them both an extra tight squeeze before turning her attention to Adam. He stood in the doorway, like he wasn't planning to stay. It didn't matter to her, but she could be polite when the situation called for it. "You can come in, you know?"

Adam nodded slowly. He stepped inside and surveyed the house as he slipped off his coat. Dane shut the door and was about to take their coats, but Adam gasped.

"What the hell are they doing here?" Adam hissed, coat back on his shoulders. He glared at Dane.

Dane arched an eyebrow to his tone and scowled. "Who are you talking about like that?" He was insulting someone who was kind enough to attend her and Nicole's first Christmas party. She didn't like him enough not to throw him out on his ass for being disrespectful.

"Them!" Adam pointed to Lynn and Henry, who thankfully looked like they were having a good conversation with Raymond and Kathleen well at the other end of the house. All four of them smiled at each other and leaned in close, so they could hear each other.

"Them who?" Dane asked because it made no sense for him to upset with any of them.

Adam growled with fire in his eyes. "Don't act stupid. You know how much pain and grief those people put Mom through."

Rearing back slightly, Dane turned her head. "Those people? Wait, pain they put Mom through?" Dane's eyes widened. She couldn't believe this bullshit. "You're the one acting stupid."

With a sharp frown, Adam shook his head. "I don't know what shit you're playing at, but I'm not letting my kids spend any time around those monsters."

Dane glared right back at him. "I don't know what the hell you're talking about, but I'm not going to stand by and let you insult anyone in this house. They're not monsters. They're angels. They were better parents to me than yours."

"That's rich coming from a juvenile delinquent!" He threw his hands out in her direction. "You never appreciated anything and always did your best to ruin things."

Dane flinched. *I ruin things?* That's what he thought of her. It shouldn't surprise her, but it did. It was like having acid thrown in her face. How dare he blame her for what his parents did? For what his siblings did to her? She was better, and he refused to see it, like he refused to understand anything about her. He gave into the lies every other Wolfe murmured about her.

Nicole rushed in, like she had a sixth sense for when Dane and Adam were getting into it. There was no way even her angel could salvage what was left of the moment. Nicole smiled as she looked between Dane and Adam. "What's going on over here?"

Adam huffed and had the nerve to glower at Nicole. "I should ask you that. What are you trying to pull? First you threaten me to let the boys go to some crappy Christmas show and now you're trying to have them around people who deliberately hurt my mother every chance they got."

"You're a liar. No one here hurt your mother," Dane said. *What the hell did Christine tell him while I was growing up with the neighbors? What did she tell everyone?*

"Of course, you'd say that because you get off on hurting Mom." Adam threw his hands up again.

Dane narrowed her gaze and her blood boiled. Really, what the hell was her life through his eyes? "Think you have that backwards. Not that you'd know a damn thing about me since you never bothered to look at me."

"Why don't you stop whining and grow up?"

"Funny, I'd say the same about you. Maybe you should tell your wife to let your balls outta her purse every now and then."

"You know what, forget this. Luke, Thomas, let's go!" Adam motioned to the door with a swift sweep his hand.

Somewhere in the middle of this exchange, Luke and Thomas had wisely escaped. They were off playing with Eddie, Sabrina, and Ben and hadn't even bothered to take off their coats. Adam's face burned bright red when he noticed the boys deeper in the house. Dane's heart sank as she heard the laughter she had missed and knew it was about to vanish, possibly forever.

"Luke, Thomas!" Adam called loudly. He yanked the door open. "We're leaving!"

Thomas groaned, bending into a slump, his arms limp and hands dangling. "Aw!"

Luke pouted. "We just got here!"

"Doesn't matter. Let's go." Adam turned to open the door.

"Can't you at least leave the boys?" Nicole asked, with a touch of imploring in her voice.

Adam sneered at her and looked at her as if she was beneath him. "No. I don't want them around people who will teach them to disrespect their grandmother."

"No one here has plans to do that," Henry spoke up, making his way to the scene. He was calm as he stared Adam down.

"Like I believe you." Adam curled his upper lip, grabbed both of his sons, and dragged them out of the door.

Dane looked out into the cold, dark winter as the night engulfed her nephews. If she tried, she could imagine it was the cruel night stealing her nephews from her. She didn't want to try. It was her brother robbing her of the only blood connection she had who didn't scorn her. A wound tore open inside of her. This might be the last time she laid eyes on the boys. *Fuck you, Adam. Fuck you so hard.*

"Danny." She felt a hand slid into hers and she could only assume it was Nicole's. The soft hand squeezed as Adam's car faded into the blackness. "Danny, it's okay."

That was patently untrue, but Dane swallowed that. It tasted bitter and seared her insides, but she appreciated Nicole's attempt to comfort her. Plus, there was still a party. Still so many people who wanted to celebrate with her. She wouldn't let Adam and his tantrum ruin the day for her. She took a deep breath and forced out a smile.

"You're right." Dane held her head up high. She wasn't sure how her voice didn't crack. "Now, something called *The Grinch* is on and I don't think I've ever seen it."

Henry laughed and clapped her on the shoulder. "Yeah, right, kid. We watched it every year."

Dane would take his word on that. She didn't remember. She had learned over the past couple of months that she had forgotten some things from her childhood. It was nice to find out she had done some things, for both her and Nicole. To understand when she was a child there were people out there who loved and cared for her. There had been people who didn't view her as an abomination. She doubted she'd ever be able to express how much that meant to her.

She went off, back to the party. Her heart still hurt, and her throat burned. There was a void now. Some of her joy was gone and the decrease was noticeable. She wanted her nephews here, having a good time, and experiencing this wonderful moment with her. *Why'd he have to do that? Why'd he have to take them away?*

About an hour after Adam's scene, the bell rang. Dane doubted it was her brother again, so she scanned the party to see if someone stepped out. Everyone seemed to be there. She caught eyes with Nicole, who shrugged. Okay, they had an uninvited guest. Dane went to see who it was and gasped.

"Christine." Her mother stood before her, cheeks paler than ever thanks to the cold, but her long, blonde hair perfect as always despite the wind. They hadn't invited her, because Dane still wasn't sure where they stood. She couldn't guess why Christine was there, even though Luke and Thomas were with her.

Luke and Thomas charged in while Dane stood there, dumbstruck. Christine offered her a small smile, which didn't help Dane find her tongue. She managed to step aside, in case Christine wanted to come in. Christine took her up on the silent offer and she shut the door.

"You brought them back," Dane said. Mentally, she patted herself on the back for being able to speak at all. *What the hell is she playing at? Why did she do this?* She hated Christine had done something that meant so much to her, and she'd never be able to let her know.

"They cried about wanting to be here for your first Christmas party," Christine replied. Her blue eyes drifted over the crowd, but settled back on Dane. A ghost of a smile played on her pale, pink lips, but her eyes glistened.

Briefly, Dane wondered who told the boys it was her first Christmas party. They probably guessed since they knew a lot of things were firsts for her. Nicole was at her side before she could say anything else and her body relaxed enough to where she felt she could speak. Hopefully, there wouldn't be any more drama.

"What time should I come back for them?" Christine inquired.

"You can stay if you'd like." Nicole, polite all the way to the end.

Christine scanned the party again, more thoroughly this time, and undoubtedly spotted Henry and Lynn. A tiny frown tensed her face. Dane wouldn't be sad to see her go, but she was curious about the lies this woman told her family and others about Lynn and Henry over the years.

Shaking her head, Christine pulled her thick fur coat tighter around her. "I don't want to spoil the party. When should I come back?"

"Well, we don't really have a stop time, but nine should be good," Nicole answered. There was no school tomorrow for parents or children to worry about.

Christine nodded and took a lingering look about the house before leaving. Dane let loose a breath as soon as the door shut. She hadn't realized how taut she was pulled until it finally let go. Nicole stared at Dane for a second, but Dane smiled.

"I'm fine. Come on. I have to let Henry spoil more of this movie for me and get you some more sugar cookies with snowman faces before they're gone," Dane said.

Dane grabbed a couple of cookies for Nicole, and they went back to watch the movie, sitting on the floor with the children. Eventually, they served dinner and got several compliments for the meal.

"You cook now, too?" Lynn asked Dane with a grin as she looked over the many dishes on display. The meal was set up like a buffet with pans of food lined up on the table. There was no way they'd be able to seat everyone at the table. There were baked chicken cutlets, fried chicken, roast beef, yellow and white rice, macaroni and cheese, biscuits, roasted potatoes, mixed vegetables, and cranberry sauce. For drinks, there was iced tea, fruit punch, cola, and, of course, eggnog.

Dane chuckled. "The one good thing I picked up at my parents' house and then perfected here."

Lynn's elegant eyebrows knitted in close. "Who cooked at your parents' house?"

"The black chef, who they assumed could watch me by virtue of being black together." Dane rolled her eyes. This would never cease to be the dumbest thing ever to her.

Lynn laughed like it was the most ridiculous thing she'd ever heard, and really it probably was. But, she looked at Dane and stopped. Her expression sobered, and her eyes widened.

"Oh, my god, you're serious," Lynn replied.

"Totally serious. Nasir wasn't as happy to have me around as you guys. He wasn't a jerk or anything, but he didn't feel it was his job to babysit me and he was right. He found out I was into music and used to put these amazing headphones on me when he needed me out of the way and turned me onto a lot of different types of music. When he let me help, he showed me how to make all these different dishes. It was okay, but he wasn't you guys." The day he quit, he cited the way Russell treated her as one of the many reasons he'd never return to the house and hoped something of biblical proportions happened to the Wolfes.

Lynn nodded like she understood, but Dane doubted it. Few people would ever understand what it was like being in that house, having only

Nasir to depend on and him not being the true caregiver she needed, wondering why the Briarmoors didn't want her anymore. For so long, she'd been certain something was wrong with her.

Lynn put a hand on her shoulder and at first Dane thought it was to show support, but Lynn led her away. They ended up by the glass doors of the backyard, away from the din of the party. Lynn held her hand for a second, tracing each finger with her thumb. Dane held in a relaxed sigh, thinking that might be weird.

"You always had long fingers," Lynn said.

"You guys called 'em spider fingers," Dane replied. She never really understood what that meant and for a time, forgot they said it, but whenever she met someone with long fingers, she'd tell them the same thing.

Lynn snickered. "This is an awesome party." There was a little awe in her voice.

"Thanks. Had a lot of help." Dane couldn't help glancing at Nicole, who was making a plate for Thomas as he bounced next to her. Thomas looked dangerously close to knocking the plate out of her hands. "Maybe I should go help her with the kids and then we can talk."

Lynn smiled. "I'd like to talk."

Dane nodded, but went to help Nicole. Her stomach flipped at the notion of talking with Lynn and she liked to pretend she didn't know why. She talked to Lynn all the time. But, this time would be different. They hadn't seriously spoken since reuniting. They'd mostly tried to get to know each other again, relearn each other, and enjoy their time together. *Not gonna mess that up.*

Dane shook her thoughts away as Nicole beamed when she arrived at the table. She smiled back and started making a plate for Luke and then Ben came out of nowhere, wanting her help as well. She ruffled Ben's hair, earning a huge grin and giggle from him. The fact that he and Allison seemed to enjoy her attention made her heart flutter each time they smiled at her.

"Is this gonna be as good as the cookies you made?" Ben asked, eyeing the pile of food on his plate. His mouth dropped open, and it wouldn't have been a surprise if he drooled.

Dane chuckled. "Well, me and Nick made everything, so I hope it is."

"Nick is a great cook. They make good stuff," Luke assured Ben.

Dane smirked. "Thanks for the vote of confidence."

Luke nodded. Ben looked up at her and then turned his attention to Luke. For a second, he frowned, and Dane feared something might've happened that she didn't get.

"You're lucky you get to spend so much time with Dane," Ben said with a dreamy sigh.

Luke grinned. "I know. Dane and Nick are the best. We're always happy to hang out with them. Maybe you'll get to hang out more and we can all hang out together."

"I bet we will," Ben stated with confidence.

Dane held in a joyous grin as she prepared their plates. *They really like us.* Carefully, she handed them their plates and watched them trot over to Eddie. They all seemed to be getting along. Terri came, slapping her on the back.

"You throw a good party. It's good to see me and Crow aren't your only friends, too. I mean, I worry," Terri teased as she pulled Dane close, into a tight side hug. It was great that she wasn't dressed in one of the so-called ugly Christmas sweaters. She had on jeans and a regular, button-down shirt, so Dane felt like she was dressed all right in her usual clothes.

Dane rolled her eyes and allowed Terri to lead her off somewhere. "Did you eat already?"

Terri scoffed, moving her short blonde hair from her face. "Twice. You're a surprisingly good cook."

Dane arched an eyebrow. "Is that supposed to be a compliment?"

Terri tilted her head in Nicole's direction. "You want me to just give all the credit to your hot girlfriend? I can easily do that."

"What have I told you about checking out my girlfriend?"

"Anyway. I'm gonna grab some cookies before the kids get back to them. Although, I think I've had more than all the kids combined."

Dane didn't doubt that. Terri could eat. But, she was tall and physical, so it made sense. Terri pushed her a little, wanting her to go with her to get treats. She glanced over at Lynn, who was eating. Her throat tightened and her stomach locked up. She decided to go off with Terri. Crow came out of nowhere and made herself at home with them. It was nice her two friends got along. Sure, not to the level of Mina and Clara, but it was still awesome.

Chapter Four

NICOLE SMILED AS SHE watched Danny walk off with her friends. The children were entranced with Haydn, who ate up the attention, rubbing his head against them and licking them. He wasn't rough with them, more protective. He seemed to realize with the children, he could hurt them if he wasn't careful, unlike when he charged Nicole and Danny. Nicole made her way over to Henry, who was in a corner watching it all.

"How are you doing?" Nicole asked.

"I'm enjoying myself. Watching her. Listening to the kids tell me about it being her first Christmas party. I wish we'd had just one Christmas with her," Henry replied, shaking his head. Lines appeared under his eyes, and he seemed quite stricken.

Nicole blinked. "No Christmases? She said she never had a birthday party either, but you guys seem like good parents. I mean, whenever we talk to Allison and Ben, they've had all these incredible experiences and they're well mannered, intelligent, and sweet. Why didn't you do that with Danny?"

A half smile settled on his face. "We do things with them that we wanted to do with her. We didn't get her on Christmases, and we didn't know when her birthday was considering her mother didn't socialize with us much. By the time she was able to tell us when it was, we only had her a few more years and her mother..." His face twisted into a snarl and a fire shot up in his eyes for a second.

Nicole scrunched her face up. "Her mother?"

Henry gritted his teeth for a moment, like he held back a flood of insults he wished to heap upon Christine. His eyes glimmered. "I don't understand that woman. I never have, never will. She gave us this amazing little bundle of pure joy, this perfect little being, and then she took her from us and ruined her." He sniffed, balling his hands into tight fists.

Nicole watched Danny joking around with her friends. "Not ruined. Delayed maybe." Danny was too good to be ruined, even back when she was filled with pain and scarred by life.

He looked at Danny, too, his eyes misty and haunted. "Yeah, delayed. I'm just happy she didn't kill herself along the way."

Nicole nodded, pained to know that could've been a possible outcome. "That makes two of us, but why do you say her mother took her from you? I mean, you guys admitted you brought her back to her parents because she needed them."

"She did. That was probably our fault."

Nicole inhaled. *They feel guilty over what happened. They're not as horrible as they seem to think they are.* Well, she had to tell herself that to hold onto Danny's hope. "You're going to talk to her about that, right?"

He glanced at Lynn. "We really should. Maybe today. She'll be more understanding, knowing there are people out there who care."

"I think that's good." Danny needed to understand why the people she saw as her parents hadn't done as much for her as they did their biological children and what had gone wrong.

Henry and Lynn hadn't spoken much about when Danny was with them or what her parents might've done to interfere with the relationship. It was probably painful for them, like it was for Danny. They needed to start somewhere, though. Sometime.

"You won't lose her, you know," Nicole said.

Henry took a breath and scratched his forehead. "We can only hope. You know, having her until she was eight was like having a daughter. We raised Allison and Ben to know they had, essentially, a sister out there. They've always been fascinated with the idea of her, Allison especially. The idea of a sister meant somewhere she had a built-in friend, someone who'd accept her for who she was and wouldn't think she was weird or awkward. Ben loved hearing about how adventurous Dane was, even though we couldn't really take her anywhere. Now, knowing her, I don't want to risk them losing that. I don't think any of us would be able to take it."

Nicole glanced at Danny again. She was still with her friends, but the kids had made their way over to them. She wasn't sure what was going on, but it definitely looked like chaos with a bunch of jumping bodies, tugging three adults. It was a little amusing to see Terri and Crow yanked around, too. They all laughed, and Terri lost some cookies in the struggle.

"I think she needs it. She needs to know what happened. She's happy to have you guys. You're her family. She won't give up on you so easily."

With a nod, Henry put his hand to his heart. "I have fear."

Nicole gave Danny another look and locked onto her bright grey eyes. "Don't." She strolled away, going to 'save' Danny from all the children.

***

The party began to wind down, causing a pout to settle on Dane's face. She was sad to see everyone go. Yes, she'd see them again soon. Many of them on Christmas day but she had such a good time with everyone. The last people there were her nephews and the Briarmoors. She felt like Henry and Lynn had stuck around for her, which was proved right as they beckoned her into the library while Nicole watched something on television with the kids.

Dane swallowed as she tried to figure out where to stand in the library while Henry and Lynn stood by the door. They didn't shut it, which helped Dane breathe easy. She leaned on the desk and folded her arms across her chest. But, that didn't last more than a second. She shifted, looked around, and tried to figure out what to do with herself. She looked at Henry and Lynn and froze. Their eyes were locked on her.

Dane felt her stomach flip a little and her heart quivered. "Uh, what's up, guys?"

"We wanted to talk to you a little," Henry replied, wringing his hands together. This action didn't help settle Dane.

"About before." Lynn tilted her head.

"Before?" Dane arched an eyebrow and then it hit her. *Way before.* She held up her hands. *Escape! Escape!* "No, you don't need to. I mean, I get it. You didn't return me. It's okay." She hoped Christine showing up or Adam going off didn't trigger their need to bring up the past. She didn't want to talk about it. They were fine now, possibly family. She didn't want to reopen old wounds and risk making them bleed and fester all over again. They had only just healed.

"No, it's not okay. We owe you more than 'we didn't return you.' You've gone through so much," Henry said.

"But, I'm okay," Dane replied. She was okay now, anyway, and now was what mattered to her. She had Nicole. She had good friends, a family. She had it better than lots of people. She had met those people, experienced it, and could appreciate what she had so deeply. There was no reason to go over the crap again.

"You're awesome. We wish we had more to do with it," Henry said.

Dane shook her head. "You did more than you had to. I wasn't your kid." That was fine. They didn't owe her anything. *I know that. I accept that.* Her heart didn't slow down, though.

"No, but we looked at you as if you were ours," Lynn replied. Henry wrapped his arms around Lynn and nodded.

Dane tried to hold in a wince and failed. She might've looked at them as parents, but she never really bought that they saw her as a daughter. She was passed around too much for that to be true. They both frowned.

"We didn't have a great way of showing it. I could offer you tons of excuses, but you were one of those things in life where you don't know how great it is until it's gone," Henry said.

Dane wasn't sure how she felt about that, but her stomach knotted up from the words to the point she feared she'd vomit. If this continued, she might crumble and blow away like sand in the wind. They took her for granted? They didn't realize how much they wanted her until she was never coming back? They didn't think they loved her until she was gone? Did she really want to know?

"Isn't it kinda late?" Dane wanted this torture to end before they revealed something that cut her deep and left her empty. She needed to be able to look them in their faces. She wanted them around for the rest of her life. They could pick up again tomorrow, go on like everything was fine. "I really want to move forward."

"We do, too. I think the most important thing for us is that you know we're not going anywhere this time," Lynn said, grabbing Dane's hand with both of hers. She squeezed and looked at Dane with pleading eyes. "We're not going to let you get hurt again."

"I trust you." Well, she wanted to trust them. She was learning to trust them again. She knew it'd take time. "I'm not going anywhere either. If this is all because of Adam, you don't have to worry about it. I don't know what his problem is."

"This isn't about Adam. This is about you knowing we're here and you're loved. You didn't miss out on things in your childhood because we didn't care," Henry said.

"Then why?" Dane blurted out and then slapped her hand over her mouth. "You don't have to answer that." *I don't wanna know. I don't wanna know.*

"But, we want you to understand. We saw you as a daughter. All the birthdays, Christmases, and even Easters we missed weren't because we didn't care," Lynn said.

"Then why?" Dane asked again. At least she could get what made her disposable, even to decent people. She took a deep breath. *Won't let this crush me. I'm strong.*

"For a while, we didn't know your birthday, but when we figured it out, we noticed a pattern. Every year, there was about a two-to-three-week period where we didn't see you. It seemed random, in the middle of the summer," Lynn replied.

Henry's hand flexed around Lynn. "It was like you vanished from the face of the Earth. We didn't get any calls about you or anything. Not that they ever called us regardless of who had you."

Dane leaned on the desk and had to take another deep breath, which pained her ribs. *Maybe this will crush me.* She released the breath as she turned away from the Briarmoors and ran her shaking hand through her hair. They couldn't be serious, but then again, she shouldn't be surprised. That didn't stop her whole chest from hurting. Were her ribs about to shred everything they were supposed to protect and leave her to collapse in on herself?

"She would actually keep me away from you on my birthday?" Dane inquired, her voice shaking. *Fuck you, Christine. Fuck you so hard.*

"I don't know about keep. We had always hoped she was at least doing something with you, but when we asked, you always said you didn't do anything for your birthday. We offered to throw you a party, but you didn't want one so late after your birthday," Henry replied.

"You always said it was stupid." Lynn sighed.

Henry took a breath, his mouth trembling. "We tried once. You were four, I believe, and you freaked out so badly as soon as you realized what it was. You hid in the doghouse for the whole day, crying."

Lynn nodded and tears slid down her cheeks. "We thought we traumatized you. We listened every time you said no after that."

Dane swallowed, trying her best to keep from exploding. "What about other stuff? We never even had a Christmas."

Henry looked down and shook his head. "She kept you most holidays. We got you Christmas gifts, but you opened them sometime in January. It's not the same thing and we could see it in your face. You knew you were missing out, but we tried. We tried."

Dane had to take another breath, but it did little to settle the turmoil rumbling through her body. Her stomach churned, her muscles jumped, and her lungs burned. The air felt hot, heavy, like it might destroy her, squash her like an insignificant bug under its unforgiving shoe. Her mother always managed to ruin something about her past. How low had that woman sunk back then? Who the hell robbed their child of a birthday celebration? Of Halloween and Easter egg hunts, and who the hell knew what else?

"And why we didn't go places?" Dane's voice was low, broken. She was almost scared to find out this answer. Talking to Allison and Ben, she knew they went tons of places already. Museums, concerts, amusement parks, food festivals, carnivals, and more. They had done countless activities, including hiking, going on bike trails, go-carting, and kite flying. Their parents weren't shy about taking them out, so why hadn't she gotten that treatment if they claimed they saw her as theirs?

Lynn wiped away more tears and then wrung her hands together. "We did go places when you turned about three. We felt like you comprehended the world enough and you should get to explore. You loved the Children's Science Museum. I think we went there about three times before you turned four."

"One day we took you out to the mall or something. Your mother was waiting when we got back. She looked like she had a panic attack mixed with a conniption fit. I think she was actually scared," Henry said.

"Scared of what?" Dane doubted her mother gave a damn.

"Either scared we took you or scared something happened. Either way, she made us swear we'd ask her permission before we took you anywhere else. She never gave us a means of contacting her to do so," Henry replied, shaking his head.

Frowning, Dane stared at the floor for a long moment. "Then, you never took me anywhere else?"

"Well, not never. Just much less frequently. It stopped after she threatened to call the police and have us arrested for kidnapping if we didn't ask her to take you somewhere. Again, no means of contact, so we never could," Lynn replied.

"This is why I only had one Halloween?" Dane asked in a whisper. It had been such a cool Halloween, too. She had been three years old and mini-Mozart. It touched her soul that Lynn saw the music in her even at that age. There was infinite candy to her young mind. She remembered lots of ladies calling her cute, but most of all she remembered how Lynn smiled as she led Dane on her trick-or-treating adventure. *Good thing I didn't smoke that memory away.*

"Afraid so," Lynn replied.

Looking away, Dane had to walk the room for a second or she'd put her good hand through the wall. She felt like she was coming apart at the seams, and if one string was pulled, she'd be done for, never to be put back together again. Her mother had thrown her away and then purposely made sure she didn't have a childhood. Added to that, she probably told Adam lies about Henry and Lynn. *How could Christine badmouth these people? What the hell is wrong with her?* Maybe her mother was worse than her father. At least Russell was honest about his feelings. What the hell was Christine beyond a filthy liar and a rotten fraud?

"Do you have pictures of us doing stuff?" Dane asked, sounding like she was out of breath. It felt like she was on the verge of passing out.

Henry arched an eyebrow, but he looked confused. "For proof?"

"No, for me. I have one goddamn baby picture." Dane pressed her hands to her chest. "I have no idea what I looked like as a kid beyond my own memory and that's not the most reliable witness. I'd love to see." She wanted to see the few times she was happy and loved. She wanted to see the few times in her youth when she wasn't a thing to be abused.

"Yes, we have plenty of pictures. Next time you come to the house, we'll look through photo albums," Lynn replied with a smile.

Dane's nerves calmed, but she had to take several deep breaths before she could breathe at a normal rate. She managed to smile back. "Okay."

"Okay?" the couple echoed.

"Yeah, okay. Guys, we're cool." Dane drew in another deep breath and ran her hand through her hair. They wanted her, they saw her as family, and they'd probably remain with her. This was a good talk. *So, yeah, heart, you can slow down any second now.* She felt like she walked through fire and had come out stronger.

"You don't look okay," Henry said.

Shaking her head, Dane could only imagine what she looked like. On the inside, she was jumbled, despite the fact the conversation was okay. She sighed and leaned against the desk again. She still felt like she might throw up or laugh hysterically. *People laugh at times like this, right? I'm not just being crazy, right?*

"It's not you. It's Christine. She talks all this crap about starting over and pretends that she cares about me in some way, but never tells me the many and various ways she screwed me over growing up. All the way up until this very moment, I just thought you guys didn't care when I was a kid. I didn't have a problem with it because I'm not your kid, but this is..." Dane let out a breath and threw her hands up.

"Of course, we care!" Henry stepped forward, pulling Lynn with him.

"We didn't tell you this to mess up your relationship with your mother," Lynn insisted.

Dane looked at them. "Oh, no, I know. Believe me, I know." They weren't those types of people. And there might not be a relationship with Christine to mess up now. "It's just that, there's all this stuff she didn't tell me and then she acts like we can have a real relationship." Dane shook her head. Christine was beyond full of shit. "Look, guys, we're cool. I think...I think I need to talk to Christine, though." Or maybe she needed to punch Christine. She'd find out when the woman was right in front of her.

"Are you sure?" Henry asked with worry lines still underneath his eyes. He reached out and rubbed her shoulder. Under his hand, her body relaxed and settled. Cracks inside of her healed.

Dane nodded. "Yeah. I think more than anything, I need to know why she did this crap. I mean, you took me off her hands, she didn't have to worry about me anymore, and yet." She could only make wild, meaningless hand gestures. Why had her mother stood in the way of her having a childhood, stood in the way of her happiness, stood in the way of her mattering to someone? If her mother cared about her even a little bit, she'd have left Dane with the Briarmoors and never looked back.

They nodded, but still appeared troubled. "Just know, we wanted to do things with you," Lynn said with tears still sliding from her eyes.

Dane nodded again and managed to make a controlled exit from the library. She was overwhelmed, and she wasn't even sure why. Was it the knowledge the people she saw as parents saw her as a daughter or the fact that her biological mother seemed to get off on ruining her life? Maybe both. It was all too much.

Henry and Lynn were right behind her, announcing it was time to go. This was good. They probably all needed time to process this. Allison and Ben hugged Nicole and Dane as well as bid Luke and Thomas goodbye. With the Briarmoors gone, Nicole and Dane were left waiting for Christine to come get the boys. They sat on the couch, still watching cartoons. Dane had no idea what it was about, but that was mostly due to not paying attention. She pondered confronting her mother as soon as she showed up.

Christine had a lot of nerve. What type of person ruined someone's life—her daughter no less—and then tried to act like it was all forgive and forget? Dane thought of every bad moment, muscles jumping as she recalled each agony while her so-called mother looked the other way. She wanted to tear Christine apart with her bare hands.

In the end, she decided 'tis the season to be jolly. It was such a good party, she didn't want to ruin it for Nicole or the boys by arguing with Christine. When her mother showed up, Dane helped put Luke and Thomas into their coats and got them out the door in a timely fashion. She'd call Christine tomorrow. For the moment, she wished her a Merry Christmas and sighed as soon as the door was closed.

"Honey, are you okay?" Nicole asked as soon as the door was locked.

Dane rubbed her eyes, drained of every drop of energy. "I will be. Let's clean up and go to bed."

Nicole took her hand. "Tell me what's bothering you."

Dane sighed. She should tell Nicole. They didn't keep things from each other, and she shouldn't try to protect Nicole from her crappy past anymore.

"I just found out Christine is the reason I didn't have a childhood and not in the way you think," Dane said. Nicole squinted and shook her head. "I'll tell you after we clean all of this up." She moved to clear the clutter of the party away.

***

Nicole's chest was tight. She was nervous to find out what happened between Danny and the Briarmoors. She had encouraged them to talk, thinking it'd be good for all involved. But, what if she was wrong? She had been wrong about so much with Danny, especially when it came to family. What if she had done something to get Danny hurt yet again? What time will be the last time? *I'm so tired of hurting her and of her hurting.*

Doing her best to hide her anxiety, Nicole moved around with Danny to clean up. They talked about what a success the party was. Danny wanted to try something similar when the weather got better.

"I'd really like us to have a barbecue," Danny said, glancing at the patio doors that led to the backyard.

"I think we can arrange that. The backyard is big enough," Nicole replied. It'd be fun.

Danny smiled. "Then, birthday barbecue?"

Nicole grinned back. "I think that can be arranged if that's what you really want for your birthday."

"Well, if we did it for your birthday, we'd all freeze to death," Danny said, earning a laugh from Nicole.

It was good Danny was thinking of the future, planning events and such. It helped settle Nicole's nerves a bit. She was able to focus and breathe easier when they settled in for bed. She didn't press Danny for what happened. They were side by side, staring at shadows the ceiling. The air was still, even though the wind outside whistled. It took Danny a couple of minutes, but she jumped into things on her own.

"Henry and Lynn talked to me about why my childhood was so shitty," Danny said, finger drawing light, odd patterns on Nicole's abdomen.

"What did they say?" Nicole asked. The gentle drawing on her skin helped soothe her, like a lullaby, but her heart raced over what could have happened.

Danny sighed. "Christine."

Nicole turned onto her side, staring at Danny, and wiggled close enough to be pressed against Danny. Danny's eyes remained on the ceiling, but there were lines etched in her face, shadows dancing across her features, aging her for the moment. "What do you mean?"

"It was her. She took me from them during holidays and my birthday and didn't even celebrate with me. She just didn't want me to celebrate with them or them to celebrate with me. I dunno."

"That's awful." How the hell could a mother do that? Of course, Nicole still couldn't figure out how Christine could damn near give Danny away or allow Russell to abuse her. Something was wrong with that woman.

Danny shrugged. "Not really surprised, but I am. I mean, why else wouldn't they celebrate at least a birthday with me or something? They said they tried, but I freaked out or whatever. Don't remember any of that. But, they tried and she blocked them at every corner, keeping me from them or threatening them. This seems so...I dunno...beyond or something. Like, does she hate me that much?"

Nicole kissed Danny's cheek. "I don't think she hates you. But, I'm not sure what she was doing. I don't understand the point of leaving you with them every average day, but keeping you on holidays."

Danny huffed. "To not do anything with me at that. What the hell?"

"I don't know, baby." Nicole sighed. Christine didn't make sense and probably never would. "You freaked out during a birthday party?"

"They said I hid in the doghouse. Don't remember any of that.

Makes me wonder why I'd react like that. Probably some more Christine bullshit."

Nicole took a deep breath and nuzzled Danny. "I'm sorry, love."

"Gonna talk to her about it. Maybe tomorrow or something. You'll be there?"

Nicole kissed the end of Danny's nose. "I'm always there for you."

Danny sighed and cuddled in close. "I know. I love you."

"I love you, too." Nicole breathed a sigh of relief. She hadn't messed things up for once, and Danny wanted her there when she spoke to Christine. That was good.

Knowing she wasn't to blame for anything didn't help Nicole fall asleep any faster. She watched Danny sleep, which didn't help either. How could Christine keep Danny from having a childhood? What type of mother not only didn't celebrate her child's birthday, but also prevented others from doing so?

Nothing would ever make up for that missed time. But, more importantly, would Danny ever be able to move forward? With Christine actively wreaking havoc against her until she had moved out of the house? Nicole wanted to make things better, but how?

No, no, no. She stopped herself from thinking that. Things worked best with her and Danny when she supported Danny's decisions rather than going out and trying to do something. She'd support Danny speaking with Christine and be there for her regardless of what happened, as Danny would do the same for her. Danny had done the same her. *I'll be there. I'll always be there.*

Chapter Five

NICOLE HELD DANNY'S HAND as they sat on their couch and waited for Christine. Danny had paced the whole morning before managing to call Christine. Poor dear could barely get out that she needed to talk. Christine hopped on the invitation, undoubtedly taking the need to talk in some other way than Danny intended. Nicole wondered how Christine would take it when Danny looked at her as the monster she might possibly be.

Nicole tried her best to give Christine the benefit of the doubt, to somehow convince herself there was a mother in there somewhere for Danny. Sure, she wasn't trying to push Danny to find that mother anymore, but the emotion was there. Now, she wasn't certain. *When Christine looks at Danny—looked at Danny as a child—maybe she only saw something that belonged to her. Something she didn't want, but didn't want others to have either.*

Unfortunately, since Danny wasn't some toy, Christine's selfish behavior had utterly disrupted her life. Could Christine see that? Did she care? Did it bother her? Well, they might find out soon. Nicole didn't plan on talking, but she was there for support if those answers came or failed to come.

The doorbell rang, and Danny almost jumped out of her skin, bouncing on the sofa as her eyes shot to the door, wide open along with her mouth. Haydn whined and backed up from his space at Danny's feet. Even Nicole's muscles twitched from the sound. Suddenly it was hard to breathe, like the air could strangle them. If she felt this nervous, she could only imagine how Danny felt. Tension piped through the house like the heat.

"I've got it," Nicole said, patting Danny's hand and standing.

Danny nodded, rose to her feet, and went back to pacing, limping through the living room, while Nicole answered the door. Christine smiled at her as she stepped in. Nicole didn't even have it in her to fake a smile. *How can this woman smile? How can she go on?*

Nicole turned away to shut the door while Christine shrugged out of her thick fur coat. Her flowery perfume, which usually seemed subtle, wafted and the smell of it gagged Nicole. She hung Christine's coat up, if only to escape the deadly scent.

"Dane, you wished to talk," Christine said, practically chirped, having no idea what she was in for.

Danny paused mid-step and locked eyes with Christine. Those grey eyes burned with the intensity of the flames of Hell. For the first time, Danny looked at Christine as if she hated her. There was no confusion, no mixed emotions, just pure disdain. Christine sniffed, possibly trying to keep her composure. Nicole hurried to Danny's side, in case she snapped.

"Christine, nice of you to make it," Danny said through gritted teeth. Her stance was rigid, and she leaned to put more weight on her left leg. Nicole was tempted to suggest her lover sit down, but decided against it. She'd let Danny handle the situation.

"Is this about Adam's reaction to the Briarmoors? I assure you that won't happen again," Christine replied.

Danny tilted her head and gnawed the corner of her bottom lip briefly. "Why did it happen in the first place?"

Christine glanced away and took a deep breath. It seemed like she was going to just stand there. Danny glared at her.

"Well?" Danny pushed, her voice a little louder and much harsher than before. Christine winced. "Why did Adam seem to think the Briarmoors hurt you when we both know it was the other way around?"

Gasping, Christine looked up with wide, blue eyes, like she was shocked by the accusation. "What do you mean? What did they say?" Her voice shook as she glanced around the room.

Danny waved the question off. "It doesn't matter what they said. What the hell is wrong with you? Playing at this game of wanting something from me when you've done so much shit to me. Do you realize they were my last shot at a normal life?" She threw her hand out, and her mother flinched. "Do you even grasp how messed up I was? Do you even care?"

"Of course, I care," Christine insisted. She leaned forward, like she was about to move, but she remained rooted in place.

"No, you care now!" Danny pointed at her, jabbing at the air with a tense hand. "Did you care back then? Did you care I never had a birthday party? Did you care I never got Christmas presents? Did you care about my grades? Did you care if I had a bedtime? Hell, if I had a fucking bed? Did you care if I had clothes on my back? Did you care if I ate? Did you care about anything at all about me?"

Christine nibbled her lip, like she was thinking of a lie. Danny's hand ran through her already mussed ebony hair, and she went back to pacing. Nicole let her go. The movement might help her work through the frustration.

"You never cared, did you? You tell yourself you did because you want to feel something like a human being, but you didn't care." Danny shook her head. "How could I ever think you cared?"

Christine opened her mouth, but nothing came out. She put her hand over her mouth and made a noise that almost seemed like a sob. The sound thumped through Nicole, and her nerves jumped. It felt like she might fall apart and they hadn't even started really, and she wasn't even a part of the argument. Haydn whimpered and went by the back door, focusing on the yard, before retreating to the music room. Nicole wished she could leave the room, but she couldn't abandon Danny.

"It's complicated," Christine muttered through a quivering mouth.

"Un-complicate it for me," Danny said as her face turned bright red. "Un-complicate how you pull away a child who just wanted to be loved from the people who actually fucking loved her? What the hell did you want them to do with me? Keep me in the yard like one of the fucking dogs?"

Christine took a shivering breath and looked at Danny with wet eyes, like she was about to cry. Like she deserved to cry! It made no sense at all. *This manipulative cow.* That was the only reason Nicole could figure out Christine dared to tear up. She was trying to manipulate Danny's emotions, gain sympathy, and possibly get off scot-free.

"I couldn't stand the idea that you liked them so much!" Christine blurted out. She gasped again and put her hand over her mouth once more.

Nicole's eyes went wide. Dear lord, she truly was like a spoiled brat with a toy she didn't want, but also didn't want others to have. Nicole looked at Danny, wanting to gauge her reaction. She didn't even flinch, seemingly immune to Christine's words.

Danny stared at Christine with an arched eyebrow. "Of course, I liked them! They treated me like a kid. Like a fucking person. Like I mattered. What the fuck did you ever treat me as?"

Christine whimpered and slinked back a little. "I understood you were a kid."

"The fuck you did!" Danny slapped her hands together, and the noise made Christine jump. "You fucking gave me to them and then fucking fucked up all of our shit because they tried to act like fucking parents and wanted the fucking best for me! Do you realize how fucked up that is?" Danny tapped against her temple.

"That was the problem. I complained all the time that they were trying to steal you from me, steal your affections, become your parents. They weren't your parents. I was." Christine clawed at the air, as if she was trying to tear the heavens down. "It burned me up that they could have what was denied to me, and I did horrible things, yes."

Letting loose a loud scoff, Danny stepped a little closer, eyes boring into Christine. "You were denied being my parent? You fucking really think that? You chose not to be my parent. Then, to keep screwing me over, you made that choice for them as well because you're petty as fuck."

Christine took another breath, but her chest heaved like she couldn't get enough air. "I suppose I did." Her voice was small, tearful.

Danny ceased to move mid-stride as her mouth fell all the way open. "What?"

Nicole wanted to say the same thing, but managed to keep her mouth shut. Who would've expected Christine to admit she was wrong? Was this more emotional manipulation? Was this something else that'd come back to haunt Danny? Nicole held the questions in, but she planned to say something if she thought she needed to.

Shaking her head, Christine sighed, her narrow shoulders dropping. "You're right. I have to stop acting like I haven't done anything wrong. I mean it every time I tell you I want us to have something. I wanted it back then, too, but I didn't want it at the same time. I was scared and selfish. I'd like to think I'm not that anymore."

Danny collapsed onto the couch, eyes locked onto the floor. Hopefully, she knew the sofa was there and hadn't simply buckled under the weight of the confession. Nicole sat down right next to her, and Danny grabbed her hand, holding it tight. Danny's face was flushed a deep crimson and she couldn't even look at Christine, who stared at her with shimmering eyes.

"Dane, I know I've done terrible things to you, just by virtue of not being there. It seems I've done even worse when I was there. I don't want to keep doing that." Christine pressed her hands together as if pleading with Danny to understand.

Danny put her hand to her forehead. "How can I trust that? How the hell can I ever trust you're here because you want to know me? You had a chance, and you ruined it for everyone involved, several times over. Who else besides Adam thinks the Briarmoors did something to you? The whole neighborhood? What lies did you tell to people to cover up why they had your child?" Danny shook her head, as if trying to make sense of any of this.

Nicole rubbed her finger against her chin. Danny had good questions. That'd help her keep her mouth shut. But, she hoped Christine had "good" answers. Nothing Christine said could be truly good, but something to help Danny move forward.

Christine looked away for a moment, her jaw trembling as tears slid down her cheeks. "Clearly, I've done things in the past I'm ashamed of. Surely, you understand that."

Danny glared at Christine so hard she had to take a full step back. "Are you really throwing my shitty life at me like it wasn't your fault?"

Christine put her hands up in surrender. "I didn't mean it that way. I just mean, you know what it's like to do something you regret."

Danny shot up to her feet. "I didn't know any better when I was fucking up, and I don't have a whole lifetime of fucking up someone else's life in my wake!" She threw her hand out behind her. Nicole stood next to her, tense, ready to catch Danny if she fell, in every possible way.

Sighing, Christine wiped away her tears. "No, you don't. Making you the better person out of the two of us."

Danny growled. "Don't you dare try to sweet talk me. Don't try to act sorry now that you got caught in another massive web of lies. You say you're ashamed, but that's probably only because you got caught. If I didn't know this shit, you'd have never said anything and lived life like you're totally fine."

That rang true considering what Christine continued to do. Christine seemed like she opened up to Danny that one time when she showed up with her box of keepsakes and then pressed on like everything else was fine, pressed on like she hadn't done tons of terrible things. What else had Christine not mentioned that might come to light? Nicole wondered if Christine was actually a sociopath and enjoyed messing with Danny's mind. All of this, the sorrow and remorse, was an act. Everything was an act.

Christine wrung her hands together. *Out damn spot*. But, was it right to even think of Christine as Lady MacBeth? Time would tell, if Danny allowed it.

Christine swallowed hard, her throat moving up and down for them to see. "I know what I did in the past was horrible. I cost you everything, and my actions, or inaction in some cases, started you on a hard road. I am sincere with you every single time I say I want to have something with you. I've always wanted to have something with you."

Danny scoffed, but Nicole conceded maybe Christine had always wanted something with Danny. It was that desire that led her to do despicable things. Instead of trying to have something with Danny, she had taken away others' chances to have something with Danny. It was psychotic. *Who is this woman? How does she even exist?* Nicole rubbed the bridge of her nose, trying to hold a headache off.

"I want to change all of this between us. I know it's not going to happen overnight. Well, I know that now, anyway." There was yet another deep breath and more tears slipped from Christine's eyes. She wiped her face with both hands, not even bothering to do it daintily, not caring that her makeup went from running to smeared. "I know I can't make the past right, but I want to have some kind of future with you. I know you don't need me. Hell, maybe you don't even want me, especially with Lynn Briarmoor back in your life, but I can't just give up. I've learned this since the day you were born. I can't give up." Those words should sound encouraging coming from a mother, but they had the aura of a plea from Christine. With her history, it could be seen as a threat.

Danny swallowed and stared Christine down. "Maybe you need to. It might be the right thing to do." She said that as if it was the final word. With that, she stormed out of the room as best she could.

Christine watched her go, which was probably the best thing she had ever done for Danny. Nicole sighed and leaned back on the couch. Haydn poked his head out of the music room and rushed to Nicole, nuzzling her stomach. She scratched his ear and he whimpered. Was he comforting or looking for comfort? Maybe both. Either way, Nicole was glad for it.

"Do you think...do you think that was it?" Christine's voice broke, and she sniffled. It did nothing to stop her tears.

"With you two..." Nicole shrugged.

If there ever was a deal-breaker, maybe this was it. Nicole wouldn't blame Danny if it was the end. She couldn't imagine any mother hurting a child like this. Christine was more than a piece of work. For a moment, Nicole stared at her, studied her, tried to see down to her bones, tried to figure out if she had a soul. She needed answers. What the hell made this woman this way?

Christine's behavior was beyond the fact she lost her parents at a young age, beyond the fact she'd been raised by hateful grandparents who kept her from her father's side of the family, and well beyond the fact she loved a racist beast of a man. Of course, maybe Christine's choice of spouse spoke louder about who she was than anything else. It couldn't take much for one monster to love another.

Eventually, Nicole had to ask. "Why? Why do this to her? You could've left her with them and let her have something. Why keep dangling it in front of her? Why take everything from her, all the time? Why stand by and watch her crumble? You must understand how poisonous this all is and, yet, you continue. Why?" She hugged Haydn to her, needing to cuddle someone.

Christine shook her head, wiping her tears again. "I don't know. I think I really wanted her. I mean, I love her. She's my daughter. But..." She traced a circle on her forehead with her index finger. "Things got muddled in here with her. I allowed many things to twist my emotions for her. I've done horrible things to her."

"Horrible doesn't even begin to cover it. Maybe you can do something to show her you understand that you've done horrible things and maybe you'd like to tell her about them, so she's not blindsided by things like this." Or maybe Christine really needed to step out of Danny's life if there were more things like this around the corner. If there were, she'd only hurt Danny again.

Christine sighed. "It's hard."

A frown cut its way onto Nicole's face before she could stop it, and she glowered at Christine like an enemy on a battlefield. "Life is hard. Repairs are hard. If you fold when things get hard, leave Danny alone. She knows what hard is. She's laughed in hard's face when it knocked her down, and she's picked herself back up. Don't complain about things being hard to her or with her. You either knuckle up or leave her the hell alone."

The nerve of Christine, acting like she was the victim, or this was some great burden to her. How dare she want to be in Danny's life, like she deserved someone like Danny! Nicole couldn't bring herself to say anything else, resisting the urge to curse Christine out. Who was she to chase Christine away if Danny might still want her?

"I should probably go." Christine started for the door.

Nicole didn't try to stop her or even get the door for her. They didn't exchange farewells and when the door closed, Nicole let loose a soothing breath, trying to cleanse her system of the poison she was exposed to in the form of Christine. She wished that was the last time they saw Christine. Toxic didn't even begin to describe her or what she had done to Danny.

Nicole scratched Haydn's head. "I hope this isn't a sign of how Christmas is going to be." Haydn whined, and she scratched his muzzle. "Well, let's find something to occupy our time for a little while and then go check on Danny. She probably needs a little space."

He whined again, and Nicole stayed on the couch, if only to collect her thoughts. She continued petting Haydn and then decided to get him a treat for making it through the tense ordeal. She also treated herself to some leftover party cookies. They didn't help settle her, though.

***

Dane paced the hallway upstairs, ignoring the jolts of pain from her knee. She needed to move, if only to escape from the desire to break something. She wasn't sure why she was so pissed off. She should've expected such crap from Christine. It shouldn't surprise her or upset her, but the thought of what could've been drove her insane. She thought about Allison and Ben, smart as hell, sports for Ben, writing workshops for Allison, and what did she get? To be alone on her birthday every freaking year of her life until she finally ditched the Hell she called home. She missed out on a loving family. She missed out on incredible parents. She missed out on a cute little sister and an awesome little brother! She missed out on everything.

"It's not fair," she snarled like a wounded animal and almost punched the wall. She only stopped when she considered she couldn't pay to have it repaired and she couldn't repair it herself. "I'm fucking useless!"

She pulled her hair, tugging hard, not caring how much of it she pulled out. How dare she ever think she could get better? Who could recover from so much damage? Who could ever rebuild when her own mother had actively set out to destroy her? She didn't even realize she was punching herself in the head as she ripped at her hair until the pain finally registered.

Taking a breath, she calmed enough to leave her hair alone, but her body shook. If not for her skin, every fiber of her being would fly off into every direction. Rushing back downstairs and ignoring the now searing agony in her knee, she grabbed the phone. Lynn picked up.

"Hey, Danny," Lynn greeted her.

"Why haven't you gotten Allison real piano lessons? Why the hell didn't you get her lessons before?" Dane demanded. Was Lynn trying to keep Allison from her? *No, that doesn't make any sense.* Lynn let her around Allison and Ben all the time. But, her mother let her around Lynn and Henry all the time and still didn't want them around her. Still took them from her. What if Lynn and Henry took Allison and Ben from her? What if the whole family left her again?

"Because she wasn't interested until you came along," Lynn answered.

Dane blinked, and it felt like every swirling emotion in her came to an abrupt halt. "Huh?"

"She never thought about it until you showed up and started talking about everything you play. Honestly, she's always been into her writing and stuff online, but nothing beyond that. We've been happy she wanted to do something else, something that might help her be a little more social."

"Social? Playing the keyboard?" Dane's music had always helped her be more alone. But, then again, it also helped attract a crowd to her.

"Yes. Hasn't she been social with you?"

Dane stopped moving completely. *Oh. Okay. Guess she told me.* "And that's why you let her take lessons with me?"

"You're the only one she wants to do it with." Lynn paused for a moment. "You don't like spending time with her?"

Dane scratched her head. "No, I really like it. Love it, actually." It was cute watching Allison try until she figured out. They got to bond, and her heart melted each time she watched Allison concentrate, work, and improve. Whenever Allison got things and looked at her with sparkling, hopeful eyes, Dane knew she'd love that kid forever and always.

"Dane, are you all right?" Lynn asked, her voice so soft, gentle. It reminded Dane of when she was little, and Lynn would put her to sleep with wild, fantastic stories or lullabies.

Taking a breath, Dane leaned against the wall and slid down to the floor. "No," her voice cracked. She rubbed an eye with the heel of her hand. *I'm way out of sorts.* Her chest hurt, and she felt like she might throw up.

"What's wrong?" Lynn's voice was practically a coo, and it wrapped around Dane like a warm embrace, but just made more agony ripple through her.

"Christine." Just saying the name made her stomach twist. It was like acid ate through her ribs, devoured her heart, and now wanted to take her soul. *Why the hell did I talk to her? Why do I bother with her?* "I talked to Christine."

"Oh, Dane." There was a sigh so full of compassion and concern, it only made Dane's stomach churn more. She wished Lynn was her true mother. Lynn never would've hurt her like this.

Dane sniffled. "Asked her about the stuff she did, and it hurts so much. I feel like she's been lying to me even now when she's acting like she wants a relationship with me. At least Russell was always upfront about it. He hates me, so he beat the shit out of me, but this woman." She took a deep, shaky breath, trying to hold herself together. *This woman. God, I don't even know.* She hated that Lynn and Henry gave her back to Christine time and time again. "I wish you guys had kidnapped me." Her voice was a whispered hiss through gritted teeth.

"Dane, you know I don't condone anything that woman did to you and I wish we'd been able to keep you, but I will always stand by the fact that as a child, you needed your parents to be parents."

To hell with that! "And?"

"Well, I think if you ever want to heal the wounds they left behind, then you have to deal with them in the way you think is right. What do you think is right with Christine? Is getting to know her worth knowing about the pain she might've caused you as a child?"

Dane took another deep breath. She wasn't too sure. Maybe she needed to walk away from Christine like she walked away from Russell and her siblings. She didn't need these things coming back on her while she was on the road to a better life. They were potholes, threatening to tear her from this new path. *Can I really be better if I don't confront these things with my past?*

"What do you think I should do?" Dane asked. She needed advice, real advice. This whole thing was such a mess, and her head felt like it might cave in.

Lynn sighed. "That one you have to decide for yourself. Dane, you know I want the best for you. If Christine is giving you too much grief, don't hold onto it or her. You have a good life, Dane. You have a loving partner, and good people around you. You're happy and not on drugs anymore."

Dane winced. "Yeah, good thing I'm not doing that."

"I'm glad." Lynn sighed, sounding like she put down a burden.

Dane rubbed her head. "Guess you know how bad it got?"

"No, we just know you almost died ten years ago. We were

incredibly relieved when you pulled through."

"Yeah?" It was good to know someone was. The idea helped steady Dane. "For a long time, I wasn't. I wasn't relieved." For a long time, underneath all the drug use and sex, she wished she died when she OD'ed, wished she froze to death when she was homeless. Hell, sometimes after she was attacked, she wondered why she survived, why she existed at all. What was the point of living if that was her life?

"You were in a lot of pain for a long time, Dane. Are you relieved now?"

Dane looked around the room, around the house she shared with the most wonderful woman she had ever met. She was about to celebrate Christmas with an outstanding family. Maybe they weren't all hers, but they could be one day. Plus, there was a family that was hers. People cared about her. Loved her. It was time to look forward instead of back.

"I am," Dane replied. She was relieved to have made it this far, to have the things she had. She'd press on, as things might get even better. Even if they didn't, if she could be with Nicole and continue as she was, then that was fine.

"That's good." She could hear Lynn's smile in her voice. "Be grateful for life, Dane. You don't have to let someone else's actions past or present ruin what you have now. Deal with Christine however you will, but don't give her any more power in your life. Don't give anyone power to ruin even your day. You've built a wonderful thing, and you should be proud of your life."

Dane's heart fluttered. *She's proud of me.* She felt giddy for a moment, like a little kid again, and that mixed weird with how upset she was. "Thank you."

"Anytime, Dane. I'm glad you called me."

"Me, too." Dane smiled a little and then glanced toward the kitchen. "I need to go."

"Talk to you later."

"Yeah."

"We love you, Dane."

Dane's heart thumped hard, and she couldn't breathe for a second. "Love you, too." She disconnected the call and picked herself up.

It wasn't surprising to find Nicole at the counter with a plate of cookies. The thing with Christine had been intense, and it tied her in knots. She had no idea how it might've affected Nicole. She wrapped her arms around Nicole's waist and placed a gentle kiss to Nicole's tempting neck as Nicole relaxed in her arms.

"Sorry you had to see that," Dane said.

"I'm sorry you had to live that," Nicole replied, reaching around to touch Dane's cheek. Tiny crumbs from her fingers pressed into Dane's flesh, but Dane didn't care.

Dane turned her head enough to place a soft kiss to Nicole's hand. "I'm not going to let it get me down. It's the past. I'm here with you, trying to be better."

"You're good, Danny. You're very good."

"Because of you. I think I'm seriously able to push through this crap. You've given me this good life."

Nicole shook her head and turned around, locking eyes with Dane. Dane could get lost in those emerald eyes and never care to find a way out. They were always full of love, but also full of pain. Nicole felt her pain, and Dane wanted to take it all away. Figuring out what to do with Christine would definitely help.

"No, you gave yourself this good life. You were strong enough to turn your life into something you want, something worthwhile. You're the one who did all of this."

Dane smiled and kissed Nicole, a lingering touch of their lips. "You're my muse, angel. You're the reason I want to turn everything around, why I want to do more. I'm not going to let this control me. We're going to have a damn Merry Christmas, a Happy New Year, and then I'm going to treat you to an awesome birthday, okay?"

Nicole moved her hands to Dane's hips and gave Dane a little kiss. "Promises, promises."

Dane grinned now. "Hey, it's not every year a girl turns thirty. You think I don't have something special planned?" She had to do something special for the woman who gave her strength, gave her purpose, gave her love.

Nicole wagged her finger in Dane's face. "I think you should not mention that age again."

"Why? You're still as sexy as the first day I saw you."

Nicole laughed. "Always the flatterer." For a moment, she searched Dane's eyes. "You sure you're okay?"

"I am. Now, let's not waste any more of this awesome Sunday." Dane kissed Nicole again.

Nicole smirked. "What did you have in mind?"

Dane smirked right back, and she helped Nicole onto the kitchen counter. Nicole squealed and laughed as Dane settled in between

Nicole's open legs and kissed her neck. The laughter turned into panting as Nicole wrapped her arms and legs around Dane. There would be no more wasted time.

***

It seemed odd to Dane that Christmas should be in the winter now that she understood what was meant by 'Christmas spirit.' Christmas was a festive explosion of molten light, pureness, and joy in the dark, bitter, biting cold. But, then again, the warm merriment of the spirit might not last long as she locked up her bike outside a small cafe in the classy part of the city. Glancing in through a slightly foggy window, she spotted Christine toward the back, tearing at a napkin.

Stepping inside the cafe, warmth and that Christmas feel wafted over her. The scent of coffee hung in the air, but she caught cookies and pastries underneath it. Nicole taught her happiness smelled like fresh baked treats. From the look on people's faces and friendly chatter, coffee and sandwiches were probably a part of the happiness equation. *Will my talk with Christine sound friendly? It's worth a shot.* It'd probably be a better shot if she could have a shot before this conversation.

"Hi," Dane said as she eased into the seat across from Christine. She let loose a low sigh as the heat fought off the chill inside of her and her muscles relaxed. Her whole leg was delighted to not be pedaling, despite the fact she loved riding her bike. She took a moment to glance out of the window they sat near. People fluttered by in their heavy coats, probably trying to get some shopping done with the big day being less than a week away.

I got everything out of the way. She almost smiled to herself, but then remembered Christine was across from her. She didn't want Christine to think she was smiling at her.

"Hi," Christine sort of mumbled and then let out a nervous laugh.

"Thanks for meeting with me." Dane hadn't been sure Christine would go through with it after their last encounter. A week had gone by, and Dane still hadn't recovered. She wasn't sure if Christine cared enough to need to recover.

"At this point, it's the least I can do. Besides, I was happy you called." A hint of a smile worked its way to Christine's face. The expression was wise not to stay.

"Well, I'm trying to move forward, and you can't do that living in the past," Dane replied. *I have to move on, keep getting better*. There were so many good people in her life, and she wanted to be good for them, especially Nicole.

Christine nodded and opened her mouth to say something, but a waiter came over. They quickly gave him orders, if only to get rid of him, and turned back to each other.

"So, moving forward, huh?" Christine said, her voice low, unsure. Her eyes drifted for a moment, sliding over to the window, and then focused back on Dane.

Dane rubbed her hands together. Her left hand ached and was stiff, which she came to expect in winter weather. "I think I've been trying to do that for a while, but now I have a real idea what it means. It's not about ignoring or forgetting the past. It's the past. I have to acknowledge and accept it happened. It made me this person, and I've grown to like this person." She tapped herself on the chest.

That was partially why Dane was happy now. She felt like she was a person, a real person. Throughout her life, she felt more like an entity maybe, or a phantom. She existed and experienced, but had no idea who she was, had no idea what to make of any of the information presented to her. She never reflected or even stopped to consider things. She never felt, beyond basic things anyway. *Is that what makes a person? Feeling?* She had no idea.

"An amazing person," Christine said.

Dane shook her head. "You don't have to flatter me. I'm coming into my own, not for you or because of you or in spite of you. What I'm becoming has almost nothing to do with you."

"Because of Nicole?"

Dane ran her hand through her hair. "Maybe, but I think I've got a better understanding of what she wants for me. I'm not supposed to be better for her or to deserve her. I should be better to be better. Being better helps me understand how I can be happy."

Nodding, Christine swallowed. "And are you?"

"Happy?" Dane shrugged. "Yeah. I'm happy. I don't think I've ever been happy, not like this anyway." Beyond happy, she was content. She had never been this way before, settling into herself rather than a bubbling mass of confused, misdirected, and wandering energy.

Christine gave her a sad look. "Not even with your music?"

"Not sure if I can ever explain what music was and is to me." Dane glanced down at her left hand. "Music connects me to everything." Music had always been the one way to know she wasn't dead and in

Hell. Music had also been her way of expressing her personal Hell. Thinking back, all her music had been about despair in some form.

"How has it been since your accident?" Christine asked.

Dane sucked her teeth. "You do know it wasn't an accident, right?" She imagined the Wolfe family went around calling it that, if it was ever brought up anyway. Her overdose at fourteen had been labeled "an accident" as well, like she'd been hit by a car rather than going into shock after too much coke.

Christine shook her head. "I don't know what else to call it, because you never explained what happened. I imagine what Bryan explained to us wasn't true."

"You never asked."

Christine glanced away again, watching faceless denizens pass by the window. "No, I didn't." She turned back to look Dane in the eye. "What happened? Was there any truth to Bryan's story?"

"There's never any truth to Bryan's anything, which is what I'm sure Russell loves about him. What happened doesn't matter. Just don't call it an accident. Don't diminish it. I was attacked. I tried to help a snake and got bit."

"You tried to help Bryan?" Christine sounded skeptical.

Dane snorted. "Continuing to prove I'm stupid."

"Helping someone is never stupid."

"Yeah, tell that to my musical ability. I don't want to talk about that." It wasn't any of Christine's business. She just never wanted to hear someone refer to it as 'an accident,' when it was a plot against her.

Christine nodded. "Never doubt that I was happy you survived. Not just that, but everything."

"I don't doubt you care about me. It's just in a destructive way. It happens. I cared about me, too, and pumped tons of drugs in my system for years without a care in the world," Dane replied.

"That doesn't sound like caring."

"Trying to stop the pain means I cared about me." Sometimes, she was certain wishing she was dead meant she cared about herself. She cared about that person inside who no one wanted and who needed the hurting to end.

Again, their conversation was interrupted as the waiter returned with their food. Dane had a simple grilled cheese with fries and a root beer. Christine had a salad with some iced tea. They didn't touch the food, but sat silently for longer than necessary, staring at their meals. Maybe it was a way to regroup.

"What do you propose we do now?" Christine asked, her shoulders slumping a little. Her blonde hair managed to droop with her shoulders.

"I'm not going to ask you about all of the shitty things you did or what you took from me as a child. It's done. People do shitty things for tons of reasons." She learned from Nicole's cousin Lily that a person could be the nicest thing in the world to you—as Nicole was with Lily— and that still didn't stop the other person from being a bitch. Sometimes, there was no rhyme or reason to it. There was no need to dwell either. She watched Nicole pick herself right up, and that was way more recent than whatever the hell Christine had done to her.

Christine nodded. "Okay, what do you propose?"

"Hi, Christine. I'm Dane," she said. This was what Christine sort of wanted, or at least suggested once. Maybe it could work.

Christine's hair moved forward as her forehead furrowed. "You're serious?"

"I think this might be best." She had stalled with Christine too long as it was. She couldn't deny she wanted some part of this woman, and it seemed like Christine wanted some part of her. But, not too much. She didn't need too much of her in her life. Maybe they could be friendly strangers, like with Adam. "It's a way to move forward and maybe we'll learn about each other along the way."

Christine smiled. "Okay." Glancing down, she played with her food a little. "It's a pleasure to meet you, Dane."

Dane took a bite of her sandwich. "I used to play music. Was in a band and everything. What about you?"

A tiny smile played on Christine's pink painted lip. "Funny, I used to play music, too."

"What instruments?" Dane was actually curious. She knew Christine played the piano, but that was like everyone knew she played guitar.

"Well, the piano is my passion, but I started out on the flute." Christine laughed, her eyes sparkling just a little. She nibbled her salad. "I'm terrible with woodwinds, though."

Dane laughed, too. "Me, too. But, I can actually hold my own with brass."

"One instrument does not count as holding your own."

"I could've improved on that one instrument or learned more at some point."

Christine shook her head, her eyes dancing. "I remember when you first picked up the trumpet. The face you made suggested you'd stomp on the next brass instrument passed to you."

Dane smirked a little and didn't deny the charges. Just like that, they were off to an actual civil and good conversation. It stuck to music, the one thing they had in common. But, it was good, almost enlightening. She didn't leave it feeling like body parts had been torn off her, which was a new thing when it came to dealing with Christine.

***

Nicole came home to a house devoid of human life. She wasn't surprised. Danny called and said she was out and about. Glancing around, the house always felt empty without Danny around, even if Haydn was there. He barked, as if to remind her of his presence and the fact that he was trapped in the music room.

She let Haydn out, greeting him with the appropriate petting, cooing, and kissing, and he followed her around the house. The noise and company were a welcome distraction. She gave him a treat since she had no idea how long he had been gated in the den. The fact that he didn't tear anything up or knock anything over was good enough for her. He nuzzled her as thanks. She leaned down to kiss the top of his head.

"You're sweet." Nicole scratched his ears before exiting the kitchen to go upstairs. She put her things away and changed into some comfortable clothing, before getting started on dinner.

When Danny came home, she had a shopping bag with her and a smile brightening her face. Nicole hugged her and gave her a kiss. Danny gave her an extra-tight squeeze.

"You're in a good mood. Christmas shopping really agrees with you," Nicole said.

"Christmas really agrees with me, but this isn't Christmas shopping." Danny grinned and wiggled a little with jubilant energy. "How long has it been since I told you I love you?"

Nicole laughed. "This morning."

"Well, I love you. And I kinda love Christmas."

"I've noticed." Nicole made a show of looking at the bag in Danny's hand. She was ecstatic to see Danny in such great spirits, especially after what happened with her mother.

"Thank you so much, angel."

Nicole shook her head and stared at her girlfriend. "You really don't have any idea, do you?" *It's actually cute she's clueless.*

Danny blinked. "What?"

"You have no idea how much better you make everything for me. Thank you, Danny."

Danny looked at her, tilting her head slightly, like she didn't understand. Well, she didn't understand. Nicole pulled Danny back to her.

"I don't tell you often enough how much better my life has been since you came. Christmas has been brighter. There's so much joy, laughter, and light in my life now. Everything seems much more vibrant and full of promise. It's because of you. You've made me much stronger thanks to your strength. So, thank you." Nicole squeezed her tight.

Danny smiled. "Are we a pair?"

"A matching pair, my love. A matching pair. Now, how about we eat and you tell me about your day? Mine, as you can imagine, was filled with idiots now that I don't have class anymore. I will be unbelievably happy when I get a few days off for Christmas."

Danny laughed. "I'll be happy, too. I think you'll like hearing about my day."

Nicole grinned and listened as Danny detailed her day, including a new start with Christine. "You think it'll be okay?"

Danny shrugged. "I'm willing to try now. If it's not, I won't let it get me down. If it is, then it's a good thing I tried."

Nicole kissed Danny. "You know I wish you the best." Maybe Christine will prove to be just as mature as Danny and things would be fine. *Please let things work out for Danny, if only to reward her Christmas spirit.* "Now, are you going to show me what's in the bag? It's killing me."

Danny snickered. "It's a surprise. You'll see tonight."

It turned out Danny bought a Santa hat and reindeer boxers. She wore them to bed. Nicole spent a full five minutes laughing. It was good Danny was in such high spirits.

Chapter Six

NICOLE WOKE UP ON Christmas day to the smell of pancakes and bacon, which didn't surprise her. The bed was empty. Last night, despite some rather energetic time together, Danny had fidgeted like a kid waiting for Christmas morning. Obviously, Danny couldn't wait. Nicole smiled.

She was probably shaking boxes before she started cooking. Nicole took a moment to picture Danny under the tree, holding a box labeled "for Danny" and shaking it to figure out what it was. The thought made her smile grow. She got out of bed and brushed her teeth before making her way downstairs.

Turned out she was wrong. Danny, still in her pajamas of shorts and a tank top with her Santa hat atop her head, was shaking boxes when Nicole came downstairs. She could only assume the cooking was done. Haydn practically stood on Danny's shoulder while she tried to figure out what her gifts were under the tree. She even held some up for Haydn to sniff, as if he could then tell her what was in the box. Nicole shook her head.

"I swear," Nicole muttered loud enough for Danny to hear.

With a grin, Danny turned to Nicole. "Merry Christmas!" Her eyes were bright and full of joy.

Nicole gave a smile back and felt a little bad that she couldn't match Danny's enthusiasm. "Definitely a Merry Christmas."

Nicole greeted her with a kiss. Danny wrapped her arms around Nicole, and they collapsed to the floor in a fit of giggles. Nicole settled on the floor with Danny pressed against her, sighing as warmth and love engulfed her. Danny pulled back a little, so they could look each other in the eyes.

"You know, it snowed a little last night, making it a white Christmas." Danny placed her hand on Nicole's cheek.

Nicole arched an eyebrow. "Enough for us to build a snowman? Provided you don't kill that one." A teasing smirk settled on her face.

Danny leaned down and kissed her again, ridding her of the expression. There was a hint of passion that might've been inappropriate for Christmas morning, but she didn't care. She returned the show of affection, opening her mouth enough for Danny's tongue to slide home. They kissed until they needed air. Haydn came in as soon as they tried to breathe, attempting to squeeze in between them, earning laughs that encouraged him. Danny gently pushed Haydn away, making him whine.

Danny stroked Nicole's cheek with her thumb. "Unfortunately, not enough for us to build a snowman. Just enough for there to be a little white on the ground to go with this awe-inspiring Christmas morning. Can we open presents now?"

Nicole laughed. *She's so cute!* She had to kiss Danny one more time, a quick peck on the lips. "Didn't you make breakfast? You don't want it to get cold, do you?"

Sighing, a pout took over Danny's face. "No, especially since there's hot chocolate involved."

Okay, she went overboard on breakfast, but there's still ways to make this morning better. She ran her hands over Danny's back. "That's tempting, but you know I like having you on top of me more than anything else."

Danny grinned. "Well, if you play your cards right and I really like what you got me..." She bit her lip, managed a light blush, and looked coy.

Chuckling, Nicole rolled her eyes. "Let's see about breakfast first." She'd love nothing more than to have Danny on top of her for the morning, but there was food to be had and she'd rather have it hot. "After all, you wore me out pretty badly last night."

Danny played with the ends of Nicole's hair. "It's not my fault you looked so sexy."

Nicole scoffed. "In a plain camisole and teddy bear pants?" She glanced down at herself, demonstrating her pajamas.

Danny gently tugged at the thin material of the red and white pajama pants. "Well, those were some sexy teddy bears."

Nicole couldn't help laughing. Danny gave her another kiss and then eased away, helping her to her feet. They went to the breakfast nook, and Nicole found her love had made quite the spread. Strawberry pancakes with whipped cream, definitely a Christmas treat. There were scrambled eggs, bacon, and hash browns as well. As soon as Nicole sat down, Danny placed a candle between them.

"You are too romantic for your own good," Nicole said before taking a sip of her hot chocolate. She moaned a little as the blast of cocoa and whipped cream hit her tongue. It was perfect. This was perfect.

"It's all for you, you know," Danny replied.

Nicole appreciated it and cut into her pancakes. "Well, this is outsiding and you're amazing."

"I wanted to celebrate this Christmas right. You know, better than that first one." Danny glanced away.

"Baby." Nicole reached over and took Danny's hand. She didn't like thinking back to that time because of the poor shape Danny had been in. "Yes, that was a hard time, but it's over. You recovered, and we're all right. This Christmas will be the first of many we celebrate together."

Danny gave her hand a squeeze. "I truly hope so, angel."

Nicole had no doubt in her mind they'd do this for many years to come. They had been through so much together, and they kept coming out better and better. The pattern would hold. *I have faith we will work out*.

"Besides, if it wasn't for that time, we wouldn't be legal partners," Nicole said. This was a silver lining for her, even though they didn't often discuss being domestic partners.

"Well, even that wasn't fair. You just did that to make sure I got taken care of. I wasn't ready for a commitment like that, even though I am now," Danny replied.

Nicole nodded and ate some of her pancakes. She took a big bite of bacon. "I'm not sure I was ready for it at the time, but I am now, too. We're definitely partners now." Yes, their domestic partnership had been rushed to get Danny health insurance, but it felt true and real now.

Danny grinned. "Glad you feel that way. I like being your partner."

Nicole smiled back and then got to work on her breakfast. Danny did the same. Everything was delicious, but the pancakes exploded with flavor, sweetness dancing on her tongue. Danny had outdone herself.

"What time do we leave for your grandparents'?" Danny asked as she cut into her pancakes. She devoured four pieces and eggs at the same time. Syrup dripped down the corner of her mouth. Nicole reached over and wiped it away with a napkin.

"We should get there a little before three," Nicole replied.

"You know, I never knew people ate dinner at three before you. Hell, I used to have breakfast at three sometimes."

Nicole chewed on some pancakes with a smile. "Oh, yeah? What kind of breakfast?"

"Usually candy and blow, which I guess actually counts as two kinds of candy." Danny shrugged and ate more eggs.

Nicole's stomach twisted, but she took Danny's casual mention of her past as a good sign. She was open to hearing it now, and Danny was willing to share. It was a big step for both.

"Did you at least drink orange juice?" Nicole asked.

Danny scoffed. "Please, I was classy. I had vodka."

Nicole laughed. "Vodka is classy?"

"Clear liquor is classy. Tequila is also classy."

"Clear liquor and foreign liquor is classy?" Nicole asked.

Danny put a finger to her chin and pretended to think. "Many things are classy. None of them beat having breakfast with you on Christmas morning, though. I was wondering if after your grandparents' place, we hit Henry and Lynn."

Nicole nodded. "Definitely. My grandparents always have dinner early to make sure everyone has time to go visit with other family members afterward. My papa will be happy we have somewhere to go now. We can deliver their presents."

"Really looking forward to that. Wish I could've seen Luke and Thomas open their gifts." A pout took over Danny's face, and Nicole reached for her hand.

"One day, love." Nicole hoped so anyway. Sharon would always be a huge obstacle. Beyond her homophobia, there seemed to be a general hatred for Danny they'd have to get through. Maybe Adam would eventually grow a backbone and stand up for his sister, but she couldn't see that happening for many years.

"Gonna be great!" Danny chirped, sitting up straight and pulling her hand away briefly. She squirmed in her seat for a moment.

Leaning forward, Nicole caressed Danny's forearm. "Yes. Now, before we open anything, you should finish eating. You don't want this great spread to get cold." She pointed to Danny's plate with her fork. All the eggs were gone, but there were still a couple of strips of bacon and half the pancakes. Not to mention, much of her whipped cream had melted into her hot chocolate. Danny nodded and went back to work on her meal, gulping down some of her beverage while there was still some cream left.

Haydn finished with his food only to come bother them. They didn't make it a point to feed him people food, but it was Christmas. So, when Danny dangled bacon in front of him, Nicole didn't say anything. Haydn snatched up the bacon and then leaped around the kitchen like he'd just gotten the best Christmas gift of them all.

"I hope I like my stuff as much as he liked that bacon," Danny said with a smile. Nicole only laughed.

Soon breakfast was done, and it was time to open gifts. They made their way to the tree and sat with Haydn crouched in front of both them. Nicole grabbed a box she wrapped, easing it into Danny's hands.

"It's not clothes, is it?" Danny asked.

Nicole scoffed. "You mean shaking the box didn't clue you in? Besides, you need clothes. No one has only three pairs of pants to their name."

"Uh, I do, so obviously at least one person."

There were clothes, but among them a couple of things for Danny to play with. She got new headphones, which she immediately put on. For a moment, she nodded like there was music coming through the headset.

"I'm so going to have sex with you with these on," Danny declared with a wide grin and bright eyes.

Nicole chortled. "Oh, no, you're not!"

"No, it's happening because these things are just that sexy." Danny ran her finger over the right headphone.

A teasing smirk worked its way onto Nicole's face. "Sexy like my teddy bear pajamas?"

Danny laughed and then glanced at the tree. "You open stuff now." She handed Nicole a box.

The gift wasn't wrapped well. She could tell there were parts where Danny tore the paper against the box and then taped it down. But, that didn't matter. The thought and effort were there. Nicole opened it with the same care she opened all gifts. Danny looked ready to burst, fidgeting in her seat.

"These gifts should be better than before. Put a lot of thought in this," Danny said.

"Danny, the last gifts were perfect. I'm still waiting for more charms for my bracelet actually," Nicole answered and then she opened the box. She laughed. "How dare you hope it's not clothes and then get me this?" She lifted the outfit up, a lovely beige skirt with a blazer and medium cut shirt.

"I figured...well, I thought it'd look nice on you for your first day at whatever job you end up working after your spring semester," Danny replied.

"Or, I could wear it for my birthday?" She liked tans and light brown colors. This outfit would definitely look nice.

"I got something else you can wear for that." Danny's eyes lit up with mischief.

"I'll bet." Nicole chuckled. "I'm sure I'll wear that, too."

"One can only hope. Open this one next since you talked about your charm bracelet." Danny handed her a wrapped jewelry box.

Just like that, she had more charms for the bracelet Danny had gifted her with that first Christmas. There were four this time. A snowman, a campfire, a cookie, and a heart. Each of them made her smile.

"I love the story you're telling," Nicole said. Every charm was a reminder of the good times in their relationship, even the campfire.

Shaking her head, Danny laughed. "This is our song."

"And it's a lovely song." Leaning over, she gave Danny a kiss.

"Come on, there's more." Danny reached for another gift.

"You have to open one first." Nicole grabbed another box and handed it to Danny.

Danny threw on an exaggerated pout. "Aw, but watching you is the best gift of all."

Nicole scoffed. "Oh, please. You're the one shaking boxes, so please, open your next gift."

Danny tore into her gift and gasped when she saw it. "Nick, this is beautiful." She held up the leather-bound journal, with embossed musical notes on it and a paw print at the bottom. She opened it to see she could add pages, too. Nicole knew that feature would come in handy.

"I felt like your music deserved to be kept someplace nice," Nicole said.

Danny ran her fingers over the leather. "I want to write in this now."

"Don't let me stop you."

Danny grinned. "Nope. I still have to watch you open more of your gifts." She handed Nicole another present.

It was a cute gift, a model of a molecule. Nicole let loose a snort of a laugh. "I'm going to put this on my desk." It'd go right next to her pens.

"There's more." Danny urged her to open her other gifts.

Nicole gave her lover a tender smile and wasted no time grabbing another present. She opened the best thing of all, a giant cookbook on how to make nothing but desserts and sweet things. "I'm cooking tomorrow." She hugged the book to her chest.

"I knew you'd love that. Now, I just fear for our stomachs and teeth."

"It's okay. We have great dental coverage."

***

Christmas at Benito and Alicia's house was as expected for Dane, namely awesome. Of course, it didn't compare to watching Nicole open her gifts. While this year her gifts weren't expensive, they were well thought out and held significance in ways her other presents hadn't. The light in Nicole's eyes, shining like emeralds, as she unwrapped each gift made Dane's heart swell. That simple thing had been everything, but Christmas with her family was the icing on the cake.

The smell of ham hung in the air, making Dane's stomach grumble. Having experienced dinner at the house several times, she knew that ham and whatever was paired with it would taste incredible. Hell, the promise of ham made Dane put on long pants. Well, technically, Nicole made her put on pants, but the threat of not being allowed out of the house was what worked. Beyond ham and family, holidays were also about dressing up.

"I got a guitar for Christmas. I brought it with me," Nicole's cousin, Philip, said the second they walked through the door. He charged over, looking dashing in a maroon suit with no tie and a short-collared shirt. It put her sweater vest to shame. *Might have to step my game up if I'm being out dressed by a kid*. But, then again, Nicole didn't really care about her outfits, just wanted to make sure she fit in wherever they were.

The couple was separated, but Dane was comfortable enough with this side of Nicole's family that it didn't bother her. She went with Philip to see his new guitar. He handed it to her like it was a prized sword, which made Dane chuckle. *This is the way I used to hold my guitar*. The thought made her heart clench a little, but then she noticed how beaming his grin was and she was fine. She inspected the instrument.

"Top of the line." It was a little much for him more than likely, but he'd probably grow into it as he continued his lessons. Christmas was the time to indulge.

"Play something now that you got the thing," Jarred, Nicole's uncle and Philip's father, requested as they stepped into the small living room. He was dressed just as sharp as his son, navy blue suit with a god-awful snowman tie. Christmas time seemed to be the time of jolly, ugly clothing.

Dane groaned like it was some great burden, which made Philip laugh. They saw right through her. After all, she used to bring her guitar to every gathering, until it had been destroyed. She had another guitar, which she couldn't touch, so never mind play. She was comfortable enough with the family to not need the icebreaker.

She checked to make sure she wasn't disturbing Benito and a football game. She wasn't, considering he looked at her expectantly. She strummed the guitar, finding it tuned perfectly. Those lessons really were paying off for Philip. Plucking it again, the clear note hummed through her in ways she missed.

Philip waved his hands, making an x formation with his arms. "No, no, no. None of that crap. Play a real song."

Dane didn't really need a push. Eddie and Sabrina came out of nowhere to listen. They giggled and she laughed, playing for a couple of minutes before giving her hand a break. She could almost play a full song now without her hand cramping up, as long as wherever she was had enough heat. Turned out physical therapy wasn't just to torture her.

"When are you going to teach me to play like that?" Philip asked with a grin.

Dane shook her head. "You have an awesome teacher. You don't need me. Hell, soon you'll probably be better than me. In fact, lemme see what you can do with this thing." She eased the guitar back into his hands.

He began playing. He sounded pretty good, especially for someone who started playing recently. She nodded as he continued.

"The boy actually sounds good," Benito said with a laugh.

"Hey, don't sound so shocked." Philip scowled at his grandfather.

Dane nodded. "You're doing fine. Definitely stick with your teacher."

Before she could hear more, Eddie and Sabrina dragged her away. They ended up playing with the dogs in the backyard, despite the winter frost and the small snowfall. Haydn was much bigger than Beanie, the kids' beagle, but the canines were good friends. Beanie was fearless and Haydn was friendly, so there wasn't much danger with their size difference. The dogs and the kids didn't seem to notice the chill in the air, and Dane moved around as best she could to stay warm.

"When it snows more, we can build a snowman with you, Danny," Sabrina said.

Dane nodded. "I'd love to."

"Yes!" Sabrina threw her fist in the air and then turned back to her brother and the dogs.

Dinner was served at three o'clock sharp. It always amazed Dane that everyone could fit around the table. She couldn't help thinking of every holiday meal she saw on television as she checked out the dishes laid out before them. There was the picture-perfect ham, an equally perfect turkey for those who didn't eat ham, a bowl of mashed potatoes, rice and peas, string beans, broccoli, corn on the cob, and fluffy biscuits full of butter. Her mouth watered from the food, but her heart glowed from the family around her. They held hands and said grace. Well, Dane listened to them say grace, as she still didn't know the words of the prayer. Regardless, she liked it, felt a part of something wonderful. Beyond that, she felt the love these people all had for each other and for her.

"Don't eat too much," Nicole said to her.

Dane's brow furrowed briefly and then it dawned on her. "Right! Lynn cooked."

"You're going somewhere after this?" Benito inquired from his space at the head of the table.

"Yeah, we're going to..." Dane trailed off. She wasn't sure what to call Henry and Lynn.

"We're going to see Danny's family," Nicole filled in. Dane perked up hearing that. *Oh, that works.*

"Family?" Benito echoed, and Alicia leaned in.

"The family from your party?" Raymond asked. His green eyes widened, like he worried if they planned to go anywhere else.

Dane nodded. "Well, yeah, I guess."

"Family from the party? We missed that," Alicia said. "I think we saw your mother when your nephews ran in."

Dane shook her head. "No, that's not who I mean. I'd never go see the Wolfes on Christmas, or ever really, at this point. There was this couple who used to take care of me when I was little and they're back in my life now. I should've introduced you at our party. They met Kathleen and Raymond. We're going to have a second dinner with them."

Benito smiled. "That's good. Family is important."

With a grin, Dane nodded. She understood the importance of

family more each day. She could almost understand why Nicole had tried to push her to be closer to her family before. She just wished the family Nicole had pushed her to initially had been the Briarmoors. Of course, Nicole hadn't known about them because Dane hadn't been open about them.

"They seemed like lovely people," Raymond said. Kathleen grunted, almost like she didn't agree.

"Mommy," Nicole said.

"I'm not going to just give a blank stamp of approval over one meeting. Besides, I'm a little skeptical considering the bit I know about Danny's life," Kathleen replied.

Dane had to give Kathleen that, but moreover, this statement suggested Kathleen was concerned for her. The worry would take some getting used to. Sometimes, she still reeled over the fact that Kathleen approved of her relationship with Nicole. *And people say violence doesn't solve anything.*

"Mommy, that wasn't their fault. They did what they could. Now, let's eat and enjoy each other. Maybe as time passes, you'll get to know the Briarmoors better and find they are lovely people like Daddy said," Nicole said.

Kathleen opened her mouth, but seemed to think better of it. She turned her attention to her food, and other conversations sprang up. Nicole smiled at Dane, who grinned. She might have to tell Nicole that she was flattered by Kathleen's unease. Hell, maybe she'd even tell Kathleen. She'd probably like to know she was appreciated.

***

"Uh...Kathleen." Dane rubbed the back of her neck as she approached Nicole's mother once dinner was done. She was in the kitchen, helping her sisters clear away the mess.

Kathleen turned to her. "Yes?"

"Can I...well." Dane wasn't sure how to say this, how to even approach the topic.

Kimber chuckled. "Have mercy and go talk to the poor dear in private, Kate."

Kathleen rolled her eyes. "I'll be right back." She waved Dane off with her, and they ducked into Benito's office. Surprisingly, Jody wasn't in there dismantling the computer as she often was.

"Look, I just wanted to say...well, thanks, I guess, for being worried about me," Dane said, trying her best not to fidget.

Kathleen snorted. "Not so much you, but the child you once were. Children shouldn't be put through such ordeals."

Dane smiled a little. "I guess."

"Next time just say that. I thought something happened with Nikki the way you're bouncing around," Kathleen huffed, folding her arms across her chest.

"Oh, no! Nick's cool. I swear." Dane did her best to assure Kathleen, but an odd, nervous chuckle escaped her. *Calm down. It's not like she's going to eat you, not after the big dinner we just had anyway.*

Kathleen eyed her hard. "You sure?"

Dane gave a strong nod and took a breath to steady herself. "Positive. Nicole is completely fine."

"That's good. Her father and I...well, we didn't want to talk to her about it at your party or here, but has she made plans for when school ends?" Kathleen asked, lines appearing under her eyes.

Dane shook her head. "Not really. We've just been kinda enjoying the holiday season and all."

Kathleen nodded. "There's no pressure or anything. She has a perfectly good career."

"Yeah. Probably not gonna think about it until she has the degree in her hand since she does have a job and all." Dane didn't want to crush Kathleen's dreams of Nicole staying at the firm, but they both knew Nicole would put that chemistry degree to good use as soon as she could.

"I suppose. I hope she talks to us before making any decisions," Kathleen said.

"I'm sure she will. Nick's real responsible. She's not gonna throw away a career before she's got another one lined up. We'd starve to death, after all." Dane laughed, but Kathleen pinned her with a stern gaze.

"Now, if only someone else had a career." Kathleen looked her up and down.

Dane winced. "I'll work on that." Her lack of a career would forever be a bit of tension between her and Kathleen, but Kathleen was right. Part of being better would be making enough money to pay real bills.

"How?" Kathleen's voice matched her hard look. It was intense, frightening. In the past, she would've mistaken it for hatred, but now Dane knew it was concern and love for Nicole's future. She respected that.

Dane flexed her hand. "I'll get more gigs." She could now. Her hand was better, not great, but better.

Shaking her head, Kathleen chuckled. "Musicians. It's cute you think that counts as a career." And, no matter what their relationship, Kathleen would probably always be a snob.

Dane only shrugged. Music was all she ever wanted to do. It was probably the only thing that would hold her attention enough to make money. Before she could explain that, Nicole called her. They needed to get going. She looked at Kathleen, who literally shooed her away, with the hand movements and everything. Dane wasn't sure how she held in a fit of giggles.

After long goodbyes from everyone, Dane and Nicole set out for the Briarmoor home. Dane's stomach tossed a little, but she knew there was nothing to be nervous about. *They want you. It's fine.*

"Are you okay, love?" Nicole reached over and took Dane's hand, which helped calm her.

Dane took a deep breath. "Yeah, of course."

Nicole stared at her with an intensity she wasn't used to. "You sure?"

Dane's heart hammered in her chest, but she nodded. "Yeah. Why do you ask?"

A small smile danced onto Nicole's face. "Because we pulled up to the house, and you haven't moved yet."

Turning, she saw the house decorated in bright lights with a Santa workshop scene on the lawn. Dane yelped and then rushed to get out of the car. Her seat belt trapped her briefly, making her yowl as it snapped her back inside, but she untangled herself. She helped Nicole out of the car before grabbing a bag with the gifts from the backseat. Nicole grabbed Allison's, as it was too big to fit in the bag. Dane tried to take it from her, but she was stubborn.

"Let me help," Nicole said, and Dane nodded. They went to the front door. The smell of cookies greeted them along with Allison and Lynn. There were smiles all around.

"Come in. Come in." Lynn ushered them into the house with a wave. The heat wrapped around them as soon as they were inside.

"Come see the cookies I made," Allison said, taking Nicole's hand and dragging her to the kitchen. Nicole was a willing prisoner if the grin on her face meant anything.

"We're not going to get any cookies, you know that, right?" Dane winked at Lynn.

"I don't imagine Allison planned it that way."

"I'm glad she likes Nicole."

"She likes both of you, and I'm happy she does. I'm also happy you're back in our lives, and that you decided to spend Christmas with us." Lynn looped their arms together.

Dane allowed Lynn to lead her to the living room. Ben was there, playing a video game. Dane eased in right next to him, putting the bag of gifts by the arm of the couch. Henry was on the sofa, and Dane leaned over, shaking his hand.

"All right, what are we doing here?" Dane asked Ben. It looked like the typical racing game.

"Racing," Ben said absently and then he turned. His face lit up, and Dane felt special. "When did you get here?" He paused the game, throwing an arm around her to hug her.

Dane hugged him right back. "Just now. You got this for Christmas?"

"Yeah. Mom and Dad won't get me a cell phone," Ben pouted.

"You're too young," Henry chimed in.

"My friends got 'em." Ben pouted more, poking out his lip and folding his arms across his chest.

Chuckling, Dane mussed his hair. "I don't have a cell phone, so you're not alone."

He gave her a sidelong glance as his mouth turned up a little. "You don't?"

Shrugging, she shook her head. "Nope. Don't need one either. Everyone I care about knows exactly where to reach me."

"Home?"

"Yup." She mussed his hair again. "Glad you know where to find me."

He smiled. "Me, too."

***

"Allison, these are too good." Nicole moaned, biting into yet another chocolate chip cookie.

A blush stained Allison's cheeks, and she glanced down. She twiddled her fingers for a moment. She tended to do that when alone with Nicole. Nicole decided to finish her cookie before she approached the subject of why. While enjoying chocolate melting in her mouth, she looked around the kitchen. It put hers to shame.

"Have another cookie. Have as many as you want." Allison motioned to the half-full glass jar.

"Did you make these for me?" Nicole asked. She was tempted to have another, but she already had three. She didn't want to eat them all. *I'm going to have to live at the gym next month.*

"Well, you and Ben."

Nicole squinted a bit, trying to figure out the connection. "Me and Ben?"

"It's my little Christmas tradition." Allison rubbed her hands together and glanced away briefly.

Attention away from chocolaty goodness, Nicole arched an eyebrow. "What do you mean?"

"Well, I started making them for Ben when he was about three. I believed in the whole Santa business and I was kind of mean to him and to avoid getting on the naughty list, I made Ben cookies on Christmas Eve. This year, I made some for you, too."

Nicole's brow wrinkled. "But, you're not mean to me."

"I know." Allison bit her lip and shook her head. A blush burned up her cheeks. "I like you, Nicole. I mean, I like Dane, too, and I show it with her...I guess. I don't think I show you. I want you...I want you to know." Allison had to take a breath. "I want you to know I like you."

Nicole smiled. This girl was adorable. "I never had any doubts, but thanks for the cookies anyway. They're great, like you."

A shy smile twitched onto Allison's face as an even darker blush scorched its way up her neck. "I'm glad."

"I'm glad you like Danny, too."

Allison laughed. "She's nice, like Mom and Dad said, but, you know, the big kid version. Having a sister is nice. I mean, if she sees us that way!" She put her hands up. That blush might live on her face now.

Nicole smiled. "You bet she does."

Allison's eyes twinkled and her mouth ticked up for a second. Sighing, she scratched her head. "I feel like she needs us as much as she wants us and we want her."

Nicole put her arm around Allison, pulling her into a semi-hug. She usually made it a point to give Allison space, but felt like they turned a bit of a corner. Allison returned the embrace.

"You're pretty insightful, you know that?"

Allison giggled. They strolled out into the living room, joining the rest of the family. Danny and Ben were engrossed in some racecar video game. Their laughter filled the room and warmed Nicole's heart.

"You're cheating!" Dane said as Ben practically jumped on her, probably to win the race. It looked like it could be dangerous to get in between them.

"Hey, show me some of your gifts," Nicole said to Allison.

Nicole settled in, and Allison went through everything she had received. Then, there was the gift Danny and Nicole bought her. She cheered when she unwrapped it. Of course, she blushed immediately after as everyone laughed.

"You gonna play us something or leave us all in suspense?" Danny asked as Allison ran her fingers along the keyboard.

Allison smiled. "You know it's not the one I wanted."

Danny grinned. "No, but I got one just like it and I know it's pretty good." The one she had was purchased by Nicole's father for Danny's birthday. It had taken a lot for her to talk Lynn and Henry out of buying Allison the expensive one she wanted and they'd probably got at least one disappointed look from her when she finished opening her gifts that morning.

Allison regarded her with a tilted head. "You're going to play, too?"

"I didn't say all that." Danny paused the game to move to play. No one had to twist her arm to do it.

Danny used to travel with a guitar, after all. Nicole bought her a replacement after her cousin destroyed Danny's guitar. She didn't seem to love the instrument as much. She didn't play it and didn't take it everywhere she went like the old one. Nicole ached, knowing even though Danny tried to act all right with the new guitar, but it was obvious things weren't okay.

"You deserve something special," Danny said to Allison as she set up the keyboard.

Danny played the keyboard. It was a treat to hear her, especially with her hand somewhat improved. Allison watched Danny's fingers move with raw fascination and awe. Danny was magic with the keyboard as much as she was with the guitar. After a few minutes, she had to stop and crack the knuckles in her left hand.

This was the first time Nicole felt like she saw Danny just have fun with her music. Yes, she played around with Luke and Thomas, but that was generally their make-believe band. When she played with Philip, it was almost like he was one of her students. This was something else.

"That was unbelievable," Allison said while everyone else applauded.

"It'll sound even better when you play this." Danny pointed down at the keyboard. "And I play your other keyboard."

Allison nodded and eagerly went behind her keyboard. Danny fetched the other keyboard, the one she taught Allison on, and set it up. By that time, Lynn had to check on dinner. Nicole liked that Lynn cooked for her family, even though Nicole was certain the Briarmoors could afford a chef or afford to go out every night. Lynn seemed to like cooking.

"I didn't miss the concert, did I?" Lynn asked, easing into the seat next to her husband.

"We waited for you," Danny replied and then she turned to Allison. "Okay, let's put on a show, kid."

Allison started to play. It was soft, smooth, jazzy. For a moment, Danny listened with light in her eyes and her shoulders squared. Danny was so damned proud. It was beautiful.

And then Danny started to play, taking her lead from Allison. Allison smiled so brightly it made Nicole melt. Maybe Allison's insight in the kitchen went beyond Danny. They played for a few minutes before Lynn decided it was time for dinner and they gathered around the table.

It was the second dinner of the day, but rather different. For one, there was no prayer said around the table. The foods weren't the same thankfully. It was easier to eat a second dinner a couple of hours after the first with different food. Here, the main dish was turkey instead of ham. There were roasted potatoes, broccoli with cheese, white rice, yams, spinach, biscuits, cranberry sauce, and noodle casserole.

"Dane, where'd you learn all that music stuff from anyway? Mom and Dad don't play," Ben said, twirling his fork around. Henry gave him a stern look, and his fork ceased its random movement, returning to his loaded plate.

Danny took a moment to finish chewing and probably think of a proper response. "Yeah, but my biological mom plays the piano, among other things. She got me lessons. Found out music kinda flows through me."

Ben chuckled. "Playing video games kinda flows through me." He earned a couple of snickers. Allison cracked a smile.

"I should blame you for this." Lynn pointed at Henry with her fork.

Henry balked, pressing his hand to his chest dramatically. "Me? I didn't even know what a computer was before you came into my life."

Lynn smirked and arched an eyebrow. "Oh, really? Then, whose tech consulting business did I merge with?"

Henry chuckled, and the table fell into a comfortable silence for a while. Nicole watched when the chatter started up again. Danny was comfortable, chiming in all the time with confidence.

"Allison's doing well with the keyboard, yeah?" Henry said.

Danny nodded. "She sounds great. Stick with it."

"I like it. It helps me think," Allison said.

"Music helps me order my world," Danny replied.

Lynn smiled. "That's good."

"You should become, like, a huge rock star and make some real money," Ben said.

Danny let out a slightly uncomfortable laugh. "Actually used to be. But..." She held up her hand and flexed it a bit.

Ben's eyes couldn't have gotten any wider. "You were a rock star?"

Danny rocked her head from side to side. "Locally, yeah."

"But, because of your hand..." Allison grimaced and glanced away, like she knew the utter tragedy behind everything.

"It's better, but not great. It'll never be like it used to. Still, sometimes I play sets. I'm going to try to play more often. I'll be sure to let you guys know my next gig," Danny said.

"We'd like that," Henry replied.

Danny smiled. Nicole smiled, too. That'd be nice. This whole thing was nice, not just with the Briarmoors, but also with her family. The day showed just how good life could be.

***

They ended Christmas day on the couch. Dane pulled Nicole close as they settled on the sofa, in their pajamas. Dane wore her Santa hat, until Nicole took it away from her. Nicole looked better in it as far as Dane was concerned. Nicole insisted they watch some Christmas show Dane never heard of. It was funny, especially when the kid got his tongue stuck to a pole. It was a nice way to end a good day. And then the phone rang.

"Who is it?" Nicole asked as Dane leaned over to see the caller ID.

"Spider." Nicole's cousin, who until a certain camping trip, had been one of Nicole's favorite people in the world.

Nicole groaned. "Do I really want to talk to him?"

"He's not really the one likely to mess up your day." Dane understood Nicole's issues with her cousins, but she also understood Nicole's underlying desire to reconnect with them. They weren't just family. They'd been the friends she could be herself with and they'd betrayed her trust. "You know, you don't have to stay pissed at them for my sake. I don't give a shit about them."

Nicole sighed. "I do. They hurt you, badly."

"Not Spider. Does silence count as betrayal?" Dane wasn't sure how it worked. She hated that Spider and Junior never told Nicole about what their sister had done, but Beth never said anything either and Nicole still spoke with her. Spider hadn't been the one to punch Dane repeatedly for finally doing something about Lillian, nor had he been the one to smash her guitar for revenge.

"I don't want to talk to him."

Dane knew that feeling. "Then you don't have to."

Nodding, Nicole cuddled in closer. "I'm sorry."

"It wasn't your fault." Dane didn't blame Nicole for any of it. "You wanted to share something special and it was. Plus, I'm looking forward to the weather getting better so we can go camping alone. And, then, maybe the kids, but not all the kids."

Nicole laughed. "Never all the kids ever again."

"Live and learn."

"Exactly."

They settled again, watching the movie. Nicole's cell phone went off a few minutes later. Unsurprisingly, Nicole ignored it. A few more minutes passed and then the house phone rang again. Dane groaned, checking the caller ID.

"Who is it?" Nicole asked.

"Christine. Probably calling to say Merry Christmas or something."

"Are you going to answer?"

Dane shrugged, but she reached for the phone. "Hey."

"Merry Christmas," Christine said.

"Merry Christmas."

"Did you have a good one?"

Dane gave Nicole a squeeze. "It was amazing." Better than anything she had experienced when it came to holidays. She wasn't even taking a shot at Christine.

"That's good. I wanted you to know, I kind of got you a gift."

"You kinda got me a gift?" Not that Dane wanted anything from Christine. The last thing Christine gave her left her feeling a little dirty and bought. *I still need to really do something with that money.* She was mostly funneling it into the joint account she had with Nicole.

"Well, I'm not sure if you're aware, but I'm on the board of several arts committees and heavily involved in the arts in the city."

Dane shrugged. "Sounds right." Christine had to do something to keep busy and undoubtedly take her mind off the fact that she was married to the world's biggest douche and had at least one psychopathic offspring.

"I have a friend who is producing a play. He's looking for someone to write music for it."

"Like a musical?"

"Well, no. It's a play with dialogue and no songs, but he wants a score to help set the tone. I volunteered your name, if you don't mind."

"Never done anything like that." She wrote music for the stage in the sense that it would be performed by a band in front of live audience. She never composed a soundtrack before.

"I think you'll be fine with it. It's not a done deal. He'll call you in for an interview, but you have the position as long as you show him your musical capabilities. I promise you."

Dane frowned, but her stomach bubbled a bit. She wasn't sure if that was from anxiety or eagerness. "Wow. Need to think about this." This was crazy. She had an actual job waiting for her. But, it was more a favor to Christine than something gained through her own talent. *Shit, did she just buy me again?*

"You have time. He's not going to see you until after the New Year. If it's all right with you, I'll give him your number. I can also text Nicole any information that needs to be passed on, all right?"

"Um...yeah. Okay."

An awkward beat of silence passed. "Well, Merry Christmas again."

"Yeah." Dane disconnected the call, her mind swirling. Trying to figure out what happened, she ran her hand through her hair and then scratched the side of her nose.

"Danny? Baby, you okay?" Nicole rubbed Dane's thigh.

"Yeah. Crazy stuff." Dane shook her head. "Tell you about it later. Right now, let's watch the movie." She wanted to end Christmas on a less crazy note. "Hey, question."

"Yes?"

"Do people get laid on Christmas?"

Nicole laughed and glanced at the time. "There's two hours left for you to find out." Dane grinned. She felt like that was more than enough time to have her question answered.

Chapter Seven

NICOLE WOKE WITH A smile on her face and Danny in her arms. She could feel the season's nip in the air, but it couldn't be warmer cuddled under the covers with her girlfriend. Danny kissed her softly, which made her giggle. Danny lit up the dark room with her cheerful presence.

"Just to be sure, we don't celebrate Boxing Day, right?" Danny's voice was low, mellow.

Sighing, Nicole kissed the end of her nose. "No, but we do have the day off. Unless you're tutoring."

Danny leaned in closer, burying her nose in Nicole's neck. "You know better. If you're off then I'm off." She inhaled, her breath tickling Nicole's skin. "You smell good."

"You're too sweet."

Danny pressed their foreheads together and caressed Nicole's cheek. "You always say that."

"Because you are. I don't make it a point to lie." Nicole gave her a small kiss. "You okay?"

Danny sighed as her thumb made gentle circles on Nicole's cheek. "Of course, I am. Lying here with the best woman I know after a mind-blowing Christmas with so much cool stuff. Why wouldn't I be okay?" She played with a lock of Nicole's hair.

Nicole's hand glided across Danny's bare hip. "Because I know you went to bed thinking about Christine and that job."

Turning her eyes to the ceiling, Danny shifted a bit onto her back. "I wouldn't say I went to bed thinking about her." They had done things to keep her mind off it. "She completely threw me for a loop. I almost wish she gave me more details. Hate when she tries to be relevant in my life like this. Why can't she just do normal stuff? Call me to have tea or walk the dog or sacrifice a goat or something? Whenever she gives me stuff, it's weird. It's like a knee-jerk reaction."

Nicole pressed herself closer to Danny. "You think it's like when she gave you the trust." She ran her fingers through Danny's hair and scratched her scalp.

Danny purred and stretched. "Yeah, I do. You don't think so?"

Nicole wasn't sure what Christine was trying to do. "I don't know if I have enough information to make a real judgment call here." *I don't want to give her the benefit of the doubt, but I can't help my nature. I don't want this to bite Danny on the ass.* She wasn't sure how much more jerking around Danny could take from Christine before she snapped.

Grey eyes narrowed, but remained on the ceiling. "She gave me a job. What more do you need?"

"A lot of people get jobs because they know someone."

Danny's forehead wrinkled. "This could be something normal?"

With a shrug, Nicole smiled a little. "It could be." She hoped it'd be like that. Danny might not survive Christine letting her down again. She scratched Danny's scalp once more, threading her fingers through soft, ebony locks to help soothe her beloved.

Danny made a contented noise and tried to settle in deeper to the mattress. "Do you think all I have to do is show up and I get the gig?"

Nicole sighed. That was a possibility, but she doubted Danny wanted things to go that way. "Again, this is normal. Hell, all Mina had to do was show up. I didn't even have to show up!"

Danny laughed. "I'm sure you had to show up."

"Well, of course when work started, but I wasn't interviewed or anything. Go see what this is all about. I'll be there with you. It could be something special."

Danny pulled her close and nuzzled her neck again. "Maybe..." She shook her head. "But, I don't want to think of that now. I just want to snuggle up to you and think about how we're going to spend your birthday. I mean, it's the big 3-0."

Laughing, Nicole narrowed her gaze. "As if I don't know Mina and Clara have already planned some crazy vacation thing." Her friends were too predictable for that to not be the case.

"But, you don't know where and how long."

Nicole blew out a breath. "Clara can't be gone long as she has a son, Mina has the meeting of the century on the eighth, and I now have to drive you to a job interview on the tenth."

Danny clicked her tongue. "By the tenth."

"Either way. We won't be jet setting too far for too long." She didn't care where they went. She'd have her girlfriend and her best friends with her. It sounded like the best birthday she could ask for.

Danny's forehead wrinkled. "Why do you know everyone's schedule like that?"

"Someone has to keep track of things." Nicole knew Clara's schedule fairly well, too, just in case something happened, or they needed to plan something quickly, and Clara and Mina were the same with her. None of them were hard to keep up with.

Danny snorted. "Anyway. We're still expected to do dinner with your parents, right?"

"Of course." Nicole suspected she'd have birthday dinners with her parents until they were all dead. She didn't mind it, especially since they liked Danny now.

"Enough of that nonsense. Time to waste this day."

Nicole was about to ask what Danny meant, but sweet lips on her mouth was an excellent clue. She immediately returned the kiss. This was a post-Christmas tradition she could like.

"Not to make things depressing or anything, but you know this has been the most normal and best Christmas time for me."

Nicole groaned. She didn't want to think about why that was, or she might talk Danny out of the job arranged by Christine.

Danny stared down at her. "We're going to build many good Christmas memories, right?" Her eyes looked worried, but hopeful.

Nicole cupped Danny's face with both hands and kissed her. "Of course."

"Then, it's all right. Don't hurt for me. Everything got us to this point, and I don't regret it. I actually like knowing why my childhood was so screwed up, though. I'm not mad about it anymore."

Nicole tried to smile, but deep down, she hurt for Danny. She caressed Danny's cheek with one thumb, and Danny took hold of her hand.

"How did you get this way?" Nicole breathed. Danny was some kind of unicorn or other mythological creature. She knew how to walk away from a fight, knew how to accept the past was the past, and kept going despite all the horrible things hurled at her.

Danny grinned. "Why, don't you know, this is all you? You made me this way. Screw what happened in the past. I know I have a happy future with you and that's enough."

"That is enough." Nicole kissed her again. "Okay. Anything you want to tell me then is fine."

"I don't think there's anything right now. I mean, all my holidays were spent alone in my room as a kid and my teen life was an unending party. This is nice and wholesome. It's order where there used to be chaos, light where there used to be darkness, warmth when it used to be freezing, and best of all, healing where there were gaping, bleeding wounds. I love it. There were years I didn't even know it was Christmas."

How can you miss Christmas time? She looked deep into Danny's eyes. "Never again."

"I know."

"No more messed up birthdays either. We'll celebrate any and all holidays. There'll definitely be more parties."

Danny's face lit up. "Then, we're definitely having a cookout when it gets warm?"

The brightness on Danny's face made Nicole grin. "Didn't I already agree to this?"

"Who works the grill if we have a cookout?"

For some reason, the question made Nicole burst into a fit of giggles. "Does it matter?"

"Your dad thinks it'll be you because I'm the housewife, but I could work the grill. I mean, it doesn't look hard." Danny sounded too eager.

Nicole laughed even more. "Baby, if you want to work the grill you can, but I thought you liked being the housewife."

"I do, but I can work a grill!" Danny held her head up high, tilting her chin in an almost superhero-like pose. Then, she squinted and her brow wrinkled. "Um, I think anyway." She looked back at Nicole. "I've never done it before."

That was far from a surprise. "Well, we'll have several over the course of years. You'll get comfortable with it and you'll be great at it and if not, I've got it. Okay?"

Nodding, Danny smiled. "We're staying in bed all day?"

"I don't have a problem with that." Of course, they'd probably only make it through the morning, but that was enough. They'd have to get Haydn eventually and take him for a walk. For now, she was exactly where she wanted to be. She leaned in for another kiss while Danny's hands wandered her back.

***

Once the excitement of Christmas and Nicole's birthday passed, Dane found herself meeting with Christine's friend about the play. Nicole wanted to drive her and took time off from work. Dane appreciated the support, as butterflies conquered her whole chest. She had never been so nervous about a gig before.

Maybe it was because she had never done anything like this. Writing a score was different from playing in a band. Was she expected to lead the score while the play went on? She had no idea. Added to that, this could be a huge step for her. It could be a real job, maybe a real career. *Holy shit.* The pressure from the thought felt like it might break her ribs.

"Breathe, love. Breathe." Nicole's voice sounded distant and low, but she was right next to Dane.

Breathing in and out, Dane felt a delicate hand making comforting circles at the small of her back. She could feel the pleasant pressure through her winter coat.

Rubbing her hands together, Dane took a deep breath as they pulled up to the theater, but her lungs burned as if she was drowning. Why was it so hard to breathe? Was the air getting thinner? That could happen in the winter, right? She took another deep breath, but it didn't seem like enough.

"Is this crazy? This seems crazy."

Nicole parked the car and the theater seemed to loom before them, casting a shadow over Dane's entire sense of being. The theater wasn't anything special. It looked like a little movie theater, with narrow red ticket booths on the side and a blank marquee with green lights, but for Dane, it seemed like some mutant monster that might devour them. The lobby doors were like a threatening maw and shadows in her mind created claws, ready to drag her to her demise.

With a smile, Nicole used her free hand to give Dane's hand a squeeze, which helped her get a little more air somehow. "My love, it's fine. It's far from crazy. Give it a try. It'll be like when we saw the Christmas show with the kids, and you wanted to do things differently. This is your chance."

Dane managed to scoff while doing her best to not hyperventilate. The day wouldn't get any easier with a trip to the hospital. "Since when do plays have music, anyway? I mean, like a real score. It's weird. Maybe Christine's pranking me." That made more sense to her than anything else right now.

Nicole gave her a deadpan look. "Danny, Christine has done a lot to you in life, but has she ever pranked you?"

Dane cracked the knuckles in her left hand, only to realize it trembled. She held her left hand with her right and took another deep breath. *Heart, I really need you to calm the hell down.* "No." A prank would've taken too much energy, too much planning, and would've meant Christine paid her some mind. *Okay, the lack of oxygen is making me crazy.*

"Just go in and see what it's about. Try it on for size. What if it fits?" Nicole said.

"Then I'd owe her." The idea of owing Christine a damn thing didn't sit well with Dane and caused a sneer to cut through her face. Yeah, she was trying to do something with Christine, but she wasn't sure if she wanted this to be the "something." If this worked, she'd have a better job thanks to Christine. The idea made her want to throw up and the way her throat burned, she might.

"Baby, she didn't get you the job. She just put the bug into a friend's ear. This isn't a sure thing unless you wow them. It's you, not Christine."

Dane nodded. This was true. The gig wasn't a sure thing. Christine never said she had the job and when she got the call about it, 'the friend' didn't seem eager to give her the gig. She needed to interview. She had to impress the guy in charge. She needed to earn the gig, like any other gig.

"It'll be you, Danny, not Christine. You." Nicole squeezed her hand again and continued rubbing circles on her back. "Music flows through you, pours out of you. It's how you experience the world and you can bring others into it. You can bring others into another world of this play."

Dane finally started breathing normally and her mind stopped spinning. "I can't put it past Christine, Nick. She feels threatened by you and Lynn. There's no way for her to yoyo me like she used to do. I feel like she'll do just about anything."

Nicole shook her head. "You're right to be suspicious, but don't go in there thinking like that. You can ask the guy about his relationship with Christine if you want. You can test the waters to see if this is already a sure thing and walk away if you don't like it, but at least go in there to find out. Don't sit here assuming everything."

Dane nodded and swallowed around a lump in her throat. She wasn't sure what this fear was, but it felt like something deeper than doubting Christine. What if this was fear of moving forward? Fear of being better? If she got the gig, then it was something real. It was a paycheck beyond the pocket change she picked up tutoring. She wouldn't have any excuses anymore. She would suddenly be living a real adult life. This was scary.

"Come on, love. You don't want to be late." Nicole kissed the corner of Dane's mouth.

Dane sighed, but Nicole was right. She didn't want to mess up an incredible opportunity. If she was late and still got the gig, then it was a sure thing, right? It meant Christine had set everything up and tried to buy her affection once again. Then, maybe she did want to be late, not that Nicole would let her. If the game wasn't rigged, then she was certain she could wow them. If the game was rigged, then she'd run away from the whole mess as fast as she could. She wouldn't let Christine ruin her life again.

"Wish me luck." Dane opened her door.

"You'll do fine," Nicole assured her with a bright smile.

Dane wasn't sure about that, but grinned at Nicole anyway. The cold air hit Dane and managed to help focus her. She marched into the small theater, looking for the producer. She went from the tiny, deserted lobby into the theater proper. There wasn't much life in the building beyond what looked like auditions on the stage. There were a few people there, holding scripts, but they didn't seem to be doing anything else. She figured one of the guys sitting in the audience was the man she needed to see. Before she could get down to them and ask, another man came up to her.

"Hey, are you here for auditions?"

"No, my name is Dane. I'm here to see Calvin Mason about music."

He nodded. "He said something about you showing up. Hold on. I'll get him." He rushed over to two of the men and pointed back at her. They nodded and rose.

"Dane Wolfe?" the older and taller of the two men asked. He was dressed in a sharp, black suit and reminded her a little of Raymond. He had facial hair that was so well groomed, it had to be done by a professional. His brown hair was done in a perfect, short haircut.

"Calvin Mason?" Dane put her hand.

"Yes." Calvin shook her hand, giving her a firm grip. "This is the director, Andrew Mason." He motioned to the younger man by his side. He was dressed casually in skinny, brown pants and a button-down red shirt with the sleeves rolled up. He had no facial hair and a tumble of messy dark brown curls on the top of his head.

"Nice to meet you." Dane went to shake Andrew's hand. It was weak, and he pulled his hand back quickly, his lip curling into a sneer. *Maybe this isn't a sure thing.* The director didn't seem impressed with her and turned away from her as soon as he could.

"I'll have someone show you to the office. Give us a second to finish up with this," Calvin said, motioning to the stage.

Dane nodded. "That's fine."

She allowed herself to be led to a desk backstage by a wall. It wasn't a well-lit space, but it was away from the traffic of production. It smelled of dust, wood, and stale air. *When was the last time this place actually saw a play?*

There were plenty of props and objects littering the place, creepy masks, bowling pins, a pile of clothes, broken tree cutouts, ballet shoes, and other things. She noticed a bent, discolored trumpet, snare drum, and a dusty piano off to the side, but didn't think anything of them. In the corner, it looked like there might be more instruments, but they were blocked by a ladder and tarp. They'd have to clean the place up, unless they wanted everyone to work in a junkyard. She unzipped her coat and took a few breaths to make sure to stay calm. Barely a couple of minutes later, Calvin and Andrew sat across from her.

"Sorry for the mess and the fact that this is the office for the moment. The theater was full of junk we don't need, so we're trying to clear away the clutter and the office is a temporary storage area, as are most of the rooms," Calvin explained.

Dane shook her head. "It's fine." She didn't care about the mess now that the guys in charge were in front of her.

Calvin smiled a little and leaned forward. "You came highly recommended for this project by Christine Wolfe."

Dane wasn't sure what to make of that. Surely Calvin knew she was related to Christine, same last name and all. Did he know Christine was her birth mother? It was kind of an open secret around their neighborhood and certain social circles, like everyone knew, but no one said anything. They pretended Dane fell out of the sky or was born from a rock and the Wolfes had been magnanimous enough to allow her to dwell among them. She wasn't sure how it worked outside the neighborhood, though. People probably gossiped. He had to know.

"She seems to think I'd be a good fit for this, but I don't even know what this is," Dane admitted. Why the hell did a play need a score when it wasn't a musical?

Andrew grunted. "Then what are you doing here?"

"Because I make music and you need music," Dane replied as if it was obvious. This was feeling less and less like a sure thing because of Andrew. He seemed to have something against her already, glaring at her as if she had done him wrong.

Andrew crossed his arms. "We don't need music," he spoke through gritted teeth.

"Excuse us for a second." Calvin stood and pulled Andrew away.

Dane watched them go off to the far end of the room, as if they were about to walk back to the audience. Calvin was all glowers with his hands on his hips with Andrew waving his arms. Director and producer seemed to be at odds over the play having music. Dane wondered if this was some kind of compromise, like Calvin had wanted a musical and Andrew didn't, so they settled on a play with music. In the end, Calvin returned to the table while Andrew disappeared back into the audience area.

"Forgive me," Calvin said as he sat down.

"It's all right."

"Like I said, Christine Wolfe sang your praises when I told her I was looking for someone to produce a score for this play. Unfortunately, for all her wonderful words, she didn't have any recent music of yours for me to sample. Everything was years old, but it was enough for me to want to meet with you."

Dane's brow furrowed. Christine had samples of her music? It was probably one of Christine's weird ways of 'keeping track of her' and being close without being close. *Whatever.*

"I haven't really made anything recently. I've mostly been tutoring people on different instruments, but if you want to hear something." Dane nodded toward the instruments in the back, hoping there was more than what she first saw. It hadn't occurred to her to bring recorded samples of her work, not that she had any. "You can go pick any one of those at random and then pick an emotion and I bet I can make you feel it." *Is this the right thing to say on an interview? Is it even an interview?* Her mother seemed connected to Calvin, not Andrew. Calvin also seemed to be the boss.

Leaning forward on the creaky, dusty desk, Calvin rubbed his palms together. His brown eyes danced. "Confident, aren't you?"

Dane shrugged. "Not so much confident. Think about if someone asked you to breathe like you usually do. That's music for me."

He nodded and glanced over at the pile of instruments. "And anyone of those?"

She took a closer look. "Well, maybe not the tuba." Why there was a tuba over there baffled her. Was there a marching band scene? Maybe it was part of the 'junk' Calvin mentioned. *You're off track. Is this what people go through on job interviews all the time?*

"But, you don't have any of your own music?"

Dane scrunched up her face and held up a messy portfolio Nicole forced her to put together. "I haven't had a chance to record anything, but I've got plenty of written work." She put it on the desk. She had some equipment to record, but she never saw the point, even when this meeting loomed over her. She was used to people knowing her when she booked gigs. She hadn't thought she'd need to play here.

Calvin took the portfolio and opened it. He had to read music from the way he studied it and nodded ever so slightly. He then looked up at her.

"Play this one for me." He pushed her song in front of her.

"You wanna pick the instrument?" It seemed like it'd be a good challenge, a way to prove herself since this didn't seem to be a shoo-in.

"Christine said you're brilliant on the guitar. I think the one over there is missing strings, though. What can you do with that keyboard?"

Dane went to grab the keyboard, poking out from under the ladder hiding the other instruments. It was covered in dust, but seemed to be in working condition. With some effort, she dragged the damn thing over to the desk, hoping he didn't notice her limp. He didn't say anything as she set the keyboard on the edge of the desk and cracked the knuckles in her left hand. *Okay, hand, you're a pain in the ass, but you've gotten better since I've been using you, so let's make it through this and maybe do something in life.* She plugged the keyboard in, checked everything out, and started playing.

***

Nicole sat in the car, hoping and waiting, feeling like there was a swarm of bees buzzing under her skin. Danny had been gone for almost a half-hour already. That had to be a good sign. If things had gone sideways, Danny probably would've stormed out. She had to see signs this wasn't an automatic hook up from Christine.

Added to that, she was fairly certain the longer the interview, the more likely someone was to get the job. If Danny hadn't seen any reason to leave and was still wowing them, then that had to be a good sign. *You've got this, Danny. I know you do.* She was taken from her thoughts as her cell phone sounded. Glancing at the screen, she saw it was Crow.

"Hi," Nicole greeted her and turned down the radio. It was simple, soft classical playing, but she didn't want any distractions, knowing

Crow was as anxious as she was over this interview.

"How's it going?" Crow blurted.

"She's not out from the interview yet," Nicole reported with a smile.

"Is that good? Can that be good?" Crow's words were fast, and she squealed. She was so excited it made Nicole laugh.

"I think it is good. I'll tell her to call you as soon as she comes out."

"This is why I wanted to drive her!" Crow groaned and then yelped. "But, I totally support you in doing it."

"That's good." Nicole tittered. She and Crow got along well enough now, but sometimes there were little things to remind her that in the beginning, Crow wasn't fond of her.

"Okay, but a long interview is a good thing, right?"

"Yes. I'm sure things are going well if she's still in there." Nicole wasn't entirely sure how an interview went to write music for a play. Did Danny have to play something? Did she have to discuss music she made in the past? She hoped the portfolio came in handy. *I should've asked Crow if she had any recordings of Danny's past performances.* Her stomach dropped a little, fearful the oversight of not having recordings could cost Danny the job.

Crow sighed. "This could be big for her, right? I mean, it's back into real music. Sure, she's not performing, but she'd be creating music for a lot of people to hear, right?"

"Yes." The fact that this could be a chance to do real music again was one of the reasons why Danny was anxious. If Christine had set this all up, Danny would be in Christine's debt for something most people wouldn't even be able to understand. Danny probably looked at it as a deal with the Devil, and she'd have no choice but to sell her soul. *No child should feel like that with their mother.*

A strange, almost nervous laugh escaped Crow. "Wow. I don't even know what to make of that. It's been quite a while."

"You know this music will be different." She hoped Crow didn't hype Danny up into thinking music in the theater would be like the world of rock and roll. But, then again, Danny had gone to plays with her, so she should know what to expect, as best one could with a play that wasn't a musical.

"It'll have Dane's flare. Even listening to her play now with her hand all messed up, she's still got her own unique signature, and it still hits you right. Maybe she can't play the way she used to, but that hasn't stopped her mind. It's still going to be fucking awesome."

Nicole chuckled. Danny's injuries might stop her from playing, but she never let them lock up her mind once she finally got back to writing. Maybe she'd be able to write something for someone else to shine. Maybe the job would take her to a different level.

"Thank you," Crow said.

Nicole blinked and looked at the phone for a second. "Why are you thanking me?"

"She wouldn't have done this if you weren't there. Hell, her mother wouldn't have gotten her this chance if you weren't there. You got her back on her feet."

Nicole shook her head. "She got herself back on her feet." *Does Crow tell her that? Reinforcing this idea, I did something? Danny had to want to get back on her feet or it wouldn't have happened.*

"Yeah, but it was because she wanted to be with you. You're the one who helped her. No one else would've been able to get through to her. Hell, I didn't even know where she was, and she wouldn't have let me in if I did, anyway. Really, even my real friendship with her is possible because of you."

Those words rang true, but Nicole still didn't want to hear it. She didn't want credit for Danny's life. She wanted Danny to be all right. "It doesn't matter. What does matter is Danny landing this job."

"She'll crush this gig, no matter how small."

Small. That was a thought. Plays didn't usually have music, not something big and flashy like Danny anyway. Not to mention, this theater didn't exactly scream 'giant production.' But, maybe it was what Danny needed.

"You'll have her call me, right?"

Nicole rolled her eyes. "You're probably just going to call back in another fifteen minutes if she's not out."

Crow laughed again. "Yeah, ten minutes probably, but who's counting, right? Anybody else calling to check up on her?"

"I've been ordered to text Mina every ten minutes. I think Terri is going to survive." She spoke too soon as she got another call. "Okay, no, that's her."

"Of course. I'm gone."

Nicole chuckled once more and bid Crow farewell only to greet Terri seconds later. Terri wanted to know the same things as Crow. Nicole wished she had answers.

***

"You weren't blowing smoke up my ass about your talent." Calvin chuckled from his seat. He leaned against the desk as Dane flopped back into her chair, causing it to groan. The screeching noise against the hard floor echoed through the empty backstage.

She gave him a waning smile and flexed her hand. It hurt like hell. Sure, it was used to playing for a couple of minutes, but switching instruments and trying to make it through almost ten minutes of playing? Cramps didn't even begin to cover it. She hoped Nicole had a solution for it, because she didn't have a clue on what to do. *Is a hand massage a thing?*

"Well, I've been told if I was cut, I'd bleed musical notes." Dane was good at one thing in life, and she'd never been shy about it. Besides, he just witnessed her play the shit out of three rundown, off-key instruments.

Calvin's expression was beyond a grin. "I can believe that. I've heard a lot of different musicians for this, a lot of different songs, genres, and styles, but you are something else. I think you're exactly what this play needs."

Dane nodded. "Can I ask you a question?"

"Of course."

"A play with music that's not a musical? I don't understand what you want me to do. You want to make a score or a soundtrack or something, but not like a musical?"

Calvin nodded. "Good question. I do want something like that. I wanted to produce something different. A play with a soundtrack would be accurate. I want it to be similar to a movie in that sense. I want something that after opening night, the papers are talking about it."

"If it's a good show, wouldn't they be doing that, anyway?" For some reason, the question made him laugh. That didn't seem like a good sign.

He held up a finger. "Give me a second. I want you to have a copy of the script. Look at the scenes and start figuring out what you want to do. Be aware the script is subject to change since we haven't started anything really, but it'll give you a good idea of the storyline."

Dane nodded, but again, that didn't seem like a good sign. He was gone before she could figure out a proper way to question his response. Also, since he was getting her a script, did that mean she landed the gig? It sounded that way, but she wasn't sure.

While she waited, she noticed Andrew sneering in her general direction. Producer and director definitely weren't on the same page. She got an understanding why when Calvin put the script in front of her. The cover page said it all. Andrew was director and writer. Music probably wasn't in his vision. It had to hurt to have his art changed without his consent, and there didn't seem to be anything he could do about it beyond pout.

"Is this a go? I got the gig?" It'd hurt her ego if she thought she got the gig and he just wanted to pick her brain about music for the script.

Calvin grinned at her. "You got the gig. You will write up a score and lead the orchestra in playing it while the play runs. I think we have something special here if you can make it happen."

Dane wasn't sure. She wouldn't be sure until she read the script. "I'll see what I can do."

"Not to pressure you or anything. Come in on Monday at eight. There'll be a group of musicians here for you to start with and you're in charge of them."

She blinked. "Monday? You want me to have music by Monday?"

"No. I want you to have read the script, have ideas, and be ready to work on Monday with an orchestra of five."

Dane nodded. "I can do that." She better do it. This was a chance, a real chance. This was a real job. She could finally bring something more to the table. She could be better. "Now, how much money for this gig?" She hoped that wasn't rude. There really wasn't a number he could tell her that would be a deal breaker. She'd be able to pay bills and treat Nicole to things with money she earned.

He chuckled. "We can discuss that."

Dane nodded. She didn't know how much money she should walk away with for something like this, but it had to be more than tutoring. It probably wouldn't be as good when clubs booked her a lifetime ago, though. It didn't matter. Time to negotiate. She'd like to find out if she had any benefits, too, not that she needed them. It'd just be nice to have them without Nicole's help.

***

Nicole almost jumped as the door opened and cold air rushed in as Danny eased into the passenger seat. She wasn't sure what to make of Danny's expression, all pinched eyebrows and pursed lips. It was something new.

"You okay?" Nicole thought things were good despite the

expression. Danny had been gone for almost an hour.

For a long moment, there was silence. Danny flexed her left hand and cracked her knuckles before putting her hands together to blow on them. *I hope she wasn't trying to play for most of that time.* If Danny had overextended herself, Nicole would do everything she could to help Danny's hand feel better.

"Yeah. I mean." Danny shrugged. "I got the gig."

"That's great!" Nicole wrapped Danny into a hug. Danny returned it tightly, but when they pulled apart, Danny's face was still kind of twisted. Nicole studied her. "Is it not great? Did it turn out Christine really did arrange the whole thing?"

Danny shook her head as she sat back in her seat. "No, I don't think she did. It was just a little weird in there. Pretty sure the director and producer are related, but they don't seem to agree on how this thing should go."

Nicole scoffed. "Well, you don't have to worry about that, baby. All you have to worry about is arranging the music."

Danny's hand went through her hair and she stared straight ahead with wide eyes. "Oh, my god."

Nicole put a hand on Danny's shoulder. "What's up?"

"Baby, I got a job. Not a gig. A job!" Danny panted. She sounded like she was having trouble breathing again and possibly on the verge of a panic attack. Nicole rubbed her back.

"Yes, love, you have a job." Nicole kissed her. She couldn't believe Danny was so overwhelmed. She kissed her again, and Danny laughed before turning to face her completely.

"I got a job!" Danny threw her arms around Nicole and held her to the point it almost hurt, but Nicole didn't say anything.

"I'm proud of you. So proud," Nicole whispered.

"I'm gonna do better for you, baby. So much better," Danny promised.

Nicole pulled away and shook her head. "You're perfectly fine." She caressed Danny's cheek.

Danny's whole face was lit up, and it seemed like a halo surrounded her. Nicole's heart jumped. She wasn't sure she had ever seen Danny look happy. She couldn't wait to watch her experience this new joy.

"We have to call everyone when we go home," Nicole said. Danny grinned and wiggled her eyebrows.

Chapter Eight

NICOLE WATCHED FROM THE sofa as Danny sat on the floor with the script in her hands. Haydn tucked under Danny's elbow, trying to get her attention. From the pinch of Danny's face, Haydn had his job cut out for him. Nicole had to give it to Danny, ignoring Haydn was a tall order, especially once he started to whimper and nose around the script. Even when he hopped on Danny's back and neck, she didn't cut him a glance. Eventually, he gave up and bounded over to Nicole.

"Aw, sorry, puppy, but your mom has work to do right now," Nicole said as he nuzzled her hand. She offered him a sad smile while petting his head and back.

Out of the blue, Danny huffed and slammed the script down. "Chem, can you read this? I mean, I feel like I might be stupid."

Nicole squinted as she turned her attention to her lover. "Well, I know you're far from stupid. What's the problem?"

Danny scratched her head. "I don't get it. I'm reading this thing, and I don't get it."

Nicole arched an eyebrow and leaned over some, trying to see the script without getting up. "What don't you get?"

Rubbing her furrowed brow, Danny frowned. "Well, I'm trying to figure out if it's a retelling of Robin Hood or King Arthur."

Nicole scratched her chin. "Well, those are two distinctive legends. Is the main character an outlaw?"

"Yes."

"Okay." Sounded Robin Hood–like. She rubbed noses with Haydn to let him know she hadn't forgotten about him. He tried to lick her, but she pulled back in time. She doubted she'd ever get used to him licking her, especially in the face.

"But, he becomes king in the end."

Not quite Robin Hood. "Well, is he an archer or a swordsman?"

"Both." Danny bit her bottom lip and squinted at the script.

Yeah, this was harder than it seemed. "Is the main villain a sorceress or an evil king?"

"Evil sorcerer king."

"Wow. Is the story any good?" She never considered a mash up of Robin Hood and King Arthur. Maybe Andrew Mason made it work or maybe there was a reason no one had ever done it.

Danny held up a hand and wiggled it from side to side. "It's not bad, but it's not great either. From skimming it, it just seems weird. Like I said, I don't know what the story is beyond some generic medieval hero crap with a damsel in distress and evil king."

"A damsel in distress?" *Wow. I thought entertainment was trying to move beyond that cliché. Guess I was wrong.*

"Yup. I'm talking trapped-in-a-tower-waiting-for-the-dashing-knight-in-shining-armor-to-come-rescue-her damsel in distress. She doesn't even have any funny lines from what I can tell."

Nicole frowned and then grunted as Haydn shoved into her. She made a face at him and scratched behind his ears. "I didn't think people still went for that sort of thing. Is this a story for adults?"

Twisting her mouth up a little, Danny shook her head. "I think it's supposed to be for kids. There's a lot of magic, and there's a dragon. Probably get a better idea of it on Monday."

"Do you have any ideas for music yet?"

Danny grimaced. "Not really because I don't get the story much. Like I said, is this Robin Hood or King Arthur?"

"Well, maybe he's trying to be original. He could've taken characteristics from those and other classic heroes to build his story. Or maybe he's trying to poke fun at those stories by showing all of the clichés." She'd rather that than kids watching a damsel-in-distress and thinking girls were incapable of doing anything without a man around.

Danny nodded. "That's possible."

"If you can't get a feel for the story, what are you going to do?"

Danny shook her head. "I'll figure something out. The story isn't awful. Probably just need to get through not knowing who these characters are supposed to be."

"Just treat them as their own characters," Nicole said.

Danny nodded. "If nothing else, I could talk to Andrew, even though he seemed kinda pissed about me being there."

"Well, I'm sure he'll get over that. He undoubtedly would want the best music to go with his art, right?" It seemed logical to her, but she had also come across more than her fair share of illogical humans.

Danny shrugged. "I dunno about all that. He's not looking at it as going with his art or even enhancing his art, but possibly ruining his art. It's weird to look at someone else's art and try to add my own. I'm used to working on my own with my music. Even with a band, they played what I wrote."

"You'll figure it out."

Danny grunted and went back to the script. She needed to find her rhythm. A smile slid onto Nicole's face as she watched Danny work, jotting down notes on the script.

Haydn pushed into her face. She rubbed his head and gave him kisses. He nuzzled her, pressed his paws against her, and bumped his wet nose into her face. Giggling, she entertained him, talking to him, scratching his head, and letting him tug on his toy rope for several minutes before she looked at Danny again.

Nicole wondered if this was how she appeared when she studied for exams—intense, focused, determined with hard eyes and a tense face. Pride swelled in her chest as she watched Danny make notes on the script. *Is this how Danny feels when she watches me work?*

They were going forward. She was almost out of school. Danny had a job that would display her talent and could lead to better things. They might both have new careers this time next year. Anxiety fluttered in her chest and she tried to swallow it down, but it bubbled. Her heart pounded in her ears. She took a deep breath, exhaled slowly, and hoped to release the sudden tension. Finding that impossible, she nestled Haydn close and he pushed her over. She laughed, despite him panting his hot breath right in her face. At least he kept his tongue to himself.

"Hey, quiet over there. Trying to make sense of a script." Danny waved the script in the air. The smile on her face made her eyes twinkle.

Nicole chuckled. "Sorry. Your son's unruly today."

Danny arched an eyebrow. "Oh, he's mine when he's unruly? Now, I know what to expect when we have kids."

Nicole straightened for a second, and her heart thumped harder against her ribs. "Really? *When?*"

Danny blinked. "I said 'when'?"

Nicole smiled. "You did. Even if it was a slip, it's nice to see you have that kind of faith subconsciously."

Sighing, Danny leaned back and smiled. "It's weird to even have a thought like that." She shook her head. "Five years ago, I'd never consider it. Hell, I'd never consider this." She motioned around them with her finger and then laughed.

"It's nice, isn't it?"

Danny flashed her a monster grin. "You know it is. Then, maybe it is when."

And just like that, the anxiety was gone. Nicole wondered if her smile and faith did this to Danny. She grinned back at Danny, just in case.

***

Monday came sooner than Dane wanted, but unfortunately none of Nicole's super powers included stopping time. Not that she would've if she could. When Nicole woke up, it would've been easy to think she had the new job. She was all smiles and practically floated around the house. Dane made breakfast for them. She was in the middle of scrambling eggs when Nicole showed up.

"Baby, you should probably get dressed," Nicole said as she entered the kitchen, in her usual work clothes.

"Oh, right." Dane had somewhere to be for once. The butterflies in her stomach should've kept her mind right on that. "Right back."

"I'll finish up in here."

For some reason, the offer made Dane's already flustered belly flip. She was supposed to make breakfast. *That's my thing. I make breakfast and make sure Nick's out the door on time. This is weird.* Shaking it off, she went to get dressed.

How was she supposed to dress anyway? Was it causal? She was creating music, not saving the world. It wasn't like she'd really be interacting with people. Did it matter what she wore? Besides, this wasn't an office job. Hell, Andrew was dressed like a hipster when they met, but he was the director. She was...she didn't even know. *Probably should've asked what the heck my job title was, but at least I found out my salary.*

Scratching her head, Dane decided to play it safe. She didn't have any business clothes, but she put on some of her better gear. First and foremost, she went with black cargoes. A red long-sleeve t-shirt went underneath a plain blue short-sleeve one. It was probably good enough. Maybe. She groaned as she looked in the mirror.

"I look fine, but I feel like an ass," Dane grumbled. It felt wrong, for some reason, to be dressed and ready to go out, when there was breakfast to finish. *I should be taking care of Nick, and she needs a proper breakfast to make it through the day*.

"Danny! Food," Nicole called.

"Shit, how long have I been up here?" Dane ran her hand through her hair and looked in the mirror again. "And this is the best I can do? I look like some punk kid. Shit." *I'm gonna fuck this up*. It was too late to change, and she doubted she'd come up with something better a second time, anyway. *Maybe I should take my piercings out*. But, she met with Calvin with them in, then why take them out now? *It seems professional. Really?* Now, she was talking to herself. *Damn, this is gonna be a disaster. Can I get fired over how I look on the first day?*

Taking a breath, she marched back downstairs. Nicole had their meals plated and waiting in the nook. Dane sat down, staring at her eggs, sausage, and toast like she didn't know what it was. Food wasn't supposed to wait for her in the morning.

"Something wrong, love?" Nicole asked as she settled across from Dane.

Dane scratched her head, wrinkling her brow. Her eyes drifted to Nicole and then back to her plate. "This is weird, right?"

Nicole offered her a soft smile. "It's not weird. I think you're nervous, which makes sense. It's your first day of work, on a job you've never done before, with a script you still can't make heads or tails of. It's natural to be nervous."

Those words sounded like they made sense, especially since everything was true. She didn't want to mess up on her first day. If she didn't understand the story, how could she put the right music to it? She had an idea of what she wanted to do, but still needed several pieces to this puzzle. Then, there was the mystery band. *I'd rather pick who's in my band than have random people thrown together*. The troubling sensation clouding her thinking felt like something more than that, though. Her heart was in her throat, and her belly refused to untangle itself from the knot it was in.

"Is this how it'll be every morning? I'll start breakfast, and you'll finish it?" Dane asked, her mouth pulled to one side and her eyebrows bent in. *What the hell kind of housewife would I be if I let that happen?*

Nicole blinked and then smiled at her again, as if she knew exactly what was wrong. "Baby, we'll work up new routines. I know you like the housewife gig, but I think you'll enjoy working. You have music on a wider scale, love. Music. In front of an audience."

Sighing, Dane nodded. The idea was enough to make her heart speed up, even though she always had music that mattered. Nicole was the one who gave music back to her, gave worth back to her, but something about this was different. Something about this made her insides flutter and twist into knots.

It was as Nicole said, music on a larger scale than what Dane had now and a different level than when she was a local legend. The job, the experience might be good, but it could also be a disaster of epic proportions. She had never done anything like it before. *What if I suck?* Then a voice in her head asked a better question. *What if you don't?*

Dane needed to give the job a chance. *This could be something magnificent, and I can't let fear control me.* She took a breath and tried to settle into the change.

"You have to eat, love. We don't have a lot of time to spare to get you and me to work on time," Nicole said around a mouthful of eggs.

"True." In the end, though, Dane had to take most of her meal to go. When they got into the car, she stared down at her eggs and one sausage link, housed in a plastic container. "I don't think I'm going to finish this." She barely managed to get her toast down.

"It's okay. Hell, every first day I've had, I threw up, including going back to school," Nicole said, keeping her eyes on the road.

The revelation didn't surprise Dane, as Nicole tended to fret. "Did you think you wouldn't be good?" She couldn't help wondering why Nicole would want to put herself through changing careers after she got her degree. *Besides the fact that she works with a bunch of jerks.*

"No. Just wondering how people would act or what was ahead of on this new path. Sometimes wondering if I set high enough standards for myself or if I set too high a standard because I've misunderstood the situation."

Dane nodded. How would people at the play react to her? The director wasn't in favor of having music and might still be hostile. Would she be able to change his mind? And how would everyone else act, especially if they see the director not getting along with her? What if this job was like Nicole's and she was bombarded by assholes for most of the day? Would she be able to cope with that? *No, you need to do this. You can be better, and make Nick proud of you. You can be like a real adult.*

"You'll be fine, love. I know it." Nicole's smile made it believable, if only for a couple of minutes.

The butterflies in Dane's stomach vanished briefly, but returned and seemed to multiply as they pulled up to the theater. It got to the point she thought butterflies might burst from her gut. Before she even realized it, Dane put her hand through her hair. She was about to pull her hair when Nicole leaned over and kissed her cheek.

"You'll be fine." Nicole caressed her other cheek.

"Okay." Dane hoped that was true. Her angel tried not to steer her wrong, after all. *Yeah, but your angel certainly gets you into trouble, too, when she thinks she's doing what's best for you.*

"You'll be fine."

This didn't make her believe it anymore, but it got her out of the car. She gave Nicole a short wave, feeling the cold bite at her fingertips, before turning to look at the theater. Just like before, it loomed. For a moment, it seemed to hiss and roar. Taking a breath, she managed to walk inside.

She had expected a bustle of energy, but it was all rather muted. The lobby was empty and there weren't that many people in the theater proper. Andrew was off to the side, talking with some folks. He happened to glance up and meet her eyes. Waving the people away, Andrew approached her with a sneer already firmly affixed to his face.

"I cobbled together an orchestra for you," he said as if he had done her a favor. He looked her up and down. "You do know what an orchestra is, right?"

Oh, that's how he wants to play it? Dane scoffed. "I could ask you the same thing." She could only imagine what crippled little band he threw together to try to get rid of her and the music.

He had the nerve to frown, as if he hadn't insulted her first. "Don't think this job is a lock for you."

"Never think anything is." The only thing she ever knew for sure was that Nicole would be there for her. The rest of life was up in the air and had been that way since Henry and Lynn returned her to her parents.

He gave her another look and led her to a small room, which reminded her of a band room back in high school, where the 'orchestra' waited. It was obvious he had no idea what the hell an orchestra was. Seven people waited for them, their instruments pretty random. *Did he grab people off the street while they were playing their instruments?*

"Did you put up a poster of instruments and throw darts to find musicians?" Dane inquired. There was a violin, a trumpet, a piccolo, a tambourine, a piano, a sax, and a harp. *This guy seriously got someone who plays the harp? Is he hoping to add class to his confusing mash-up?* "Was a sitar player unavailable?" Of course, she might've been able to do some fun things with a sitar. *Probably could with a harp, too, but I probably won't have the chance to be that artsy.*

He scowled, his blue eyes trying to cut into her. "This is what you have. Work with it."

He can't be serious. She wasn't sure if she could work with it. Her art had a process to a degree, and she might not be able to compromise it to do her job. Dane needed to be able to put her band together, if only to make sense of what her universe was. This was like some mutant beast. There wasn't even a percussion instrument; well, beyond the tambourine anyway.

Glancing away from the instruments, Dane saw who came attached to them. Everyone looked roughly her age, maybe a little older. She wouldn't judge experience by that, though. Maybe they were all good, but it didn't matter. They didn't seem bothered by her words, like they had these jobs already, like she didn't matter. To hell with that.

"Okay, I was led to believe I'd have creative control over the music, which would also mean having creative control over the orchestra," Dane said. She thought Calvin would put something together and trusted he'd do something serious. Instead, Andrew tried to give her a mess.

Andrew scoffed, folding his arms across his narrow chest. "Who told you that?"

"The man who hired me." Maybe if this so-called orchestra was Calvin's doing, she'd try to do something with it, but that wasn't the case. She'd have to be a little difficult and not let Andrew set the tone of their relationship by walking all over her. Besides, she'd like for the music to not suck. Her music had to touch people, make them feel, make her feel, and connect them to the story more than the story itself already did. She couldn't do that with this group of instruments.

Andrew stared at her, as if trying to force her to back down. He pointed to the floor with authority. "This is my show."

"I don't doubt that. Your name is on the script twice, after all. In fact, I'd like to talk to you about that. I want to better understand your vision and do it justice. I'm supposed to be in charge of the music, though, and I wanna make awesome music." She motioned to his collection. "This is noise."

Andrew's square jaw tensed. "Oh, you can't make any music with this? I guess you're not the genius Calvin thinks you are."

Dane tilted her head. He said "Calvin" in a weird way, beyond obviously making fun of her. She already suspected they were related, but she felt like Calvin had to be his dad because he didn't seem comfortable with saying his given name.

"Yes, well, I'm not sure how much sound you expect to get out of the tambourine, but if this is the sound you want, I'm sure I can make something out of it that won't suck and have people ripping into your work." She shrugged, but had to roll her eyes. *Sound? Who are we kidding here?* Now, this shit made no difference to her. She'd do her best with this madness and let the critics yammer on about the work.

He flinched. "My work doesn't need music."

"Not saying it does, but Calvin wants it and I'm guessing the buck stops there."

"I'm the writer and director." He puffed out his chest.

"Fine. Call Calvin. We can settle this, see who picks the orchestra, who makes the music, and move on with our lives." She wouldn't let him push her around, even if he was the director. She wanted to do her best and if she could get better than this, she'd like that. She needed the instruments to go together in some order. *Maybe he doesn't take his art seriously, but I do.*

Folding his arms across his chest again, Andrew glowered at her. Seconds ticked by, but she refused to look away. She wouldn't back down. She had a real gig, a job. She could step up her game, make actual money, and take care of Nicole, like Raymond wanted her to, like Kathleen wanted her to, like she wanted to. She wouldn't let this ass screw that up for her.

"If you think you can do better, then fire these guys and hire new ones. Just don't go over budget," Andrew hissed before slinking away.

Dane shrugged. She had no idea what the budget was. Calvin was supposed to handle that part of things. Why hadn't he? Where was her five-piece orchestra rather than this seven-piece collection? She shook that off. She'd fix this, find out the budget, as she'd need to hire new musicians. *I still need to talk to Andrew to figure out what the hell he's trying to do, then I can write music for it.* Turning, she took in the orchestra.

"Okay, tambourine, do you play anything else?" Dane asked. A tambourine wouldn't come in handy, but maybe there were other talents there.

The woman, possibly the only person over thirty among them, rolled her eyes. "No. What does it matter?"

Dane nodded. "I'm sure you're awesome at what you do, but it's not 1970." She pointed behind her with her thumb.

"You can't just fire me," the woman protested.

Dane had some experience in cutting people loose, in the sense that she told club managers where to go when she was at the top of her game. "Sorta just did. Thanks for your time."

"The director said I was hired."

"Go chat with him, then. Maybe he didn't tell you, but I'm in charge of music." Dane motioned to the door with both hands. She didn't have time to argue. She really needed to see what she was working with.

The tambourine player huffed, stomped her foot on the painted cement floor, and marched off. Dane turned her attention to the others. The harp player looked at her, and they seemed to come to an understanding.

"I was wondering why I got hired for this in the first place," the woman said.

"As much as I'd like to get a chance to compose with a harp, I don't think it'll work, especially for this play," Dane replied. She needed a string instrument with a little more range. Surely working with a harpist would be an experience, but she wouldn't experiment right now. *Maybe one day I'll be established enough to try that.* And maybe one day she'd understand the story enough to feel comfortable experimenting.

"I'm always up for a challenge if you do get a reason for a harp."

Dane chuckled. "I'll keep that in mind."

The woman marched off without the harp, which easily could've been one of the many instruments dumped backstage. *Maybe Andrew told her not to bring her instrument.* Traveling with a harp couldn't be easy. Before she was totally gone, Dane noticed the woman roll her eyes. Dane ignored the snub and turned her attention back to the orchestra. *Should I make more cuts?*

The way the other musicians looked at her, Dane knew they awaited her next dismissal. The sax was a little out of place, but she might be able to make it work. There was always room for jazz. She'd need to find a drummer. Before that, she wanted to see what these guys could do. Finding out their abilities could help her come up with a plan. Maybe things wouldn't be about cutting the instruments, but cutting the players.

"All right. I've got some music and I'd like to hear each of you play," Dane said.

"Is it 'Pop Goes the Weasel'?" The trumpet player smirked, devilish happiness twinkling in his green eyes. He earned snickers from the others.

Dane shrugged. She wasn't new to mockery, even in music. She remembered being fifteen, stepping on stage, hearing laughs, jeers, and taunts. Until she played her guitar. From that moment, she'd been a snake charmer and the crowd had been her cobras. It still happened whenever she ventured into new places, like jazz clubs. Blues clubs had never taken her seriously until the music started.

"Joke all you want, but I'm running this orchestra." She had to roll her eyes, but she managed to keep in a groan. More like she was running this mismatched band of misfits, which already felt like running a marathon with weights around her neck. *No, no, no. Stay positive. This thing could work.* "Let's get to it."

Grabbing a stand, Dane pulled a piece of paper out of her pocket and put it the stand. It was crumpled and slumped. It certainly didn't look professional and probably didn't add to her credibility, but it was what it was. She'd have to start carrying around that portfolio Nicole bought her if this panned out.

"We can introduce ourselves and everyone gets to see what everyone has. I'm Dane Wolfe, and this piece I wrote is possibly the start of scene two. Do I have a volunteer to play first?"

The musicians all looked at each other before the trumpeter swaggered up. He was an average guy with a goatee that he had to think was hip. Dane struggled not to roll her eyes again as he squared his shoulders and held his horn like a mighty weapon, ready to take down any who challenged his might. He probably thought he'd read the music and get a good laugh at her. Whatever. If he didn't impress her, she'd be the one laughing while showing him the door.

"I'm Louis Graham. Let's get this out of the way." He smirked as he stared at the music and then put his trumpet to his lips.

He wasn't horrible, but she could think of several other trumpet players she'd grab instead. In fact, they'd probably be grateful for a steady gig and they'd be easier to get along with.

"Thank you, but no," Dane said.

Louis folded his arms across his barrel chest. "I hadn't planned on working for an obvious poser like you anyway. What the hell do you know about music?"

"You'll never know. Thanks, goodbye." Dane pointed to the door.

He sucked his teeth and left. She ended up keeping the sax player, Pedro Martinez. He was too good to let go, even though a sax would never be her first pick in a horns section. She had to figure out what she'd do with him and his talent.

The pianist, Evie Miller, was good. She had a keyboard, which Dane would prefer for the different sounds they'd get, but she was told she'd play the piano set up in the corner of the depressing blue-grey room. *Were they going for modern asylum when they painted this place?* The piano wasn't tuned, but Evie did the best anyone could ask of her and it was worthwhile.

"You definitely need to bring the keyboard," Dane said.

Evie nodded. "Hey, as long as I'm not fired, I'll bring it."

"Nope, not fired. Next up." Dane motioned to the music stand.

The piccolo player, Dougie Clark, was the hardest. He was spectacular, but Dane wasn't sure what she'd do with a piccolo. He also played the flute and clarinet. She'd be able to use that versatility. Unfortunately, he was also a jerk, being friends with Louis the trumpeter and not at all happy she fired him. Still, she could work with him.

The one who stole the show was Samiyah Caro, the violinist. She'd probably be able to beat the Devil in a fiddling contest. As soon as she was done, Dane knew who her star was and knew who to highlight. Andrew couldn't have possibly hired these guys, not on purpose. They were too talented. Maybe Calvin had put together an orchestra and then Andrew tried to sabotage it in protest. Whatever the case, she needed to glue together more of an orchestra than what she had and needed to know what sort of money she had to work with.

"Okay, guys. Take a break. I need to go talk with our director." Dane could only imagine how that'd go. *Gotta get it outta the way, though.*

Marching out of the room, Dane went to the front and found Andrew talking with a group of people. Standing off to the side, she waited for him to finish. He glanced at her and then turned his attention to his clipboard.

"You and your scarf can ignore me all you want, but I'm not going anywhere." Dane couldn't believe he actually had the scarf on inside. *All he needs is a slouch hat or some khaki pants and he'll have a douche uniform on.*

Andrew sighed and scowled as he turned to her. "What do you want?"

"To talk about the script, your vision." Despite his attitude, she wanted to do his work justice, one artist to another.

Snorting, he waved her off. "I don't have time for that. I've got way too much to do. The theater still needs cleaning and I need to hire real talent. Read the script. You can read, right?" He looked her up and down, like that answered his question.

"Just to be clear, you don't want any input in helping with the music, right?"

"Didn't you just say you're in charge of the score? You fired the people I brought in. Go be with your music." He turned away, going to boss some other people around.

"Okay." Dane shrugged. She'd do her own thing with the music, then. She'd also do her best to avoid interacting with Andrew. No reason to be insulted every time she had a question. Well, best to find out what the budget was and talk to Calvin about the orchestra and his expectations for a score.

***

Nicole reached for her desk phone for the umpteenth time that morning. She wanted to call Danny, but Danny hadn't left her a number to call. A couple of times, she tripped up and called home. Haydn probably freaked out when the phone rang.

"Danny has a job." Nicole smiled, needing to hold back titters. She felt good for Danny. Tutoring wasn't as fulfilling for her, no matter how much she tried to act like it was.

She hated that Danny put up a front for her and probably for her parents as well. It was all right for her to need things, all right for her to be unhappy with circumstances. She wanted Danny to pursue things that brought her joy.

"Danny should have this," Nicole said aloud. Her heart beat a little quick, though. *Change is good and Danny deserves this, so settle down.* Still, there was a little bubble in her chest.

Taking a deep breath, Nicole tried to focus on her work. *Change brought Danny to you. Get some work done.* Trying to work only made her think about how in a few months she wouldn't be here anymore. The world almost felt tilted to her, and she hadn't even left yet.

Taking a moment, she looked around her office. Would there be an office at the next job? Would there be people who appreciated her on the same level as her current clients did? Would she be happy to be away from law in general? She never had a real problem with law itself, just corporate law. While she was great at it, it never fit her well, like shoes that were a half size too small.

She didn't get through much work before there was a knock at her door. For once, she was fine with the distraction. At first, she thought it was Mina, calling her to lunch. It was too early for that, and then she remembered she had an appointment with a client.

"Karisa, how are you today?" Nicole greeted the woman as she closed the door behind her.

"I'm doing well. How are you?" Karisa Collins replied with a bright smile. Her mocha eyes sparkled and the few lines on her face seemed to fall right into place.

Nicole stood to shake the older woman's hand. Karisa had to switch her purse to her other hand for a proper greeting. "Wonderful. Please, have a seat." Nicole motioned to the seat to the right of Karisa's hip.

Karisa nodded and shrugged off her heavy coat and placed it, along with her bag, in the empty seat next to the chair by her. She eased into the leather chair with unnecessary, but possibly inherent grace. She smoothed a phantom wrinkle on her tan skirt as she crossed her legs at the ankle and leaned back, brushing her wavy blond hair out of her face.

Karisa was one of Nicole's favorite clients. She was easy to get along with and almost never high strung. She wasn't argumentative and never treated Nicole as if she didn't know what she was doing. Karisa carried herself with a soft dignity and elegance that never seemed to leave her, regardless of what was going on around her. Plus, she was sweet.

"Give me a moment to get everything I worked up for you," Nicole said, going into a side drawer on her desk. She pulled out a folder and brought up the work on her computer.

"Take your time. I'm sure Jason is just happy to have me out of the office and will not lament if I'm kept out as long as possible. I'm almost surprised he didn't call you and ask you to stall me," Karisa said.

Nicole laughed. "He didn't, I assure you. How is Jason?"

Karisa waved a manicured hand, but her eyes twinkled. "I'm driving him crazy according to him. But, if he thinks he's going to run my business one day, he needs to learn to do it the right way."

Nicole smiled. She couldn't help thinking of her own parents when Karisa spoke of Jason. Jason had voluntarily followed in his mother's footsteps, but Karisa was always on top of him about operations. She had no doubt Karisa looked forward to the day when she'd gift Jason her natural household cleaning company and he'd definitely jump for joy. Nicole's parents wanted her name to be on their firm one day and she always thought it'd come to that, but not lately. *Soon, I'll be somewhere else, building something of my own.* A sharp pain shot through her heart and her insides felt shredded. It only lasted a moment, but it made her nerves jump. *What the hell?*

"I'm sure he thinks he's doing it the right way," Nicole said.

Karisa nodded. "He's good at marketing, but this is more than marketing. I wanted to show you the new ads he came up with, but let's get this all out of the way before I take up your time with my son's things. Of course, you'll have to promise to never let him know I bragged about him."

Nicole laughed again. Karisa was a fascinating distraction. Before Nicole realized it, almost an hour had gone by. Karisa took up most of the time telling her about Jason's marketing strategy for the company. Karisa even praised other business ideas Jason had, even though Nicole knew she probably teased him.

"He'll be good one day when he's in charge," Karisa said. "I'm sure your parents feel the same about you."

Nicole shifted in her seat and blushed. "Well, you know." Certainly, the plan had been for her to inherit the firm, but she wasn't sure if that was in the cards anymore.

Karisa's brow furrowed, and she pursed her lips briefly. "Your parents wouldn't let anyone else run this place."

"No, I know. It's just, I'm about finished with my masters in organic chemistry, and I want to see where that will take me. Law is their passion, not mine."

Karisa nodded. "Well, marketing is Jason's passion, but he still wanted to work with me, even though the business is mine."

"I think it's a little more difficult to connect chemistry and law than business and marketing."

"This is true, but it's not impossible."

Nicole knew that was true, but she still wanted to explore her passion for a while. Karisa had never pressured Jason to follow in her footsteps like her parents. Plus, Karisa was a little more laid back than Nicole's mother.

"It'll work out," Karisa said, as if she just knew.

Sometimes Nicole believed mothers did just know. "I hope so."

Karisa shook her head. "No reason to hope. It will. But, I will say this, I'll miss coming here to see you over legal matters. You're brilliant."

"Thank you." Nicole liked to think she was brilliant at everything she put her mind to, with certain exceptions. Still, being brilliant at her current vocation didn't mean she wanted to do it for the rest of her life. She felt smothered at the firm, and some of that was more than the usual suspects. While her parents had backed off, there was a time when their very presence made her teeth itch, afraid to fail, scared to disappoint, too shook to ever dream of stepping off their path. There was a world out there she only now thought to explore.

Part of her still hurt at the thought of leaving forever, at abandoning her parents' second child to people who didn't know the work, passion, and love that went into the place. *Their legacy deserves so much more.* And who would treat her parents' firm with the same love as her parents? *Me.* But, would it be her pleasure or prison? Of course, that'd be a moot point if she followed her dreams.

"Congratulations on your degree. If you find at the end of the day, you want to do something with it, well, I do make all-natural cleaning supplies." Karisa smiled.

Nicole blinked. Did she just get a job offer? Part of her wanted to jump for joy and another part of her made her stomach twist. *I always thought when this moment came, I'd feel nothing but happiness. Why does it feel like I might laugh and throw up at the same time?*

"I'll keep that in mind," Nicole managed to say around the lump in her throat.

"Good luck then. I'll see you later."

Karisa stood and took her leave right after Nicole bid her farewell. Nicole barely had a chance to let out a sigh before her phone rang. She hoped it was Danny, and her heart jumped to find it was 'King Theater' calling. She almost dropped the phone.

"Nicole Cardell," she said with as much professionalism as she could muster in case this wasn't Danny.

"Hey, Chem." Danny's voice seemed to sing through the phone. Nicole's heart fluttered again.

"How's your day going so far, baby?"

Danny groaned. "It's definitely something. Andrew tried to sabotage the orchestra. How petty is that? He got pissed when I let three of the musicians go, but what the hell was I supposed to do? What am I going to do with a tambourine player?"

Nicole's eyebrows furrowed. *Her day does sound adventurous.* "A tambourine player? Was he serious?"

"I don't know. He argued with me over that and how I can't fire people without telling him, but I'm pretty sure I can. I'm supposed to be in charge of the music. Think there's a title that goes with it and everything. I tried talking to him about the script, but he doesn't want to. He doesn't want to tell me how much money I have for the music either."

"Talk to Calvin then, Danny. Don't let Andrew push you around. If he's not going to cooperate with you, you must go over his head. Calvin seemed like he was the one in charge when you met with them, right?"

"Yeah."

"Then, talk to him and get everything settled. Make sure he gives you clear lines as to what you're supposed to do. Try to work out any deadlines he might have for you and see how much power Andrew wields in your domain, if any. And maybe find out what your title is. You might like it." Nicole smiled.

"Okay. I was gonna do that." Danny sighed. "Not used to this, you know? Even when I had gigs, I didn't do a lot of fighting. I could walk away."

"Do you want to walk away?"

"No. I think I could do something cool here. There's a violinist. She's…" Danny blew out a breath. "Incredible doesn't even do it justice. I want to make music for her."

Nicole swallowed at those words, and her nerves twitched. For a moment, a buzzing in her head drowned out whatever Danny talked about. The sound of excitement brought her back, though.

"…and the others are pretty amazing, too. I think I could do something here as soon as I get all the pieces together."

"I knew you'd like it."

"I do so far."

"Have you eaten yet?" Nicole asked. She wasn't sure why. She probably should've let Danny go on about her job, but she was worried the excitement might have Danny forget basic things. "You didn't eat breakfast. You have to be hungry."

"I'm going to go eat as soon as I'm done on the phone. I just wanted to check in on you."

"I'd like to be able to return the favor. Do you have a number here?"

Danny made a low humming sound. "I dunno. I'll have to ask around and see if there is one. The phone I'm calling from is built into the wall behind the stage, looks like an old pay phone without the coin slot. I don't know the number for it. Have you eaten yet?"

"No, but I will."

"Okay, well, I want you to eat. We can catch up later. You're gonna come get me, right?"

"Of course." She'd like taking Danny to work and picking her up. The only problem would come when school started, but that wasn't for almost another two weeks. She'd worry about it then. She'd worry about everything else later. For now, she wanted to be happy for Danny.

Chapter Nine

NICOLE GRABBED DANNY'S HAND as they drove home after a day of work. Danny used her other hand to rub her eyes, which she had done every couple of minutes since she got in car. The day had obviously been stressful, and Danny was probably worn out. Nicole wanted to give her a minute to gather herself before she asked about everything.

"Are people always stupid?" Danny murmured, glancing at her with stricken eyes. Danny might need a little massage when they got in if only to relieve her tension. Hopefully, the surprise she picked up for Danny during her lunch earlier might help lift her spirits.

"You know what I think about that." Nicole gave people the benefit of the doubt. Beyond that, she felt like people were more manipulative and lazy than stupid. "What happened?"

Danny rubbed her face. "Andrew's an ass. He fought me every step of the way on little things."

"Did you speak with Calvin?" Nicole knew what it was like to have an asshole stand in her way. Sometimes, the only way to get the person out of the way was to go over their heads.

"I talked to him right after I talked to you, and then we talked to Andrew, and then Andrew continued to be an ass. Gotta assume that's his personality."

Nicole didn't doubt that. "Well, sometimes that is someone's personality."

Danny sighed, rubbing her eyes. "Forgot the world was populated with assholes."

Nicole gave her hand a squeeze. "That's good."

Scrunching up her face, Danny raised an eyebrow. "Good?"

"It means life has improved, right? It's good to be able to forget assholes exist, even if they eventually remind you that they're there."

Danny's mouth twitched downward. "Yeah, I guess you're right. Life has been damned good." A tiny smile settled on her face.

"Beyond Andrew, how was everything?" Nicole wanted Danny to

focus on the positive of this job.

This got a real smile out of Danny and that beaming light returned to her eyes. "Well, thanks to Andrew trying to mess things up for me early on, I actually get a seven-piece orchestra instead of five-piece because of Andrew being an ass. Calvin felt like it wasn't fair for me to think I had seven people to work with and then reduce it after Andrew got my hopes up. So, he's making room in the overall budget for two additional musicians."

Nicole laughed. "Really?"

"I'm serious. He said he'd make it happen and he came back to me in the afternoon to say it was a go. I'm gonna get a drummer, and I want a guitarist." Grey eyes lit up once more at the idea. "I'm also going to grab a trumpeter since Andrew put that in my head. The one he grabbed was nothing special."

"I'm assuming you know the ones you want."

Danny nodded, and her smile remained. She glowed. "Oh, and I do have a title." She sat up straight. Her voice was a chirp.

"And what is your title?"

"Musical director." Danny grinned. "Doesn't it sound official?"

Nicole giggled. "Yes, love, it does. As musical director, do you have complete control over the music?"

"Well, complete in the instance that Andrew can't just come change whatever I do on a whim. Calvin has the final say, but I think it's like that with the whole production."

Nicole nodded. "Good."

They pulled up to the house, and Haydn rushed the doorway, halted by the music room gate. He whined so loudly he drowned out the music they left playing for him, but his yelps weren't enough. He stood on the gate and could jump it if he was inclined.

"Let's set you free." Danny opened the gate, and Haydn went right for her. He tugged her right back to the door and scratched at the doorknob with his paws. Danny shook her head. "Need to be careful. One day we're gonna come in, and he'll have let himself out and the entire world in."

"Well, he'll definitely be grounded then." Nicole chuckled. She petted his head, and he pushed against her before turning his attention back to Danny.

Danny hugged him around the neck. "He's hyped."

"Do you want to take him for a walk?" Nicole asked. They'd have to think of something for him when she started school again. It was obvious being alone for nine hours wouldn't work. She might be able to pop in and check on him, but she wasn't sure if that'd work. He was too spoiled.

"Probably should. He's been in the room all day. It's pretty cramped for him," Danny replied. He was used to being in the room for a couple of hours, but nothing like today. This was totally unfair to him, and a little shocking he hadn't wrecked the room.

Nicole nodded. "We'll figure something out."

Danny left with Haydn. Maybe Danny needed the walk just as much as he did, trying to unwind from her first day at work. It must've been tough since Danny hadn't asked Nicole if she wanted to walk with her.

"But, then again, she's used to me coming in and getting comfortable before this walk," Nicole muttered. *Now, I have a chance to wrap my gift.*

While Danny took care of Haydn, Nicole decided to take care of her. She'd do dinner and hopefully it'd be almost ready by the time Danny came back. She hoped to hear more about Danny's day when they ate. Afterward, she'd see if Danny wanted a massage or something else to relax. Best of all, she'd get to give Danny the present to celebrate her first day.

Nicole moved about the kitchen, preparing a familiar meal for them. *I should've gone shopping and got something special.* Cooking wasn't on her mind much, though. It almost seemed like unfamiliar territory, making dinner from start to finish. When was the last time she made a full meal on her own? It had been quite a long time. Usually if she wanted to give Danny a break in the kitchen, they ordered takeout. Nicole couldn't help wondering if her using the kitchen was all right.

"Why shouldn't it be all right? Danny's got a full-time job. She can't be my housewife and work all day. I should help. She walks the dog. I make the food. Why should that be a problem?" Nicole asked the air.

Her insides churned and her nerves jumped under her skin. She knew it hadn't been all right when she finished up breakfast. Would Danny want her to make their entire evening meal? Would these changes affect their whole dynamic? Tilt them so far off their axis that they couldn't recover? What if this was the thing to end them, after all they had come through?

No. Nicole shook her head and she convinced herself this was all right. Cooking and doing things around the house was all right. She went to the refrigerator to see what she had to work with. Nicole wanted to be able to take care of her lover. She pressed on through dinner, preparing pepper steak with white rice and black beans.

If I can't handle Danny having a job, what happens when school starts? What happens when I graduate? What happens when I change careers? She shook her head again, trying to banish those thoughts. *Focus on dinner.* She wasn't sure how, but she managed to follow that advice, seasoning the steak, and getting everything to the stovetop.

***

"Oh, man, Haydn. I moved too fast. I should've seen if your other mom wanted to come," Dane muttered as Haydn tugged her down the street. Haydn wasn't paying her any mind, happy to be in the great big world. She laughed and shook her head. "I understand."

A happy feeling spilled through Dane as she watched Haydn bound from tree to tree. They'd have to figure what to do with their poor pup. He wouldn't survive five whole days in the music room. Even if they left him to wander the house with music playing and the television on, he'd need attention. Not to mention, he'd have to pee. They could use pads, but they'd have to train him, and they didn't have time for that. Plus, he was accustomed to at least one walk in the afternoon. *Damn, why didn't we think about this?*

Dane scratched the bridge of her nose. "How is any of this gonna work? I've got all these responsibilities at home and now I'm trying to work? I gotta work, though. Can't just bum off Nick, right, Haydn?"

Haydn yapped and tugged her a bit, which she didn't think was a good answer. Dane sighed, being tugged in two different directions and it had nothing to do with Haydn. She wanted to take care of their home, wanted to be there for their pup, but also desired be a proper partner to Nicole.

"Nick shouldn't have to take care of me and this job thing could be fun. I mean, it's music, you know? Real music. I mean, yeah, I don't get the script, and there could be changes, and Andrew's an asshole, but it's still music. Music that'd get reactions from an audience." Dane inhaled and a calm settled on her. "It's been a while."

Haydn glanced back at her and then charged forward, yanking her along. Dane yelped and had to pull back a little. Haydn looked back again and moved at a reasonable clip, aware she couldn't hurry thanks to her knee. His eagerness was a sign she should've brought Nicole along. He could pull Nicole all he wanted and she'd jog with him, give him the freedom of movement he craved.

"You're not helping at all, you know that, boy? I expected more advice from you. I guess your day didn't go as good as mine for you to want to talk things out. That's another thing. I really like working. I'm sure I could have fun with this. Working with those musicians alone will be worth it. I can put up with Andrew and whatever else. We could do something really special."

Dane took a breath and shook her head. *Look, Nick wants me to work. She pushed me to go to the interview, and she's cool with this.* She turned her attention back to Haydn, who took a keen interest in another tree.

***

Everything was on the stove and the table was set, waiting for the food, by the time Nicole heard the door open. Haydn charged into the kitchen, barking merrily as he nuzzled her stomach. Nicole leaned down to kiss the top of his head. He jumped up and bumped noses with her. She laughed before turning to the entryway to see Danny standing there, eyes wide and her nostrils flared. Nicole's heart leaped into her throat. Maybe this wasn't all right.

"How was our young man on his evening walk?" Nicole asked, wanting to distract Danny. Maybe if Danny had a second, she could process everything and figure out she didn't need to do everything. Then, they could move on.

"He was good as always, but there's not much for him to chase in this weather," Danny sort of mumbled, her attention more on the nook than anything else. "I could've cooked, Chem."

"I know, love, but you took the pup for a walk. We're a team, right?" They were supposed to be there for each other. *If we're a team, then we can stand these new changes.*

Danny's mouth twisted to the side briefly. "We are, but you know, this is what I do. I mean, you work all day—"

Nicole jumped in before Danny could finish. "And now so do you and I think you're a little more stressed since your job is new. Let me do this for you. We can have a nice quiet meal, talk about our days while I massage your leg, watch a movie, and top it all off with a bath together. What do you say?"

Danny seemed to chew it over, literally with the way she ground her teeth together. Her shoulders slumped, and she eased her way into the kitchen nook. Nicole wanted to smile, but Danny seemed defeated.

We're a team. Maybe Danny was just as worried over these changes and how they might affect their relationship. *Well, maybe we can talk it out.*

"Danny, I want to take care of you, like you take care of me. This is always a two-way street." Nicole hoped the idea of give-and-take wasn't always going to be an issue. She didn't want Danny to feel like she always needed to shoulder so much work.

Sighing, a small pout settled on Danny's face. Nicole slid into the seat across from her and grabbed her hand. She squeezed Danny's hand until Danny stared at her and squeezed back. Some of the tension eased out of Nicole, and she caressed Danny's thumb with her own. *She's just as worried as I am.*

"Love, we can't keep coming to this point. We're in this together, we're here for each other, and we both need and want each other, right?" Nicole said. It was good to say aloud, as it reminded her of the same.

Danny sighed. "I know, I know. It's just..." She put her free hand through her hair. "You know I always think you do more than me and now you're doing what I usually do."

"Okay, but I don't do more than you and you're stepping out to do more for yourself. I support you in taking care of yourself. You deserve to be happy, love."

Danny looked at her. "I was happy. I am happy."

"The job makes you happier, right? You get to work with music in a more fulfilling way, yes?"

Danny blew out a breath. "Yeah."

"And that's fine, baby. I want you to be happy. I want you to work this out and see where it takes you if that's what you want. Your life doesn't have to revolve around me. It doesn't have to revolve around just taking care of me. Your own health should be a priority."

Finally, a small smile ticked onto Danny's face. "Thank you."

"No, thank you for being here and for being yourself. I understand why you're nervous. Believe it or not, I'm a little troubled, too."

Grey eyes went wide. "You okay?"

With a small smile, Nicole nodded. "We're going through changes and things will keep changing. I worry we'll grow apart."

"Never." Danny's vow was powerful, like it could've moved the heavens and it came with a matching gaze. "We've been through a lot of changes and we come out better. We're not the same people we were when we met, but we evolve together. We're like..." Danny rubbed her chin with her free hand. "Okay, I don't know any chemistry things to make a good metaphor, but we're like stable chemicals mixed together and changing states, but staying stable, if that makes sense."

Nicole chuckled. *I can only imagine the mess I'd make of a music metaphor.* "I appreciate the effort. You're completely and totally right." They'd been through plenty of things, tough times. Why shouldn't they survive Danny with a real job and her changing careers? *We must stay positive, and go with it. We'll work it out as it goes.*

Danny beamed and sat up a little straighter. "Like being right."

Nicole laughed a little more. "Now, let's eat. Plus, I have something for you. Like a congratulations gift."

Danny's brow furrowed in confusion, which just made Nicole smile. Leaning over, she gave Danny a small kiss at the corner of her mouth before going to check on the food. Danny got up and met her at the stove. "Why don't you take a shower and let me finish up here?"

Nicole was about to protest, but felt like it'd be a little hypocritical to do so. Instead, she kissed Danny again before going off to take a quick shower.

By the time Nicole returned, freshly showered and in-house clothes, Danny had their plates made. Haydn was being his usual self, whining for treats and bumping Danny's legs as she went to the refrigerator for drinks. Nicole whistled for him and he bolted over to her, fussing for treats again. Chuckling, she petted his head.

"Did he eat?" Nicole asked.

"He hasn't touched his food. He seems to think just by being cute he'll get treats, even if he doesn't eat dinner."

With another giggle, Nicole rubbed Haydn's head. "Sorry, pup. You need to eat your dinner. No treats until you do."

Haydn whimpered and Nicole had to kiss his head. He was too cute, especially when he nuzzled her. He seemed to understand there'd be no treats and he crept over to his food bowl. Nicole attached herself to Danny's side, who pulled her close. Danny was also too cute.

"Ready to eat?" Nicole asked.

"Of course. Good shower?" Danny replied.

"It would've been better had you been in there with me."

Danny grinned. "Well, I was promised a bath later."

"And that invitation is always open." It was relaxing for both of them whenever they took a bath together.

Danny's grin widened. They sat down for dinner and discussed their days. Despite Danny's trouble with Andrew, she seemed optimistic.

"Music's supposed to enhance an experience, right?" Danny asked, tapping her fork against her plate.

"Unless it is the experience," Nicole replied before eating some rice with peppers mixed in.

Danny nodded. "See, I think I wanna go with both on this. I wanna make something powerful." She held her hands together, linking them like a chain.

"I'm sure you will. Musical genius and all."

A cute blush flared up on Danny's cheeks and she glanced away briefly. "Wouldn't say genius."

Nicole couldn't help winking at her. "I would."

"Anyway. What about you? What did you do today?" Danny mixed her steak and rice even more than it already was and then shoveled a forkful into her mouth.

Nicole sighed and shrugged. "I think a client sort of offered me a job, but also made it seem like she knew I'd figure out how to fuse my love of chemistry with my skilled law practice." The idea shouldn't appeal as much as it did, but she already found herself dreaming. *I used to dream of chemistry and getting out of law. Why the change? It's in reach. That felt like the answer and insanity.*

Danny scratched her chin. "Can you do that?"

"She seems to think so." *And I want that to be true.* Nicole wasn't sure how to make it so, why she wanted to make it. *Why cling to what makes me crazy? Because I'm crazy.*

"But, if you can't, she offered you a job?"

Nicole nodded. The job offer was second in her mind to the idea of marrying her current job with her future degree. "Well, her company makes natural cleaning supplies, so organic chemistry definitely could come in handy." Working for Karisa probably wouldn't be too bad.

"Do you want the job?" Danny asked in a soft voice, as if she knew Nicole wasn't jumping for joy.

"I should." But, for some reason, she wasn't sure. Maybe it was just the hot knot of uncertainty about their future with changes. Whenever everything seemed to come up roses, she knew there were thorns among the beauty. It sat like a molten stone in her guts and quicksand under her feet. She had to be careful or she'd drown in it. "I think I need some time to adjust. Hopefully, the job will be there when I figure it out."

Danny nodded. "Sounds good."

They settled on watching a movie after dinner, saving the bath for right before bed. Nicole grabbed her gift while Danny found a show for them to watch. They met on the couch, having to make some room for Haydn. He took up almost as much space as the two of them.

"What's this?" Danny asked as Nicole eased a wrapped box in her hands.

"Open it and see."

Danny carefully did so. Nicole waited patiently as Danny inspected the box. Her eyebrows knitted close together as she held up the gift and removed the leather-bound portfolio from the container. This one was more elaborate than the one Danny already owned. It had a pocket for a tablet, if Danny ever got one, a pocket for other items, a place for business cards, notes, and other tidbits along with personalized stationery that had music notes at the corners.

"Chem, it's beautiful," Danny whispered as she flipped through each section of the portfolio.

Nicole smiled. "I bought it this afternoon. I thought you'd like it. I know you already have one, but it's full of work you've already done. This is brand new for this momentous occasion. Use it to make some kickass music for this play. Write your heart in this, love. Okay?"

Danny grabbed her into a hug, and the embrace was enough of a promise. It was sealed with a kiss and then Nicole curled in close to Danny, who held onto the portfolio through the whole movie. Nicole rubbed Danny's knee as best she could while they cuddled.

Before retiring for the evening, they took Haydn out one more time. He trotted ahead of them proudly before running back to them every now and then, nuzzling them for a few seconds. When they came back home, they took that bath together and settled into bed. Danny explored her portfolio, running her fingers along the pockets. Nicole laughed.

"I'm glad you like it."

"I can do this, right?"

"You can do this and more. Look at me, love." Despite those words, Nicole shifted her body, straddling Danny's abdomen. Danny looked up at her, and she cupped Danny's face with both hands. "You know what your world is. You're a master of your art, and he can't take that away from you. You've got this."

Danny put her hands-on Nicole's hips. The cold leather of the portfolio pressed against her bare thigh, but she ignored that as Danny tapped her fingertips against Nicole's legs. Nicole caressed gentle circles on Danny's cheeks with her thumbs.

"I've got this," Danny said.

"I know you do. Go in there every day and show them just how you earned the title of goddess of rock and roll. You're awesome."

Grey eyes sparkled like polished silver and it was clear Danny was all right now. Nicole hoped she carried that confidence with her for the rest of her stint as musical director. Danny could do much more than shine with her new job.

***

Dane made sure to wake up early enough to make breakfast and get dressed. Yes, she understood their relationship was a two-way street and everything, but she liked her household tasks. She liked taking care of Nicole, and making music wasn't as hard as handling idiots in a law firm or settling serious business matters.

By the time Nicole made her way downstairs, everything was ready. She handed Nicole a cup of coffee and smiled at her. Nicole grinned back, which set Dane at ease. She thought Nicole might be upset with her for making breakfast. Maybe Nicole understood the housework was something Dane needed to do to keep peace in her heart.

"We're going to have to figure out something for Haydn," Nicole said as they sat down to eat. "I don't think he'll get used to both of us being out of the house for this long."

Dane nodded. "I don't want to leave him alone for this long anyway. You think Jody or Philip might be able to come over? I think we'd all like him to have his afternoon walk."

"I'll ask them. Jody might have time, depending on the day."

Dane nodded. Philip had college courses, but he also had a band he played in now. They weren't very good, but they weren't horrible either. They were all late bloomers when it came to learning instruments and enjoyed playing together. Between their practicing and their few gigs, Philip wouldn't have a lot of time to pup-sit.

"What about Allison? We could pay her," Nicole said.

"Is she old enough to be here by herself?" Of course, when Dane was Allison's age, she used to be drunk and wandering the streets. Allison had her beat in that regard.

"We'll talk to her parents about it. First, I'll ask Jody. I'm sure she'd love a valid excuse to be away from people."

"She is not that antisocial." Dane liked Jody, who was exceptionally introverted. She respected that because Jody was also extremely focused on her own passion and worked a computer the way Dane worked her guitar.

"Please, if Jody woke up one day and found that everyone on Earth had disappeared, she'd breathe a sigh of relief and go on to build her android army."

Dane snickered. Nicole teased Jody about these things. She wouldn't mind seeing more of Jody. It'd be nice to build more of a relationship with her. They were sort of family, after all.

***

Nicole drove Dane to work. They exchanged a kiss that reinforced Dane's steely soul, and Dane turned her attention to the theater. Today would be a good day, damn it. She clutched her portfolio to her chest. She'd crush this gig. *Just like Nick said I would.*

Taking a breath, she marched into the theater. Andrew was already busy with something by the stage area and if it didn't have anything to do with her, she wanted to keep things that way. Calvin was nowhere in sight, but she had been told yesterday he wouldn't be around much once things got settled. She went to the band room.

Samiyah was the only one there. She stood in a corner of the room by the slender windows, sunlight highlighting cracks in the wall, but also causing her to glow. Chocolate skin had a halo around it as Samiyah's bow glided across her violin strings. The music sounded divine, and Samiyah was in her own world as she played.

Dane's body buzzed and the world was brighter as her mind rushed for ideas on what to do with Samiyah. She had to do Samiyah's talent justice in the score and people had to leave the play feeling like Samiyah had given them new pieces of themselves, like friends they just made. Dane let loose a loud breath, which caught Samiyah's attention.

"Hey, Dane." Samiyah smiled as she put down her violin.

"You sound better now than you did yesterday,"

Samiyah's high cheekbones were on display as she smiled and shrugged. "Well, I'm more familiar with the classics than what you came up with."

"I hope you get as familiar with my work. You sound awesome." She was giddy at the thought of composing for her. The inner child she thought died when she was eight giggled and danced.

Samiyah glanced away briefly. They were cut off as Evie came in, struggling with her keyboard. Dane moved to help, forgetting about her leg until the keyboard was in her hands. It wasn't as bad as it would've been if she hadn't had that surgery, and wasn't wearing her brace, but thankfully she didn't have to take it far. Evie and Samiyah greeted each other with short waves.

"I'm going to leave this here from now on," Evie said, motioning to the keyboard. "My boyfriend was not happy helping me drag this thing down to the car."

"I'll bet." Dane ran her hand across the keyboard, a little jealous. She had a good one, but this was beyond her imagination.

Evie must've noticed her affection. "You play?"

Dane shrugged. "A little."

"Let's get it set up and hear what you got, director." Evie winked. There was a bit of a challenge in her voice, like she didn't think Dane was much with instruments.

Dane shrugged again. There wasn't any reason to hold back and they'd probably respect her more if they knew she was musician as well as a composer. She cracked her knuckles just for the show of it and flexed her left hand. Just as she was about to press the keys, Dougie and Pedro strolled in.

"Hey, boss." Pedro smiled at Dane.

Boss? Dane blinked. *Whoa.* She was the boss. The idea was different from when she was in *Destined for Nowhere*. She'd been in charge back then, but no one openly acknowledged it, not even her. The group just did what she said. Maybe the acknowledgment could be better, though. The job itself was her second chance. *I can make it better. I will do something with this.*

Dane clapped and twirled her finger. "Let's get started." She grabbed a nearby seat while the others found spots to park themselves. "After talking to the producer, Calvin Mason, he's going to let me add three more players. We need a drummer. I'm going with a trumpeter as well."

"You should've kept Louis then," Dougie hissed.

"Why? Louis sucked," Dane replied.

"Like you know good music."

"I know what sucks and Louis has vacuums beat. Now, drummer, trumpeter, and a guitarist," Dane said.

"A guitarist?" Evie asked with a furrowed brow.

"I've decided to let each instrument represent a character. I think it'll help make the characters more dynamic. I need a badass guitar player for the villain," Dane explained.

Since she didn't have the best understanding of the overall story, it seemed like having instruments play the characters might be a good way to work with the script. If she couldn't figure out the story, maybe they'd be able to figure out the characters. "Anybody know anyone looking for a gig fitting those descriptions?"

They were musicians. Maybe they had friends who needed gigs. If not, she knew plenty of people. In fact, she already knew who she'd grab for the drummer. *God help us.* She had a couple of ideas for a trumpeter and had called them up to come, but the orchestra might have friends who were better.

"You want us to save your sorry little production already?" Dougie scoffed, throwing his head to the side.

"No, I want your input. I don't want this to be a dictatorship. If you have valid information, please share. If you don't have any, I know plenty of people searching for a gig." She'd go haunt *Melody* for a while if she didn't get a decent trumpeter. They'd probably have suggestions for her down there anyway. Crow might be able to point her to a guitarist. She called her last night to spread the word. Crow was more than happy to do so.

"It's cool you want to include us," Pedro said, glancing around. He smiled, even though it didn't seem like anyone else was with him. Still, he had a cherubic face that could set pretty much anyone at ease.

Dane shrugged off their indifference. "Okay, if you know anybody who fits the description and needs a gig, call 'em now. Dougie, did you bring your flute and clarinet?"

"I did," he grumbled, glowering.

"Okay, I want to hear you on those and then we'll talk about what we're going to do with these characters." Dane motioned to the script, which sat next to her new portfolio on a small office desk. "With our remaining time, we'll practice some songs together to get used to playing together."

Dougie went for his instruments while the others made some phone calls. Thankfully, they respectfully took the calls into the hall without needing to be told. Dougie sounded fantastic with both woodwinds, as promised. She nodded as he played, and she picked out bits of his sound. The ideas she had could work. By the time she was done, she had ideas for the others as well.

"You'll be seeing a few of my friends in a couple of hours," Evie said.

"Mine, too," Pedro said.

"Good. Let's get to other things while we wait. Have you guys read the script?" Dane asked.

They shook their heads. "I didn't get one," Samiyah said and the others nodded.

Dane groaned. *How do they expect us to get anything done if we don't know the story?* "Lemme go get some scripts."

Dane hated that she'd have to interact with Andrew, but it was a necessary evil. She needed the musicians to know the characters and the story, so they could understand her vision as they played. She'd also like feedback, in case they thought something she made didn't match the scene or didn't match the character. Plus, they might be able to figure out the story Andrew was trying to tell, beyond the basic fairy tale anyway.

"Andrew," Dane called for him as she spotted him on stage. It looked like he was auditioning an actor. They hadn't completed casting from her understanding of things and the theater still needed to be cleaned. So much work for everyone.

"I'm busy," he snapped, not even bothering to turn to her. She didn't understand his hatred. Okay, he didn't want music, but trying to stonewall her wouldn't help his play in the long run. After all, there'd be a score going with the production opening night no matter what. She figured he'd rather it be awesome than terrible, as the music would reflect on him regardless of how he felt about it. He didn't seem to follow the same logic, though.

"I'm sure you are. I just need a few copies of the scripts for my orchestra," she replied.

With a sneer, he glared at her. "They're just playing music. They don't need it."

She squinted. *That's really his answer?* "They do. They need to know and understand the show to play the music for it and why the music goes with what's happening." *Why do I even have to explain this?*

His eyes dug into her in ways that reminded her of how her parents' friends looked at her. "They don't need to understand anything. They're not actors. They just need to play some stupid music."

Dane frowned, but wouldn't let this jackass get to her. *Keep calm. Do your best and make Nick proud.* "The music will enhance the story."

"The story doesn't need enhancing," he barked, slapping his hands against his sides. "I don't care what my stupid father thinks!"

Ah, Calvin was his father. That made some sense. Maybe Nicole was right about people getting jobs through personal connections. She felt a little better, but she still needed to get scripts for her people.

"I still need scripts," Dane said.

"I'm busy," he hissed and turned away again.

Dane rolled her eyes and asked the crew who milled about the place. Eventually, someone got her copies of the script. She made sure to thank him and find out his name. She'd need to make friends with the crew to get things done. Now, to get to work.

***

Nicole had a spare minute, so she decided to get in touch with Jody. She wasn't sure how long they'd need Jody, but after talking to Danny, she was certain Danny would see the job all the way through. They'd need someone to watch Haydn for a few months, probably.

"Hey, Nicole," Jody greeted her over the phone.

"Hey, Jody. How's everything going?"

"Fine, the usual."

"Ah, school and computers, but nothing else. You still keep your blog?"

"Of course."

"That's good. It still taking you places?"

"I got an invite out to this thing over in the spring, but it's a while from now. I've made a couple of apps, too. You should tell Aunt Katie to get me IT work at the firm. She's acting like she doesn't know what I'm talking about."

"She might not. Mommy isn't completely up-to-date on the firm's network. I'll put a bug in my father's ear about it." It'd be nice to help Jody out, and the firm would benefit in having her around.

"I didn't even think to ask him."

"He'll be okay with it. He knows you're brilliant."

Jody laughed. "I am."

"Now, humble on the other hand..." Nicole trailed off into a snicker.

"I'm humble enough."

Nicole rolled her eyes. "I'm fairly certain that's not how humble works. Now, if you'll forgive me, but I was calling to ask a favor of you." She kept working since she doubted Jody would want to stay on the line for long.

"Well, I just asked you a favor. Tit for tat. What do you need?"

"Danny has a regular job now, and we need someone to watch Haydn." Nicole grabbed a few folders and flipped through them. Once she found the one she needed, she grabbed a pen.

"She got the job writing music for that play?"

"Yes. She got the gig." Nicole couldn't stop a smile as she made a few notes about the file in front of her.

"Awesome! I have classes three days a week, though. I'm not sure what I can do."

"If you could just go over and check on him whenever you get a chance. He's by himself from eight to five-thirty now. It might be later than that when Danny really gets into work and when I have school." They would have to do something before classes started for her. She didn't want Haydn to suffer because they didn't plan.

Jody made a humming noise. "I'll do what I can. It shouldn't be too hard. You're not far from school, and I scheduled stuff in the morning."

"Great. Can you start tomorrow? I'll leave you a key in the mailbox."

"Sounds good."

"Thank you so much."

Jody scoffed. "Are you kidding me? You've helped me tons of times in my short life. I'm glad you trust me enough to take care of your precious pup."

"I know you're responsible." She frowned at her notes and went into her desk drawer, needing a paper that should've been pinned to the folder.

"Yeah. You also know I'm going to mess with your computer, right?"

"I imagined you would." As long as Jody didn't do anything dramatic to it.

"I'm going to play Danny's game system and possibly ruin any places she saved."

"Figured." She even warned Danny, but Danny didn't seem to mind.

"I'm also going to eat all of your food."

"We're well stocked." But, they'd have to figure out who would go shopping when they started running low. It would probably have to be her at some point since she drove. *Or maybe we can do it together, one day after I get her from work and Jody can stay with Haydn for a little longer.*

They bid each other farewell. Smiling, Nicole was glad it was easy to figure out what to do with Haydn. She hoped it gave her and Danny a chance to spend a little one-on-one time with Jody as well. If Jody hung out for a little while, anyway. They could play video games and bond some.

Finally, time to leave, Nicole picked up Danny, who seemed to be in good spirits. Well, a smile danced on her face anyway. They greeted each other with a kiss.

"How was work?" Nicole asked as she pulled away from the theater.

Dane's caramel cheeks flushed a light pink. "I think this is going to work out. I hired musicians today. I mean, I got to hire people. Got everyone, except a drummer. The dude I want is going to show up tomorrow. He's great. Bad with time, but unbelievable on drums. The group's going to finish reading the script tonight, and we'll be able to talk music and the play tomorrow, start getting to know each other and learning how to play together."

Nicole couldn't help her grin. She listened as Danny went on about her plans for the show, if she could get her orchestra behind her. It was adorable whenever Danny used the phrase 'my orchestra.'

"I think I'm going to let Samiyah represent the main character. It might seem weird for a hero to have violin music as a theme, but she'd crush whatever I write."

"You seem to really like her. Are you having instrument envy?" Nicole teased, even though her skin prickled a bit. It was odd to have Danny openly talk about a woman to her. It'd take some getting used to.

Danny laughed. "I couldn't match her with the violin, even before my hand. And this says a lot about her, because I used to be awesome with my violin. She'd smoke me like a cheap cigarette. I think she's going to be the thing that makes this special."

"I think you're going to be the thing to make this special. Have you seen how enthused you are about this?"

Danny tittered, like a little girl with a new toy. Nicole left it alone, figuring Danny was trying to play it cool. Too bad the giggling blew it. However, Danny wanted to play her mood was fine with Nicole, as long as she was happy with her work.

What Nicole wasn't fine with was Danny trying to dive right into the household chores as soon as they came in. She didn't want Danny to burn herself out trying to be a housewife and breadwinner. It was possible, but it wasn't necessary. Besides, they were a team.

"Danny, you don't have to do that," Nicole said as Danny went to the vacuum.

"Can't let Haydn's hair build up. Besides, it's been a while since the floor got cleaned." Danny didn't turn the vacuum on, but she was in prime position to get started.

Nicole folded her arms across her chest. "And let me guess, after that, you'll go make dinner?"

Danny shrugged. "Why shouldn't I?"

"Because we're partners. We can do things together."

Danny's shoulders dropped, but she nodded. The agreement didn't stop her from turning on the vacuum. Nicole sighed and rubbed her chin. She sorted through the mail and picked up a few of Haydn's things while he tried to take them from her. She turned back to Danny once the vacuum powered down.

"Danny, let me handle dinner. Take Haydn out," Nicole insisted as Danny rushed into the kitchen. She had allowed Danny to handle breakfast that morning without making a fuss because she suspected Danny needed bits of her routine, but she refused to let Danny try to be everything.

"I've got it."

"Love." Nicole wrapped her hands around Danny's waist and snuggled her shoulder. "You don't have to do this. You're not meant to run yourself into the ground for me."

Danny sighed. "I like taking care of you."

"I'm not going to leave you because you don't make dinner or clean the house. Before you came along, I handled every meal, cleaned every room, did all the laundry, and that was for someone who was ungrateful. You had breakfast. Let me do this. Let's be a team." She'd love the chance to do for Danny what she had done for too many unappreciative lovers.

Danny put her hands on Nicole's hands and lightly caressed her skin. She gnawed at her bottom lip. "I don't want this to turn into your other relationships."

Nicole laughed. "The fact that you want that means it won't happen, but there's a simple solution."

"Which is?"

"Don't let it happen. You don't make demands of me, love. We're arguing over who's going to make dinner right now." It seemed silly to Nicole. *How could I be worried over us? She wants us to work just as much as I do.*

"Not arguing," Danny grumbled.

"Okay, no, we're not, but it's on its way. You think I've had this argument before? No. No one ever volunteered to make dinner for me after a long day at work for both of us. How about we make a deal?" She'd be able to negotiate something they could both live with and help them ease into this new phase.

"A deal?"

"Neither of us tries to do everything. We clean together. Walk Haydn together when we can. One makes breakfast and the other makes dinner." Nicole suspected dinner would become her meal. Danny always woke up before her, and she doubted she'd ever be able to work herself into the habit of getting up before Danny.

Silence reigned supreme. Nicole wasn't sure what she'd do if Danny turned it down. Haydn rushed in, the noise of his paws on the tile cut through the quiet. He nudged them both with his nose before brushing his muzzle against Danny's hand.

"Fine. I'll take this little brat for his walk," Danny said, rubbing Haydn's head.

Nicole laughed and released Danny. She'd have to remember to give Haydn a treat later for his help. He was such a good pup.

Chapter Ten

DANE LISTENED TO LENNOX Peterson strumming his guitar. He was a friend of Evie's, but Dane was familiar with him to a degree. She'd seen him play a couple of times. She mentioned his name to Crow, who had seen him almost a dozen times and couldn't say enough good things about him. He was worth the hype. She felt damned lucky he wanted a job.

"I'm going to have you represent the villain," Dane said, moving to make a note in her portfolio sitting on the small desk in the orchestra room. Before, it was something she considered, but now she was certain the guitar worked for the villain. The way his thick fingers glided along the strings of his guitar, he had to be someone powerful in the story. The modern sound of the electric guitar with the classical notes of the violin for the paladin would be a good mix.

"You mean Lord Vadar?" Lennox smirked, pushing long, dark dreadlocks out of his face. He dropped into a nearby seat, which groaned a little, and secured his guitar next to him.

Dane chuckled. "I see you've read the whole script."

"I've read some of it. Evie showed it to me and explained what was going on before she got me to get off my butt and come play for you. I don't get it. Is every hero story that similar or is this guy as much of a tool as he comes across?" Lennox wiggled his eyebrows as he crossed one leg over the other and held his ankle. Evie probably told him about Andrew as well.

"I don't think it's that bad," Evie replied from across the room. Her fingers tapped at her keyboard, but with the power off, no sound came from her beyond the click of the keys.

"No, it's worse," Samiyah said. Pedro guffawed and then a maroon blush painted his cheeks. He tried to hide behind his sax.

"Forget that crap. Let's take it back to the beginning. Why should this newbie get the part of the villain?" Dougie glared at the group with hard green eyes. "I'm going to be putting in three times as much work as he is. I should at least get a bigger part."

"Or to avoid putting too much on your shoulders, we let Lennox do his thing. It'll be a good contrast to Samiyah's hero violin." Dane liked the idea of the two biggest roles going to similar instruments. People would feel contrasting emotions through strings, which she hoped would intensify the show and maybe make them think a little when it was over. She also wanted to get people to root for the instrument they usually wouldn't consider with a guitar in the mix.

"Wait, she's getting the hero? The hell?" Dougie jabbed his thumb toward Samiyah.

A scowl settled on Samiyah's umber face, and she placed a hand on her side, cocking her hip out. "And why shouldn't I play the hero? I could play you into the ground right now."

"I'd destroy you." Dougie held his chin up high.

Before she could stop herself, Dane scoffed, but thankfully everyone else did, too. She had to step in and do something. The last thing she needed was infighting. They didn't have time for that. They needed to start practicing together to make sure they had the best sound possible on opening night.

"All right. I've already made my decision. Samiyah is the hero. Lennox is the villain. Pedro, sidekick," Dane said. Pedro smiled, as if he liked that role. To each his own.

"You better not make me the freaking damsel in distress." Dougie gnashed his teeth.

"Well, I want Evie to be the dragon." Dane motioned to the keyboard.

Evie grinned. "I'd make an awesome dragon." Modesty didn't seem to be a thing amongst any of them.

"No! No way am I going to be the damsel," Dougie huffed, holding his arms across his chest.

"The fact that there is a damsel in distress is nuts. Most people would've at least made her a sassy princess or something. I mean, who the hell makes a traditional princess now?" Lennox scratched his forehead.

"I think that's what he's going for, this classical fairytale feel," Evie said.

"I guess that explains why you like it," Lennox replied. Evie stuck her tongue out at him. He gave her the finger, and they both laughed.

"No, he does hit the classical fairytale, I'll give him that," Dane said. It wasn't a horrible thing. It just wasn't terribly original either. The story was beyond generic and bordered on boring, except there was magic, sword fights, and dragons. Kids would probably be engaged. But, it wasn't sold as a children's show, and she didn't want to bad mouth the play to the orchestra. Maybe Andrew would change things during rewrites or once he had every character cast, which could impact the music. She'd need to keep an eye on that. "Anyway, Dougie, someone has to play for the princess and that's you."

"Why don't you get your stupid drummer who hasn't bothered to show up be the princess?" Dougie's face turned bright red.

"Because I'm musical director," Dane replied. And who the hell ever heard of a drum playing a princess?

"Well, how about I go speak with the actual director?" Dougie stormed off before Dane could retort. She could hear him stomping all the way down the long hallway to the stage.

"What a baby." Lennox chuckled and shook his head, his long locks slapping him in the face thanks to the overly exaggerated gesture.

"You probably should've fired him when you had the chance," Pedro said to Dane.

Dane shook her head, even though she could still fire him. "Nah. He's good at those pipes. Attitude is shit, though." She saw a lot of headaches and temper tantrums in the future.

"Unfortunately, he has a point. Where's your drummer?" Evie asked.

Sighing, Dane waved the question off. "He'll be late every day. I don't think he's ever been on time for anything in his life, even his birth. He always says he was born a week past due and even then it took him two more days to come out. He's the type who'll be late to his own funeral."

"Well, that won't be good for when the show starts," Samiyah replied.

"Of course not, which is why we will all lie to him about when anything starts. It's best to tell him ninety minutes earlier. He'll show up on time if we do that," Dane said, and she was dead serious. She'd seen the strategy work many times. She used it to get him to come in today. She should've gone with two hours.

They nodded. One of the things Dane liked about dealing with artists was that they expected people to be eccentric. They accepted this. It also seemed like they spoke up the drummer. Ryan Garner wandered in, looking like he just woke up, complete with a wrinkled plain t-shirt and wild, short brown hair.

"Wow, Ryan, only two hours later than I need you," Dane said. She wouldn't care if he sounded good and got along with the orchestra.

With a yawn, Ryan scratched the top of his head, mussing his wavy brown hair more. "I had to find someone to drive over my kit. Took forever. How the hell do you guys not have a drum set here?"

That was something Dane wondered herself, especially considering the tuba. "I don't know. I didn't make the theater or fill it with junk." She drew her eyebrows in close together as she realized his whole statement. "Why don't you drive yet?" She figured by now he'd have his act somewhat together.

"I dunno. Why don't you drive yet?" he countered seriously, as she should have her act together by now, too.

She rolled her eyes. "Touché."

"Anyway, I need help setting the kit up."

Groaning, Dane shook her head. Her knee throbbed at the thought of moving stuff. Just when walking had become comfortable, she suddenly had to carry stuff. She and the others went to help Ryan get his kit from the back of a friend's van. Along the way, the trumpeter she hired showed up and lent a hand. *I love how no one is on time. Making me look real good here.* They finished in time for Andrew to get in her face right outside the band room. Dane could feel the makings of a headache thumping right between her eyes.

"What sort of monkey show are you running back here? Musicians shouldn't be complaining to me about your poor management," Andrew said, glaring at her. Good thing he couldn't shoot lasers from his eyes or he'd have burned her to crisp.

Sighing, Dane forced herself not to roll her eyes or strangle Andrew with his 'fashionable' scarf. "I've got things coming together. Dougie's just being a baby and seems to think you're going to help him. You don't have to white knight for him and run to his rescue."

He growled. "I'm not running to anyone's rescue. I don't need your people running to me when I've got more important things to do. Now, I'm here to tell you to get your shit together."

"My shit is together. Don't entertain the musicians if you don't want to bother with the music." It seemed simple enough to Dane. If an actor came to her about something, she'd point them right to Andrew, unless it had to do with music.

Andrew's fiery eyes narrowed as he pointed a thick finger at her. "Keep your damned musicians in here."

"Dougie, you hear that? Stop being a baby. What I say goes," Dane called to him hiding at the end of the hall.

Andrew's eyes seemed to ignite with even more fury. His nostrils flared. "What you say most certainly doesn't go. This is my show." He patted himself in the chest. Stupid declarations like that would be the reason Dougie kept bothering him about the music he didn't care about.

Dane sighed. "And my music. Either I'm in charge of the music or you are. Make up your mind."

"I'm in charge of everything," Andrew replied, throwing his hands up in a dramatic fashion.

"Okay. You're in charge of everything. Good?" Dane hoped this got him to go away. She wanted to get a feel for this blended band. She didn't need Andrew in her face about anything. It was time to make some music, damn it.

Andrew snorted. He stormed out of the room, and Dougie made his way back inside with his head hung low. Dane ignored them and turned her attention back to the rest of the group.

"All right, the band's altogether." She glanced over at the trumpeter in the corner. Greg Little seemed shy, but he played a mean trumpet. "Greg, I need you here on time from now on."

Greg's brown eyes went wide and nodded more than necessary. He bowed to her a little. "I know. I've never taken the train here before and got lost several times. I called, but no one picked up." His voice was small and he stared at the floor. Pedro eased over next to him. Pedro would be kind to him and help him along the way through these massive, often loud personalities.

"Well, at least you tried." Dane sighed.

"Now, what, boss?" Lennox asked.

"Now, we play together and see what happens." Dane already had ideas now that she had assigned each character an instrument, but they would also need music for scenes. Things were coming along nicely, despite the few bumps in the road.

***

Nicole sat at her desk at work. She had barely been at work an hour and had checked her class schedule four times, wondering if there was a way for her to change it. She worried about seeing Haydn and Danny getting home. But, she needed these specific courses for her thesis and to graduate. There was no way around it. She sighed while her heart clenched. She massaged the center of her chest with two fingers.

"I shouldn't worry. This is it. I finish this, and I have my degree. I don't need to be attached Danny every moment of the day," Nicole told herself, as if saying it aloud would make her believe it. Her stomach trembled, but she knew that was true. She needed to keep it together.

It was unhealthy to want to be around Danny all the time. Besides, they had both worried about changing and agreed they'd be fine. She knew this was true, too, but her body didn't want to believe it. Anxiety danced down her every nerve and gnawed at every bit of her. She took a breath, refusing to let the anxiety turn into a tornado and rip her apart.

Taking a deep breath and holding it, Nicole turned her attention back to her work. Still, she thought of Danny. She hadn't gotten a phone call yet. Glancing at her clock, it was early. Well, it was still morning anyway. Maybe Danny would call her after lunch.

"Maybe I am too dependent on her," Nicole muttered, shaking her head.

"No, she just brightens your day," Mina said, stepping into the office.

Nicole snorted and rolled her eyes. "You don't even know who I'm talking about."

Mina turned her mouth up to one side. "You're kidding, right? You're in here moping and sighing over being too dependent on someone. If you're not talking about Danny, I'm going to tell her you're cheating on her with another housewife."

Nicole chuckled. "She's not a housewife anymore. She's got a job."

"Impressive," Mina said, as if she didn't know Danny had a job, even though Nicole made sure to tell everyone. A proud smile settled on Mina's face. "How is that working for her?"

"She seems to enjoy it. The director of the play is giving her a bit of a hard time, but other than that, she's happy to be making music again."

With a nod, Mina grinned. "I can't wait to see this thing."

"The script is a little cheesy, but I think Danny's going to knock the music out of the park. I'm sure she'll be happy when we're all there to hear it."

"Yes, so you should let her work and not worry about it."

"I know." Nicole sighed to the point where her shoulders dropped. "I've gotten used to her calling. It seems weird for her not to reach out. I mean, even if she didn't call, I could call the house. Now, I don't know what to do."

Mina's forehead wrinkled. "Wait, she didn't give you the number to the theater?"

"I asked her for it, but the number she calls from is just a random phone in the hall. If no one's by it, no one will pick up. I looked online and the number from there just rings. I don't know what's up with that one. There's still a lot of work going on at the theater, so maybe the phones are a part of that. She doesn't know the number for the office. She can't give it to me until Andrew gives it to her and he doesn't seem eager to share information of any kind with her."

Mina shook her head. "We have got to get Danny into full-adult mode. What she needs is a cell phone, especially for when you go back to school."

Nicole rubbed her chin. She'd like for Danny to get a cell phone. It'd come in handy when school started. They'd probably worry about each other less. But, she didn't want to make it seem like she wanted to keep track of Danny. Maybe they should take the time apart and use it to grow as people.

A scoff echoed in Nicole's brain. *You're full of it.* Okay, having a cell phone and being able to call each other wasn't about keeping track of each other. It was about being in contact with each other, especially on long, late nights. She needed to bring this up with Danny.

Mina smiled. "You're already putting together notes when you present this idea, aren't you?"

Rubbing her forehead, Nicole chuckled. "You know me too well."

Mina shrugged. "You're practically my sister."

"At least I know you'd never betray me." Unlike the last person she declared her sister.

"Please. Only idiots throw you away, Nicole, and I think we've established I'm not the idiot around here. Now, stop worrying about Danny. You're not dependent on her for wanting her to call. You care about her. Also, don't stress yourself out about her not calling. She's probably busy. She's in charge of making music, and she's got a band to worry about."

"An orchestra," Nicole absently corrected.

Mina arched an eyebrow. "A what?"

"She calls it her orchestra. I think there's only seven of them, but the title seems appropriate as they're working for a play."

Mina tittered. "That's damned cute. Don't tell her I said that, though. I'm not trying to ruin our friendship."

Nicole smiled. "That'll stay between us. Thanks for the talk."

"Anytime."

"What brings you by, though?"

"Your presence has been requested. I think they're about to tag us both in on something, which is good. I need a competent partner, and you obviously need the distraction."

Nicole furrowed her brow. "They're going to get us both to work on something?" That was extremely rare, but she enjoyed working with Mina on the few occasions it had been allowed to happen. Mina was beyond competent at what they did and possessed a passion for it that Nicole never could manage.

"Yes. Don't tell anyone I said this, but I think the partners are starting to feel the pressure of you possibly leaving. One more semester and then you're a trained scientist with little reason to stick around and they know they haven't treated you the best because they always thought you'd be here."

That made sense. Nicole knew she was valuable for the firm, even if sometimes it was hard to tell. She had plenty of clients. One of the reasons people always came to bother her was because she was exceptional. She always brought her best to the table because this was her parents' dream. Now, she had dreams of her own.

It was good to know the firm understood her importance, though, and to see them make an effort to keep her. A few years ago, the effort wouldn't have been made. There was always this expectation of her. Now, they were nervous about her leaving. *Just like me.*

"It'll be cool working with you again. I like when we get to do that." Mina stood up a little taller.

"I like it too, of course."

"Then, let's get going." Mina jabbed both thumbs in the direction of the door. Nicole nodded and followed Mina to a brief meeting with some higher-ups to learn what was expected of them, and leaped into preparing for the actual task.

Mina and Nicole had been teamed up to dazzle new clients and assure them this was the firm for them. They'd have to come up with ironclad work to meet with the clients in a few days, especially since the clients had deep wallets. It was a good distraction, especially when Mina started throwing ideas at her. It got her mind working and before she realized it, they had the whole presentation mapped out. It was easy. Fun. She looked forward to when they'd speak with the clients.

If I get another job, we might not be able to do this again. The thought made her heart sink, swallowed by disappoints and sorrows she never considered before. Her thoughts didn't get any better once they were done. Mina decided it was time for lunch. *Wow, there won't be any more lunches with my friends if I leave.* Even though daily lunch dates were recent for them, she wasn't ready to give it up. *I guess it would depend on where I end up. If I'm across town, this ends.* Nicole shook it away, not wanting to worry about it right now.

"I think we did a damn good job and deserve a reward," Mina said, packing up her notebook in her briefcase.

Nicole chuckled. "We didn't even do the presentation yet and you're trying to get us the Nobel Prize."

"They should give it to us right after the show, actually. Let's go grab Clara," Mina said as they made their way out of the conference room.

"And our coats. We'll freeze outside if we don't," Nicole reminded her.

Mina laughed. "Well, obviously."

They picked up their coats and their friend and made their way to their usual cafe, sitting at one of the round tables near the back. While there weren't a lot of people, they didn't want to disturb anyone or be disturbed by others.

Right after they ordered drinks, Nicole's phone went off. There was a number she didn't know, but she answered. It was probably Danny.

"Nicole Cardell," she said.

"Hey, Chem," Danny replied.

A light smile floated across her face. "Hey. I was hoping you'd call."

"Yeah, sorry I'm a little late. I got caught up in this thing with Samiyah. She's taunting Dougie with her talent," Danny laughed.

Nicole wasn't sure what that meant, but it tickled Danny. "Is everything all right over there?"

"It's fine. I imagine this is what running a kindergarten must be like. I'm waiting for Dougie to wet himself. Pedro's trying to befriend my new shy kid, Greg. Beyond that, I'm working on getting these guys to play together and to get Samiyah to be a little humble. She sounds incredible, yes, but she doesn't need to keep telling Dougie that."

Nicole's face scrunched up a little as she searched her mind for details on Dougie, Pedro, and Greg. She couldn't remember a Greg, but Danny said he was new, so she probably just hired him. "Is Dougie the one who gave you attitude?"

"Yeah. He seems to be that way with everyone. He's upset I gave Samiyah the part of the hero while he's the damsel in distress."

Nicole laughed. "Don't you think you need to learn the characters' names if you're going to assign them instruments?"

Danny scoffed. "Nope. Lennox and Pedro want to call them by their instrument, and I think I'm going to go along with that."

"Lennox?" The name was familiar, but Nicole couldn't remember what he did.

"My new guitarist. I was telling you about him before. He's the one Crow went on about after I said I might hire him. I think he'll add an interesting dynamic to the villain. He already wants to change up between guitar and bass when he can. He has a vision, which I like."

"As long as it doesn't end up clashing with your vision."

Danny chuckled. "He can have all the vision he likes, but once it tries to clash with mine, we're doing my thing. I'm musical director, after all." It sounded like she said the title with her head held high and her chest puffed out.

Nicole smiled. "Sounds like you're enjoying yourself."

"It's all right. Oh, I've got to get back to them. Ryan's about to fall asleep. See you later."

"Of course. I love you."

"Love you, too." Danny disconnected the call.

Nicole sighed as she put the phone down. Looking up, she noticed Mina smirking at her. The light in Mina's eyes made her groan.

"Mina, don't," Clara said.

Mina grinned. "What? I didn't say anything. And, now the moment's passed, so I can't say anything."

Nicole gave her a deadpan look. "When has that ever stopped you?"

Mina smiled more. "You know I kid because I love, right?"

"I'm sure that's it," Nicole said.

"What's Danny up to?" Clara asked, undoubtedly to cut off any smart aleck remark clinging to Mina's tongue.

"She's having a good time, even though she doesn't want to say that. She's rather taken with her violinist." Nicole tried not to think about it. It was about the music, nothing more. *But, I bet she's cute.* If she had eyes in her brain, she'd roll them.

"Her violinist?" Clara echoed, arching an eyebrow.

"A woman named Samiyah. Danny can't stop singing her praises. I've never actually seen her so enthused about the violin, even though she plays it. I don't think she imagined someone could play it the way Samiyah does." Nicole was certain that was the reason Danny kept bringing Samiyah up, but her stomach twisted again. She forced herself to settle down. It was nothing.

"Then, she's got a good group of musicians?" Mina asked as their drinks were delivered. They paused to order some sandwiches and salads.

"According to her, yes. She's excited about this whole thing, even though I think the director has it out for her and she thinks so, too."

"Hey, if she's having fun with it and getting a paycheck for it, she's doing better than most." A teasing smile lit up Mina's face and she motioned between her and Clara. "Well, not me and Clara obviously, but most."

Nicole stuck her tongue out at Mina and kicked her in the shin. Mina yelped and glared at her. Nicole glared right back.

"Mina, be nice," Clara scolded her.

"Why should I when she's the one sticking her filthy tongue at me?" Mina winked.

Nicole pretended to gasp. "Who says my tongue is filthy?"

Mina wiggled her eyebrows. "Danny told me."

"She doesn't kiss and tell."

"Or so you hope." Mina winked at her again.

"And just when I was having fun working with you." Nicole sneered in her best friend's direction. She took a bite of her tuna salad sandwich and popped a fry as Mina offered her a peacekeeping smile.

"I'm only playing. Anyway, what's the deal with the director?" Mina asked before picking up her grilled cheese sandwich and nibbling it a bit.

Nicole shrugged. "He doesn't want his play to have a score. He thinks the story stands well on its own."

Mina nodded and swallowed her food. "Does it?"

Nicole shook her head. "I definitely think the producer, Calvin, was right to go with music. He needs something to make the play stand out. It's a fairly generic fairytale, with a generic hero and villain complete with a princess who needs to be saved."

Mina's face scrunched up. "Is it a kiddie play? I was looking forward to seeing this."

Clara's face lit up at the mention. "Oh, then it's fine if I bring my son."

"I'm not sure if it's a kiddie play, but you can bring him. I think it's just a fairytale, so if you like fairytales, you'd probably enjoy this. I'll know more about it when Danny does. So far, we've only had a chance to read the script, but I'm hoping there'll be some changes. The dialogue is a little cheesy, and the female character is...well, Danny and her crew have been calling her 'damsel in distress,'" Nicole said.

Mina groaned as a deep pout settled on her face. "I was looking forward to this."

"Hey, the music will be outstanding," Clara reminded her.

That much they all knew was true. Mina nodded and sat up a little more. Nicole was happy her friends looked forward to seeing Danny in action. Despite Mina being annoying on purpose much of the time, Nicole knew she couldn't ask for more supportive friends.

They had their lunch and returned to the firm. Nicole finished up for the day and then went to go pick up Danny. She had to wait a while for Danny and watched several people leave. One of those people was a woman with a violin case. While bundled up to guard against the cold, if this was Samiyah, she had gorgeous dark skin, a curvy figure, and expressive hazel eyes. *I was wrong. She's not cute. She's beautiful.* Bitterness nipped at her insides in ways the cold never could, and she refused to give it a name.

Nicole shook the feeling away. It didn't matter. Samiyah was with three other people, another woman and two men also carrying instruments, and they seemed to be talking excitedly. They didn't even glance over at her.

Nicole wished she had an excuse to get out and introduce herself, just to meet Danny's orchestra if they were that. It could get awkward quickly if they weren't. Hell, it could still get awkward if they were.

***

Dane couldn't wait to get out of the theater. Nicole was already outside waiting for her, but Andrew felt the need to keep her back to complain about Ryan's lateness. Like it had anything to do with him. He wanted her to know how moving Ryan's kit was distracting to everyone else. She'd get Ryan under control. *Or I'll have to replace him.* The thought didn't sit well with her. *He fits my plan so well. Damn it, Ryan, don't make me have to fire you.*

"Look, we have to get his kit in here and distracting to who? You have people moving stuff through the place all day," Dane said.

"They're doing their job," Andrew said, nostrils flaring.

"Okay, as was he. He needs his drums here to play the drums." It seemed logical enough to her, but the way the veins in his neck bulged, she assumed he didn't think so.

"If this is the type of ship you're running, I think you should get off now before you sink," Andrew said, putting his chin in the air. There were still people milling about, so he was essentially reprimanding her in front of his staff, trying to flex his muscle. She wouldn't give him the satisfaction.

Dane rolled her eyes. "You having fun trying to chase me off or are you getting off at looking big around the guys you pay?"

His face turned red, and he puffed out his cheeks for a moment. "I'm not trying anything. You're not cutting it. This is serious. It's not some back-alley bar or something. I won't have you messing up my show."

"You focus on everything. I've got the music. It won't be the thing to mess up the show." She doubted he believed that, but he was annoying and she needed him to back off.

He scowled, obviously getting the buried insult there, and put one finger up. "You've never done anything like this and the only reason you're here is because of Christine Wolfe. I'm sure it's only a matter of time before you screw up."

"Gotta start somewhere. And are you really here on merit alone?" Dane countered with an eyebrow cocked up.

He made a fist and his hand shook. Pinching the bridge of her nose, she had enough. Between him and Dougie, Dane fought off a headache all day. She was a champion for making it through those two with her sanity intact. She left, relieved to see Nicole outside in the car. She practically jumped into the passenger seat and was almost tempted to yell at Nicole to drive like they had robbed a bank.

"Hey, love." Nicole leaned in for a kiss, which Dane was all too happy to give her. The kiss helped alleviate some of Dane's tension. Nicole pulled away from the curb. Settling into her seat felt like settling into hot bath after a long day. *It can't always be this way, right? Gotta be because I just started.*

"Hey. How was your day?" Dane felt bad for calling Nicole so late and then not even having the chance to really talk to her.

"Fine. Mina thinks the partners are starting to worry about me leaving once the school semester is done. They're letting us work on something together, and it was nice. I wish I could do it more often."

Dane smiled. "They know how much you're worth. I'm sure they'll start showering you with all sorts of goodies. Your parents in on it?"

"I don't think so. I think they're ready to let me go." A small smile slid across her face.

Dane nodded. *Do her parents know how much good they've done for their relationship by letting her have this without butting in anymore?* Nicole should be allowed to spread her wings. Her angel could go far on her own. "They're worried a little, but I think you're right."

An auburn eyebrow arched. "They said something to you?"

"Your mother. She wanted to know if you had a plan."

Nicole nodded. "At least she hasn't cornered me about it. Maybe she's trying to let me go."

"Are you ready?" Dane asked before she realized what she said. *A better question would be, am I ready?* What would happen when Nicole finally achieved her dream? When Nicole was finally where she wanted to be? Nicole kept assuring her that they were in this together and they were forever, but nothing lasted forever. Would Nicole still need her there cheerleading for her once school was over and she had what she longed for?

Nicole let out a weird laugh. "I am, but I'm a little nervous. I've never actually had this much control over my life, you know?" Then, she laughed again. "Well, I suppose it would be different for you."

Dane shook her head. "I never had much control, just the freedom to not have control."

"Freedom." Nicole sighed for some reason.

"You okay?"

"I'm fine. You mention your freedom, and everyone values their freedom."

Squinting, Dane shook her head. "Chem, what's up?" *Geez, are we already not a team? I thought we were good.* Of course, she had considered what could happen once Nicole achieved her dream and it hadn't been a happy thought. *What is wrong with us?*

"I was wondering if you'd be willing to get a cell phone," Nicole sort of blurted out. Then, her eyes went wide, like she was horrified.

Dane laughed, but it sounded awkward because her heart and her lungs had been ready to explode. "Is that all? You scared me for a second." *Okay, still a team. Still good. We'll be okay.*

"Well, I'm not sure about your stance on them. I know before you never felt like you needed one because you're almost always home or near home. Now, we're both out and about. It's okay if you don't want one. I think I have the theater's number now since you called before." Nicole shook her head.

Dane's face scrunched up as she studied her girlfriend. "You're nervous about this, huh?" *Nick's just trying to do what she thinks makes me comfortable, even though she's worried about me and wants to talk to me.*

"Like I said, I know you never wanted one before and I don't want you to think I'm trying to put a leash on you or anything."

Dane grinned. "Angel, I think we both know you already got me on a leash. You joke about it all the time. Can't believe you're so nervous about this."

Nicole shook her head again. "I can't believe I am, too. I had a real argument mapped out before you got in the car."

"I'll bet you did, and we both know I don't win arguments against you. Maybe I should get a cell phone. Trying to make phone calls in that madhouse is madness."

A frown marred Nicole's features. "Why?"

"There's always so much going on with the phone in the hall and from what I can tell there's only one other place with a phone, which is the office, which is Andrew's. Wanna punch him in the face when I go to use the phone. 'Why?' 'Who are you calling?' 'You've been on for a few minutes now. You should probably get back to work.' Are bosses generally this annoying?"

"Bosses, yes. Leaders, no. From what you tell me with Andrew, he seems insecure and wants everyone to think he's in charge because he doesn't feel like he's really in charge."

"Yeah, maybe a cell phone. This way, you can call me, too. I can't even imagine what Andrew might do if you called the office and asked for me. A cell phone might be the way to go."

"It'll also help in case your orchestra needs to catch up with you after hours," Nicole said.

"That is good." It'd come in handy with Ryan most definitely.

"We'll get you on my plan."

Dane frowned. "Are you going to be paying for it?" Money was one of the main reasons she never wanted a cell phone. She couldn't afford one and didn't want Nicole footing yet another bill for her.

"You'll be getting a steady paycheck. We can divide up bills, okay?" Nicole replied.

Dane nodded. *Awesome, I can really start carrying my weight around here.* "That's a great idea. I can pay the phone bill, then. I can pay bills now." There was her trust money, but this was different. This was her money.

"Yes, you can."

Dane felt light enough to float off to space. "And now I'm happy I can pay a bill." *Nick is totally a witch. I'm bewitched. I'm happy to pay bills.* Being able to pay the phone bill and getting a phone seemed reasonable enough.

Holy shit, I have responsibilities. I'm like a real freaking adult. Pride had her high, but she'd have to come down sometime. That was how things worked. Dane had to take a deep breath. They were evolving into something better. She was better. She had a job. She could support herself and support Nicole. *Then, stop feeling like you're going to throw up.* She had never come down that fast before.

Chapter Eleven

MINA GAVE NICOLE A high-five and Nicole managed to keep in a giggle fit. Mina must have noticed, grabbing Nicole around the shoulders as they walked down the hall of the law firm, away from the conference room, and from the newest clients of the firm. Nicole let loose a high pitch laugh.

"We were on fire in there!" Mina squeezed her shoulders.

Nicole lost a fight to a smile and nodded. "We were pretty outstanding."

The clients had been enamored with her and Mina. She couldn't blame them. Mina had a silver tongue coated in honey, and Nicole always chimed in with her own sweetness. It was like an old dance, like when they did projects back in college. Nicole had fought back giggles there, too. They worked well together. *I love working with Mina.*

"We are good at this," Mina said, inviting herself into Nicole's office.

"We are that."

"We should go celebrate." Mina dropped into the seat by the desk.

"Mina, it's ten in the morning. We are not celebrating." Nicole made her way around her desk and sighed as she settled into her chair.

"Later then."

Nicole shook her head. "Classes start tonight."

Mina snorted. "Classes start at six. We'll catch a drink before you go to class. We'll do it quick, even grab Clara. You know we won't be long because she's got to get home to the kid and you have to get to class."

It'd be nice to hang out with her friends. It'd help keep nervousness from nipping at her brain. First day of classes. Last semester. What happened next? The question never entered her head before. She knew what happened after undergrad and then she knew what happened after law school. What happened post-degree?

Mina snapped in front of her face. "Hey, you still in there?"

Nicole blinked several times. "Sorry. You were saying something?"

"Nothing. Just about us being an awesome duo. Always have been."

"Do you ever wonder about when I get my degree and if I'm not here anymore?"

Mina took a loud breath. "Honestly, I try not to think about it. You know I'll be happy for you, but it won't be the same for me here without you. Look, I know how this place has been for you, but I also know what it means to you."

Nicole wasn't sure what that meant. "Then, I shouldn't go for the degree?"

"What? Fuck, yeah, you should. I just know this place is more than a workplace for you. You shouldn't let that hold you back, though. I do this because I like it. You do this because you inherited it. It ties you in knots, which is understandable. You're the heir, but you're the heir who wants to do her own thing. You should be able to, just like anyone else."

"Why in the hell do you know me so well?" It blew Nicole's mind.

"Didn't we already establish sisterly bond? Anyway, don't let it bug you. You're allowed to want your own thing."

"But, what about…" Nicole motioned around the room.

Mina shrugged. "Someone'll figure it out. You're smart. Your parents are smart. I'm smart. One of us will come up with something. Besides, I wouldn't let this place turn to shit."

She hadn't thought of that. Mina would be there. Mina would guard the firm. But, Nicole wasn't sure if she liked that. She was the heir, after all, and she wasn't one to let go of responsibility.

"Nicole, no matter what, it'll be fine. Here or there. We'll figure it out," Mina said with her usual confidence, as if the universe was tailor-made for her while Nicole felt like she needed to work hard to make things fit. Nicole nodded and took a deep breath, trying to breathe in Mina's words, her confidence. Everything would work out.

***

"Lennox, you're killing me here." Dane groaned, throwing her hands in the air. Her portfolio dropped to the ground with a soft thud. Pages of notes flipped open and settled on a random sheet.

"What? I thought that was good," Lennox replied, dropping his guitar with a scowl. He looked pissed, like he wasn't the one messing everyone else up. Everyone else glared at him.

"You can't overpower everyone else." Dane paced in front of the orchestra.

She had the musicians lined up like they'd be in the orchestra pit. Everyone knew where they went and could get used to their spots. It was probably the easiest thing, even though they even argued over that. Even when she explained why she wanted them where she put them, they still needed to backtalk and drive her crazy. Now, they played together. Well, they tried, but it was a struggle.

Dane's limp became more pronounced as she moved, as she had been on her feet all morning. Her knee ached a little, and her muscles burned. Ignoring the pain, she focused on her people and hoped like hell they could make it through the day without her having to kill someone. *And, surprisingly, I won't even start with Dougie.*

"Not all the time. Just that part. It cries out for my axe, man." Lennox held up his guitar in triumph. A collective scoff echoed through the room.

"It cries out for you to be in step with everyone else. I get enough of this leader of the band shit from Dougie." Dane motioned to Dougie, who rolled his eyes.

"All I'm saying is we could do with more flute solos," Dougie chimed in.

Dane sighed and rubbed her eyes with both hands. "First off, I'm not even halfway done writing the score. You don't know where your solos might be, even if you go based on your character. Second, we need to play together for this. The flute will come in when the damsel does. Right now, we're doing the opening scene and no one's in the lead. Now, can we play together?" She eyed Lennox, tired of going over this with him.

"Play together? Have you seen this thing?" Dougie motioned around them, talking about the orchestra.

"Yes, I've seen this thing and it's fucking unbelievable. It could be awesome if you guys just play together. I know you're used to being the best guy out there and you wanna do solos and lead the band, but at some point we have to be the orchestra I keep claiming we are." A small headache knocked at the side of Dane's skull, but she ignored it. She put her hand in the air. "Now, from the top!"

Ryan started up and Evie came in right on time. Dane sighed, relief coursing through her, and signaled for Samiyah. Lennox came in right behind. She glanced at Dougie to make sure he didn't try anything and then back to Lennox to make sure he didn't try anything, either. For the first time that morning, she had hoped they'd make it through one song. And then a phone went off. Dane wanted to jump through the roof.

"What the hell? Guys, I told you, vibrate or silent mode," Dane said. The phone kept ringing, and Dane was certain she could hear her blood pressure rise. How many times would she have to tell them the same thing?

Evie shot her eyes up to the usual suspect. "Lennox."

Lennox held up his hands. "It's not me this time, I swear!" It frequently was him, even when he swore it wasn't. He eyed Dane. "Um, I think it's you, boss."

"Yeah, sounds like it's coming from you," Pedro said, nodding toward her.

"Me?" Dane echoed and then she patted down her pockets. "Right! I have a phone now." She hit herself in the forehead. *Gonna have to get used to this*. She grabbed it from the pocket opposite her wallet. Picking up, she stared at it and then answered. "Terri?"

"Hey! I was just checking to see if you really had a phone, and you weren't punking me when you called yesterday," Terri said.

"Okay, yeah, not joking. I'm working, so...is this just to make fun of me having a phone?"

"I'm surprised you know how to answer the damned thing. Is it a flip phone?"

Dane scowled. "No, it's not a flip phone. I'm not totally behind the times, you know?" Besides, she knew how to operate Nicole's smartphone. She'd get the hang of her own.

"You sure? You download any games, yet?"

Sighing, Dane covered her face with her hand. Well, she knew what Terri would be doing the next time they saw each other. Either way, she needed to get back to work. "Terri, working now."

"Oh, right! How's the job going?"

Apparently, 'working' didn't mean anything to Terri. "You're determined to talk to me while I can't talk, aren't you?"

Terri laughed. "Nah, you know I'm fucking with you. I'll catch you later. Show you how to use whatever stupid phone you got."

"Shut up. Bye."

"Bye."

Dane groaned and slipped the phone back into her pocket. Looking up, she found her orchestra laughing at her.

"All right, all right. Sorry about that. Let's get back to it. We finally got something going." Dane smiled at them.

"You might want to put it on vibrate first, boss," Evie said.

Dane's brow furrowed, and she pulled out the phone. It shouldn't seem so complicated. It was a tiny thing that fit easily in her hand. A button in the middle at the bottom, a couple on the left side, which she knew to be the volume, and one on the right, which she knew was the power button. Maybe the protective case around it hid some other buttons to put it on vibrate. Okay, she didn't know as much about the phone as she thought. Nicole showed her some basic things when they got it the other day, and she played with it last night. She fiddled with it.

"New phone?" Samiyah asked.

"Yeah. Very new."

"Let me see it." Samiyah held her hand out for it.

Dane didn't put up a fight. Samiyah worked quickly and then handed it back. "Thanks." Dane slipped the phone back into her pocket.

"No problem. I've got the same one." She offered Dane an impish smile. "You might want to put a password on it, though."

"Yeah, because I've got so much stuff on here to be stolen." Nicole tried to put one on for her, but she didn't think she needed one.

"Well, not now obviously, but eventually," Pedro replied.

Scoffing, Dane shook her head. "I highly doubt it."

"You do realize you can store music on it," Lennox said.

Okay, that was something worth looking into. "Good to know." Dane twirled her finger in the air. "Back to work!"

There were some mock groans, but everyone fell in line. Dane felt like they were getting somewhere. She spent a lot of time at home on the couch writing in her portfolio, usually after walking Haydn while Nicole worked on dinner. She still handled breakfast in the morning. It was a nice balance, just as Nicole tried to assure her it would be. But, there was something...missing. When she was at home, writing, there was an emptiness. When Nicole was working on dinner, there was a little void inside of her. Just thinking about it made her heart clench. *It'll be fine. It'll be fine.*

Ryan starting up brought Dane's mind back to her musicians. The orchestra finally managed to make it through the song. It didn't sound bad, but it definitely needed work. The orchestra didn't seem to agree. They exchanged high-fives when it was over. Evie smiled at her.

"We killed it!" Lennox took a bow.

Evie smiled. "It sounds really good."

"Well, it's not horrible," Dane replied. It could be better. She needed to figure out what was missing.

"That's not a ringing endorsement," Pedro said.

"I know, but it's our first time getting through it. There was something in it that just..." Dane trailed off and shook her head. "It needs more, and I have to figure it out."

"We'll help," Evie said.

Dane nodded. "Good. I'd like that. Let's go to the next song and then come back to this one. I might be able to figure it out or one of you might get an idea while we go through it."

"You certainly like the idea of us chiming in. You got nothing, boss?" Dougie said, giving the unofficial title a hiss.

"We're all musicians here. I'm open minded, and I like to think we can all build something together," Dane answered with a shrug.

Dougie scoffed. He motioned to the orchestra. "Yeah, we're all musicians. You're just some poser." His upper lip pulled into a sneer.

Dane arched an eyebrow. "Excuse me?"

"What do you play?" Dougie challenged her, climbing to his feet. If he had been taller than she was, he probably would've enjoyed literally looking down at her.

She felt like Dougie didn't truly understand art, even music. The idea that she needed to play an instrument to create music seemed ridiculous to her. Art was about experience and connection. Music, at least for her, was about going through her own emotions and hoping others connected with her on some level, any level.

Dane looked back at Dougie, face calm, but eyes hard. "What do I play? What does it matter? If I couldn't play the spoons, that doesn't change the fact that I'm musical director or that I want your opinions."

"Do you play anything?" Lennox asked, his face scrunched up a little as he studied her.

"Why does it matter?" Dane folded her arms across her chest. While she didn't mind playing, she didn't have anything to prove to them. She was in charge, and they needed to get used to it.

Lennox held up his hands in surrender. "It doesn't."

It did if everyone's faces meant anything. They'd probably respect her more if they knew she played something. It might even get Dougie off her back.

"Fine. Take your pick," Dane said, leveling a look at Dougie.

Dougie blinked. "Huh?"

"Pick. Anyone of them." She motioned to their orchestra. "Pick one."

Dougie laughed. "You're kidding, right?"

"Kidding? Nope. Pick one."

Dougie laughed more and then looked around at the orchestra. They all shrugged. He shrugged, too. He turned his attention to their instruments and rubbed his chin. She didn't give a damn what he picked. She'd rock the crap out of it, unless of course he picked one of his damned woodwinds. Then she was screwed.

"Nothing she's gotta put her mouth on," Pedro said, holding his sax to his chest.

"Please." Dane agreed with that. Just like they didn't know where she'd been, she didn't know where they'd been. Of course, if they'd been similar places she'd been, none of them would want their mouths in contact with the same things.

"And sometime today," Lennox requested.

"I figure a poser knows something about the guitar and drums. Those are popular. Play the violin," Dougie said.

Samiyah made a noise and then frowned. "I don't like people touching my violin." She glanced at Dane. "Sorry, boss."

"No, I get it." She never liked people touching her violin either, but probably because it had been a gift from her mother. She'd been protective of her guitars back when she was in *Destined for Nowhere*. Eventually even that fell to the wayside when she'd been injured, and the world lost its luster. Even when music came back to her, it wasn't the same. She wasn't the same.

"You're just looking for an excuse. You can't play it," Dougie said. A smirk eased onto his face and his eyes seemed satisfied, like he won something.

Dane rolled her eyes. "Watch this." She wouldn't touch Samiyah's violin without permission, but she could wow this lot fairly easily.

She moved behind the drums and got started. She tapped out a simple beat for a moment before getting a little more complex. It had been a while since she played the drums, but it came flooding back the more she hit the drums. She gave it about a minute, watching them. They seemed a little less skeptical, but not wholly impressed.

Cracking her knuckles, she reached for Lennox's guitar. She grabbed his pick and strummed the guitar, playing a light melody. She picked up the pace and now wide eyes watched her as she went along. Her hand wouldn't allow her to play for long, but she managed two minutes before her hand begged her to stop. She put the guitar down and eased behind the keyboard. She started with only her right hand and once her left hand was rested, she got a little more complicated in her riff. She drifted a jazzy tune into classical and then turned to them.

"Holy crap," Evie muttered with wide eyes.

"Yeah," Lennox agreed with a similar expression.

Samiyah let out a breath. "Wow."

"Good enough for you, your highness?" Dane asked Dougie.

He stared at her, mouth dropped open. "Uh...yeah."

"I play, guys. Not as well as I used to, but I play. If you dare doubt me, go ask around. I know music in more ways than most. I want to make music with you guys. Can we do that?"

"Yeah," they all mumbled.

"Good. Instruments up." Dane whirled a finger in the air, wanting to get back to their opening song, and do it right.

***

Class started in less than an hour. Nicole had a drink with Mina and Clara, and they celebrated the victory from the morning. It was uplifting and fun, but brief. She went back to her office to kill a little more time after that. Mina's pep talk seemed like a lifetime ago rather than just that morning. Butterflies flittered in Nicole's stomach. It was a daunting idea that she'd be done in four months. What would she do after that? Who would she become after that?

"It's not like I'll have to search for a job right away," Nicole muttered, pushing away from her desk. *Hell, I might not have to search for a job at all.*

Just as with all her other classes, she planned to stay late at work until she had to leave for school. Crow had promised to get Danny, which was fine, but Nicole had come to enjoy their drive back home. Now, two days out of the week, that time would be Crow's. It might prove more days considering she had a thesis this term and would have to spend loads of time in the library.

"I wonder if Mina would say this wasn't dependent behavior as well." Nicole sighed and she packed up her briefcase. *What if...*She shook her head and made her way to the car. She refused to go where her mind wanted, refused to doubt Danny. Danny was nothing like anyone she had dated. Danny hadn't led her wrong yet. "I owe her this if nothing else, considering all the shit I've put her through."

Of course, that reminder led to more unease. Danny had gone through so much because of her. Was it hard to believe that once Danny could truly support herself, she'd try to get as far away from Nicole as possible? It could be for survival.

"Danny's not like that. I've got to focus on class. Can't afford to fail anything now." She had put in too much hard work to let it all fall apart now, especially on insecurities. "God, I just turned thirty. I'm acting like a fifteen-year-old."

She couldn't help it. Lovers had conditioned her over the years. She was accustomed to being used until she couldn't take it anymore. Soon Danny would have no use for her. *You're kidding, right? If Danny wanted to be done with you, she'd have walked away when her mother gave her that trust.*

Shaking it off, Nicole managed to get herself together to pay attention in class, read the syllabus, and find out what was expected of her. Taking a breath, she assured herself that she had this. She could handle school, graduating, and the new aspects of her relationship. Change was good.

"Change is one of the reasons I like chemistry. It'll be fine," Nicole muttered as she made her way back to the car. Class was done and seemed promising. Now, she looked forward to this final semester.

When she got in, the house was quiet. Haydn rushed up to her. He rubbed his head against her and then led her into the living room. A soft smile settled on her face as she stared at Danny, asleep on the couch.

"She's cute, isn't she, Haydn?" Nicole asked. He gave a yelp and nudged her leg. "I know she is. Let's let her sleep and see about getting a late snack."

Haydn let out a little bark and followed her into the kitchen. Much to Nicole's surprise, dinner waited on the counter. Fresh dishes sat in the rack. Nicole sighed. Danny made dinner and did the dishes.

"Well, I guess that explains why she's asleep. We're supposed to be a team," Nicole said. Her heart sank a little. *I don't want to burden Danny.*

There was only one plate. At least Danny had eaten rather than waiting for her to do so. Moving the wrapper on top of the plate, Nicole was greeted by chicken breast, yellow rice, and broccoli. She heated it up in the microwave and then went to go wake Danny, knowing she'd want to have dinner with her even if she already ate.

"Danny, sweetheart." Nicole gently shook her lover.

Danny groaned and turned over onto her side. Nicole chuckled and shook Danny a bit more. Grey eyes fluttered open. There were a couple of blinks and then a smile curled onto Danny's lips.

Danny yawned. "Hey, love. You're home."

"And you're asleep." Nicole leaned down to kiss Danny.

Danny kissed her back and then rubbed her eyes. "Didn't mean to fall asleep."

Nicole offered her a soft smile. "I'm sure you didn't. I woke you up because I figured you'd want to sit with me for a while."

Danny nodded and slowly made her way off the couch. She sat across from Nicole in the kitchen nook. Nicole started in on her food while Danny drank some juice.

"You didn't have to cook," Nicole said. She'd have to try to wake up early and make breakfast. Of course, that might not do much since Danny could easily claim dinner tomorrow.

"I don't want you to come home hungry. Besides, I gotta eat, too," Danny replied.

True. Nicole couldn't expect Danny to get takeout on days she had class. She knew there was no way in hell Danny would let her eat out when she had class either. She loved this particular care about Danny, but it was a little annoying, too.

"How was your day?" Nicole asked.

"It's coming along. The orchestra's having trouble playing together. Everybody wants to be in charge, ya know?" Danny replied.

A smile settled on Nicole's face. "You'll pull them together."

"I'm trying. It's hard. Didn't think Lennox would be as annoying as he is. He's got a damned ego on him."

Nodding, Nicole ate a little more before saying something. "Is he good enough to have that ego?"

Danny laughed a little. "Hell, yeah. They should all have the egos they do. Hell, even Pedro, Greg, and Evie, who aren't problems, but aren't exactly humble either. They all have a reason for it. In my head, this thing is gonna be awesome, partially because they're all as good as they think they are. I'm hoping like hell it turns out like that in the show."

Nicole nodded. "You'll pull it off. I mean, you had to do it with your band, right?"

"Yeah." Danny tilted her head and squinted a little. "Have I told you about my band?"

"Not much."

It was a little surprising Danny didn't talk about them more. Yes, Bryan had been a part of the group, but she could talk about them without mentioning that traitorous bastard. Had someone else wronged her in the group or did it cause her too much pain to think about back when she was pretty much a celebrity?

"I know they were a big part of your life. I wasn't sure if you wanted to forget about that time, and that's why you haven't said anything." Nicole now knew better than most to never push hard for anything.

Danny shook her head and looked down at her left hand. "No, I don't like to think about it much. I mean, not gonna be that good again. Why think about it?"

"Because it was a special time," Nicole replied, taking Danny's hand and giving it a squeeze. She didn't want to say it was a happy or good time for Danny, but it wasn't awful. "You're allowed to remember it and even feel good about it, even if there's some pain there."

"Yeah. Plus, I want to share with you. I want you to know about stuff like that." Danny sighed as she put her hand through her hair. Maybe she didn't know where to begin or how to put it into words. "What do you want to know?"

"Anything. Just talk to me," Nicole replied.

Danny put a finger to her chin. "We called ourselves *Destined for Nowhere* because we'd all been told that's what we were once or twice. Now, we've got this great band, and it was like a big middle finger to all of them. Beyond that, we were friends, I guess. We played pranks on each other all the time. Harmless, stupid stuff. Crap I imagine little kids do to each other. It was fun, though."

Nicole tilted her head. "You guys would laugh them off?"

"All the time. The only thing that was off limit were our instruments. Anything else was fair game. I remember one time, someone put shaving cream in one of my shoes. It was gross, but I laughed. I put a fake bug on Fae's, our other guitarist, pizza once. She screamed so loud. Did stupid stuff like that all the time."

Nicole's smile grew. It certainly sounded like harmless kid stuff. Maybe everyone in the band was immature or missed out on a childhood like Danny. "That's good. Were they all as good as you with their instruments?"

Danny shrugged. "We were good. If I was gonna put together a band, I'd pick them every time, except for the douche bag."

Bryan. She'd met him twice, and that was too many times. She couldn't understand how someone's best friend could hurt them the way he hurt Danny.

"Of course," Nicole managed to say once she realized the conversation paused because of her.

"They were willing to take risks with me, which is what I'm trying to get the orchestra to do. I want to be able to do things different, but I want them to also know I'm going to pull them through."

Nicole nodded. "Your band was like that?"

"Yup. Stuck with me through weird shit. I wrote a song that called for fucking water glasses one time and they were like, 'well, shit if Dane wants to do it, then let her do it.'"

"Water glasses?" Nicole had to laugh. "How did that go over?"

"Pretty good, but we only did it a couple of times. I kept accidentally drinking the water. Too high to remember it's part of the set. I love when I get to combine hip-hop and rock. I love bringing elements of jazz into rock or back into rock, I guess, since jazz is the granddaddy of it all. Hell, I've had clubs jumping from swing music with *Destined for Nowhere*."

Nicole doubted she'd ever fully understand when Danny was popular, but it was great to hear about. She felt like Danny was truly at ease with her and hoped this meant Danny understood she wasn't going anywhere. Hell, she knew she needed to understand Danny wasn't going anywhere, yet her stomach knotted up thinking about the possibility.

"My hope is to be able to pull stuff like that off with these guys."

"You have ideas?" Nicole guessed. Of course, she had seen Danny writing in her portfolio every night, but those ideas might have remained just that.

"A ton, but sometimes my ideas are actually fantasy and I've come to accept that. I like being able to run stuff by my orchestra. They can pull me back if I'm getting too out there. I already know what I want to do with Pedro and his sax. I have to throw Dougie's piccolo into something because he sounds..." Grey eyes glanced up, searching the ceiling. "Beautiful is the only accurate way to describe it. And, then there's Samiyah." Danny groaned, and the noise hit Nicole in her suddenly knotted stomach.

Danny certainly was enamored with Samiyah. *It's just for music, though*. Still, Nicole couldn't help the burn in her throat at the mention of the violinist.

"You're really impressed with her, huh?" Nicole did her best to sound normal, casual even.

"I'm impressed with them all, but I feel like having her is good luck. She's going to be the thing to make this something beyond regular music. Everyone else is good, but she's heads above them."

Nicole nodded. She wished she could share the passion of music with Danny. Yes, in a way she could, but not as deeply as she wanted to. It was still fun to see and experience.

Dinner went quickly, and they took Haydn for a short walk outside, strolling gloved hand in gloved hand. It was mostly quiet with Danny telling her more about her band experience. Her music had allowed her to travel to many places.

"I never left the country. Couldn't get a passport. Made the band miss a few things because of that," Danny said.

Nicole took her hand. "We can go get you one and then plan a trip." *Something to look forward to. Plans for the future.*

Danny smiled. "I'd like that."

Those words soothed anxiety in Nicole that she had been trying to ignore since the mention of Samiyah. Danny made plans with her, wanted to do things with her, wanted to be with her. Everything else was work.

***

Dane rubbed her eyes with both hands as she flopped down into one of the hard chairs in the orchestra room. New day, same problems, plus some. The orchestra couldn't get themselves together, from seating to playing together to playing at the right volume. Then, there were script rewrites and she didn't hear about them from Andrew. She managed to make friends with a few of the play's crew and some of the actors and the orchestra had done the same. Now, she had to consider the rewrites when she worked on the score. She waved the orchestra out, missing her band a little.

Destined for Nowhere did what she asked because she asked. Her orchestra talked back even when what she said made sense. It wasn't as much as before, but they still needed so much direction. And she still needed to write. *Might as well get home and get on with it.*

It was Nicole's second day of school. Crow picked her up. They exchanged greetings and light pleasantries and then Dane lost herself in her portfolio. She needed to do something to include the rewrites in what she already had.

"You okay?" Crow asked.

Dane took a deep breath. "Yeah, a little tired, but that's about it."

"Well, when you get home, you can take a nap."

The idea should've sounded like music to her ears, but Dane wasn't in favor of it. The other day when she was at home alone, it was quiet and boring. She only accidentally fell asleep after doing chores. She'd rather not go home, but she had to get to Haydn.

"Thanks for the ride," Dane said as they pulled up to the house.

"Anytime, kid," Crow replied.

Dane let out a snicker and wished she could stall, but she had to go inside. Jody gave her a wave while Haydn charged her. His greeting was enough to lift her spirits.

"Catch you tomorrow," Jody said, shouldering her messenger bag.

"You don't wanna stick around and play some games?" Dane nodded toward the television.

"Nah, I got schoolwork to start on. I spend a lot of my day here working on non-school stuff."

Dane arched an eyebrow. "Why?"

"The change of environment seems to help. I go home, and my mind wanders. I can focus on school stuff at home, but not other work. I dunno." Jody scratched the top of her head.

Dane nodded. A change in environment? It was something to consider. For now, she had home. Jody saw herself out and Dane flopped down on the couch, hoping to get to work. The silence crept through her, so she put on some music. Haydn cuddled in close to her and usually that was enough for her. But, underneath it all, there was still a crawling sensation, gnawing at her mind, and her hand was still. Sighing, she rubbed the bridge of her nose, a headache catching up with her.

"Maybe it'll be different after I make dinner," Dane said. She'd get to work after that. Of course, she said that the other night, too.

***

Classes had only been going on two weeks, but Nicole already found herself swamped. She ended up at the library after class, seeking science journals to help her project, but then hurried home. She found Danny asleep on the couch with her portfolio on her chest. Haydn was on the floor next to her, asleep as well. Food waited for her on the counter again, but she decided to let Danny sleep. It was kind of late, and Danny probably needed it. Getting a good night's sleep might help cure Danny of the writer's block she had complained about earlier.

Sitting at the nook, Nicole stared at the empty space across from her. Her heart thumped in her chest, sending chilling vibrations throughout her body. If she looked hard enough, she could picture Danny across from her, like old times, which was only a couple of weeks ago. She missed Danny's smile. How many nights would be spent like this? At least until she was done with school. That felt like an eternity with the deafening silence crushing her.

"Change is good. We're evolving," she said this aloud to remind herself that it was true. They weren't growing apart, and change wouldn't set them adrift. Besides, the thing clinging to her that felt an awful lot like loneliness wasn't permanent. It would end with school. The emptiness and the anxiety were growing pains.

Chapter Twelve

NICOLE STARED AT HER work computer, doing one thing she never did in the firm—schoolwork. She and Lisa Santos, her lab partner, had to design an experiment, explaining it and their process before completing the experiment and recording if it was successful or not. They emailed back and forth. Lisa was a working mother and she didn't have a lot of free time, but she had ideas, as did Nicole. They did their own independent research and then compared notes. A knock at her door got her attention.

"Hey, Nicole could you—" A coworker marched in.

Nicole put up her hand. "Nope. Can't do it."

"But, there's all this talk about how you wowed those new clients. I need help with a presentation," he said.

"And I said, no. I'm busy." She had finished her work for the day, cleared her emails, and now had a couple of hours of nothing to do that was work related.

"But—"

Nicole looked up and glared. "I said no. I thought it was understood or do I have to get on the phone with a partner?"

He yelped and shut her door. How bold. She didn't even have time to be annoyed before her phone rang. A boss apologizing for someone disturbing her and promising reprimands. She smiled. If only they cared that much about keeping people away from her before she went back to school. She wouldn't miss this.

"I should get out of here," Nicole said. She finished her email and was about to log out, but noticed an email from Karisa Collins. She checked it. It was thanks, but also a reminder. Karisa would make space for her in her lab if she wanted it. *Wow, she was serious about her job offer.*

It sounded good right now, but it was too much to deal with. Nicole needed to get out of there. Once Nicole was in her car, she realized she didn't have anywhere to go. Dane didn't get off work for two more hours. There had to be something.

"The fridge is almost empty. Might as well get some shopping done." Nicole pulled out of her parking spot and went straight to the supermarket. It was the least she could do considering Danny handled the cooking and cleaning when she was at class.

With the backseat and trunk full, Nicole went to pick up Danny. She watched the musicians leaving, as usual. Danny stood with them, talking, but Nicole couldn't hear. Danny's face was stern, and she made a circle motion with her finger. Her crew nodded. Danny reached out and touched Samiyah's arm. Nicole scowled, but schooled her features by the time Danny jumped in the car.

"Hey, love," Danny said, leaning over for a kiss. She settled into her seat and then glanced back. "Did you buy the grocery store?"

Nicole started for home. "We need it."

"How much did all this cost?" There was an odd urgency in Danny's tone.

That was a weird question. "Why?" She tried not to sound confused, but it couldn't be helped.

Danny shifted, putting her hand in her pocket. "I can give you half."

"You're kidding, right?" She better be kidding.

"No. Why would I be kidding? I can afford it, and I used to buy the groceries anyway."

Nicole looked at Danny from the corner of her eye. "It's not about being able to afford it. It's groceries for the house. I didn't pitch a fit when you bought them."

"I'm not pitching a fit. It's just this is my thing, and I have money now." Danny held up the bills in her wallet.

"I understand that, but you've had money before."

"Not like this." Dane kept the bills in her hand. "I can pay for groceries, just like I can pay the phone bill."

Nicole frowned. She didn't need this right now. "Okay, and so can I. Why is this an issue?"

"It's not. If we're a team, then I should be able to put fifty percent of the grocery money in. Why don't you want me to?"

Nicole ground her teeth. "Because that's not how a team works."

"Because you know so much about team work?" Danny snapped.

Nicole took a deep breath. Maybe this wasn't about groceries. Maybe it was about work. Work was taxing. Danny wasn't used to it. Danny was there for her when work got under her skin. But, she didn't want to take Danny's money. It didn't make any sense to do so.

"Danny, sweetheart, why would we start this half thing?" Nicole asked. "I'm truly curious. We never did that before."

"Because I couldn't afford it. Now, I can. Can you just take the money?" Dane shoved some money at her and then turned away, staring ahead, like that was normal behavior.

Nicole swallowed down the pain it caused her, feeling torn open. Who threw money at someone? "Fine. Fine."

The rest of the ride was spent in bone-crushing silence. This had to be what it felt like to die in space, sucked into the vacuum, and destroyed by the void. It didn't get better when they bid farewell to Jody. Haydn whined, going between them as they tried to go their separate ways. They locked eyes, and Nicole sighed.

They were a team. They couldn't let something this small come between them. She grabbed Danny's hand. Danny squeezed back. There were smiles, but Nicole's face hurt a little from forcing it and Danny's eyes didn't shine the way they used to.

"How about we go walk our young man together?" Danny said.

Nicole nodded. It could be the cure for what ailed them, for the moment anyway. She'd take it and let the world fall away because when the world came back there'd be work and school and decisions on who'd make dinner. *We need to figure this chore and money situation out.*

***

Days later, Dane sat in the dimly lit orchestra room, staring at a song that didn't want to come together. She had already sent the orchestra home for the night. They'd done well with what she had worked out, but she hadn't written a complete score yet. She was stuck.

Moving, Dane grabbed one of the rather pathetic acoustic guitars leaning in the corner. The instrument would have to do since she didn't think to bring her own instruments to work. She never thought she needed to until now. Throwing herself back into a hard, folding chair, causing it to screech and scrape the floor, she strummed the strings. It didn't sound right.

"Maybe I should do this at home, on my own guitar." Not that she had been able to do much at home lately. When it was just her and Haydn, there was an emptiness, a stillness that stayed her hand. Not to mention, a tension lived there now. "I can't hide here."

She did need to break in her guitar. She had it for a couple of months, but hadn't done much with it. Nicole bought it for her and hadn't pressed her about using it. There was something about the guitar that didn't sit well with Dane, but she couldn't leave it idle for the rest of her life. Besides, she couldn't leave Jody at home with Haydn. *She's got a life, after all.*

Dane called Crow for a ride and Crow was all too happy to take her home. *Why the hell does Crow care so much about me?* Dane liked it and returned the affection now, but she didn't understand it.

"Crow, what's the deal? Why do you help me out like this?"

Crow glanced at her. "You're kidding, right? At this point, you're basically family, Dane."

Dane nodded. "Yeah, I feel that way about you, too, but it took me a while to get here. You didn't start out like that, right?"

"No, but I've always liked you and I truly believe in your gift. I think other people need to hear it and I want to help you get back into it in some way. If it means giving you a lift from work, that's fine with me." Crow smiled.

Dane couldn't stop her grin. "My music means that much to you?"

"Hell, yeah. I heard you play for the first time at a somewhat depressing and dark point in my life, and you touched me. I kept coming back and even as I got out of that place, your music always hit spaces inside of me and made me feel...connected or something. It lets me know I'm alive. That it's okay to be alive. Sometimes, it made me feel at ease. It went beyond the usual emotions, but like I was part of something great, like there was greatness in me. I hope other people get that when they hear you."

Dane nodded. She wanted her music to do that to people. She scratched the back of her head. "I think music saved me, too."

"Music is powerful. Maybe your darkness makes light and that light seeks out other darkness, turning it the same."

"I dunno about light. Sometimes, writing and playing were the only things that kept me alive, kept me tethered to this world, gave me something to care about." It never seemed to drive the darkness out of her or bring light into her world. *Nick is my light.* But, the light dimmed a few days ago when tension moved into their home. Now, Nicole hid from her in the office and looked at her with dull eyes. *I should do something about that.*

Crow nodded and glanced at her. "You got a lot more to care about now."

"Damn right I do, friend."

"No, not friend." Crow grinned. "Fam."

"Yeah, fam. You're great family, Crow, and I mean the hell outta that."

Crow sat up a little taller. The rest of the ride was light small talk about their days. When Dane got home, she found Jody messing with the TV. She didn't bother to ask, knowing Jody was experimenting with something Dane wouldn't understand. They barely said hi and bye to each other before Jody was out the door. Even though they liked each other fine, she'd come to learn Jody preferred things that way.

With the house to herself, Dane ignored the dancing shadows that seemed to taunt her and set up her guitar to try to make this music work. Curling up in the corner of the music room, she strummed. For some reason, even after having it for a while, she couldn't get it to sound right. She had a feeling it was psychological. It was probably fine, but didn't sound like her old guitar. She doubted anything would ever sound like her old guitar. The thought bothered her enough to keep her writer's block solidly in place.

"Maybe it's because things are tense with me and Nick." She doubted that. The writer's block was before the tension. *Why the hell are things tense between us?* She snorted. It'd probably be easier to figure that out than to keep trying with her guitar. She'd talk to Nicole and sort things out.

Giving up on that guitar, she switched to her keyboard and had better luck in playing. It still didn't sound exactly like she wanted, but she played on. Jazz came naturally, flowed, but didn't fit what she needed. With some effort, it became soft rock. Eventually, she gave up. Something still wasn't right.

Grabbing her phone, she wanted to call Nicole, but she was in class. Instead, she called Allison, wanting to tell her all about her orchestra. Allison eventually put her on speakerphone, so she could tell the whole family about how things were going.

"We're very proud of you," Henry said.

"We get to see the show, right?" Ben inquired.

"Of course, you get to see the show." Dane expected she'd have to pay out of pocket, but they wanted to be there, and she wanted them there. She wanted them to see she made something of herself.

"Front row?" Ben practically yelled into the phone.

"Sure, no problem," Dane replied. She had the money now. Sure, she needed to pay bills and stuff, but there was money coming in. Oh, god, she had to tell Lynn and Henry she paid bills! They'd probably laugh at her enthusiasm, but they'd understand.

***

Nicole felt hugged by the warmth of the house as she came inside. Haydn was on her before she could shut the door. She rubbed his head and looked around the silent space. Hints of fried chicken hung in the air. Did Danny cook, or had she ordered out? Time to find out.

"Danny?" Nicole stepped into the living room to find Danny hunched on the couch, writing in her portfolio. "Danny?"

Danny's head shot up. "Huh? Oh, hey, Nick."

"You okay, baby?" Nicole walked over to Danny and gave her a kiss. It was barely returned. Nicole didn't think anything of it. They still seemed to be on shaky ground from the grocery incident.

Danny grunted and shook her head. Nicole didn't ask. She went to put her stuff away and grab something to eat. Homemade fried chicken, green beans, and mashed potatoes awaited her. She took her plate to sit with Danny. Haydn made himself comfortable on their feet.

Danny didn't offer any conversation, scribbling on her notepaper. Nicole ate silently and observed. Danny's face was pinched and for every line she wrote another got scratched out. Once Nicole was done, she went and washed her dishes. Haydn followed her.

"Aw, what's the matter, boy? Other mom not giving you attention right now? Well, her job is really important. Lots of people depend on her. Just give her time, okay?" Nicole gave Haydn a treat to make him feel better. He barked.

Nicole went back to the sofa. "Danny, how long have you been working on this?"

Danny shrugged. "A while."

"How about you pause for a second? Let me help you relax." It might help the tension in Danny's body and the strain between them.

"Not right now. I'm trying to get these notes just right. Gotta make it perfect if Samiyah's going to do it."

Nicole frowned and ignored the fact that it felt like she got kicked in the gut. Again with Samiyah. "A little break might help you think better." She put her hands on Danny's shoulders.

Danny shrugged her off. "No, I need to get this done."

If Samiyah's name was like a kick to the stomach, the brush off was like a punch to the face. Best to quit while she was only a little behind and not totally stomped into the ground. Taking a breath, Nicole scraped together what little dignity she had left and stood up.

"Fine. Sorry I offered." Nicole retreated to the library to do schoolwork. Haydn followed her and laid his head in her lap as she sat at the computer. She petted his head.

After an hour, Nicole was ready for bed. Danny was already in their room, watching her as she settled into her side. Grey eyes never left her, but told her nothing. Was Danny none the wiser of the pain she caused?

"I didn't mean to be so short with you downstairs," Danny said.

"Your work is important." Nicole didn't want to excuse Danny's behavior, but she didn't want Danny to know she hurt her either.

Danny grabbed her and pulled her close. "You're important."

"You threw money at me," Nicole found herself saying.

Danny flinched. "Excuse me?"

"The other day with the groceries. You threw money at me. Literally threw it at me and then went on like it was fine."

"Shit. I'm sorry, angel. I didn't mean that. I didn't even realize it. I just want you to have the money." Danny hugged her. "I'm letting this gig bug me out. I didn't mean. I promise. I'll do better."

"Danny, I know you're stressed. I know this is a lot. I just..." Nicole wasn't even sure what she needed to say. She didn't know what she needed, beyond respect and acknowledgement and she shouldn't have to tell Danny that. Danny knew. Danny always knew.

"I'm sorry." Danny kissed the side of her head.

Nicole had no doubt Danny was sorry, but did that mean it wouldn't happen again? Did that mean she wouldn't be shrugged away the next time she offered relief? Did that mean next time Danny was working she wouldn't kiss Nicole back? Nicole stayed awake, eyes on the ceiling as if it had the answers. Instead, she stared at the abyss and the abyss stared right back.

***

Dane hadn't slept and it wasn't helping her attitude and patience with her hardheaded band of misfits. She rubbed the center of her forehead, hoping to keep away a headache. Taking a deep breath, she released it as she stood from her chair.

"Evie, can you please step back to your position?" Dane asked, pointing to where Evie needed to be.

"I will if Pedro can step back." Evie looked behind her.

"I'm standing on a platform," Pedro said.

"What the hell does that have to do with your foot on my leg?" Evie replied.

"Hey!" Dane glared at them. "We don't have time for this. Just be in position. It gives us the best sound. And, Dougie, don't think I missed you came in late."

Dougie gasped. "I did not!"

"You did," everyone said.

"It doesn't matter. Let's all do this again." Dane clapped and then twirled her finger for them to go from the top.

They didn't look happy, but they went from the top. Dane frowned as she listened. She didn't know what she wanted. It sounded light, airy. It should. It fit the scene. *You threw money at me.* Nicole's words echoed through her head. She rubbed her eyes and shook her head. *You threw money at me.* That wasn't the actions of someone who loved Nicole.

Dane held up her hand. "Stop."

"What? That was good," Lennox said.

"Just like it was the last two times she stopped us," Samiyah said, throwing her hands up, even though they were full of her instrument and bow.

"Guys, take five." They were sick of her, and she was sick of them. She didn't even have to say it twice. They were gone. She kicked the nearest chair. "Fuck."

"You okay there, boss?" Samiyah asked.

Dane turned around. "I thought you left."

"Yeah, but Dougie tried to talk to me, so I'm back." Samiyah stepped closer.

"I wouldn't want to talk to Dougie either."

"What's wrong?"

Dane scratched the top of her head. "What makes you think anything is wrong?" Beyond the fact she was blowing this gig and her relationship all in one shot.

"You made us take a break. Usually, you're always on top of us, which we need. Plus, I just saw you kick a chair on a leg I know is killing you."

Fuck. When did the world get so observant? Dane rolled her shoulders and looked away from Samiyah. "I'll figure it out."

"Is it us?"

Dane shook her head. "Isn't it always?" She grinned.

Samiyah smiled. "We'll definitely be the thing to kill you."

Dane snickered. *Nah, I got that handled myself*. The orchestra piled back in and Dane dialed it back. It wasn't them. It was her and how she treated Nicole. She had to do something to make up for that.

At lunch, she was on her way to make up for things. There was a jewelry store not too far from the theater. It was a good place.

"Hello, ma'am. I didn't expect to see you back," the salesman said from behind the counter.

"Yeah, well, I need to make an apology." Dane needed to do something before Nicole slipped through her fingers.

"Nothing says sorry like a tennis bracelet." He motioned to the display.

Dane moved to see. Should she get Nicole another bracelet? Her eyes drifted to the necklaces. They were beautiful, like Nicole. They were also expensive, but she had the money now and a diamond heart would look good around Nicole's neck.

"Save this one for me," Dane said, pointing down to the necklace.

"You sure? It is a lovely piece, but we have better."

Dane grinned. "You already milked me once. I can't let you keep fleecing me."

He gave her a light laugh and a nod. Dane felt like a load dropped off her back. This had to work. Now, she needed to get the orchestra right, which meant she also needed to get herself right. She needed to finish the score.

***

The night was easier for Nicole and Danny, mostly because Nicole went to the library before they really had to interact with each other. She knew she was hiding, but she'd rather that than something else happen between them. Haydn joined her again, occupying himself by pushing her chair. *Time to take the wheels off this thing*. She pulled herself back to the desk for the umpteenth time.

"Hey, Nick, you busy?" Danny asked from the doorway.

Nicole looked at Danny. It was obvious she was busy, but she supposed it was nice Danny asked. It was nice Danny understood things still were a little strained between them.

"What's up?" Nicole replied.

"Can we talk?" Danny stepped into the room and ran her hand through her hair. She shifted from foot to foot.

"Of course." It was hard to be upset with Danny being so adorable in her uncertainty.

"I know I messed up hard. Saying I'm sorry can't be enough. I didn't mean to throw the money at you. I'm just happy I can pay for things, buy you things. That's important to me."

Nicole frowned. "I don't understand why, especially since you put so much money into our joint account. You haven't spent that the same. You haven't shoved it into my face."

"Because it's not mine." Danny let loose an uncomfortable laugh. "That's blood money, but this is earned and I want to shower you with it."

"You know I don't need that. I just need you to do what you've always done."

Danny's jaw flexed. "I can do more now."

"I don't need more. I just need you."

Danny nodded. "Well, what about this?" She went into the pocket of her pajama shorts and held up a necklace.

Nicole's eyes widened. "Danny, you got me a diamond necklace?"

"Yeah."

"Danny," Nicole sighed. *She doesn't know the value of money. Stay calm.* "It's beautiful, Danny." It was beautiful, but that was to be expected. It probably cost an entire paycheck.

Danny smiled and squared her shoulders. Oh, no. She was proud. Nicole tried to plot out how she could put things without popping Danny's balloon.

"Here, lemme put it on you." Danny came over to her. Haydn whined as he moved out of her way. Nicole stayed still as Danny put the necklace on her.

Nicole cupped Danny's face while she was down on Nicole's level. "Sweetheart, the necklace is lovely, but you have to be more careful with your money. I'm flattered you want to spend it on me, but you should save."

"I know. I've saved before. But, I like spending money on you. There's that." Danny stepped back and looked at Nicole. "It looks perfect on you."

"Thank you, but again, please, save your money." It didn't help that Nicole might change jobs after school. No way working in a lab would pay the same as being a lawyer. While they could live comfortably, they still needed to be smart.

And Danny's smile was gone. "Look, I know how to save money. I did it while I was high out of my mind. I've got a savings account and everything. Not a complete idiot."

"I never said you were." Okay, this was about to devolve into exactly what she didn't want it to.

"Then, can you just accept the gift and my apology?"

Nicole cocked an eyebrow. "Or else what? You'll throw more money at me or shrug me off when I try to help you out?"

Danny pinched the bridge of her nose and let out a hissing breath. "Angel, I didn't mean to do that. I'm just trying to keep my head above water here."

"I understand that." Nicole took Danny's hand. "I know this is hard. I'm just asking you show me some respect rather than trying to literally and figurative throw money at me. An apology from the heart is as good as a necklace. Talking to me is even better."

Danny's free hand went through her hair, and she sniffled. "Angel, I don't know how to do this."

The quiver in her voice rippled through Nicole. She hugged Danny. "Yes, you do. We've been doing it for a long time now. You're just stressed. It happens." With luck, it wouldn't happen again, and this was the hardest thing they'd have to deal with for a while.

Danny buried her face in Nicole's neck. "I'm really sorry, Nick. I love you, and I didn't mean to be an asshole."

"I know." Nicole would take this all as a bump in the road for them, not a sign. Danny got derailed by pressure. She wasn't going to turn into the lovers Nicole had who didn't respect her. Danny still did way too much for her to turn into that person. "Let's go to bed." It was the best thing she could think to say to let Danny know it was all right.

Danny nodded, and they called it a night. Settling into bed, Danny didn't let go of her, which was fine, but Danny started kissing her and Nicole wasn't sure she was in the mood. For a second, she was going to keep going, thinking Danny was in a fragile place and she didn't want to shatter her, but no. Danny wouldn't feel better if she found out Nicole slept with her to avoid her feeling rejected. And Nicole wouldn't feel any better either.

Nicole pulled away. "Not tonight, love. I really want to go to sleep." They could start fresh tomorrow, like a redo.

Danny's face, covered in shadows, twitched. She licked her lips and nodded. "Oh. Okay."

"School and work are doing me in." Not to mention their little tiff. She was spent, physically and emotionally.

Danny nodded again. "I get it. I'm all tied up, too. Dunno what I was thinking."

"Let's go to sleep. We can rest up and then spend the whole weekend together." *Oh, my god, did I just try to write sex into our schedule?* That didn't mean anything, right?

"Yeah. Cool."

They rested on their sides with Danny spooning Nicole. She could feel Danny breathing against her and she could tell Danny wasn't asleep. The tension remained, like a brick wall between them, even when they pressed together. Nicole held onto Danny's hand, giving it a soft squeeze. They were both stressed. They'd work through it. She hoped. *No, we will. I need to stop second guessing everything. I'm over that. Danny's not like my exes, and we'll be fine.*

Chapter Thirteen

DANE BARELY NOTICED THE orchestra leave for the night as she studied her notes, scowling at the paper. In the gripping, cold silence, she noted the room had a stale smell, even though they used it every day. The stillness made the place seem like a tomb. Her tomb. It wasn't the best environment to write music in, but her mind did worse things in other places.

She had tried to do her improvements at home, but inspiration escaped her in even the warmest of spaces. Mostly because when she was home, she liked spending time with Nicole, even though things were bumpy between them. Still, she'd rather be with Nicole than without, regardless of the circumstances. When it was just her home, the silence was oppressive. Lately, she simply fell asleep if Nicole wasn't there. She used sleep to escape the pressing quiet and the spreading emptiness. But, it didn't help, not now and not years ago. Haydn wasn't even enough to keep her up beyond taking him for a walk.

How the hell can I still be the same if things are different? She didn't have an answer for that, but it buzzed in her mind like wasps. She had a job, made real money, and contributed to the household. That was better. *Right, which is why you can't do your job at home, right?*

Fixing her music at home hadn't been going well. She wasn't sure why. After all, it was easy to destroy quiet with music, but she couldn't muster up a single note to do it. Maybe because her guitar still bothered her and Haydn begged for attention she couldn't give since she was supposed to be writing. Maybe it was the questions floating through her mind, questions she couldn't answer. She hoped staying after would work better. Nicole had class and Jody texted her that she didn't mind staying with Haydn for a couple more hours.

Dane picked up a guitar from the corner and started to play. The guitar sounded like crap as expected, but she played anyway. She adjusted the worn instrument and strummed a classical tune. Still, she couldn't get the sound right.

Her mind drifted back to Nicole. How dare Nicole assume she didn't know how to save money? She wasn't an idiot, and she wanted to do something nice for her beloved. Then she got punished for it. *Why doesn't she want me doing nice things for her?* Probably the same reason Nicole didn't want to sleep with her.

"I'm never going to finish this song." Dane sighed, dipping her head. She resisted the urge to fling the guitar away in disgust. *It's not the guitar's fault. It's all me.* She was distracted and fed up.

"It sounds fine," Samiyah said from the doorway.

Dane's head shot up in that direction. "I'm going to have to put a bell on you. What are you doing here?"

"I left my bag behind. It's funny. I always remember my violin, but my bag…I don't even keep important stuff in it because I know I'm going to leave it everywhere," Samiyah replied with a shrug. "Anyway, what you were playing sounds fine."

"Can't settle for fine." Every note needed to go above and beyond. Not just because she wanted to rub it in Andrew's stupid face, but also because her music had to touch people. If it didn't, she failed. She couldn't fail music. She couldn't fail Nicole, who helped get her to this point. She needed to make the most of this.

Samiyah stepped closer into the room and her presence seemed to illuminate everything. Somehow, the room got lighter. Her perfume, something flowery and elegant, chased away that flat clinging fragrance. The air seemed less dense and pulverizing.

"Why can't you settle for fine? Not everything you do is going to be amazing."

Dane shook her head. "It needs to be." Even she could hear the grit and determination in her voice, bouncing off the cracked walls. It strummed in her body and fortified her a little more.

"Maybe you need to hear it on a different instrument," Samiyah said, but she sounded a little hesitant, like she meant something else. Dane could guess what the sentence was supposed to be.

Dane flexed her left hand. "Or maybe a different hand."

Samiyah gave a short nod. "It's a little stiff. When you played before, it looked like you wanted to go faster than it could."

"Good eye or ear, whichever you caught it with."

"Both." Samiyah smirked.

Dane blew out a breath. "Yeah, I don't think I'll ever actually get used to it like this. It's been a good while." Three years and she still couldn't accept it. Her left hand wouldn't be able to do the things her mind wanted ever again.

"What happened?" Samiyah's hazel eyes went wide, and she waved the question off. "If you don't mind my asking."

Dane shook her head. "An old injury." Something she felt she should be over, but doubted she ever would be with the eternal reminder that was her left hand. *I don't regret it.*

Samiyah's perfectly curved eyebrows curled up a little. "It bothers you?"

"Not as much as it used to." Sure, she'd never be able to play like she used to, but as Dane often reminded herself the broken bones eventually led her to Nicole. If she had it all to do over again, she'd do it. Music would've probably killed her eventually, anyway. Nicole made her live.

Samiyah tilted her head to the side a little, curling hair swaying with her. "Do you want help?"

Taking a breath, Dane figured help might be the best way to get through work. "Can you play this?" She handed Samiyah her song pad.

Samiyah examined the paper and nodded. She unpacked her violin case and began playing. Dane focused on the sound. She tried to imagine what she wanted to use to fill the deafening abyss overpowering the whole piece. Listening, she thought maybe the piano should come in...and then it hit her.

"You and the flute!" Dane slapped her hands together and jumped up.

"Hmm?" Samiyah said. Her hand stilled and the music faded.

"I've been trying to cram everyone in the orchestra into this piece, thinking it'd work with the scene, but it should just be you and the flute. I'll sprinkle in Evie, but it doesn't have to be everybody." Dane rubbed her forehead. "That's been killing me, but it should work."

"Don't you think Pedro and Greg need more parts?"

Dane nodded. She needed to do more with her horns. She only had them representing the bit players in the play, even with Pedro being the sidekick, and needed to do a song that highlighted them. She could use them to set a scene.

"I need a trumpet," Dane grumbled, falling back into her seat. She'd have to make a note of that.

"You could use me if you have any ideas," Samiyah said.

Dane cocked an eyebrow. "Don't you want to leave? It's late. I'm sure you have someplace to be."

Samiyah shook her head. "No, not really. I was just going to watch

TV at home and practice on my violin."

"Really?" The news surprised Dane. Samiyah didn't strike her as a loner. She'd expect to hear quiet Greg was the introvert of their little orchestra.

"You don't get as good as I am by hanging out every night."

Dane nodded, but that was something she didn't understand. It wasn't that she was a slouch when she played her guitar or any other instruments, but she'd done more than her fair share of partying. In fact, she probably could've split up her day—partying and playing. *Imagine what I could've done if I had done less partying and more playing.*

"You okay?" Samiyah asked.

Dane blinked. "Just thinking I should've probably practiced more."

Samiyah nodded to the guitar. "It's never too late."

"This is true." Dane wanted to pick up guitar again. Maybe she'd start bringing it with her. She could play a little, even with them, and continue building on what she already had. It'd help her get used to the new guitar, as well.

"You want to use me?" Samiyah smirked and held up her violin.

"Sure, why not? Two goods hands will work better than one and you'll be able to fill in blanks with me." Once the orchestra got into it, they had done that with other songs.

"Of course. And, I know we don't tell you and we bicker like kids when we're together, but we all appreciate you including us in the creation process." Samiyah winked.

"That's good to know." Dane smiled a bit.

***

Nicole found herself needing the library more often. A huge research project wouldn't be accomplished with her home library. There was the university library. First to pick up a book and then to study for a moment, taking notes from a journal she couldn't remove from the library. A moment became ten minutes, which became twenty minutes, mostly because her notes didn't support her project. That wasn't good. When she realized how late it was, she was about to get up and leave, but barely made it away from the table.

"Hey, you're in my class, right?" a young man asked. His brow wrinkled, and he squinted, like he was trying to place her face.

"Yeah," Nicole answered, her own forehead furrowing. She wasn't sure where he was going with this, but hoped it only took a second. *I don't want Danny to think I'm avoiding her*. She needed to get home.

He gave her a somewhat sheepish grin as he nervously rubbed the back of his neck. "Do you have a partner for the lab project yet? I came in late and missed it."

Oh, yeah, because that's what everyone wants, a lab partner who can't be bothered to show up on time. Fortunately, she had a lab partner already. Of course, considering how everyone should be through the first stages of their projects, everyone should have a partner and experiment already.

"I'm sorry, I already have a partner," she said with a small shrug. She made a move to leave.

He groaned and pulled at his short, sandy brown hair. "Damn it. The one I got assigned is already not working for me and the professors won't let me do it alone, regardless of how much my partner isn't pulling his weight."

"Sorry to hear that. I need to get going." She started walking, not wanting to seem like she was fleeing. She wasn't about to let someone rope her into his class issues. She had a good partner and wasn't going to problem-solve for someone when she had her own project problems to solve.

He walked with her. "Oh, no, I get it. I've seen you in here a couple of times and thought our schedules would work out."

Nicole managed to fight back a groan and stared ahead, not wanting to encourage him by making eye contact. *Okay, that's not creepy*. How many times had he seen her in the library? "No, I don't make it a point to hang around campus once class is over. I just needed books." She hoped that'd get him to leave her alone. No such luck. Well, she couldn't go to her car with him at her elbow, and she wasn't going to walk off into the night with him either. She paused in the well-lit lobby.

His shoulders slumped. "Sorry. I didn't mean to bug you. I'm a little freaked out over the whole thing with my crappy partner."

She looked at him, really looked at him, standing in the library entrance with the night sky framing him right outside of the glass doors. He had an expression that reminded her of Haydn when he wanted a treat. With a sigh, Nicole put her hand through her hair, brushing stray auburn locks from her face. *Damn it, heart, this can lead nowhere good*. She didn't have time for this on several levels. She had a project and partner of her own to worry about, and between work and school there weren't enough hours in the day. Not to mention, she had a lover at home who was stressed out and was, in turn, stressing her out.

"I know school can be stressful, but I'm sure you'll get through it. I've already got a lab partner. Even if you follow me home, it's not going to help."

He laughed, throwing his head back and everything. His eyes weren't as amused, though. There were some worry lines under his dark brown eyes. "Yeah, I know. I'm sorry. I don't mean to be a creep. I'll let you go."

"Thank you."

He ducked his head a little, an awkward nod. She gave him one last look before exiting the library. Thankfully, he didn't follow her, but to be sure, she took a winding route to her car and made sure to stay close to any campus call boxes. He didn't seem dangerous, but lots of things didn't seem dangerous and she turned out to be wrong. She felt it better to err on the side of caution tonight. She was able to make it home without problems, but it was still rather late. The glow of the house lights felt warm compared to the night chill.

"Chem?" Danny called from the living room as Haydn charged Nicole.

"Hey, love," Nicole replied, rubbing Haydn's head. He yelped and nuzzled her stomach, which growled. He barked at her abdomen and nuzzled it again, as if trying to let it know who was the alpha around here. His enthusiastic greeting was more than enough to make her feel happy.

Danny stopped dead in her tracks and gave Nicole a wide-eyed stare. "Whoa, was that your stomach? Damn it, Chem, I didn't make anything. Shit." She grabbed a handful of her onyx locks.

Nicole blinked. Danny didn't make anything? She really shouldn't care, but it still sent a shot through her, like rubbing salt in a wound. *No, let it go since you don't want her stressing herself out anymore.* She shook her head. "Baby, please, don't do that. It's okay."

"Hell, no, it's not okay. I wasn't thinking." Danny rubbed her brow. "I just got in too late."

"Danny, honey." Nicole went to Danny and grabbed her into a hug, wanting to assure both of them. Dinner didn't matter. The press of Danny, her warmth and subtle scent made up for the lack of food. *How does she make me feel like this even when we're on different pages?* It made her want to get back on the same page. "It's okay. I can fend for myself. You've been making more meals than you should anyway."

"But, I was here!" Danny stepped out of her embrace to throw her hands up wildly. "I know you're going to be hungry. You've been out all day. The least I could do is make dinner."

"I don't need you to make dinner for me when you work all day, too," Nicole insisted. Why was Danny so stubborn? *I'm sure she wonders the same about you.* "You don't need the added stress."

Danny shook her head. "I was here first, though. I just grabbed a slice of pizza after work and wasn't thinking. I could've at least got you one, too, but it would've been way too cold." Danny paced a few steps.

Nicole grabbed Danny's hand. "Baby, so what? It's not the end of the world. I'll pull something together to eat. It's late. I shouldn't have anything heavy either."

"It doesn't matter. Damn it, I could've at least had a sandwich or something waiting for you. I mean, damn." Danny made a crazy arm gesture.

Nicole stepped over to Danny again and grabbed her once more. She caressed Danny's hand with her thumb. Danny didn't pull away, but she also refused to look at Nicole. Nicole crumbled on the inside. Danny wanted to take care of her so bad, and she couldn't fault Danny that. She felt the same way. She needed to make sure Danny didn't tear herself apart trying to take care of Nicole, for both their sakes. After all, if Danny went insane, Nicole would have to follow.

"Danny, it's not that serious," Nicole said, sneaking a little kiss.

Danny sighed. "I just want to take care of you and instead, I got wrapped up in my stupid music."

"Hey!" Nicole gave her lover's hand a tug, which got Danny to look at her. "Your music is not stupid. It's important. Your job is important. It's equal to my work and school. You're not second to me, Danny. We're equal in this."

Danny pouted, lip poked out and everything. "But, I got home first."

Nicole gave her another hug, hoping it helped. "So, what? If I was really thinking or as hungry as my stomach makes me out to be, I'd have stopped for something on the way."

Danny frowned. "Why would you? I cook all the time."

"But, you don't have to."

"I want to!" Danny stomped her foot.

Nicole wanted to scoff, but offered a soft smile and reached up to caress Danny's cheek. "Love, you know I appreciate it, but this isn't the end of the world. You don't need to be so upset. Can we sit down and talk for a while? You don't need to get worked up."

"I've been ignoring you, not treating you right."

"No, you haven't. You got wrapped up in your work, and you made it up to me with an apology and a gift." Nicole wasn't exactly over it yet, but time would heal that sore and once Danny wasn't as tightly wound as she was, they'd be able to move on. "It's all right. We're all right."

Danny looked down at the floor and nodded, but gnashed her teeth and had fists clench tight enough her hands shook. It hurt to see Danny out of sorts. She knew completing the score weighed on Danny's shoulders, but she hoped Danny wasn't collapse under that weight.

"Love, let's go upstairs and you can tell me all about your day," Nicole suggested with a smile. She'd like to be able to give Danny a massage and hear about what was going on. Maybe they could even do a little more, if it played out right. It had been a while since they were intimate.

Danny arched an eyebrow. "You're sure? You don't want something to eat?"

"It's fine. Come on." She tugged Danny toward the stairs. Whatever was troubling Danny was more important.

"But…" Danny whimpered and glanced toward the kitchen. "Dishes."

"Let them sit until morning. It's fine."

"And Haydn."

"He can be spoiled for a day and come with. God knows he hasn't seen enough of me in the past couple of weeks."

School was expectedly consuming, but she missed their little family. Haydn could spend the night with them. They prepared for bed while Haydn made himself comfortable at the foot of the bed. Once Danny was down, Nicole settled behind her and began rubbing her shoulders.

"Angel, you don't have to." Danny tried to shrug off her hands.

"I want to. Take it and tell me about your day." Nicole kneaded tense muscles. Massaging Danny, being allowed to do this, soothed Nicole like hot tea on a cold morning. She kissed the top of Danny's back tattoo, the one that read "demon."

"It was pretty normal. Andrew came in at one point to tell us to calm down the noise, whatever the hell that means. He's like a cranky neighbor on TV or something. Dougie still insists there needs to be more woodwinds in everything. Pedro almost swallowed his sax trying to play a bit I wrote for him the other day." Danny laughed a little, like the day was fun because of these things rather than in spite of them.

"Are you writing overly complicated things?" Nicole asked, teasing a little.

"Nothing these guys can't handle. Pedro eventually got it and it sounded on point. Lennox came up with a good riff for a piece me and Samiyah came up with the other day."

Nicole stiffened for a moment. Her stomach twisted and turned. Danny spent a lot of time with Samiyah. *You already know that. It's nothing. It shouldn't bother me. No, it doesn't bother me. Okay, it bothers me a little.* Samiyah got to see more of Danny than she did and they seemed to be on better terms than Nicole felt she was with Danny. It wasn't fair.

"You're enjoying it?" Nicole hit a particular spot that made Danny moan. *Can Samiyah do that?* God, she hoped not.

"The rubdown or the gig?" Danny shifted and mewed a little.

"I can guess the answer to the former."

Danny laughed. "But, not the latter?"

"You sound like you're having fun, even when you have writer's block or have to deal with Andrew."

Danny shrugged and hunched over a little. Nicole worked lower. There were more moans and little purrs. Nicole missed these sounds. They had both been too busy the past couple of weeks to do more than cuddle when they got into bed. She hadn't been in the mood to try anything more and Danny hadn't made any moves since the necklace incident. *Maybe that's why I feel a little raw when she brings up Samiyah.*

Leaning in, Nicole kissed down Danny's spine, hitting each letter in the demon tattoo. Danny shivered, and Nicole couldn't help going in for another kiss while her fingers traced the angel wings Danny had tattooed on her back in Nicole's honor. Danny turned at that one.

"Kisses are better done here." Danny pointed to her lips.

"Maybe I want to trace your tattoos with my tongue." Nicole smirked. She retraced the right angel wing on Danny's shoulder.

Danny trembled a little. "Such dirty talk."

Nicole chuckled. "Wow, this qualifies as dirty talk? It's been awhile, huh?"

Danny turned all the way around and gathered Nicole up in her arms. "Since your birthday."

That was over a month ago. It didn't feel like a month, but it felt like they hadn't connected enough lately. She kissed Danny and Danny kissed her back. Next thing Nicole knew, the firm mattress was pressed against her back and Danny was above her. The press of Danny's body was a soothing welcome. She clutched Danny's shoulders, trying to pull her even closer. And then, the next thing she knew, she was asleep.

***

Dane could only smile at Nicole when she drifted off when they broke for air. Nicole falling asleep didn't hurt like it did when Nicole flat out rejected her, saying she wasn't in the mood. Nicole had been willing this time, but her body wasn't able. Nicole had been out of the house for over fourteen hours. In the past, Dane wouldn't have understood how arduous that could be, but now with a steady gig and a loving home, she knew how bothersome it could be to be gone for hours on end.

"Sleep well, angel." Dane kissed Nicole's forehead before getting her under the covers. She pulled Nicole close and closed her eyes.

Exhaling, she held onto the loose feeling Nicole rubbed into her muscles. *I have to take it easy. She still wants me.* Nicole didn't need her to be perfect. It was like Samiyah told her. Some things needed to be fine. Nicole wanted her to be fine. *I have to take it easy, but I must do this job right.* The thoughts alone hurt her head. She blew out a slow sigh.

When Dane woke up, she was alone in bed. That was new and she wasn't sure she liked it. As she suspected, Nicole was downstairs making breakfast. After such a tiresome day, she didn't want Nicole starting off another day with a task she didn't need to do. Besides, she could make up for not having dinner ready.

Not bothering to get dressed, Dane rushed downstairs, hoping she'd be able to step in and finish up breakfast. Unfortunately, things seemed to be done. Nicole was still in her pajamas with Haydn moving around her, but breakfast was on the counter, along with a glass of orange juice.

"Good morning," Nicole said, smiling. She blatantly checked Dane out, as if her basketball shorts and tattered tee were sexy.

"Good morning. You know you didn't have to do this," Dane replied. The drowning feeling was back, and she wasn't sure how long she'd be able to keep her head above water.

Nicole sighed, but continued to smile at her. "Danny, baby, can I please do something around here? I live here, too. Just like you're happy to pay bills, I'm happy to do chores."

Nicole was right, but Dane still had this driving desire to be a housewife. She wanted to keep Nicole from throwing her away, like everyone else in her life, but she also knew Nicole wouldn't throw her away. The notion that Nicole would keep her no matter what made her want to do everything and more as thanks.

Dane was aware she had to fight against this instinct to basically be Nicole's servant. Nicole didn't want a servant. Nicole wanted a companion, a lover, a partner. And Dane honestly wanted to be a partner. *Stop trying to do it all. Let her be there for you. She's not going to throw you away, idiot*. Dane wished she could believe that, but her mind got lost in the rejection from days ago.

Dane put her hand through her hair. "I'm sorry, Nick." She shook her head.

"Baby, we're a team, right?"

Dane nodded. They were a team. They made each other better. They supported each other and pushed each other through hard times. *We've proven that. Then, why is it suddenly so hard to believe?*

"It sucks to know I have stupid abandonment issues," Dane grumbled. *Feel like such a fucking cliché.*

Nicole took Dane's hand. She liked when Nicole held her hand. It tethered her to the world. She wasn't sure why, but it reminded her that there were good things in the world, good things that wanted to connect with her. She pulled her close, giving her a proper hug and kiss.

"It's okay, love. We're in a relationship and we want to maintain it," Nicole said, holding Dane tight.

"Yeah, we are. Again, I'm sorry."

"Don't be sorry. We both know from experience there'll be ups and downs. We just must press on. Let's eat and then get dressed. Just so you know, I'll also handle dinner tonight, okay?"

Dane wanted to argue, but it didn't make sense to do that. *I need to let Nicole do things. I have to act like we're a team because we are.* They ate and dressed and were off to work. Slowly, the ball of anxiety in her chest unraveled, but never truly left. She'd be able to forget about it at work, though.

"Dane, tell your crew of savages to keep their asses in that room!" Andrew barked before she was even all the way in the damned theater.

Dane rolled her eyes. "And good morning to you, too, Andrew." She blew him a kiss. He glared at her, and she couldn't help smirking. *Sometimes, I wish I could see into his head and know how much it pisses him off when I look at him like this.* "Look, whatever Lennox did, I'm not responsible for him." Lennox could be immature when he had free time on his hands. It was possible he was harassing the actors or asking the prop people if there was anything they'd let him take home.

"He's a menace and your responsibility. Keep your musicians back there or I'll start firing people, starting with you." Andrew stuck his finger in her face.

Her eyes rolled once more. *I better be careful before my eyes fall outta my damn head with this guy.* To save her eyes and her sanity, she escaped by sidestepping him. "Uh-huh."

"You think I can't? Just because one producer likes you doesn't mean anything. I could have you out of here like that." Andrew snapped his fingers.

Dane waved him off. If she could get through the day without one of the musicians doing something silly, ridiculous, or immature, she marked it as a success. At least they tended to keep their shenanigans in the music room.

"Everybody here? Great! Let's begin," Dane announced as she marched into the orchestra room. She wasn't even sure if everyone was there.

"I've got stuff to share after talking to my acting counterpart," Lennox said with a grin. It was good to know he wasn't wasting time when he was 'bothering' the actors.

"Good. Everybody, let's get to it." Dane clapped her hands.

Her motley band assembled—thankfully they were all there—and went through their rounds with new insight since they had spoken with the actors. They tended to practice the songs in the order of the scenes of the play. Each time they did it, they improved, but it was noticeable now that they had better understandings of the characters. They made it through three songs before they had a surprise guest. Calvin showed up. Dane paused the practice to go greet him at the door.

"Hey, sir," Dane said, leaning over to shake his hand. He hovered around the theater some days, but not often. This was the first time he made it to their little space. She wasn't sure if it was because he trusted her or if he had other things to worry about.

"Hey, Dane. Just coming to check on the production. I watched the actors go through some scenes. Now, I thought I'd sit in with you guys for a while."

That sounded logical, especially since she didn't know how these sorts of things worked. If not that, then she suspected Andrew gave

Calvin a call, possibly knowing she had writer's block on a few pieces. If that was the case, the joke was on him. She had a good deal of the score worked out enough to show Calvin her work. As long as everyone played like they had been, and no one decided they needed a solo, things should be fine.

"Sure. Here, meet the orchestra." Dane introduced him around.

Calvin made sure to shake everyone's hand and find out what they played. Then he took a seat, which creaked and scratched the floor. Everyone winced at the sound, and Dane hoped it didn't squash their vibe. They went back to work.

Dane pretended Calvin wasn't there. Thankfully, they acted professional with the play producer sitting there. Calvin sat with them for an hour, the smoothest hour she had with her group. It was almost a little boring, but it allowed them to troubleshoot different spots.

"Evie, you should come in sooner on that last song. I think it'll make it sound lighter," Dane said, making a note of it in her portfolio.

"Actually, I was thinking we should add this riff to it." Evie played a light melody.

Dane nodded. "Dougie, jump in with the piccolo, playing the same thing."

Dougie started in and Evie played with him. Dane liked it. She jotted down notes on that song. She hoped Calvin showed up more often if they could be this productive.

"Well, folks, thanks for having me, but I have other business today. The music sounds wonderful," Calvin said.

"Well, you can thank our great musical director for that." Samiyah motioned to Dane.

Calvin nodded with a small smile. "It seems like a group effort."

"She encourages us to give input," Pedro said.

"She also builds unique songs to showcase our talents, which allows us to come up with other ideas," Greg said.

"And she understands our strengths and weaknesses to bring things together," Ryan said.

Calvin's grin grew wider. "You have a supportive ship here, Dane. I think this is special little group. Everything I heard sounds wonderful, and you're still tweaking things to sound better."

"You'll get the best possible mix from us by the time the show opens," Dane replied.

"I have no doubt. Thanks for having me. Good day." And just like that Calvin was gone. Dane breathed a sigh of relief.

"Good work, crew!" Lennox gave a round of high fives to everyone, except Dougie. With a sneer on his lips, it seemed Dougie was grateful to be left out.

"Good work, yes, but we still have a long road ahead of us. From the top!" Dane clapped her hands and then twirled her index finger.

"Slave driver! Can we get a break? We've been playing all morning nonstop." Lennox wiggled his fingers at her.

Dane glanced at the clock. "Ten minutes and then from the top." The room cleared quickly. She laughed until Andrew showed up at the door, glaring at her. "What now?"

"Your band is a menace. They're out there harassing the actors and Dougie is in my face again."

"None of that sounds like my problem." *Why the hell does he keep thinking this is my problem? Of course, he must know how annoying this whole song and dance is and that's probably why he's doing it.*

He scowled. "You have to keep them under control."

Scoffing, she waved him off. "They're on break, and they're probably just talking to people who aren't rehearsing. They've been getting good feedback about the characters, the scenery, and scenes to help them with the music. Maybe if you were willing to have a conversation with any of us, they wouldn't be doing that." She'd go check to make sure as soon as Andrew was out of her face. She didn't want the orchestra to mess up someone else's practice.

"I don't have to talk to you or them. Now, go get them."

Dane sighed and scratched an eyebrow, coming close to pulling a piercing. "They're on break."

"They're in my way."

Dane rolled her eyes. Andrew was in his own way and his head was up his ass. His little visit made her think he had called Calvin on her, but she didn't care. He helped her if he did. She'd return the favor, in the sense that she'd go check on her orchestra. As suspected, her orchestra was socializing with actors who weren't rehearsing. Dane gave Andrew a glance and dismissed the whole matter. With a few minutes to spare, she decided to call Nicole.

"We need to talk more anyway," Dane muttered as she fell into the nearest chair. It clattered under her weight, but didn't feel like it'd crumble under her like most chairs in the band room.

"Hey, baby," Nicole said, a smile in her voice. "How are you?"

The question was simple, but it got Dane talking. She explained how she got so much done and Nicole listened. It was nice. *This has to be how Nick feels when I listen to her.*

"I'm happy you weren't intimidated by Calvin walking in. It's good you understand how great your work is," Nicole said.

Dane preened, even though Nicole couldn't see. "Thank you, Chem."

Nicole laughed. "You don't have to thank me, Danny. It's good you're enjoying yourself."

Dane nodded. She wanted to know about Nicole's morning, but Nicole was more interested in talking about her. Dane grinned. Nicole was interested and invested in her. *She wants me.* The thought made her giggle and in her heart she felt light and loved.

***

Nicole felt settled and content for the first time in a while. It was astonishing what one phone call from Danny could do for her. Just hearing from Danny made any day better. *I hope I do that for her.* But, it was more than just hearing from Danny. It was making breakfast that morning. It was about pulling her weight.

She could understand Danny's desire to do so much. She hoped Danny finally understood the balance of it. This morning felt like a rhythm. *Hope it felt like that for her.*

Nicole went to lunch with her friends, but her thoughts were on what she'd make for dinner. She wanted it to be special, something like a celebration, but also intimate. She'd make one of Danny's favorites. *Which one, though?* They didn't have much at home for her to whip together a meal, either. She'd have to go to the store and she remembered the last time that happened. *Well, no, I can't be scared to do stuff.* Just how Danny settled into her making breakfast, Danny would settle into her grocery shopping.

"Hey, Nicole, you with us?" Clara asked, waving a hand in front of her face.

Nicole blinked. "Hmm? Yeah."

"You don't even know what we're talking about," Mina said.

Nicole chuckled. "No, I really don't."

"What's on your mind?" Clara inquired.

Nicole had to shrug. "I'm thinking about what to make for dinner. Danny's been burning herself out making breakfast and dinner whenever I have class and she doesn't want to admit it. I told her I could make dinner, but she insists on doing everything."

"Wait, wait, wait." Mina waved her hand. "Please, don't tell me you two had an argument over who would cook."

Nicole frowned. "So, what if we did?"

Mina laughed, putting a hand to her forehead. Her eyes sparkled with mirth as she looked back at Nicole. "You two are so tooth-rotting adorable. I might have diabetes from knowing you. That's how sweet you are."

Nicole rolled her eyes. "Oh, shut up." The arguments didn't feel cute, and they shouldn't be laughed at. They left her feeling useless, discarded, and disrespected.

"You really had an argument over who would make meals?" Clara asked.

Sighing, Nicole rubbed her eye. "She's burning herself out, and I want to do things as well. We should take care of each other."

Clara chuckled a little and leaned on the table. "Okay, no, I think Mina's right. This is way too cute."

Nicole made a mocking face at her friends. "Mina, how do you and Shawn find the right balance? You're both busy with demanding careers and since Shawn hasn't killed you yet, I'm assuming you guys have it all figured out."

With a smile, Mina gave Nicole a side-eye look. "Shawn is the one who's dying if it's anybody in this marriage. We eat a lot of take out and clean up after ourselves. If we're going to have people over, we make sure to let the other know as soon as possible. Whenever one of us thinks we haven't seen enough of each other, we make sure to tell the other and plan something out. We still go on dates. But, most importantly, for us anyway, is we joke around with each other all the time. It keeps our relationship light and carefree. If we take a joke too far, we trust each other enough to talk about it or if we feel like a joke was the truth but told as a joke, we talk about it."

Nicole nodded. She and Danny could be playful, but they didn't joke like Mina and her husband did. Of course, Mina had been with her husband for many years and they were comfortable with their relationship. Nicole was certain she and Danny would get there, but not yet. This was a step, though.

Mina reached across the table and tapped her hand. "You'll get there. And on the way, you'll have more sugary, sweet arguments."

Nicole sucked her teeth and pretended to glare at Mina. "Why do I tell you anything?"

"Love," Mina answered and Clara nodded. Of course, she was right about that, too. "I'm serious. You'll get there. It takes time and, yes, the arguments are going to sound silly to us, but they'll be nuclear war to you. You'll get over it. You never let the blow up blow you apart."

"I'll do my best."

S. L. Kassidy

Chapter Fourteen

NICOLE'S PHONE VIBRATED, AND a smile ticked onto her face. Danny was still getting the hang of having a cell phone, but she discovered texting recently and seemed to find it as acceptable as the rest of the world.

The best part of it was that she got little text messages along with Danny's usual call. Nicole had tried calling, but they could only talk for a couple of minutes before Danny had to rein in the madness that was her orchestra. From then on, they agreed Danny would call when she could.

After finishing up an email, Nicole checked the text. It said, "I miss you." She texted back the same and added an emoji blowing a kiss. Danny hadn't figured out emojis yet. It'd tickle her. "How's rehearsal?" She knew it'd be several minutes before Danny could respond and went back to work. Danny could only reply during breaks or at the end of songs.

It took longer than she thought, but Danny replied. "Lennox is childish when no one's watching him."

Nicole laughed. Danny wrote out full, proper sentences in text messages. She didn't seem to know any of the abridged language. Nicole tried to avoid it with her because Danny always asked what something meant, which distracted from the conversation. It'd come with time.

Nicole's fingers glided across her phone. "What did he do?" She always thought Dougie would be the real problem for Danny, but Lennox seemed to get on her nerves.

"It's too long to explain here. I'll tell you at home."

Nicole smiled. They had been trying to make time for each other, but it wasn't working the way they wanted. It was going to get harder before it got easier. She had tons of schoolwork and Danny wanted to practice with the orchestra more. The show would open soon, and Danny was stressed over being perfect, which Nicole understood. But, they seemed to be more stable than before.

There was a lot at stake for Danny. It could lead to more work. The world needed music that could touch places inside people they might not even know exist and make them feel on levels beyond their expectations. Nicole couldn't wait to see the show. Well, really, she couldn't wait to hear the music.

"It'll be amazing." Nicole knew that for a fact and focused on her own work.

And Danny won't have to work with Samiyah anymore once this is done. She knew it was wrong and possibly a little petty, but every time Danny mentioned Samiyah, Nicole's stomach quivered. Danny seemed hung up on Samiyah and spoke about her as if she was some musical demigod. *No one wanted to hear their partner speak of someone else in such glowing terms. Right?*

Nicole shook her head, physically trying to rid herself of those troubling thoughts. "It's nothing. Danny's just impressed with her talent." In her heart, Nicole knew that was the truth, but it scratched her insides. *There's too much of this right now.* Too much knowing the truth, but feeling anxiety over the opposite anyway. *This has got to stop.*

Nicole focused back on her work. The day passed by as usual. The only hiccup came as she packed up. She got a text from Danny. "Still working. Can you pick me up in an hour?"

The request didn't surprise Nicole. She knew when she had class, Danny tended to stay late at work. She thought Danny might be lonely at the house now, especially since they made up, but she couldn't be sure. She'd ask about it later. For now, she replied, "No problem." She could go to her campus library for a few minutes and get some more research books for her experiment and the accompanying research paper. She and Lisa had hit many speed bumps. Another library trip would be useful.

"Hey, Jody," Nicole called her cousin while she was on the way to school.

"How's it going, Nikki?" Jody replied.

"I wanted to know if you're all right with staying late."

"Oh, yeah. I get more done at your house than anywhere else. I'm learning that one day, I will much enjoy living alone."

Nicole chuckled. "I'm sure one day you'll find someone who makes you want to at least be alone with them."

Jody snorted. "Doubtful, but I might get a dog. The dog must be as cool as Haydn, though. He's too chill."

"Most of the time, yes. I'm going to my school's library and Danny's working late. Do you want me to bring you anything? Food? Books? A life?" she teased.

Jody tittered. "The life sounds tempting. Bring me some food, though. I'm actually sick of pizza. Spoil me."

"I'd love nothing more. Your favorite meal will be delivered."

"And you remain my favorite cousin. Thank you."

Nicole laughed. "No, thank you. Love you."

"Love you, too."

In the library, she ran into the young man who had tried to be her lab partner. His name was Dwayne and after their awkward meeting and interacting with him in class, she found he was an upstanding guy. He just had a habit of running late with everything. Maybe he could only work under pressure? She was glad she wasn't his lab partner. She'd have pulled her hair out trying to work with him.

"Hey, Nicole," Dwayne smiled at her as she stepped over to the shelf of books where he was.

"Hey, Dwayne, working on your paper?" Nicole asked, eyeing the four books tucked under his arms.

He tried to shrug, but almost lost his grip on his books. "Trying. You really should've saved me and been my partner when I first asked you. The guy I'm working with is worse than I am with deadlines."

Nicole laughed. "You'll be all right. You're good in class." He really was. He probably would've been a good partner as far as academics went, but she couldn't work with someone who thought handing work in at the last minute was a good thing.

He squared his shoulders. "I'd be better with a competent partner."

"You can't charm me, sir," she replied with a wink.

He laughed. "Of course, I can't. I'm a nerd. I'd never even try."

She couldn't help arching an eyebrow. "You're a nerd?" Dwayne couldn't look more like an average guy if he tried.

"Oh, yeah. Total nerd. This is my second master's degree. My first is in biology. I work in a lab. I have dorky glasses." He only wore the glasses in class, possibly for reading. "Oh, and a totally ironic t-shirt."

Nicole drew back a little. "Your second degree? Seriously?"

"Oh, yeah. Now, you're impressed with my nerdiness." He smirked and held his head up high, but then he laughed.

Nicole tittered. "You can't even say that with a straight face."

"I can't. But, you are impressed. We can both admit that, eh?" He wiggled his eyebrows.

"I will admit I need books, but nothing else. Oh, and that t-shirt isn't even ironic," she replied. His shirt said 'smart remark loading' with the loading graphic underneath.

"It's totally ironic." He tried to tug at his shirt, but his hands were full of books and he couldn't quite maneuver them enough. He almost dropped them again, but righted himself before they tumbled. "Look, I don't want to keep you and I need to go anyway. Talk to you in class?"

She nodded. "Definitely."

Dwayne went on his way while Nicole quickly located the science journals she needed. Nicole dumped her books in the back of the car and then drove to get Danny. By the time she made it to the theater, she expected to see Danny waiting. No one was outside, though. She gave Danny a call.

"Hey, baby, I'm outside."

"Oh. Shit. Lost track of time. I'll be right out."

Nicole sighed, but didn't think anything about it. About a minute later, Danny emerged from the theater. Samiyah walked alongside Danny. Nicole never confirmed she was Samiyah, but the violin case was a dead giveaway. Danny was about to confirm it, though, as she waved Nicole out of the car.

"Nick, want you to meet Samiyah, the brilliant violinist keeping this whole ship from sinking," Danny said, motioning to Samiyah. "Samiyah, this is the woman who keeps me sane, Nicole."

"Pleasure to meet you," Samiyah said, offering a bright smile and her hand.

"Likewise." Nicole shook Samiyah's hand. It was a normal handshake, and Samiyah was obviously a normal person. But, something about her ate at Nicole with jagged teeth.

Danny pulled Nicole close and wrapped her arm around Nicole's waist. Nicole felt warm despite the chill in the air. Glancing up, she locked eyes with Danny to see them sparkling and a small smile lit up Danny's face. *What the hell am I worried about?*

Why did she ask that question? Her mind came up with almost a dozen worries in a second. They couldn't stop arguing about chores. Danny spent money on outrageous gifts. They hadn't spent many waking hours together. They hadn't had sex in several weeks. *To be fair, the last one was your fault.* That made it worse. *And this is why we need some time alone, time to really reconnect.*

"Sorry for making you wait, angel," Danny said.

"It's fine. I hope you got a lot of work done."

"She's muddling along," Samiyah said.

Danny chuckled. "Thankfully, she's helping. Her playing is much better than mine, especially when it's cold." Danny flexed her hand.

"Well, I'm glad you have help," Nicole said. That wasn't really a lie. Despite her reservations about Samiyah, she knew how weather messed with Danny's body.

"It's a shame she can't play the way she wants. She comes up with such great music. I'd love to hear her full take on it," Samiyah replied.

Danny's cheeks turned red and it wasn't from the cold. Nicole fought off a frown and pressed herself closer to Danny. They all stood there for a moment, tension pulsing.

"Well, I should get going." Samiyah nodded her head off to the right. A dark blue wool cap on her head shifted a bit.

"Do you need a ride?" Nicole offered to be polite.

"No, no. It's fine, thanks."

"Are you sure?" Internally, Nicole cheered and then instantly withered. *Really, I'm happy not to give someone a ride? How crappy is that?*

"I've got a ride coming for me. I need to pick up food to make sure she's not pissed when she finally shows up," Samiyah said.

Nicole wasn't sure if that was the truth or if it was a way to avoid spending more awkward time together. Nicole and Danny got in the car and started off for their home with a minor detour along the way.

"I promised Jody I'd get food."

Danny patted her stomach. "Good. Can't remember when I ate, and I think it was just an energy bar or something."

Nicole reached over and rubbed Danny's soft tummy. "Oh, no, baby. Definitely have to feed you."

"Have to feed you, too. I know you haven't eaten since sometime in the afternoon."

Nicole couldn't call Danny a liar there. She smiled. Danny grinned back, and they sat quietly for a while. Nicole tried not to think about Samiyah. She was tall, seemingly elegant, and beautiful. Her dark mocha skin had a radiating glow to it, like the sun. And, in her mind, she could picture it drawing Danny in. *No, stop it. Danny's with you. Stop worrying about things that won't happen.*

"Samiyah plays for you when you stay late?" Nicole was thankful she managed to sound curious, which she was, instead of upset, which she wished she wasn't.

"Yeah. I can't seem to get the sound right, but she does it perfectly," Danny answered as if it was nothing.

"Why don't you play at home? You don't have to worry about it being too cold."

Danny sighed. "Tried that. I don't want you to think I don't like it, but the guitar..." She puffed out her cheeks, eyes falling to her feet. "I'm an asshole."

Nicole shook her head and took Danny's hand. "You're not. You want your other guitar. I understand. That one meant...I couldn't begin to understand or describe what it meant to you. This one will never replace it." She understood how much sentiment Danny's old guitar had, and she might never completely forgive her stupid cousin Junior for destroying it. *Bastard.*

"I know it's all in my stupid head." Danny knocked against her forehead. "I don't want you to think I don't like it."

Nicole squeezed Danny's hand. "Baby, I understand it'll take you awhile to get used to it and to like it. I'm sorry my cousin is the real asshole." She scowled. Her cousin's stupidity seemed to be the gift that kept on hurting. "Is that why you've been working late? Because Samiyah will stay and play for you since you don't want to play?" She refused to say Danny 'can't' play. That would always be a lie to her.

"Well, that and it's weird being home without you."

"That used to be your whole day." It was a little nice to know Danny didn't want to be home without her, even though they weren't really interacting.

"I know, but now it's weird. I miss you when you're gone."

"Aw, love." Nicole smiled. *That's sweet. And I'm worried about her being with Samiyah. How insecure am I?* "Hey, how about we go on a date? We've both allowed work to consume our time these last couple of months. Let's go be together for a couple of hours." She had quite a bit of work to do, but this felt necessary.

Danny blinked. "Right now?"

"Yes, right now." Nicole knew it was spur of the moment and she knew how Danny felt about dates, but they needed this time together.

"You think Jody will be okay with that?"

"We can call and ask."

***

Dane wasn't surprised Jody had no problem with staying with

Haydn a couple more hours. Jody seemed to get a lot of work done and no one bothered her, which seemed to be her dream come true. Once upon a time, Dane would've appreciated that, but she wanted to be around people now, especially Nicole. *I'm happy Nick wants to be around me.*

"Do you have any idea where we should go?" Nicole asked once they delivered Jody's meal, curry chicken with rice and beans. Jody practically slammed the door in their faces after they handed it over. Dane had laughed, which made Nicole laugh.

"Anywhere is good. Let's go someplace close, so we don't waste time searching," Dane answered.

Nicole nodded and steered them to the closest restaurant. There was some silence between them, and Dane felt her phone vibrate against her leg. Pulling it from her pocket, she saw Samiyah texted her to let her know she made it home safe. Dane texted the short message of "that's good" back. She didn't like texting with Samiyah much because Samiyah tended to tease her about not knowing how to text. She hated hearing that since she clearly did know how to text.

Nicole glanced at her as she put her phone back in her pocket. Dane didn't think anything of the look as Nicole pulled into a parking lot. Staring out the window, Dane saw they'd be spending their date at a place called *Sam's*.

"Ever been here before?" Dane asked.

"A couple of times. They're the closest place I know with fairly good food."

A chuckle escaped Dane. "Not a ringing endorsement." It didn't matter to her. She'd eat anything anyway.

Nicole smirked. "You'll like it."

Dane shrugged. She had no doubt she would. She'd be sitting with Nicole, after all. They entered the little diner and were greeted with soft, generic rock music and mixed smells. They were seated within moments on thinly cushioned wooden chairs by the wall at a cozy table for two. As soon as they were down, Dane reached out for Nicole's hand and wasn't disappointed. She sighed as soon as Nicole's hand was in hers and her thumb wasted no time drawing circles on Nicole's soft skin. It felt like her exhaustion raced out of her now that she could feel Nicole.

"I know we see each other most days, but I still miss you so much," Dane said. It felt like they saw each other in glimpses, ships passing in the night, with work bogging them down.

Nicole smiled. "I know what you mean. We just must make it a couple more months. Things will be better once I finish school and plus your show opens soon. It'll be okay."

Dane nodded. *Will it be okay?* After school, Nicole would probably get a new job. *She'll like it and might be surrounded by much better people. Who knows who she might meet and what they could offer her.* The world would have a new shine for Nicole. Once her gig was done, though, Dane would go back to being an unemployed musician, who could barely play and who could barely make ends meet.

"Will it?" Dane whispered.

Nicole tilted her head, watching Dane with concerned emerald eyes. "Of course, love. I mean, you still want me, right?"

Dane blinked at the question. Why the hell was that even a question? Had she not proven time and time again that she'd walk through fire for her angel? If anything, she should worry about Nicole still wanting her.

"Of course," Dane managed to respond. *Maybe this isn't about me. Nick can be sensitive, too.* After all, Nicole had doubts early on. "Do you doubt I do?"

Nicole hesitated, which wasn't a good sign at all. Why even a second of indecision? Dane frowned a little. *Is she worried about us?* But, then again, why wouldn't she be worried? It wasn't like Dane had been the best partner.

"I don't doubt," Nicole said, and Dane leveled her a look. "Much."

Dane sucked in a breath. It took a moment for her to find a simple question. "Why would you doubt?"

"Same reason you do. We're changing. I get scared you're going to leave me behind. Eventually, you'll find someone who doesn't put you through Hell all the time."

Dane felt her face twist as shock rippled through her. "Angel, never, ever think that. Life is going to throw crazy things at us, and you're the only person I want to face those things with. Besides, who the hell is going to put up with me like you do?"

Nicole gave her a watery smile. Dane felt bad. Nicole should never doubt her affections. Never fear for their relationship. Dane wasn't sure what to say or do to make this better, though. They'd continue to be swamped for a while. She couldn't quit her job, knowing that'd only hurt Nicole more. Besides, she liked her gig and was determined to see it through. Added to that, she knew Nicole wanted her to have this, even if it made her anxious.

Dane was about to ask what she should do, but the waitress came over, taking their drink orders and informing them about specials. Dane didn't listen to any of it, focusing instead on Nicole and her hand. Turning Nicole's hand over, she opened it a little. She drew small circles in Nicole's palm until they were alone.

"It's like you said before, angel. Things are changing, but we are, too. We'll make it through this. We're stronger than anything life can throw at us," Dane said. She hoped that was true. She needed to tell herself that more often to make sure she believed it. There was no reason for her to be insecure if Nicole was the same way. *Now, if only I could stop doing stupid stuff while thinking stupid thoughts.*

"I know. Hey, what if, once I graduate, we take a little trip? We can spend some alone time together with no stress."

Dane loved trips with Nicole. "Yes, please."

She had a feeling they'd come out of this situation just as well as they did everything else, but there was still this underlying nervousness that made her skin kind of crawl. *I keep talking about being better and I feel like I'm getting there, but it's like two steps forward and one step back. I won't let her slip through my fingers.*

Nicole smiled at her, and they slipped into less serious conversation, talking about their days. Dane finally understood how different things could happen in Nicole's day, but she still described them as 'the usual' or 'normal.' While she only had to put up with two jerks—Andrew and Dougie—they got on her nerves routinely. Then, there was Lennox and his childishness. Same shit, different day.

"You'd do this all over again if you could, though, right?" Nicole asked, as if she needed to be sure.

Nodding, Dane sat up a little taller. "Yeah. It's good to be this involved again."

"Good. I can see so much joy in your eyes when you talk about things, even when Dougie is complaining. I hope you get a chance to do it again. You think Calvin likes you, right?"

"Yeah. Well, he seems to appreciate me and the music."

"Maybe when he produces the musical he really seems to want, he'll keep you in mind. Things like that happen."

Dane smiled at that idea. "You think so?"

That was one of the reasons Dane wanted things to be perfect. The fact that Nicole thought it could happen made it valid to her. Calvin seemed to like her. He had popped up a few more times to listen in and seemed pleased with the score. Maybe he'd keep her in mind if he did something like this again or at least recommend her to other producers. *I might have a career.* Her heart fluttered at the thought. *Damn, I really want this.*

"If not him, I'm sure other people in the industry will see the play and hear your extraordinary music."

Dane nodded. That sounded good for her. She'd be able to pay more bills, maybe even help with the mortgage. Doing the same job a second time might be better with Nicole done with school. There wouldn't be all that missed time. Nicole might even be at a better job, more relaxed. This could be perfect for them. *This will work.*

"If that happens, I'd have a career again," Dane said. She'd be able to appreciate having a career now.

"Yes. It'd be different from being on stage, but you'd make music."

Dane nodded. "Our domestic partnership will be more like a partnership then."

Nicole tilted her head with her brow wrinkled. Before she could say anything, their drinks and food were brought. Dane had gone with a simple burger while Nicole had some chicken and shrimp pasta thing. It looked good and smelled great. Dane decided to sample her lover's meal, stealing a shrimp.

"You think our domestic partnership isn't a partnership?" Nicole asked, moving some noodles around with her fork. There were some worry lines under her eyes. Dane had to explain this carefully.

"Well, you know, I always feel like you're doing more since you're making all the money." Dane had been working on the feeling, but it was tough. Yes, she was happy being a housewife, but part of her didn't seem to be built for it.

"You'll be more comfortable now that you're paying your way?"

Sighing, Dane shook her head. "I know that's not how it is. I feel better about it. I mean, even our domestic partnership...you did that because I needed healthcare. Without you, I'm screwed. You can't tell me there's not a little imbalance here." She needed Nicole for everything. Nicole shouldn't have to take care of a grown ass woman like this. It wasn't fair to her.

Nicole sighed. "I'm not going to belittle your feelings. They're valid, of course. If you feel you need to do this for us to be more balanced, then so be it. Just remember, not everything we bring to the table is material. You've done so much for me that can't be measured." Nicole tapped the center of her chest. "You've become not just the keeper of my heart or the protector of my heart, but my heart. You've balanced me and given me confidence and love and everything."

Dane's soul soared at those words. She knew that, but it was hard to focus on when she felt like she should do more. Maybe it was because she wasn't at a place in her life that she felt she should be, which technically had nothing to do with Nicole. *Chem always wants me to do things for me. Maybe that's what this really should be about.*

"I get it. I really get it." Dane tapped her heart. In this quiet moment, after being apart and sorting through how much they both missed each other, things weren't about her doing this to deserve Nicole or be on the same level. *I have to do this for me, which will then be for her and us.*

"Then, let's enjoy our date." Nicole smiled at her before taking a bite of her meal.

"Yes. I just want to say one more thing. I need you to understand, I want to be able to take care of you on the same level as you do with me. Everything I give you emotionally, you give me. This is a little more than that."

Nicole nodded. "I know. I understand."

"Now, how about you tell me what's going on with school." Dane took a bite of her burger. Nicole smiled and went on about school. Dane was glad to listen.

***

Nicole was happy to sit across from Danny and tell her about her thesis project. It reminded her of old times when she told Danny about work, except this was more pleasant, despite the trouble the project gave her and her lab partner. Danny hung on her every word, even though she probably didn't have a clue what Nicole was talking about. The chocolate cake they shared at dessert helped keep things mellow between them.

There had been a chance to talk about Samiyah, but Nicole passed on that. Danny's words about how they'd make it through the stress was enough. She shouldn't be jealous, even if Samiyah got to spend more time with Danny or Danny talked about her constantly. She didn't have to worry, not over Samiyah or her disagreements with Danny. They'd make it through. She felt encouraged by Danny's words and claimed she understood she gave enough emotionally that she didn't have to keep harping about the material.

But, it hurt to know Danny still thought money was the great equalizer between them. How often were they going to have that argument? Often, she found out when the check came.

"I got this," Danny said.

Nicole was about to let it go, but felt like that only reinforced Danny's thoughts. "What if we split it?" Surely that wouldn't lead to an argument, right?

"It's not a big deal, Nick. Lemme get this one. It's nothing."

It really was nothing. A little over thirty dollars. "Then, we can split it."

Danny scowled. "Chem, I just told you I like being able to pay my way."

"And we just discussed how everything isn't material. We've argued over who's doing what chores. Now we have to fight about who's going to pay the check?" Nicole frowned.

"Why can't you just let me get this? You know how it makes me feel and you said you didn't want to invalidate my feelings. Now that I have a job it's like you want me to do less stuff than ever, like you don't want me to pay for anything."

"I never said that, but you act like you don't want me to do anything. I make dinner and you have a problem. I clean the living room, problem. Do you realize I haven't walked Haydn alone in weeks?" Nicole asked.

Danny scoffed, tossing her head to the side. "I'm keeping you from walking the dog?"

"You think I baby you, but you really want to baby me." Nicole pointed to Danny and then to herself.

Danny folded her arms across her chest. "Oh, you'd rather I treat you like crap? Like everyone has in the past?"

Nicole flinched. She almost brought up the money incident, but swallowed it. It tasted like broken glass. It was incredible how quick things decayed here. She looked around, noticing some stares. They weren't going to be a show.

"Okay, Danny, please, pay the check," Nicole said. Anything to get out of here. They could talk in the car.

Danny opened her mouth, but glanced around and then closed it. She tossed some money on the table, reminding Nicole of in the car. Nicole put down some money as well. Danny glowered at her.

"For the tip," Nicole said.

Danny's face twitched, but she said nothing. They retreated to the car. Nicole didn't start the engine. They stared ahead.

"I'm sorry," Danny said.

"For what?" Nicole didn't want Danny to turn into a person who apologized just to apologize. "If it's the money thing, save it. Because all this showed me was that this is always going to be a thing with us, even when you say you get it."

"You're not even trying to see it from my side. It's thirty dollars. Why can't you let me get it? I'd have gotten it when I was tutor."

"Because we talked about balance and then you reach for the check. When was the last time I got anything without a fight?" Nicole asked.

"When you got anything? You got the house. This car. The bed I sleep in!" Danny threw her arm around, grazing her knuckles against the roof of the car.

"Then, what do we need to do buy a new house, car, and bed together? When does it end?" Nicole ticked an item off each finger. When did any of this madness end?

Danny took a loud, deep breath and put her hands over her face. "I never thought getting a job and having money would make this harder. I'm trying to adjust, angel. I am."

"I understand, but can we at least stop arguing over money? Dates, household things, stuff like that? We've worked out bills. We can work this out."

Danny nodded. "Partners."

"Yes, partners." Nicole rubbed her temples. She thought about what Mina said. Their arguments might sound silly to others, but they'd be nuclear war for them. So far, she felt like there wasn't an explosion. Was their relationship now a ticking time bomb?

"I'll remember it. I get it," Danny said, as if she hadn't just said that an hour ago and displayed she didn't get it at all.

Nicole didn't reply. She'd wait and see. It was the best she could since talking to Danny didn't seem to be getting her anywhere.

***

Dane felt like she might come apart at the seams. Hopefully, the one thread holding her together was hidden and made of steel. It wouldn't take much for one of these idiots at work to unravel the one thing keeping her whole. She messed up with Nicole, even though Nicole tried hard to make it seem like everything was all right last night. She had to stop doing things where Nicole ate her feelings. No way was that healthy.

It wasn't that things went in one ear and out the other. Dane wanted to treat Nicole the way Nicole treated her and beyond. It wasn't fair, she understood that. She needed to stop or this relationship she loved so much, this woman she loved so much, would get away. She couldn't let that happen, but paying for things was her way of trying not to let that happen.

She shook her head, getting rid of that thought. Worrying over Nicole and the state of their relationship would drive her crazy. Even though, she was almost certain her gig would send her over the deep end first. Pinching the bridge of nose, she motioned for the orchestra to stop once again.

"I swear to all that is holy, Ryan, if you hit that snare again before it's time, I'm going to beat you to death with your own sticks," Dane said. How hard was it to come in on time, crying out loud?

"It sounds better," Ryan insisted.

"You can't change the beat in the middle of the song," Pedro huffed.

"It makes it more interesting," Ryan said, earning more glares.

"You're messing up the horns," Dane motioned to Pedro and Greg. They were really her most sensitive artists. They seemed to feel when one of the others was about to step off, and it threw them off immediately.

"I'm improving the horns," Ryan replied.

"No. You're not dragging us into bullshit like this again, Ryan," Dane snarled. They'd been through the same argument more times than any of them cared to think about. "We all know the songs, so play the damned songs. We don't have the time to screw around like this. We need to get it right. Opening night is coming up fast."

Ryan grumbled, but stopped annoying everyone. Andrew popped in, trying to take over the annoying bit, but they ignored him, including Dougie. They had come too far and Dougie didn't seem to want to make waves right now. Andrew complained about 'the noise,' but eventually gave up when none of them reacted. They did their best to focus and make it through the day. The way practice went now was getting more and more typical for them as opening night drew closer. Dane chalked it up to stress, and she didn't know what to do about that. She wasn't used to pressure on all sides. *I guess drugs made sure stuff like that didn't make it through.*

At the end of the day, Samiyah stuck around as usual. Dane handed her a few pages, which she played. Dane listened. Most of her editing was tightening things up now. It was too late to make real changes, too close to show time.

"I think this one is done," Dane said.

"It seems perfect," Samiyah replied.

"I really want to make sure 'Shock' is good. You want to go?"

Samiyah smirked. "You think you can?"

Dane flexed her hand. It wasn't too cold in the room as it often was. She should be able to handle one song. She grabbed a guitar and gave Samiyah a nod. Samiyah shouldered her violin again and put her bow to the strings. Dane got started. Samiyah came in perfectly. They were halfway through the song when Samiyah missed a note.

"Shit. Sorry." Samiyah tapped her bow against her shoulder and put it back to the strings again.

Dane smiled. "It's okay. Better now than during the show."

"You know, hearing you play is a little shocking. I guess when the room is nice, you're okay." Samiyah smiled, as if to get her to understand by 'okay' she meant emotionally rather than her playing.

Dane nodded. "I'm all right."

"No, you're really good. Playing with you is different than practicing with Lennox. You get this more because this is your work. I can feel it more with you." Samiyah smiled a little more.

Snorting, Dane shook her head. "Well, we need to get Lennox to feel it, too. He's the one who'll be playing this in front of an audience."

Samiyah grinned as short laugh escaped her. "I'm sure once that thought finally hits him, he'll get it together."

"I'd like that thought to hit him before I do."

Another light laugh escaped Samiyah. They continued playing. They made it through the piece. Dane made a mental note on what to fix, what needed to be taken into consideration for Lennox and his style, and what would give the song the right amount of power.

"All right. I know what I want to do. Gimme a second." Dane needed her hand to recover. "Hey, do you think everyone's anxious over the show and that's why they're more annoying?"

Samiyah shrugged. "Of course, everyone gets nervous about opening night. Plus, we can tell when you're distracted."

Dane blinked. "What?"

"We can tell when your mind is wandering. Today, Ryan could tell your mind was only halfway here. That makes everyone a little more antsy and that's why he started acting up."

Dane rubbed her chin. "Any idea on what I should do to make them know it'll be okay?"

"Well, stay as focused as you keep us, of course. Plus, you could always just say it."

Dane wrinkled her brow. "That easy?" Saying stuff didn't seem to be working out for her in other areas of life.

"You're pretty encouraging when it comes to figuring out music for us and our strengths. You're competent. Every now and then telling us it'll be okay would help. No matter what, we're going to be nervous, but nice words should help."

"Okay. Never thought of that, but I can do it. Thanks, and I'll make sure you guys get my all." Dane flexed her hand. "Let's get back to work."

Dane walked Samiyah through the minor corrections she wanted for the song. They played it again with the edits. Dane liked it better and jotted down the tweaks to make them permanent. At the end of the day, they parted ways. Crow came to pick Dane up, as she did every time Nicole had class. As soon as she hopped in, she texted Samiyah to find out if she caught her ride. Crow glanced at her.

"You still sending those long ass texts?" Crow laughed.

Dane frowned. "Between you and Samiyah, someone has to show me the damn class for texting."

Crow rolled her eyes. "There's actually a thing called text speak, and you don't speak it."

Dane stuck her tongue out at Crow, who cackled. Thankfully, her phone vibrated, giving her a good distraction. Samiyah had texted back, letting her know she got her ride and asking about the score. The question led to a conversation, which had Crow looking at her.

"You talking to the princess?" Crow asked.

"No, Nick's in class." Nicole would have Dane's hide if she interrupted her class. Of course, texting Nicole might be the only way to say the right thing nowadays. She got plenty of smiley faces, blown kisses, and loving hearts in texts, which was more than she got in real life.

Crow's eyebrows drew in close together. "Then who the hell are you texting like that?"

"Samiyah."

"Is she the person you're always texting when you get in the car?"

Dane shrugged. "Usually."

Crow's eyes, nearly black today, went wide. "Crap. Do you do this shit around the princess, too?"

Dane's brow furrowed. "Sometimes."

Crow sighed and took her hand off the steering wheel to rub between her eyes for a second. "Goddamn it. Okay, I know you're new to this 'having a phone' thing and you probably don't realize how personal texting really is, but you need to stop that."

Dane arched an eyebrow and looked at Crow like a crazy person. "Why?"

"Because if you're texting someone constantly and it's not your girlfriend, it looks bad, especially in front of your girlfriend."

"Nick knows I'm not doing anything." *Of course, she did ask if I would still want her. Does she think there's something up between me and Samiyah from texting? Shit, how much of this am I fucking up?*

Crow shook her head. "If you say so, but I'd still cut that shit out if I were you. It'll get suspicious. I don't think you want to have that argument, even if it's nothing. You're putting it out there, and you don't want to get to the point where your girlfriend wants to search through your phone."

Dane nodded. Crow had more relationship experience than she did. She didn't understand why texting would seem like anything at all. It was kind of a hassle to her. It was easier to have a phone conversation than this mess of typing it out, but everyone seemed to text.

"Any other phone etiquette I should know? Is it all right for me to answer this text?" Dane asked.

"Just so you know, one of the best things about texting is that you don't have to answer immediately, and for fuck's sake, you don't need to use perfect grammar, punctuation, or spelling," Crow replied.

Dane nodded. "Samiyah told me."

Crow gave her a look. "Okay, yeah, don't answer that text right now and from now on, when Samiyah texts you, you wait two to five minutes before you respond."

"Why?"

"You don't mess anything up. Trust me."

Dane nodded and decided to take Crow's word for it. She was already on shaky ground with Nicole. Now she had to watch the texting thing. *Who the hell made adulting so damn hard?*

***

Nicole yawned as class wrapped up. Her head throbbed and she wanted nothing more than to fall into bed. She packed up her books, but Dwayne made his way over to her. She openly rolled her eyes at his smile.

"What, Dwayne? Should I just tell you no right now? My partner is still here." Nicole pointed over to Lisa, her lab partner.

Lisa eyed Dwayne and gave him a mock-scowl. "I keep hearing about you trying to steal my partner. Back off, man. Don't make me have to hurt you!" She waved her hand at him as if she had a knife.

Dwayne held up his hands and laughed. "I'm not poaching. I promise. It's way too late in the game for that, anyway."

Lisa seemed appeased with that and gave Nicole a wave. "I'll email you later tonight."

Nicole nodded. "Yeah, we can put everything together then and hope it works out like it should this time." Lisa disappeared, and Nicole turned her attention back to Dwayne. "Okay, what's up?"

"I just want to pick your brain a little. Do you have five minutes?"

Nicole sighed. Really, she didn't. She wanted to go home and cuddle up with Danny, who was undoubtedly asleep on the couch already if she left work on time. But, if that was the case, she supposed she could spare five minutes. Besides, if Danny was asleep, she'd spend about an hour, staring at her, mind whirling on how to get them back on track. It wouldn't help her budding headache.

"Just five minutes," Nicole said. *Really, Nikki? You're going to let school turn into the new work, where you just help everyone who asks?* There was a difference, of course. Most of the jerks at work she was forced to help. Dwayne was oddly charming and she liked him. She didn't mind helping him.

"Five minutes."

They strolled to an all-night cafe and ordered hot chocolate. The warm, sweetness helped ease the tension bumping at the base of Nicole's skull. Five minutes of discussing class turned into ten and then fifteen. At that point, Nicole practically ran back to her car hardly bidding Dwayne goodnight. Danny was asleep by the time she got home. She didn't have the heart to wake her, scared to talk now, especially since it was late. She didn't want to explain why she just came in. She made herself some dinner and didn't wake Danny until it was time to go to bed. They didn't exchange more than three words that night.

Chapter Fifteen

A WEEK AND SOME days had passed since Nicole's impulsive date with Danny. Unfortunately, they hadn't been able to sneak much more time together. They hadn't been able to talk, even though that seemed to go in one ear and out the other with Danny. Even on days Nicole didn't have school, she went to the library after work. Danny didn't seem to mind, staying late at her job, too. During quiet moments, she feared they were avoiding each other. They weren't even two ships passing in the night. Just two bodies sleeping near each other, and it felt like rats eating through her.

Nicole wanted to try to connect again, even if it was only for a little while. If she kept at it, Danny would get there eventually. Yes, it'd hurt each time they had to start over, but every little bit counted. It wasn't like she could give up. *Sometimes, you should.*

"Hopefully, this isn't going too far," Nicole said, pulling up outside of the theater. She texted Danny earlier to make sure she was there.

She wanted to have a surprise lunch together. There was a little pizza restaurant up the street. Hopefully, it'd be fine for Danny. Nicole knew a surprise lunch date was rather hypocritical of her to do. If a lover ever showed up to her job, she'd probably lose her mind. It was annoying when Tyler used to do it and they worked in the same place. She also used to work through lunch. Danny had changed her mind on taking personal calls at work, so if Danny showed up to take her to lunch, she was certain she wouldn't be bothered.

"Maybe Danny won't be bothered by this." Nicole bit her lip.

Still, she had to take a deep breath. She wasn't sure how the idea might go over. Danny might not like the added distraction. Or she might appreciate the effort. They'd have to find out. Now, if only she could get the butterflies in her stomach to stop before she vomited.

Going inside, she confused the first person she saw by asking for Danny. Everyone here seemed to her know as Dane. *I must remember she introduces herself as Dane.* Once she switched names, she was pointed in the proper direction, navigating her way through a wave of people who didn't pay her any mind. Soon, only their noise remained, but even that began to sound distant. Finding the small room tucked into a corner behind stage, Nicole caught sight of Danny's back.

"Pedro, you gotta pick it up, man. You're letting Lennox drown you out," Danny said.

"Of course, he's drowning me out. He'd drown out thunder," came the response from someone Nicole couldn't see.

"Don't even try it! I'm at the same level as everyone else," the guitarist huffed, glaring off to a corner of the room.

"Pedro, often, yes, it's Lennox's fault, but this time it isn't. I need you to shine here. It's your moment and you're fantastic at what you do. Bring it," Danny urged him.

Danny seemed really busy, and suddenly this felt like a bad idea. Nicole considered turning around, pretending she was never there.

"Hey, somebody order a cute redhead?" the guitarist, Lennox, asked, looking at her.

"Cute redhead?" Danny turned and blinked. "Chem, is everything okay? What are you doing here?"

A nervous laugh escaped Nicole as the butterflies in her stomach morphed into sharp spikes. "Uh...I thought we could have lunch together."

Danny inhaled deeply, enough for Nicole to see her chest puff out. *God, this was a bad idea. A horrible, terrible idea. What the hell was I thinking? I wouldn't want someone to do this to me, especially not when I'm stressed.* Of course, she'd undoubtedly make the exception for Danny. Still, that didn't mean this wasn't the worst idea ever. *Now, how the fuck do I get out of this without messing this up even more?*

"You know, now is the perfect time for lunch. Take some time to relax, feed your body and soul. Decompress. Reassemble in an hour, people, where we will be amazing," Danny called out before walking over to Nicole, who breathed a sigh of relief. A burning sensation in her chest faded as quickly as it ignited.

"Hey, you're not going to introduce us to the girl, boss?" Lennox asked with a smile, sliding over. Sweat patches marked his t-shirt even though room was chilly. He held out his hand and wiggled his eyebrows. "I'm Lennox, and I play the guitar. I'm awesome at it by the way."

"I'm Nicole and also taken by an awesome guitarist," she replied, motioning to Danny.

"Damn, boss. Your lady is fine," Lennox said and then made a show of biting his lower lip.

Nicole giggled a little. She could see every story Danny told about him had to be true, just from this moment. "Thank you, I suppose."

Danny shook her head and put her hand through her hair. "Nicole, this is the orchestra. Orchestra, this is Nicole." Danny pointed to each member of the orchestra. "Evie on the keyboard. Ryan on drums. Pedro on sax. Greg on trumpet. Dougie on the woodwinds. Annoying on guitar, aka Lennox. And Samiyah."

Nicole smiled at them all. "Nice to meet you." They waved and grumbled back, but didn't get a chance to say much as Danny escorted her out of the room. It sounded like they began arguing with each other, but it was muted thanks to all the noise going on around the theater.

"Where do you want to go to eat? How much time do you have left?" Danny asked as they made their way out of the chaos.

Nicole shrugged. "As long as I go back within the next couple of hours, I'm good." That was partially due to hard work and partially due to being the daughter of the firm's founders.

"That's good. I, unfortunately, only have an hour. A minute over and Andrew will be all in my ass, like he literally clocks the time I leave. Any place around here you want to go?"

"I've only seen the pizza place around here, but I thought it might be good enough."

Danny nodded. "We order from there sometimes when we get caught up in practice and no one really wants to leave."

"There are times like that?" Hearing stories and seeing Danny now, it seemed like the orchestra couldn't wait to get away from each other.

Danny chuckled. "Yeah, they're spoiled brats, but they're also dedicated artists. They want to get this right. We want to get this right. There are times when we just keep it going and eat pizza like it's ambrosia."

Nicole smiled and took Danny's hand. "You'll be awesome when the show opens."

Danny squeezed her hand while blowing out a loud breath. "If we keep practicing. I really need Pedro and Greg to get it together, especially when Lennox starts trying to play over everyone. Let's not talk about that. There's a couple of places around here to eat if you don't want pizza."

"Pizza's fine, love. I just want to spend time with you."

Danny smiled at her and Nicole finally felt herself relax. Her heart slowed down, and it was only then she realized how hard it had been beating before. *Why was I so nervous?* It seemed beyond silly now.

Exiting the theater wasn't as easy as entering. Eyes watched them go. Nicole assumed they were watching Danny leave.

"Does Andrew have spies or something?" Nicole asked. The firm had plenty of those for various bosses and partners, her parents included.

Danny looked around. "It's that or they're all checking to see if I'm leaving, then they know the orchestra is on break. The orchestra's quite popular with the rest of the crew."

Nicole nodded. "As long as I'm not getting you in any trouble."

A loud scoff escaped Danny. "Oh, please. I'm always in trouble here, anyway." She flashed Nicole a huge grin, earning a laugh as they left the building.

They sat down in the pizza restaurant, munching on slices. Nicole went simple with pepperoni while Danny had ordered two slices. She only got toppings, pepperoni, and sausage, on one, which Nicole was happy for. Danny was trying to rein in her poor diet habits with junk food, finally accepting she didn't have to keep up her habits from being homeless. Best of all, Danny let Nicole pay for the food.

Their talks weren't going in one ear and out the other. *I just need to be patient.* Of course, that was proving to be easier said than done.

"This is nice. Can we do this again sometime?" Danny asked before taking a swig of her bottled iced tea.

"Of course. I'll call when I get a moment," Nicole answered. *Okay, this turned out to be a pretty good idea.* Small quiet moments might be the way for them to pull through this busy period of their relationship.

Danny chuckled and smiled at her, as if she were silly. "You don't have to call. Just show up."

Nicole blinked. "You sure?"

"Yeah. It's cool."

Nicole grinned quite wide. It almost hurt her face, but the delight within her pushed that aside and those spiked balls in her gut dissolved. *Please, let this be it.* She wasn't sure how much more back and forth she could take. Not when just the thought of seeing Danny had caused her distress.

"I know this is moot since you'd have a harder time doing this with me, but you could if the mood strikes you," Nicole said.

Danny placed her slice back on the plate. "You sure? I mean, I know I don't have a car or anything, but I'd like to be able to surprise you if I can."

"Danny, you know I'm always happy to see you, even if I'm working. Hearing from you brightens my day."

"It's good to hear. One day, I'm gonna test this out, though. I don't know how, but I will."

"I look forward to it."

After lunch, they walked back to the theater and Nicole's car. Before she got in, Danny caressed her cheek and leaned down, giving her a tender kiss. Nicole practically melted. It was like all the distress they had gone through never happened.

As they pulled apart and she stared into those grey eyes, she got hit with something that never occurred to her before. A part of her thought Danny would be the person who destroyed her. No matter what Danny did to her, she'd come back, she'd try harder, and she wouldn't give up. But, she was probably the same for Danny. If anyone studied their history, they'd see how Nicole sinned against Danny. Were they meant to be each other's destruction with sweet words and determination?

"I really needed this. Thanks," Danny said.

Nicole shook her head. *I really needed this, too.* "Never thank me for spending time with you. This makes my day, you know?" And might be the calm before the storm, just as their last few times together had been.

Danny gave her another kiss before Nicole got into the car. They said a couple of goodbyes before she could muster the strength to drive away. Danny watched her from the street until she had to turn the corner.

***

Dane wanted to clap and click her heels as she watched Nicole leave, but just grinned, watching her breath escape her open mouth. She hadn't realized how tense she had been until she saw Nicole. Beyond the lunch and spending time with Nicole, she felt forgiven. She left work with a million pounds on her shoulders and came back as if she were reborn into light without anything heavy in her heart.

"My angel." Dane tapped her heart before turning to go into the theater.

Andrew was in her face almost immediately. "It's about time you got back," he huffed, throwing his hands down like a petulant child.

"I'm entitled to an hour lunch last I checked," Dane replied. She'd been gone exactly an hour.

Dane was about to walk off, but Andrew grabbed her by the arm. He might as well have flipped a switch in her. With a snarl, Dane yanked her bicep back. She glared at him with fire in her eyes and lava in her belly, more than ready to explode all over him. He winced. All her tension was back, plus more. *How many women has he grabbed in his life and thought it was okay?* If she didn't have to work with him, she'd put him on his ass.

Dane put her finger in his face. "I don't know who the hell you think you are, but you don't have the right to touch me. Now, listen carefully, you don't ever fucking touch me again. In fact, don't let me see you touch another fucking person like that."

He swallowed and opened his mouth, but nothing came out. He had to swallow again and worked hard to glower at her, but he did it with red, bloated cheeks. "Get your stupid band." He pointed to the orchestra room.

Dane scowled, pointing at him. "Just because you don't want music doesn't mean the orchestra's stupid. They're working just as hard as your actors and pulling together to bring this piece of shit you call a play into something worthwhile. Why don't you learn to appreciate it?"

"You can't talk to me that way," he replied, trying to puff himself back up, almost like a raccoon.

Dane arched an eyebrow. "What way? The way where I tell you not to fucking touch me again?" Never in her life had she contemplated a lawsuit before, but she'd get Nicole to sue the shit out of him if he dared put his hands on her again. Mina and Clara would help once they knew the story. Hell, Kathleen might even help.

Folding his arms across his chest, he narrowed his gaze and widened his stance. "If Calvin knew you allowed the band to wander around like lost babies while you went to get laid by some chick, he wouldn't think so highly of you."

Dane's hand balled into a fist, trembling. Taking a deep breath, she kept herself from hitting him. Calvin wouldn't understand why she gave his son a black eye, even if he listened for the explanation. She focused on him.

"First of all, what I do on my lunch break isn't any of your concern. Second, the orchestras on lunch and what they do is none of your concern. I get that this doesn't seem to register with you, but that's how it is. I don't know what your problem is, but from now on, don't get in my face with them. If you want to tell your father, then you go right ahead. But, if you touch me again, I'm laying you out on your ass and I'm suing the ever-loving shit outta you. Tell your father that, too, if necessary."

Andrew flinched at the words 'your father,' like she wasn't supposed to know that. He gathered himself, eyes boring into her as if trying to make her crumble to dust. She gave as good as she got.

"You think I got this job because my father's the producer, huh?" he hissed.

She squared her shoulders and folded her arms across her chest. "Isn't that how it worked?"

"Not everyone gets a job because of their parent, but you don't know shit about that, do you?"

She scoffed. "You're the one standing here who hasn't got a clue on how to get on without a parent holding your hand. What exactly is your issue? You're pissed Daddy wanted music to go with your mediocre story or mad that my girlfriend looks better than yours?"

He snarled and stomped his foot. "Your girlfriend can't prance into our rehearsals! You're not special."

"Never said I was and she showed up for lunch. I've seen plenty of other people get visitors during lunch. Is that really what has your panties in a bunch?" Dane had to shake her head. He was quite petty. He always came after her for the dumbest things. She came in everyday on time, did her job, and didn't bother anyone.

He grunted. "You can't just have people wandering through. It's distracting to everyone working."

Okay, that was probably true. "She showed up to surprise me."

"She's your responsibility, whether or not you knew she was coming."

She grunted. Damn it, he had her there. "True."

"Yeah, I know it's true. You and your lot aren't the only ones working here. Your work isn't more important than everyone else."

Dane put her hands up. "Yeah, I got it. We don't think our work is more important."

"But, you act like it. If any of my people wandered in and out of the band room, harassing your people, you'd probably pitch a fit."

Okay, he had an inch and now he wanted a mile. "Not if they were all on break. Sometimes, your guys do come back there and talk to us, but apparently, you're not keeping track of them like that. We don't mind. In fact, we appreciate it. Now, if you don't mind, I have practice to get back to. See you later." Dane waved him off with one finger and went about her business.

By the time Dane got back to the orchestra room, Lennox was already there. Barely a minute later, everyone reassembled in their spots. Practice picked up and went on like normal for a while. And then Andrew was at the door. *Wow, he went from an inch to a mile to he wants the whole damn country?*

"Hey, your noise is carrying. We need quiet," Andrew said.

"And we need to practice," Dane replied. Besides, she knew the music carrying was bullshit. There was always too much going on for anyone to hear what they were up to. If the music carried, they'd gotten complaints about it early during the production from people other than Andrew. No one even casually mentioned it.

He held up a finger, as if reprimanding her. "We're rehearsing the final scene. We need to get this just right."

Dane was about to tell him off, but then got an idea. "Guys, let's go watch." She had a feeling she would regret the suggestion, but it felt like the right thing to do right now. *We should've done this sooner.* Having the actual visual compared to what they imagined from the script and what the actors and other crew members told them probably would've given them a greater understanding of the story.

Andrew's mouth dropped open as they all filed out of the room to go see this unbelievable, vivid climax. It was underwhelming as expected, but caused an unexpected argument within the orchestra as they made their way back to their room. In their heads, the climax had been way more epic, and their music had matched.

"We need to talk to Carlos and Peter about the climax again. They need to show it in the same way they built it up," Dane said, walking a little behind her group. Carlos and Peter were the actors playing the hero and the villain respectively. They came to the music room every now and then, discussed their parts, and what they tried to do with the characters. Their talk was bigger than their actions.

"Why the hell should Samiyah get the drums with her during that? I'd kill with the drums behind me. You should get the damn keyboard," Lennox said, motioning to Evie.

Evie drew back, genuinely insulted. "Hey! The fuck, dude?"

Samiyah rolled her eyes. "Please. You're lucky Dane is brilliant, or I'd bury you in any other song."

"Hold on, why are you both acting like there's something wrong with my keyboard?" Evie scowled at them.

"Because it's weak," Dougie chimed in.

Dane winced. *Oh, damn it.* "Guys, no." She tried to step between them, but that didn't stop a damn thing. It was like an avalanche.

"Oh, you mean like flute playing," Evie shot back, jabbing her finger at Dougie as if he was the damn devil.

"My flute kills! I easily dominate over you and the horns." Dougie motioned to Pedro and Greg.

"You play over us when you're not supposed to, messing up the whole set," Pedro replied, which wasn't a lie. "That's not dominating. That's being a dick."

Oh, wow. Pedro might've been holding that one in for a while. "Guys, I know we're all on edge, but this isn't helping," Dane said, but it didn't even register.

"Well, he is a dick," Evie agreed with a nod.

"The fact that you guys let a sissy ass piccolo play over you in and of itself is weak," Lennox said. Greg gave him such a scathing look, Lennox should've dropped dead right there in the dusty hallway.

They entered the room, but that wasn't the end of it. "Oh, yeah, and you're such a big man that you can't even follow directions," Samiyah said.

"Okay!" Dane banged her hand against the desk. All eyes went to her. "Like I said, we're all on edge. Attacking each other isn't helping. We're a team, and we've been playing like one most of the time. We can't fall apart now."

"A team? Lennox wouldn't know a team if one stomped him in an alley," Pedro said.

"Dougie, too," Greg said.

"That's not true. We're doing good." It seemed good to Dane, but then again, maybe she didn't know what a team was. When was she really part of a team, beyond Nicole? And she couldn't even get her act together with Nicole. The thought of Nicole gnawed at her. Nicole got her in trouble. Nicole made Andrew right. Nicole got her into this whole headache. It was all Nicole. *Fuck.* She didn't need this.

"How is this good?" Ryan threw his hands up.

"Obviously not this. We've been playing well for the most part and together. We're okay. We're okay," Dane said, pleading with them to get it. They were okay. The way their eyes drifted from her, they couldn't believe her.

It was clear the orchestra had been in their box too long. Dane decided today they'd end early, even though she was certain Andrew would end up in her ass again over the decision. Would he be right on that one, too? She didn't want this headache, though. She hoped they'd apologize to each other without her having to direct that tomorrow.

"All right, everyone. Go home. Come back fresh tomorrow," Dane ordered, making a shooing motion to get rid of them. If there was a tomorrow, she wasn't sure she looked forward to it.

She didn't have to tell them a second time, which really showed how much they needed the break. Usually, they'd be all about practicing for however long they were supposed to. Even Samiyah didn't stick around.

Dane fell into a chair as soon as she was alone. The scratching across the floor screeched up her spine, making the base of her skull throb. A migraine came on, even though she thought she'd avoid it once those clowns were gone. And then Andrew came in, and she could already feel her head explode. It was going to be a long day, even though technically the day was done.

***

Sighing, Nicole rubbed her eyes as she roamed her school's library once again. Each step was like pulling a ball and chain. The smell of the books, usually a familiar comfort, set her already raw nerves on edge today. She had been here too many times for her taste and her lab partner felt the same way. At least her relationship with that partner wasn't wringing her out like a soaked washrag.

She and Lisa kept hitting rough spots in their research, no matter what they did. And every time they thought they had a brilliant solution, another problem sprang up. School was halfway over. They didn't need these roadblocks. Sure, it'd make for a great paper eventually, but they needed to finish if they wanted to pass and graduate.

"Hey, fancy running into you," Dwayne said as he ambled up to her with a smile.

Nicole smiled back, but it was a little forced. Her face ached with tension, even her teeth had a small thump echoing through them. The paper would be the death of her. She didn't have time for Dwayne and his humor. In fact, she was a little resentful of the light in his eyes, knowing hers had lost any luster.

"Dwayne, I'm going to start thinking you're following me," she said, doing her best to sound amused rather than tired.

He chuckled and tilted his strong chin up. "Nah, I think I'm here for similar reasons."

She glanced at the shelf. "Books?" It was a library. Of course, that'd be his reason.

He laughed. "I meant the lab thing. I keep running into you, because we're both doing more research. Me because my partner is lazy as hell. You?"

"Every time Lisa and I think we have things figured out, something else goes wrong. It's beyond annoying."

He nodded. "I saw Lisa earlier. She had a bag of books. What do you two do, email back and forth? I never see you together."

"Email, calling, and texting work best for us. We both have full time jobs. Hell, Lisa has kids." As soon as they partnered up and went through their usual days, they both knew they'd have to treat their partnership like a long-distance business deal. They pulled their weight, just not together. They'd be done if their project decided to stop being a bitch.

"Yeah, when I saw her, she told me she's married and driving her husband nuts because of the paper. What about you?"

Nicole sighed and thought about Danny. Pins and needles shot through her. "Definitely neglecting a relationship for this. You?"

He chuckled and shrugged. "I've got work and school. Nothing else, not even friends. I'm not good at multitasking."

"I find that hard to believe." She thought someone who always ran late had to figure out how to juggle more.

"Nah, I might act cool and all, but I can only do one thing at a time. My mom thinks I'm the most boring nerd on Earth."

Nicole gave a weak laugh. "I'm sure you're fine."

"I'm hopeless. Hey, I know you're usually in a rush with me, but I could use another brain. Can I just run some ideas by you? My partner is worthless. Honestly, I'm not sure how he made it this far unless he cheated."

Nicole should go home. Danny waited for her, in some shape or form anyway. She wasn't sure if she was ready to face Danny, even though lunch went fine on the surface. Underneath, after her epiphany, she was drained, like she'd been walking through a storm, against the wind, and now she was at the eye of the hurricane. Going home would mean returning to that storm.

Besides, Dwayne was friendly and seemed to need her help. She helped at work all the time with people who weren't grateful. Dwayne would be appreciative, and she'd like to help a friend.

Nicole found herself in a twenty-four-hour coffee shop with

Dwayne again. He had his notes with him. Nicole flipped through his notes while she sipped a hot chocolate. Dwayne talked her through it while having tea.

"This looks good," Nicole said.

"Yeah, but I need a lot more."

Nicole nodded. She had suggestions for him, and he jotted down what he liked. They talked about different things he could do and then next thing she knew an hour had passed. *Shit*. She wouldn't solve any of her problems by not going home. Besides, her troubles this time were all in her mind. She was spooked by a thought.

"Dwayne, this has been fun and all, but I have to get home."

"Ah, duty calls with the neglected relationship. Good luck." He smiled.

"Thanks." She dashed off. Checking her phone, she was surprised Danny hadn't texted or called. She'd been out late at the library so often, Danny probably expected it.

As she pulled up to the house, Nicole worked on an apology. It was late, even for her. Danny might be in bed already, not asleep on the couch. Instead, Danny was up on her phone, fingers working on a text message unless she learned to download games, and Haydn whimpered at her feet. As soon as he noticed Nicole, he rushed over to her and tried to tug her to the door.

"No, pup. It's too late for a walk," Nicole said, petting his head. He whined more, trying to push her back to the door. She looked up at Danny. "Hey, love."

"Hey." Danny didn't bother to look up from her phone, probably texting with Samiyah, the most important thing in her life.

"Have you let Haydn out? He's begging." He had her by the sleeve, yanking her to the door.

"Opened the backyard for him and he wouldn't go out." Danny kept working the keyboard on her phone.

Nicole fought off a scowl. Now Danny couldn't be bothered to walk the dog. Before she couldn't be stopped from doing everything. "Well, he's begging now."

"Okay. Can you let him out then?"

"I'm going to," Nicole replied, maybe snippier than she should have. She was tired and annoyed that Danny texted someone so late while their dog entreated her to go outside.

Danny didn't seem to notice her attitude as Nicole let Haydn out. He had a little spot in the backyard that was all his. He was out and in fairly quickly. It was too cold even for him. She returned to the living room to see Danny still on her phone.

"Who are you texting, love?" Nicole asked as she made her way to the kitchen. She frowned. "Babe, what's up with the pile of dishes?"

"Huh?"

"The dishes. Why are there a mountain of dishes in the sink?" Nicole couldn't believe her eyes. It looked like Danny had people over.

"I had to take out a bunch of stuff from the fridge that went bad."

"And you didn't wash the dishes after?" The kitchen looked like an experiment gone wrong.

Danny scoffed. "Do I have to do everything?" she grumbled.

"What the hell?" Nicole turned right around to go look at Danny, who was glued to her phone. "Danny, look at me."

Danny glanced at her. "What? What is the problem? It's damn near midnight and you're just walking in and you have a problem."

"I don't have a problem. You left a pile of dishes in the sink."

"Oh, then, I should've let the food in the fridge turn into one of your damn science experiments?" Danny huffed.

"Of course not, but could you do the whole job if you're going to clean something? This is way half-assed." Nicole motioned to the sink.

"At least I did something."

Nicole frowned. "Okay, you made a mess. Congratulations. Why can't you just clean it up? You're too busy texting Samiyah at midnight."

Grey eyes narrowed as Danny focused on her. She stood up, looming in a way she never had before. "So, what if I'm texting Samiyah? You think I'm fooling around with her?"

"I didn't say that. I think you're paying her more attention than anything else."

"Like you're doing with school?" Danny replied.

Nicole blinked twice, hard enough to where she thought she heard her eyelids smack together. It would've been less shocking to be struck by lightning. "Then, you don't want me to go to school?"

Danny flinched and her mouth gaped open. "What the hell? Of course not, but you can't be in my ass about anything when you're never here. Why the hell is this even a problem? I cleaned the fridge. Shouldn't I get a thank you? No, it's obviously too much trouble for me to get any thanks for anything, like it's too much trouble for you to be here. It's not like you were going to clean the damned thing."

"You didn't finish the job." Nicole pointed behind her to the kitchen.

"Oh, now I'm getting in trouble for not doing stuff. First, I was doing too much and now I'm not doing enough, is that it?" Danny frowned. "What the hell do you want me to do? You want the impossible all the time."

"I'd like you to just finish whatever you start and since you want to act like Haydn is your sole responsibility, maybe you could take care of him."

Danny put her hand to her chest. "Oh, now he's my responsibility. Fuck the team thing, huh? Just like with this dishes BS. Why don't you just finish the dishes? Oh, lemme guess, you're too tired from school or got too much work to do. You'll go hunker down in the library now."

Nicole ground her teeth together. "Now I should just be happy to clean up behind you? I should take your scraps is what you're saying? And you probably didn't finish because you're too busy texting with Samiyah. Why don't you invite her over while you're at it? I'm sure she could keep you company while I'm being a bitch for being at school and having work."

Danny pointed at her. "Didn't even say that, Nick. This is bullshit. You know Samiyah's helping me a lot with the music."

Folding her arms across her chest, Nicole scowled. "That's the real bullshit. You don't need help. You're fucking brilliant, but you're so damned scared. You don't want to pick up that new guitar, not because it doesn't sound like the old one, but because it means starting new, becoming someone new. You're so terrified of turning into someone other than the goddess of rock and roll."

Danny's face turned red. "Are you fucking kidding me? I'm trying to be someone better for you! I'm doing this all for you. And all you do is fuck me over left and right. In fact, that's the only way you fuck me now and you try to act like I'm the one who's cheating."

The world spun. Nicole licked her lips to help any words come out. "Excuse me?"

"When was the last time we had sex, Nick? Whenever I try, you're always too tired or you don't want to or my favorite—you fell asleep on me. But, like I said, I guess you're getting off on other things, like fucking me over at work."

The words were like a shot through the heart, and Nicole stepped back. "I fuck you over at work?"

"Yeah, like today. Your little lunch surprise? You distracted the crew and messed up the rehearsal." Dane jabbed her finger in Nicole's direction.

Nicole pointed to herself with her hands. "Really? I messed up rehearsal. I fuck things up for you. Okay, then I'm the reason you stopped doing gigs. Not fear, but me?" *Is this what Danny really thinks of me? I'm fucking up her life?* A traitorous voice in the back of her head dared to ask if Danny was wrong.

"I didn't do as many gigs because I had to be here. Someone has to take care of the house." Dane ground her teeth as she motioned around them with a sweeping arm gesture.

Nicole shook her head at this weak excuse, especially since it seemed like the truth had already come out. She was holding Danny back. "The house doesn't need you twenty-four hours a day."

Danny's nostrils flared. "Do you mean you don't need me twenty-four hours a day?"

Her eyes burned as she somehow kept tears at bay. "I didn't say that."

Danny sneered. "Well, now you see how it feels to have someone put words in your mouth."

Nicole scoffed. "Do you really think I don't know how that feels? Besides, didn't you just basically say I'm holding you back? I got you in trouble. I fucked up your life." Her insides felt shredded, and she wasn't sure how she managed to stay on her feet. This was her worst nightmare.

Danny's neck tensed, and she squared her shoulders. "There you go with more words in my mouth. I'm just telling you like it is."

Nicole sniffled. *She's telling you like it is. You're a stone around her neck.* "You're dodging the issues here, like you have a habit of doing."

Danny rolled her eyes. "Oh, you mean the dishes in the sink?"

Nicole took a deep breath to keep her voice from trembling. She needed to stay on task. "I mean the fact that it's midnight and you're texting Samiyah when you're perfectly capable of writing music on your own. I mean the fact that you have a perfectly good guitar in that room, but you're too scared to touch it."

"I wouldn't need to touch it if your fucking cousin hadn't smashed my good guitar against a tree!" Danny snarled. Her eyes blazed.

Nicole went ramrod straight, muscles all tensed, and acid flowed through her. Her vision blurred and narrowed to a point. That was true. Not just true, but proof she did ruin Danny's life. Danny losing her guitar was pretty much at her feet, with blazing destruction in its wake. All caused by her. No, she hadn't broken the guitar, but she had put Danny in the situation. She always put Danny in tough situations. She had probably even done that here. Maybe this situation was worse than it seemed, but Danny was a soldier. She always took things and kept on marching, especially when Nicole put her in harm's way. *Shit.*

It really is all my fault. Everything. Danny wasn't the storm. *I am.* She ruined everything for Danny. She ruined them. It was more than a broken guitar. *I broke Danny.* Her heart shattered in chest, turning into fine powder.

"You're right. This is all because of me." Tears flooded her eyes as Nicole threw up her hands. It was over. She was over. Everything inside of her was dust. "I've been wondering why you put up with me, but now I see why you talk to Samiyah all the time. You can't stand to talk to me. You can't stand me."

"Not when you're like this. Not when you're impossible. I'm just trying to do right by you and you make it seem like the worst thing I've ever done. I've stood by you pushing me to my stupid fucking parents. I've stood by you through your family, and you just keep wanting more. And now you're going to blow this fucking gig for me and then probably bitch me out about that, too." Danny sucked her teeth and turned her head. "Can you just leave me the fuck alone?"

"You're absolutely right. That's exactly what I'll do. I will not bother you again, never hurt you again." She turned and fled. *Why keep this up? I'm the reason every single time something goes to shit around here. I'm probably the reason every single relationship I've ever had failed.*

"Nick," Danny called after her.

Nicole ran off, knowing Danny wouldn't be able to catch her. By the time Danny got upstairs, she was already in the bathroom. In the shower, she purposely let the spray hit her in the face to hide her tears.

***

"Fuck," Dane growled from the top of the stairs and hit the wall with the side of her fist. Her knee might be better, but it was no match for two healthy ones. "Why the fuck did I say that?"

She hadn't handled that with any sort of grace, but then again, neither had Nicole. It was like Nicole didn't even know what she wanted from Dane. *How the hell am I supposed to know, then?*

"You should know not to blame Nick for every pissy thing that's happened," Dane said as she made her way back to the couch. She thought she'd feel better after getting all of that off her chest, but she felt like she had been impaled with a splintered stake. She was rundown and exhausted and wanted to get the show out of the way.

She wanted everything done. And, maybe everything was done. Nicole certainly sounded like she was done. Dane wouldn't blame her if she was. And she was so messed up right now that she didn't know if she'd lament it or celebrate it. Too many missteps and now open wounds.

"She shouldn't be telling me what I'm scared of. What the hell does she know? She's never been phenomenal at something and forced to quit. She's never had this sort of pain in her life." Dane punched the sofa cushion several times. Her eyes burned like sand was poured in them, which went well with an intense need to retch. She held it back.

Nicole didn't know anything about what it was like to be her. Nicole didn't even know what the hell she wanted, not out of their relationship and not out of their life. But, she wanted to tell Dane how to live her life? Who was Nicole to judge? Fuck Nicole.

Nicole, who could barely even stand to be in the same room as her, but wanted to pretend their problems were Dane's fault. Nicole, who wanted to act like Dane's texting was more than it was, but also didn't want to touch her. It was obvious now Nicole didn't really want her. Dane was worn to the point where she wouldn't mind letting go.

Her phone vibrated, signaling Samiyah texted her again. She glanced at it and then threw the phone. She wasn't cheating, and she wasn't scared.

"I was fucking getting better for her. I'm being better," Dane said, even though she didn't feel that way at the moment. To hell with Nicole.

Chapter Sixteen

THE CAR RIDE TO work that next morning was tense, and that was being kind about it. Last night was the nuclear war and this morning was the fallout. The air was poisonous, slowly suffocating Nicole. Haydn wandered and whined between them until they left the house for the car. No freedom to be found there. The pressure felt like it might crush the car and the air was just as toxic in the car as it was in the house, eroding every inch of Nicole. Nicole glanced at Danny often, wondering if Danny felt as horrible as she did. She doubted it since Danny was on her damned phone, undoubtedly texting Samiyah.

Now, in the pit of her stomach, Nicole was afraid something could be going on with Danny and Samiyah. It hadn't been a serious fear of hers, even though she was jealous of Samiyah getting to spend time with Danny. It was different after finding out Danny blamed her for many things in her life going wrong and her facing the fact that Danny was right. They also hadn't had sex in quite a while and that was her fault, too. There probably was something going on between Samiyah and Danny, something to soothe the ache. Maybe nothing physical, but something emotional and possibly spiritual, considering Danny's religion was music. She'd never be able to touch Danny on that level, not like Samiyah could. Beyond that, she feared Danny was using Samiyah as a crutch and using her new guitar as an excuse.

The more Nicole thought about it, the more she feared Danny was still traumatized by her injuries, haunted by her limitations to the point of not realizing she was boundless if she only tried. She might not say it and she tended to act normal, but now, watching her work, there was obviously something there. Danny wasn't going to talk to her about it. Hell, Danny might never talk to her again and she wouldn't blame Danny if that was the case. Who wanted to talk to the person that ruined her?

That left Nicole to stew on what Danny snapped about, what might cost her everything that brought her joy. Yes, she was never home, but school wasn't going to be forever and Danny wanted her to graduate.

Danny pushed her to do this, to see school all the way through. That was probably huffed out of frustration and a useful comeback when she got on Danny about the dishes.

Maybe I shouldn't have said anything about the dishes. It was nice that Danny cleaned the refrigerator. The fridge needed it. *But, why do a half-assed job?* Danny never did that. She was also a little annoyed over how anxious Haydn had been to go outside. Sure, maybe he hadn't gone out when Danny opened the door, but he begged by the time she came in. Surely, he had begged Danny before.

It was like texting Samiyah had been more important than Haydn and that wasn't like Danny. Nicole had to wonder if working in music again, trying to find her place in the world, was something even more traumatizing to Danny. She feared she pushed Danny to do the wrong thing again, like when she threw Danny to the Wolfes. *Have I always been this much of a fuck up?* It didn't feel true, until now anyway.

Maybe I am the reason my relationships fail. It's not them. It's me. Nicole hadn't been able to see it before and no one close to her wanted to tell her the truth. It wouldn't be the first time. Maybe she never did anything right. Maybe that was why Lillian hated her. Maybe that was why Danny had to do everything.

Nicole's thoughts had wandered, but came back to the proper train of thought. Had she left everything to Danny before? She wanted them to work on being balanced. It was all she wanted. Danny had always insisted on doing more than she needed, but maybe it was because she didn't want Nicole to mess things up.

I can see why she doesn't want me. The idea was like a hot knife through her. She wasn't sure how she'd survive without Danny. She wasn't sure she wanted to survive without Danny. *I can do better for her.* Nicole decided right then and there, she'd stop using school as an excuse. She'd get home, be there for Danny, and make sure she did the right thing for their family, if it meant they could stay together. If schoolwork suffered, then ah well. *My family is the most important thing, always.* Unfortunately, she wasn't sure if she still had a family.

They pulled up to the theater. *What if this is it?* What if Danny got out of the car and never came back? After all, nuclear war vaporized things too close to the blast, like love, affection. Wiped away all traces and made sterner stuff vanish into thin air.

Nicole gripped the steering wheel and stared ahead. It felt like the only way to keep from flying apart. The world had come to an end and she needed words to acknowledge it. After all, one couldn't look the apocalypse in the face and not say anything.

"Have a good day. Bye, baby," Nicole said, her voice low, a little uncomfortable. It wasn't the best thing to say during Armageddon, but it seemed appropriate. This could be her last goodbye and she couldn't handle it, but she didn't want to break down. How pathetic would it look to turn into a sobbing mess right in front of Danny's job? She didn't need to do anything else that might reflect poorly on Danny.

Danny leaned over and gave Nicole a little kiss right at the corner of her mouth. Her heart skipped a beat, but as she returned the kiss, Danny pulled away, like she hadn't expected it. She caressed Danny's cheek and got her to pause long enough to kiss her back. Her eyes stung with hot tears. Was that a goodbye kiss? She couldn't ask.

"You have a good day, too. Goodbye, angel," Danny said and she exited the car.

For a moment, Danny stood there in the cold morning air. She looked in the car, like she wanted to say something. But, in the end, she entered the theater. For several seconds, Nicole stared at the door, unable to move. She wasn't sure how she got to work. She couldn't even remember driving off.

Nicole went to her office and stared at her desk for a while. She didn't turn on her computer or take anything out. She barely recognized where she was. The world didn't exist anymore.

She needed to take time to let her body unravel all the unease from the morning. She and Danny had moved around the house woodenly, like they didn't want to shatter the other. They didn't hover around each other, even when they had breakfast. Poor Haydn put himself in the music room by the time they left, and they merely pushed the gate shut.

"I should tell Jody to give him a little extra exercise or something," Nicole muttered. Haydn needed something to help ease his mind. The call should help distract her a little, too.

"I'll take Haydn outside some. I could pretend to jog or something." Jody snickered. They both knew Jody wouldn't even feign jogging.

"Thank you."

Jody snorted. "No problem. He's all over me anyway. Maybe he knows you're on the phone. Let's do a video chat and he can talk to you."

Nicole laughed, but she indulged Jody, if only to keep her mind off things. They hung up and Jody called her back. Haydn showed up on her phone screen.

"Hey there, big man," Nicole cooed. Haydn barked and whined.

"Sounds like he misses you, Mom," Jody laughed.

Though her cousin was teasing, the words shot Nicole in the heart. "I'm sorry I'm not around more, Haydn, but that doesn't mean you stop being my little guy...not that you're a little guy anymore. You're so big now. You be good for Jody. She's practically your foster mom."

Jody scoffed. "Please. I feel like he pushes me out of the door when you guys show up. He loves you."

"Well, we love him, and I love you, Jody."

Jody grinned. "Yeah, yeah, yeah. You're trying to butter me up. I'm already here and watching this dude, you know?"

"I know, but I appreciate what you do." *I appreciate Danny, too, but I guess I'm not good at showing it.*

"You think I don't know that? Go ahead and work, Nikki. I've got your pup."

"Thank you."

Jody disconnected the call. Taking a deep breath, Nicole tried to focus on her work. A knock on her door interrupted her. Not bothering to glance up, she was about to dismiss whoever it was. She didn't have time to waste on the firm's usual idiots.

"Nikki, do you have a moment?" her mother asked as she shut the door behind her.

Nicole looked up and blinked. She felt like her eyes played tricks on her. Her mother almost never came to her office. If her mother needed something that required more than a phone call, she was summoned to her mother's office. If it had nothing to do with work, then it waited until after hours and her mother summoned her home.

"Yes, Mommy. Is something wrong?" Nicole asked, her heart in her stomach. *Oh, god, what if something happened to Daddy?* It really was the end of the world.

Her mother smiled, which quickly eased Nicole's nerves. Okay, she had jumped too high on the 'what could be wrong' meter. That was good. She wouldn't be able to deal with anything else wrong. She wasn't sure how she was still sane.

"There's nothing wrong. I know you're coming close to graduating," her mother said, easing into the left chair in front of Nicole's desk. Her eyes appeared a little wet, like she was trying to hold back tears.

"Yes. Two more months, actually," Nicole replied. Well, if she and Lisa could get their act together on their project. They were doing fine on the professor's weekly checks in lab, but if things didn't work at the end of the semester, then that was it.

"Do you know what you're going to do after?" her mother inquired with an intense stare, like she was trying to keep Nicole pinned in her chair.

Nicole squirmed in her seat, feeling nine years old again, and scared to move. She licked her lips and her forehead furrowed. She managed to keep back a frown. *Please, Mommy, let me walk my own path.* "Is this about continuing to work here?" She didn't have it in her to argue over things right now.

A small, sorrowful smile settled on her mother's face as she shook her head. "No. I just want to make sure you have a plan."

Oh, she's worried about me, as always. Nicole smiled. "Mommy, haven't you taught me to always have a plan?" She hadn't decided on what she might do, but she had plans.

"Then, you'll look for work in your field while continuing to work here?"

"That's one plan."

Her mother cocked an eyebrow. "There are others?"

"Yes, I have others. I have to do what's best for my family, after all." She had considered many things before Danny had a job, but never settled on a solid plan. Now that Danny had a job, she needed to think. Of course, if she and Danny were over, she wasn't sure what she might do. She wouldn't be in a good space to make any life changing decisions.

"You've discussed these plans with Danny?"

Nicole blinked as she realized something new. "Not recently." *Well, damn. I have been fucking this up for a while now. No wonder Danny's sick of me.*

Her mother laughed at her. Nicole wasn't in the mood to be mocked, especially after last night, so she glared. The expression sobered her mother up a little bit.

"Calm down, Nikki. I'm not laughing at you in a malicious way. It's just watching you and Danny in this relationship. It's actually cute."

Nicole's mouth dropped open. Yes, her mother no longer completely hated Danny after Danny stood up for her and punched out her backstabbing cousin Lil, but her mother never showed this sort of approval.

"Mommy, are you okay?"

Her mother smiled, tapping her finger to her chin as if considering her words. "I'm fine. It has taken me a long time to realize and accept that you've evolved."

"I've evolved? Don't you mean I've grown up?" Great, her mother finally accepted and respected she was an adult in a loving relationship and that was all gone.

Her mother shook her head. "No, this is evolution. You have a fight in you. I've known that all your life, but the fight has expanded. You've gone from fighting to win games and defending teammates to fighting for yourself and defending your dreams. Just because you grow up doesn't mean you'll fight for yourself or go after your dreams. Adults often play it safe due to responsibilities or comfort. You've gone out on a limb you wouldn't have gone on until now, until Danny."

"And this makes you proud?" Nicole arched an eyebrow. That didn't sound like her mother. After all, her mother hated Danny back when she thought Danny talked Nicole into returning to school. If her mother spoke the truth, she was about to be a huge disappointment because she lost the fight.

Her mother leaned forward, eyes sharp like she didn't want to miss it if Nicole did something. "It has taken a lot of talks with your father to get me to this point, but I need you to know I've always been proud of you. You've always been the best daughter I could've asked for and I never want you to doubt it."

Nicole's heart thumped in her chest. "Mommy." Her voice cracked on the simple word, broken up by so much inside of her, a swirling monsoon of emotion, dense and deep, warring with each other for who would control her reaction.

The concern was back in her mother's eyes. "Have you...have you doubted that?" Her mother swallowed and the sound seemed to echo throughout the room.

Nicole glanced away for a moment and then shook her head. She took a breath, needing to calm down. She had never truly felt like a disappointment in her life until now. Danny was fed up with her at the same time her mother had finally come around to her life choices. What would happen when her mother found out she had ruined it all? The wave of disappointment would never end, and her mother would never trust her to do anything on her own again.

"No, I've never doubted. I think I've always been scared I didn't measure up." It was a fear she carried with her all the time, she realized. Not just with her mother or father, but all her relationships. She always feared she wasn't enough, which factored into her always doing so much in relationships. Of course, there were other factors, like she was a fixer and was used to doing her best to prop up teammates, but there was the terror, too. *Wow, I've got quite a few problems, for myself and others.*

Her mother laughed again. "I think it's human to have this fear. There are times I fear I didn't measure up to be your mother or Raymond's wife. Hell, even my parents' child or my sisters' sibling. It happens. Of course, there are also times when you think you're the best in the world."

Nicole nodded. That was true. *Okay, maybe I don't have as many problems as I think I do. I just must accept I'm human.* Humans made mistakes. Humans weren't perfect. She wasn't perfect, despite being told she was often in life. Would Danny accept that, though?

"Mommy, I know we're at work and we usually don't discuss nonbusiness related things here, but can I ask you a question?" Nicole rubbed sweaty palms on her thighs out of view. Her mother might say she was proud of her, but what if in detail it turned out the reason was for something simple? What if she was proud of Nicole just because she was her daughter? What if Nicole hadn't really done anything to deserve it? What if Danny was right about Nicole ruining everything?

Her mother eyes twinkled. Nicole hadn't seen this expression in years. "Well, one, we've already been discussing nonbusiness related things. Ask me whatever you want. We both know there's a good chance you won't like the answer, though."

"Do you think I'm doing all right? I mean, I'm thirty. I might change careers. My girlfriend's trying to get a new career. We're trying to figure out how to work out both of us suddenly being busy, and it never seems like we're on the same page. Is this normal?"

"Of course, it's normal. People change careers at my age. Like you said, you want to do what's best for your family. I think Danny wants the same. You just must figure out what the best is. This is about the time when I'd give you the advice to talk to her."

Nicole was almost about to say they had talked, but arguing wasn't talking. "That is sound advice. I should've figured that out."

Her mother gave her a soft smile. "I get the feeling you're looking for more than that."

"Danny and I...things are rough. We keep fighting over things. Things that I thought were done with the first time we talk about them. And I feel like I'm not learning lessons I should."

"Relationships take time. They change as we change, and you're both going through big changes in life. You're not going to give up because something gets hard. That's not who you are, and Danny isn't going to give up when things get hard either. I've seen her stand with you through tough situations, Nikki. She'll be there for you."

Is Mommy right? Will Danny be there for me after saying I ruined her life? Part of her felt like that was true, but a bigger part of her remembered last night, remembered harsh words and even harsher truths. No, Danny had not said it was over, but that was basically the only thing she didn't say.

"She's not going to give up on you, Nikki," her mother stated as if it was a fact, like the sun would rise in the morning and Danny wouldn't give up on Nicole were on the same level. It made one of the billion cracks in her heart heal, but the rest remained fresh, open, and agonizing.

"You really think so?"

A smirk settled on her mother's face. "Sometimes, we need people to state the obvious. I do it for your father all the time. To this day, I still don't understand what the man thought he'd do with that physical education degree if he didn't want to teach gym."

Nicole chuckled and shook her head. "I don't think any of us will ever know that." She gave her mother a genuine, delighted smile. "Thanks, Mommy. I appreciate it." If nothing else, at least her relationship with her mother was stronger.

"I know I've been against Danny, but she's good for you. I've never seen anyone stand up for you the way she does and I finally understand that she's even standing up for you when she doesn't say anything to me. She could've easily come between us, but hasn't."

"I'm glad your view of her has changed. You've evolved, too."

"Well, I have to keep up with you. Besides, life seems to be enjoying proving me wrong about you. It would be foolish of me to keep fighting it. I didn't fight it because I thought you were wrong."

Nicole waved it off. "Mommy, I know."

Her mother nodded. "That's good. How's Danny's job going?"

Sighing, Nicole rubbed her forehead. "She's stressed, but I've heard some of the music she's made and it's beautiful. She's really good at what she does, Mommy." She sat up a little taller, feeling quite proud of her lover. Regardless of what happened to them, she'd always be proud of Danny.

"Do you think she'll get another job like this?"

"I sincerely hope so." Despite their troubles right now, she hoped to everything in the universe, Danny got to create a score or work on a play again. Or at least Danny would get to do something she loved, because who knew if Danny loved this job or just suffered through it because Nicole forced her to or because she thought it made her better.

Her mother nodded. "Maybe she can take care of you."

Nicole shook her head. Her mother and Danny had that one thing in common. "Mommy, that's what she's been doing since the day I met her. Her support has always been beyond belief, and she's always trying to lift me up. I hope you'll see it now that you're open to her."

Her mother nodded again, and for the first time, Nicole truly believed her mother would eventually understand what Danny did for her. Maybe not now or tomorrow or even sometime in the near future, but eventually, her mother would get there. Of course, it might be too late by then. If not, Danny would be able to sit down and have a conversation with her mother without someone needing to be a buffer. They'd share laughs and funny stories, probably embarrassing ones about Nicole. Nicole wouldn't even care as long as Danny was there.

"You'll be all right, Nikki. You're strong."

"Sometimes, I don't feel it." Hell, right now, she felt like she might collapse if the wind blew too hard.

"Well, more of the obvious, but that's normal. There are moments like that in life, you know that. And, you're allowed for that to happen. Not to mention, you have someone there for you when you don't want to be strong. It's all right to not be strong all the time, sweetheart. You have someone to lean on when you need it."

Nicole nodded, even though she wasn't too sure that was true. She broke Danny from leaning on her. Danny didn't need to be strong. Danny was allowed that. She couldn't always expect Danny to hold her up now. She smiled at her mother anyway, if only to make her feel comfortable. There were still cracks in Nicole's heart, pains of too many mistakes, too much leaning. She was shattered, just as Danny was.

***

Dane ran her hand through her hair as she walked into the theater. Her mind wasn't ready for work. She wanted to go home and wait for Nicole to come back. Hell, part of her thought maybe she could go up to Nicole's job. Everything inside of her wanted to make Nicole feel better, but there was a little voice in her head that argued against all of that. *Fuck Nicole*, the mantra of last night.

Why should Dane be the one to bridge the gap? She cleaned out the damn fridge, after all. Okay, no, she hadn't done the dishes after cleaning, but she was tired and she wanted to wait up for Nicole. It shouldn't have started a war. *Why the hell do I even bother?*

Dane massaged above her eye. Nothing she did measured up, ever. Nicole didn't want her to do everything and then suddenly wanted her to do everything. She couldn't keep the orchestra together. She'd been bitching about Andrew, but he made a point that was enough to make her reexamine her whole life. She blew up at Nicole about surprising her at lunch. But, that was Nicole's fault. Everything was Nicole's fault.

Nicole needed to know about the consequences of her behavior, needed to understand the trail of corpses in her wake as she forged a new path to who the hell knew where. *Maybe you could've put it in a better way.* And maybe Nicole could've appreciated the fact that she waited up for her, even though Nicole avoided her at home. Yeah, maybe that was the mistake.

"No," Dane mumbled to herself as she stepped by several people. They looked at her, but she barely gave them a glance. They'd figure out she wasn't talking to them.

Waiting up for Nicole was never a mistake, could never be a mistake. The mistake had been telling Nicole that she was never home after she had encouraged Nicole to go to school. Putting it all on Nicole, that was all types of wrong. Letting Nicole walk away rather than talking to her, that was wrong. That was all wrong, but Nicole was wrong, too. And a major problem was that Nicole never wanted to admit she was wrong or confused or had no idea what was going on. *Yeah, so, fuck Nicole.* She shook that accursed voice away.

Nicole didn't want to admit she was drowning just as much as Dane was. Dane didn't know how to keep her head above water, but she tried to save Nicole and one drowning victim couldn't save another. *I'm not drowning. I'm just...*She didn't have the words to explain it.

Dane wasn't always on the phone with Samiyah because Samiyah was a crutch. Samiyah was innovative and a welcome help in making the whole score. Why would she need a crutch? She was good with creating music. Once upon a time, she had been a freaking goddess, and not just because she played the guitar like she'd been born with one in her hand. Why the hell would Nicole even think she used Samiyah like that?

Of course, the idea of Samiyah being her crutch was better than Nicole thinking other things of her texting with Samiyah. When Nicole brought it up, her guts bunched up and her throat burned. Dane feared she might have to prove she wasn't cheating on Nicole. Nicole at least had faith in her being faithful.

"That's good," Dane said, not that her soul seemed to think so. It felt like something beyond her body was inflamed, torn.

But, her mind had her back when her soul wanted to back down. Nicole probably thought she had Dane on a tight leash. She could withhold sex and Dane wouldn't step out. Not that the thought crossed Dane's mind. *That leash is short.* Not short enough to keep her from tearing a chunk out of Nicole to the point that she hadn't said a word beyond their farewell in the car.

"You say something, boss?" The sound of Lennox's voice made Dane pick her head up.

Dane blinked. When had she gotten into the orchestra cell? Rubbing her forehead, she shook her head. Her mind wasn't in the game at all, which wasn't good considering how wrecked her people were yesterday. They needed her to pull them back together. How could she do that while she was in tiny pieces?

"All right. Places everyone," Dane called her motley crew to order.

"Ryan's not here yet," Evie replied.

Dane pinched the bridge of her nose. "Fuck my life. He's been doing good. Has anyone seen him?"

"By the coffeehouse not too far from here, but that was like a half-hour ago. He said he was coming," Samiyah answered. "I actually texted you that he wasn't here."

Dane grumbled something that could've been words as she retrieved her phone. She had been texting with Crow and Terri all morning, ignoring anything else, trying to block out the world, block out Nicole. She wanted validation from them, but wasn't ready to let them know what happened yet. She was raw and needed them to patch her together, as poor as it might be with minimum information. But, sure enough, there was a text from Samiyah, too. Apparently, Ryan had a wild look in his eye that morning and Samiyah worried about him showing up.

"When you say wild look, you mean feral?" Dane asked. Ryan wasn't one to do drugs, which was one of the reasons she hired him. She wasn't sure what would give him a wild look.

Samiyah shook her head. "I mean like wired. He might've had more coffee than necessary. He was drinking coffee while waiting for coffee. I think that's how he's been getting here on time, drinking coffee to stay awake."

"Oh, god. How long does it take for someone to crash when it comes to caffeine?" Dane didn't drink much coffee, and the last thing she needed was for it to ruin her orchestra. At least Ryan wasn't on drugs.

"Was he still at the coffee shop when you left?" Dougie asked, grabbing his flute from the case.

"I'm not Ryan's keeper," Samiyah replied as she put her violin down to close her case.

"No, but you know what kinda guy he is. Why not snag him while you were there?" Lennox said.

"Yeah, get him to walk with you or something," Evie added.

"Again, I'm not Ryan's keeper and he said he was getting coffee."

Evie motioned to Pedro. "Well, neither is Pedro, but he still keeps an eye on the fucker!" Pedro nodded.

Dane drowned their argument out. Scrolling through her contacts, she called Ryan. He answered before the ring was even over. She could already feel in her bones this wouldn't be fun.

"Dane? Sup?" He spoke too quickly.

"Ryan, we have practice. You coming?"

"Practice? Practice. Shit! Coming." He hung up.

Dane sighed and massaged her temple. *Yeah, this is exactly what I need after this shit with Chem and the orchestra still seems tense as hell.* "Ryan, apparently, is whatever happens when you get drunk on coffee."

"Hyper and I don't think you get drunk off of coffee," Evie said.

Dane waved that off. Whenever a drink made a person act differently, the person was drunk to Dane. When Ryan came in, he was tweaked and twitching. Pulling him together took Dane's mind off her argument with Nicole. She had to spend most of her morning keeping Ryan focused. When he wasn't playing too fast, he was getting up in the middle of a song or suddenly felt the need to compliment everyone's playing. He thanked her about a million times in the span of an hour for giving him the gig.

"Yes, Ryan, you're welcome. Can we get back to the song now?" Dane rubbed her eyes.

Sitting up, Ryan let out a sort of squeak. "Oh, yeah!"

"This is why you keep an eye on him," Evie said through gritted teeth.

Dane was glad he was making sure he was awake on time to get to practice, but he took it too far. *Maybe he's nervous about the show.* She'd have to talk to him, but she'd have to do that after lunch. He was gone as soon as she said they could go.

"Can you be addicted to coffee?" Dane wondered aloud.

"Sure can," Greg replied.

Wow, the things you miss out on when you do actual drugs. "Is Ryan?" Dane asked.

"Probably," Samiyah answered.

They had a few weeks before opening night. Dane didn't need Ryan gulping down coffee that day. She also had to do something to help get the orchestra back as a unit. Something to remind them they were in this together before they blew it for all of them. Before that, she had to get some food in her stomach and some advice from her friends. Crow was outside waiting for her and grinned when Dane jumped into her car.

"Terri said she'll meet us there," Crow said as she pulled away from the curb.

"Figured," Dane scowled.

"Oh, you're in a mood. Of course, I suspected when you texted us."

Dane felt like she was about to cave in on herself. She had a show coming up in less than a month. Nicole graduated in two. What the hell was going to happen after that? It felt like all she had in her life was problems, questions with no answers, or questions with answers she didn't like.

Am I scared because of that? Am I scared our relationship won't make through these changes? Or that they hadn't made it through changes? Didn't she already blow them out of the water by saying Nicole ruined her life? Nicole hadn't ruined it. Nicole had made it better. Nicole gave her music again, gave her life. Music was her everything, but she didn't need to be the goddess of rock and roll to enjoy it.

"You okay?" Crow asked.

Dane only shrugged. She didn't know. Before she realized it, they pulled up to the little deli where they agreed to meet Terri. A few people milled about, but Terri was inside already, sitting at one of the small tables. They dropped down next to her, chairs clattering against the linoleum floor.

"I ordered sandwiches for us already," Terri told them. She had bottled drinks waiting for them as well.

"Good, because I really just want to hear about this." Crow looked right at Dane. She didn't even look back when a guy bumped her chair moving to get to a table behind them.

Dane shrugged. "There's nothing much to hear. I mean, Nick accused me of being scared. She said I've been using Samiyah as a crutch."

Crow rolled her eyes. "We can all agree that was the best thing she could've said. She could've pulled the emotionally cheating card or the physically cheating card. Either way, the cheating card, which is hard to come back from. Because it means she doesn't trust you and that'll make you not trust her."

Dane grunted. "I'm not cheating."

"The amount of texting between you two is suspicious, and if Nicole was a little more insecure, she'd be worried about that," Crow replied, leaning on the table.

Dane scoffed. "Even if I was, it'd be her fault anyway."

Terri arched eyebrow. "You cheating would be Nicole's fault?"

"She doesn't want to have sex anymore. She barely pays any attention to me," Dane replied.

Crow raised an eyebrow. "She's going to school and has a big project that requires a lot of her time. Do you really need attention that badly right now?"

Dane scowled, but Crow glared at her. She shifted in her seat. This wasn't her fault, and she wasn't being childish for wanting attention from the woman she loved. *The woman you love? You said she ruined your life.*

"I got barked at for dishes in the sink," Dane huffed, turning her nose up at her friend, determined to stay on her path of Fuck Nicole.

"Oh, please." Terri let out a loud breath. "That's not what you got barked on for. You're both frustrated over things changing, which is to be expected. You said you guys keep having these little arguments. It's not the end of the world." She waved the whole matter off.

"No one said it was," Dane replied. *Okay, I kinda said it was last night and maybe it's better if it is.* She didn't need this type of stress in her life.

"What's really bothering you? You said something to Princess, didn't you? I'm sure she'll forgive you," Crow said.

Dane had no doubt about that, even though she had accused Nicole of some horrible things. She doubted they'd agree Nicole ruined her life. They didn't even feel her pain over the lack of attention. *Maybe this wasn't the best idea.*

"It's..." Dane rubbed the bridge of her nose, trying to figure out what to say. She was given a bit of a reprieve as their orders were called out. Terri rushed over to get them, like she knew Dane would try if only to buy more time.

"It'll be okay, you know?" Crow had a sparkle in her eye that made her words seem like the absolute truth.

Dane sighed. It'd be some form of okay, sure. But, she felt like she ended it last night, especially with the cold shoulder Nicole gave her this morning. The Arctic had nothing on that, but Nicole still drove her to work. Nicole took care of her, even before they were a couple. What the hell would she do without Nicole? Little by little, whatever held her together popped and pulled. What the fuck would she do without Nicole? Now, she was scared. Wasn't that the thing that compelled her to try to do everything? *Holy shit. Was Nicole actually right?* Dane's been scared this whole time and was holding herself back? *It's starting to sound like it. Why the hell else would I be asking myself all these stupid questions?*

"You guys are sickeningly sweet in love. It'll be okay," Crow said.

"I'm not so sure," Dane replied, voice lower than a whisper.

"All right, you were saying?" Terri asked as she eased back into her seat. She pushed a wrapped hero sandwich in front of them. They all quickly opened the white paper, revealing their lunch.

Dane wasn't sure what her sandwich was. She'd eat it, anyway. For the moment, she didn't feel like eating, though. Sometimes, food helped. *Oh, that's an idea for later, possibly heal the orchestra through food.* She ran her hand through her hair. "Do I ever come across as scared?"

"Scared of what?" Crow asked with a furrowed brow before taking a bit of her sandwich.

"Nicole thinks I'm scared to grow as a musician. Like because I can't go back to what I used to be, I've allowed myself to get stuck here."

Terri scratched her chin. "Well, I'm not sure since I didn't know you when you were all goddess'ed out, but I definitely expect more confidence out of you." She motioned to Dane before taking a huge bite out of her sandwich. Mustard gushed from the side.

Dane's eyebrows drew in close to the point she wondered if they touched. "What do you mean?" She took a small bite of her sub. Turkey with swiss, mayo, lettuce, and tomato. Any other time, happiness would've flooded her the second it hit her mouth, but right now it tasted like bitter ashes. The ashes of defeat.

Terri shrugged. "You talk yourself up, and Crow is never without something to say about your genius. I've heard you play. Hell, Crow's made sure I've listened to your CDs and burned me copies of them. I've seen how you inspire your little nephews and Nicole's cousin. But, you can never hang out now because you're revising things, or you can't talk to me because you're texting Samiyah about improvements. You're constantly wondering why something doesn't sound just right. This isn't something a person with confidence does."

Crow pointed at Terri. "All that. Everything she said. Yeah." She bit into her sandwich again and smiled as she chewed.

Groaning, Dane leaned forward and let her head hit the table. The wood let out a dull thump and their beverages clattered from the small movement. "Art needs revisions."

"Yeah, but not all day, every day," Terri replied.

"I have to make sure it's perfect," Dane grumbled. What if her revisions were the things making the orchestra so antsy?

Sucking her teeth, Crow shook her head. "No, the goddess knew when her work was perfect, and she didn't spend every waking moment changing it. You've definitely lost some confidence."

"Well, the goddess was on drugs." Dane glanced at her friends, but left her head on the table.

"Yeah, but the goddess also understood she was a goddess and knew when her stuff was how she wanted it. There weren't a million rewrites," Crow replied, giving Dane a look with pursed lips and unforgiving eyes.

Dane picked her head up to shoot Crow a heated glower. "Well, can you fucking blame me? All my life music was the one thing I had consistently, and bastards took that away from me." She flexed her left hand. *Bastards.*

Scowling, Crow shook her head. "They didn't take it away. You were never just a guitar player, Dane. You've always been more than your instrument. You compose, you write lyrics, you sing along, and play five instruments. You're like a music unicorn. You've stopped believing in yourself."

Terri gave Crow a deadpan look. "A music unicorn? You're Goth, and you come up with a music unicorn?"

"I am not my clothes," Crow replied, and Dane couldn't help chuckling. Crow was in her usual Goth attire and dark makeup.

"Clearly." Terri turned her attention to Dane. "You're scared you won't measure up to what you used to be. It happens. We're human."

"You're going to be fine," Crow added. "Maybe you're nervous because this is the first time you've done something like this and the director is a douche. His negativity might be influencing you, but remember, you impressed some guy enough to hire you."

Dane scoffed. "He knows Christine." Her future rode on a guy who knew Christine, and she ruined things with Nicole. How the hell had she hit a new low in life after what happened with Bryan? She was beyond drowning, whatever that state of existence was.

Terri rolled her eyes. "Okay, did Christine force him to give you the job?"

"Not to my knowledge."

"Then that bastard believed in you, you hear me?" Terri looked her dead in the eye.

Dane took a deep breath and nodded. Calvin had been touched by her music and hired her right there. He had to have other, more experienced people in mind, considering he produced plays as a living, but he gave the job to her. Nicole pushed her to go for the gig. Hell, even her mother put in a good word. These people trusted her, believed in her music, believed in her. Things needed to be perfect for them.

"You guys want to hear?" Dane suddenly asked. That was what was missing. She used to play her music for regular people. She got their opinions and knew if she hit her mark as she watched them experience her sound. Her music was supposed to connect her to the masses, not those already involved in sound.

Crow preened. "You know I do!"

Terri nodded before taking another large bite out of her sandwich. Dane fished out her phone and started the song. Crow gave her an odd look. Dane sighed, her shoulders slumping.

"Samiyah showed me how to do it," Dane said.

Shaking her head, Crow wagged a scolding finger at her. "You need to ask Nicole how to do these things. I bet she'd have a ball teaching you how to work a smartphone."

Dane had no doubt about that. She also had no doubt she owed Nicole an apology. It might not solve everything, but it'd definitely help. *Hopefully, Nick will be willing to hear me out and maybe we can work something out.* There had to be more to relationships than arguing over who'd do the dishes. It would explain why it felt like a piece of her was missing. She had ignored as best she could, but there was a hole in her. A Nicole-shaped hole. *Fuck.*

***

Nicole was at the library, not for her project, but to avoid Danny more than before. She wasn't ready to face her yet. Or worse, not face her. She couldn't imagine going home to find it empty, because if Danny left she'd certainly take Haydn with her. The house would be empty in every sense of the word, and it would be her fault. She wouldn't even be able to pretend otherwise.

"Nicole, you okay?" Dwayne asked as he stepped over to her.

Nicole blinked, even though she shouldn't be shocked by his presence at that point. "Yes, why do you ask?"

"You've been staring at that book since I spotted you, like thirty seconds of staring."

Nicole shook her head. "Have I?" She wasn't even aware she had a book in front of her.

He put down a stack of books and eased into the chair next to her. "Still having trouble with the project?" He scratched his cheek, probably aware of the lines under his eyes.

Sighing, she shook her head again. "No, avoiding."

"Avoiding what?" he asked with puppy eyes.

Nicole didn't want to tell him. It wasn't his business, but it wasn't like she could talk about this with Mina and Clara. She didn't want them to know the nuclear war had happened and it was her fault. She didn't want them to know she had ruined the best thing to happen to her. She didn't want them to know Danny had gutted her and left her wounded, bleeding on the side of the street like road kill, like she was disposable.

"I don't want to go home because I had an argument with my girlfriend last night," Nicole admitted. Ex-girlfriend, possibly.

He blinked hard. "Girlfriend?"

She grinned. "Yes, I have a girlfriend. That a problem?"

He laughed and held up his hands in surrender. "Of course not. Just caught me by surprise. Okay, you had an argument. Avoiding it isn't going to help. You don't strike me as the type to avoid."

She pursed her lips and tilted her head. "I don't strike you as the type?" What did he know about her? He only saw her in class and interacted with her at the library.

He threw his head to the side. "Oh, please. You and Lisa don't know when to say die. Most people would've changed their project, done something easy, but you two are pushing through, doing whatever the hell you can do because you're dead set on this project. I figured you're always this stubborn." He gave her a smirk.

She chuckled and smirked back. "I'm not stubborn at all." If only that was the case. She'd have stopped trying to get Danny to know her family or taking Danny camping or bothering Danny about chores. Her nature cost her the best thing in her life. The price was too high.

"Yeah, right. How long have you and your girlfriend been together?"

"Nearly two years." Two years of pain and suffering for Danny.

He nodded. "Cool. Think you'll be together for two more?"

"I envisioned us together for more than the next twenty." It hurt to breathe. They probably didn't have twenty seconds left. The cracks in her heart bled, decimating her soul.

His smirk was now a half-smile. "Then you'll have to go home eventually and face her. You might as well get it out of the way. The sooner you do that, the sooner you make up, and you can get started on that twenty-year thing."

Nicole sighed. "You're a pain in the ass, you know that, right?" It wasn't so much that she believed they'd make up. Time wouldn't stop for her. The future would come and her air would remain noxious. Might as well get it out of the way.

He grinned and puffed out his chest. "My mom tells me all the time."

She chuckled, even though it eviscerated her to pretend she was fine, to pretend he helped. Nothing would help, but she wouldn't tell him that. "I really like how comfortable you are with yourself."

"I like what I do and do what I like. Now, get going."

Nicole didn't argue. It was time to get things out of the way.

Chapter Seventeen

DANE SHOT UP FROM the couch like Haydn at the sound of keys in the front door. They both rushed to the front, wanting to greet Nicole. She grabbed Nicole into a hug before Nicole was even fully through the door, before Dane even got a good look at her. Haydn pushed up against them and knocked them into the door, closing it. Nicole grunted and tensed in her arms. Haydn moved around them, but Dane ignored him.

"Hey, baby," Nicole said, but her voice was small and broken.

Dane looked down to see Nicole's face was drawn, ashen. *I broke her.* Out of all the people Nicole had been with, Dane couldn't believe she was the one who broke Nicole. What did that make her? The monster Nicole tried to convince her she wasn't. Dane's throat tightened, and she sniffled.

"I'm sorry, angel. I'm so sorry." Dane couldn't stop the tears.

"It's not your fault. It's mine. It's all me," Nicole said.

The words tore a sob from Dane. She stepped away, staring down at Nicole. "No! Damn it, Chem, do not say that."

"Baby." Nicole wiped some tears from Dane's cheeks and tears poured from her eyes, flowing down sallow cheeks.

"Don't talk, just listen. I've been here all night, missing the hell out of you. I don't know what was wrong with me last night. You could never ruin my life. You gave me my life. Yes, I've been scared. Not just of music, but the idea of life without you. Hell, the idea of life with you. This whole thing is scary and frustrating and I didn't know!" Dane wanted to rip her hair out. How could she know? She never felt this way before, never had something so precious. "Please, don't leave me."

Nicole blinked. "Leave you? I thought you were leaving me. I do nothing but hurt you."

Dane cupped Nicole's face and brushed her hair to the side with one hand. "No, no, no. Never think that. I've been stupid. You're the best thing to ever happen to me and I just forgot. I've been stressed, like you said. You're not at fault for what happened to my guitar. I just said that because I was pissed over what you said. I was also pissed about the dishes, obviously."

Green eyes stared at Dane like she had no idea what Dane meant. It was like Nicole couldn't process it. Dane searched her mind for a better way to put it, a way to make sure Nicole didn't slip through her fingers.

"I'm sorry about the dishes. I'm happy you took the initiative to clean the fridge or we would be growing experiments in there at this point. I'm just exhausted and frustrated over a lot of things," Nicole said.

Dane laughed through her tears. She couldn't believe the absurdity of this. They were both bawling and wiping each other's tears, like they were both at fault somehow. Maybe they were. It took real teamwork to throw a game the way they had. "I was tired and frustrated, too, which is why I attacked you as harshly as I did. And, I don't blame you for not being home."

Nicole inhaled deeply through her nose. "I'm going to make more of an effort to be here."

Dane frowned. "No, I want you to focus on schoolwork, angel. I want you to graduate and get the job of your dreams. I meant it when I first pushed for it, and I still mean it."

Nicole squinted. "Are you sure?"

"Of course, I'm sure. I want to see you walk across that stage and smile so big when you get that diploma." She stroked Nicole's hair again. "Angel, I want you to soar, just like you want for me. And, you were right."

An auburn eyebrow ticked up. "About what?"

Dane sighed. "Maybe we should have a seat?"

Nicole nodded and allowed Dane to lead her to the sofa. Haydn followed and made himself comfortable across their legs. Dane shifted, getting him off her knee. He refused to move beyond that.

Nicole petted Haydn's head. "I guess he misses his parents."

Dane nodded. "Makes sense. I miss his mom a lot. Not just tonight, but in general."

Nicole held her hand and clutched it tight. "I miss his mom, too. Maybe you didn't mean to say I ruined your life, but isn't it true?"

Dane gasped and looked at Nicole. "No, it's not true. It was said out of anger, out of stupidity, and out of frustration. You're the best thing ever. My angel. You took me out of the darkness and showed me the light. Nothing will ever change that. It's huge, and I feel like I will never be able to return that feeling to you, which is why I will run myself into the ground and do everything in my power to do everything for you."

Nicole shook her head. "I don't want that. Just like you don't want me to treat you like a child, I don't want you to do the same. I want us to be equal, but maybe I've just been scolding you about things, reprimanding you instead of truly treating you as an equal."

"You're tired and stressed just like I am. Any little thing can set a person off like that. I think we just need a moment to really regroup. I mean, my orchestra has been crazy, but we took a moment to sit down and just be. I bought everybody subs and donuts and we just chilled for a second. Sat together, ate, talked about our lives. It was enough to take the pressure off, to forget opening night was coming, and maybe we need that."

"We've been avoiding it."

Dane nodded and leaned her forehead against Nicole's. "But, it's like you said, we'll get through this."

Nicole's smile was watery, eyes still glistening. "I'm glad you think so, too."

"I will be honest, I had a lot of stupid thoughts throughout the day. I had the nerve to think I was right. I had the nerve to think you're the reason for everything and my life would be better without you, but that's seriously the dumbest shit I've ever thought. You get me through life. You're the reason I have the audacity to think I can make it without you."

"You would be able to do it."

"But, I don't want to. This has been part of my fear. You're always being this super, magnificent person. I want to be like that with you, but just like with the score, I get scared about not living up the standard. I've lost confidence. And I think it went with this." Dane held up her left hand.

"Well, you're not the only one who was scared." Nicole patted Dane's hand. "Being scared is part of being human."

That's true. Dane hadn't even thought of that. But, then again, she never really had to acknowledge being scared.

"I don't know if I'm actually scared or nervous or traumatized over my music, but your theory was as good as any. I've been concerned over not being good enough. My introduction to music was through playing and I can't play like I used to. It's a little unsettling." It was more troubling the more Dane thought about it, but from now on, she'd remind herself that she was more than her instrument. So much more. She was more than a job. She was more than a housewife. She was a person who wanted to be loved and wanted to love. She could do that with Nicole.

Nicole nodded. "I know, but you have to grow, evolve. You've been doing it."

"I know, but...what if I can't?" Dane glanced away for a moment, swallowing with the hope it'd help get the hard lump out of her throat and get her insides to untie themselves. "I mean, what if I was only ever good because I could play while I wrote?"

Nicole chuckled, and it was wonderful to see the light in her emerald eyes. "You can still play while you write. I think part of it is that you're still in mourning, and you have every right to be upset over what happened to your guitar, over what happened to your hand."

Dane shook her head. "No, I should get over it. First, I don't have the right to blame you. My hand's improving and I made up with Christine a bit. I can face her. I don't need to hold onto that sentiment anymore." She needed to go into that music room and pick up that brand-new guitar. She needed to let go and move on. She was evolving, after all. She needed to shed bits of herself she didn't need anymore.

"If that's what you feel is right, then do that."

Dane stared into Nicole's eyes. "I meant it when I said I was sorry for accusing you of being the reason my guitar got broken in the first place, for saying you ruined my life. That wasn't your fault."

"I know. I'm still sorry. I shouldn't have put you in that position. I put you into bad situations."

Dane scoffed. "You're kidding, right? You wanted me to meet your family. I'm still happy you wanted that, wanted to share that with me, even though it didn't go as planned. You want to be close with me, Chem, and you want me to be happy. I know you always think you screw up, but that's not true. My screaming at you didn't help, I know, but I didn't mean it. I was just upset."

"Your family..." Nicole shook her head, probably not wanting to remember that episode of their lives.

"Yeah, they're assholes, but we get to see my nephews. That wouldn't have happened without you pushing me and something might've finally gotten through with Christine. Life happens, Nick."

"And your job?"

Dane's face scrunched up. "What about my job?"

Nicole swallowed and squinted, eyes searching Dane's face. "I didn't push you to do something you hate, right?"

Dane reeled for a second. "Are you seriously worried about that? I don't hate the gig, Nick, not at all. It's stressful and I know I make it sound like it's horrible, but you're trying to help me get back to being me. You're the one who picked up I wasn't fulfilled without music in some grander fashion and you were right. Just like you're right about me being scared and just like you're right that I'm mourning my guitar. Hell, I'm mourning my career, but you didn't force me into something I hate. Work can be two opposite feelings at one time." She shrugged, hoping that made sense.

Nicole sighed enough for her shoulders to slump. "Yes, I suppose."

Dane pulled Nicole closer. "It's part of life, right? And, like I said, life happens."

"A life together?"

"Of course."

Nicole eased back. She ran her hand through Dane's hair. "But, what kind of life together?"

Dane tilted her head, feeling a little unprepared for the conversation. "What do you mean?"

"Well, your show is about to be out and depending on how long it runs, you'll then have to decide if you want to pursue this career and I'm about to graduate."

Dane nodded. "True. I've worried too much over getting another gig after this that I actually haven't thought about if I want one."

"Do you?"

Hell, yeah! Dane didn't say that because she didn't want to startle Nicole. It was the first thing that jumped into her mind, though. Creating a score was quite the experience.

"I do," Dane managed in a controlled voice. "I don't hate it and I believe, under the right circumstances, I could grow to love it. Maybe not like on stage, but in a different, more wholesome way. Do you want to leave the firm when you graduate?"

Nicole breathed out of her nose and glanced around. "I've got options."

"That's not what I asked." Dane wasn't surprised Nicole had some reservations about leaving the firm. It was her parents' second child, and Nicole enjoyed being a part of their dream. The only problem was that Nicole had her own dreams. She didn't seem to know how to combine the two or work out which she was willing to chase full time.

"A client offered me a job at her lab as soon as I'm done with my degree. She said she didn't want to risk losing a brilliant mind to one of her competitors."

Dane grinned. "Okay. I remember that. Great, right?"

"Except I didn't tell you that my heart kind of sank when she made the offer. I can take the job. It would probably be phenomenal, but part of me doesn't want to leave my parents or my friends. Unfortunately, I'm still not happy practicing corporate law and I don't think I ever will be."

Dane leaned over and kissed Nicole's chin. "I'm sorry. What do you want to do?" Nicole didn't pull away or tense up. Dane danced on the inside.

"Well, there are options. I could stay at the job and then look for part time work in a lab. I could work at a lab and keep only the clients I like for law, just make sure it's not a heavy work load. I could work at the lab and leave Mina with a bunch of clients, as she's the only lawyer I'd ever have replace me. I haven't made a decision. I want to weigh in what's best for our family. I don't want to leave Haydn alone all day. I just don't think he'd get used to it, not after the way we spoiled him. I don't want to be out late anymore." Nicole's shoulders slumped again.

"Well, are there any forms of law you could do that your chemistry degree would be good in?" Dane rubbed Nicole's back. While she wasn't well versed in law by any stretch of the imagination, she knew there were plenty of different fields.

Nicole sighed. "I don't think the firm has anything like that, and I'm sure it wouldn't involve lab work. I'd like to do some lab work."

"That sucks you can't mix the two."

"It does. I'll figure it out. We'll figure it out. I'd rather seriously consider things after school is over. We've got enough stress right now. No need to add to it."

"Agreed." Dane felt a weight come off her shoulders and her guts untwist. For the first time in a long time, it didn't feel like she was breathing in shards of glass. She hadn't even realized she was so tense until right now. "Sorry things have been messed up lately."

Nicole shook her head. "Don't apologize. It's not your fault. We both have to learn to deal with it, like we're doing."

Dane nodded. "And thanks for thinking enough of me to not think I was having an affair with Samiyah."

"Honestly, I've been jealous of her for a while and I was scared for a moment, but you've been through too much with me to do that. Plus, I know we're going to be close to new people in our lives from time to time. Hell, I've made a new friend with a guy in my class, but it doesn't mean anything."

Dane made a strangled noise as she felt like her brain short-circuited. She could only imagine what her visage looked like as it felt like her face completely bugged out. *What the hell have I missed?* "A new what?" *Shit, my dumb-ass might've shoved Nick to a guy.*

Nicole chuckled. "Calm down, love. He's a friend. I'm not going anywhere without you."

"Good. I'm not letting you go." She planned to scoop Nicole into a hug, but it was hard to do with a huge dog in their laps. Still, she did the best she could, a one-armed embrace. "I do get scared about that, though, which is why I've been trying to get better."

"You say that a lot, love, but what do you mean? What does it mean to you? There's nothing for you to improve on from what I can tell."

Shaking her head, Dane felt a blush burn her cheeks. "Wish I was as perfect as you think I am, but that does let me know how stupid I am for thinking you'd go off with someone else. I always feel like someone who has it more together will eventually come by and…" Blowing out a breath, she ran her hand through her hair.

"And, what? Sweep me off my feet?" Nicole scoffed and her emerald eyes rolled hard. "Baby, I've been with people I'm sure you'd think had 'it more together' and they were awful. I want you to feel good about yourself, not for my sake, but yours. I'm not going anywhere."

Dane managed a smile. "Me neither, and I totally understand all of that. It's just…I feel like I should be doing more."

"For you or for me?"

Dane scratched her head. Dane had been happy to a degree before this job, but her music thing made her itch. She wanted, maybe even needed to do more gigs like this. It made her feel fulfilled.

"For me," Dane answered. Just for her.

"Then, I support you wholeheartedly. You're not worth less than I am, Danny. We're in this together."

Dane sighed. *I keep making her repeat this. I get it, but I don't get it.* "I know. Remind me every now and then."

"As long as you remind me of the same." Nicole smiled, and the expression made everything inside Dane lift up.

Despite being in a relationship with Nicole for over two years and knowing her for three, Dane had a long way to go in realizing the scope of how much Nicole was there for her and Nicole seemed to have things to learn, too. Leaning over, she kissed Nicole. Nicole returned the kiss and grinned at her even more.

"I don't mean to baby you," Dane said.

"I don't mind a little spoiling. I want to spoil you, too. I just need you to be open to it," Nicole replied.

"Slowly, I'm becoming this new person who can look back at the old me and not think that was the best possible version," Dane said. "And that's thanks to you. No matter what happens between us, whatever road bumps, I will never forget you are the person who's always there while I put pieces back together and try to figure out where the new ones fit. Even when I say stupid things, I'll remember that. I love you for that."

Nicole sniffled a little and her eyes moistened again. "I love you, too. I love you so much."

"I love you. And I love me, too, now," Dane said, stroking Nicole's cheek with her thumb. "You've helped me get to this point."

Tears slid down Nicole's cheek, letting Dane know she understood how powerful that was. Dane hadn't loved herself in a long time, if ever. Nicole let her know there was a person in there who was worthwhile and other people could see it. She didn't need their validation or attention like she used to. She wasn't garbage to be thrown away or an object to be passed on or a thing to be used. She was worth something.

Dane wept again. "I wish I could just show you everything inside of me to get you to understand what you've done for me. It's the reason I want to do everything for you. I understand why you need to do things, like chores and treating me and junk like that because it's the same reason I need to do things."

"I'm glad you understand, Danny. You're a super, magnificent person as well."

Dane nodded and didn't feel like she was bragging for once. This wasn't bluster or bravado. She was this person who could have a healthy relationship, hold down a gig under pressure, and have a beautiful family. Experience had taught her not everyone could manage such a thing.

"You really are special, Nick. On all sorts of levels, but one of the most beautiful things about you will always be your soul and how you could use it to put someone like me back together. I'm so happy I met you."

"I'm happy I met you, too. You were the best thing to come out of dating Tyler. In fact, I'd live everything over just the same if it meant I'd end up here in this moment with you."

Dane smiled big. "Same."

"I know, but I want you to know you're worth any pain, agony, or annoyance I've gone through. You're worth the string of horrible lovers. The users and manipulators. I'd take them all again, as long as you're at the end of the line."

"Team?"

Nicole nodded. "Team."

Dane breathed a sigh of relief and felt like the world had been lifted off her chest. She leaned over, pressing her forehead against Nicole's shoulder. It astonished her that Nicole would say as much, especially after the horrible things she said. How dare she ever think her life would be better without Nicole? Who would ever go through all of this with her?

"I'm never letting you go," Dane said.

"The same," Nicole replied.

"I'll do my very best to listen to you. We can split checks for dates or however we decide to make it happen. I won't buy crazy stuff. I won't flip out when you buy groceries. I won't—" Dane's words were cut off by Nicole's index finger.

"I appreciate it. It's good to know you've been listening. You don't have to go down the list. We'll work it out."

Giving a nod, Dane kissed Nicole once more. They sat there in silence for a while, enjoying being together with Haydn draped on them. This was only the start of the healing process. Still, being able to be with each other like this was cool water on a scorching day. Eventually, they got up. Haydn took it upon himself to go to their room and he deserved it, considering how Dane ignored him last night.

Dane and Nicole took a shower together. It was nothing sexual, even though they were naked. It was more about taking care of each other. They didn't break eye contact, but they didn't speak. They caressed each other, washed each other, and then exited the shower to crawl into bed. Haydn made himself comfortable in between them.

"How am I supposed to sleep with his hot breath in my face all night?" Dane grumbled.

Nicole chuckled. "Well, this is what happens when the baby misses his moms."

"Baby's' breath can't possibly be this hot." Dane tried to move Haydn to where he wasn't panting directly in her face.

"Just wait until he starts having that dream where he's running. Then we're in for it."

All too true. "Okay, starting tomorrow, no more neglecting Haydn. Need a real night's sleep to deal with the orchestra and Andrew."

"First one up makes breakfast and second one up finishes?" Nicole proposed.

Dane nodded. "I think I can handle that." She meant it this time.

Nicole reached over and rubbed Dane's shoulder. The simple touch was enough to help Dane drift off to sleep. Unfortunately, sometime during the night, Haydn had that running dream.

***

Opening night was upon them. Nicole hadn't even realized it was time until a couple of days earlier. She'd been too busy with school. No, she and Danny hadn't completely worked out the kinks of their schedules, but they'd been doing a bit better. They weren't snapping at each other and working things out around the house as best they could.

Nicole had stopped practically living at the college library for one. Danny stopped staying late at work, unless the orchestra needed serious practice. Danny felt like easing up on the orchestra made them less frustrated and antsy, which reduced her stress. Relaxed Danny helped Nicole relax, holding her while she worked on her paper. Sometimes, they sat together and worked, Danny tapping out instructions on her phone, sending texts to each member of her orchestra as she listened to the rehearsal playback while Nicole worked on her laptop, writing up parts of the project or sending off messages to Lisa about the project. They'd met up for lunch a few times, as well, with Nicole waiting outside for Danny rather than going in. They split the check. It worked for now.

"All right, everyone, stay together," Nicole called as her family— her mother's side and her cousin Elizabeth—gathered in the small theater lobby, which was rather busy. Dane's family—the Briarmoors, Christine, Luke, and Thomas—were there as well. Mina and Shawn were there, with Clara and her son. Of course, Crow and Terri showed up, standing close to Nicole as if they were guarding her. Everyone was dressed like they were going to the opera rather than a play. For them, they might as well be on some red carpet.

"Nick!" Thomas ran over to her and took her hand. He was dressed in a little tuxedo and bowtie. She wasn't surprised, considering how formally he and his brother were often dressed to play outside.

Nicole smiled at him and put a hand on his shoulder. "Hey, buddy."

"When do we get to see Dane?" he asked with stars in his eyes as he held his hands together.

"Not until later. First, we must watch her show. And to do that, we all must get into the auditorium and find our seats," she replied.

"Then, let's go!" Thomas threw his fist in the air.

Nicole couldn't help smiling and she tried to usher the families into the hall, but they were all chatting amongst themselves, everyone expressing joy and pride over Danny. Nicole wondered how Danny would feel when she saw everyone here to support her.

Allison made her way over to Nicole, shyly tucking hair behind her ear. There was an excited flush to her face. "Nicole, is Danny going to play anything in this? I tried to ask, but she never answered."

"She wants to surprise everyone. You'll like it," Nicole promised, wrapping an arm around Allison, pulling her close for a quick embrace. "If we can ever get in there."

Allison gave her a small smile. "I could help."

"It's all right. I've got this. I've had practice in getting stubborn people to move." Nicole didn't want Allison to do anything that might be uncomfortable for her tonight. Tonight was about enjoying themselves.

Eventually they piled into the auditorium and found their seats, taking up a decent chunk of the front row. With the size of the theater, they could've sat in the back and still had a great view, but being in the front gave them just a little glimpse into the orchestra pit. Thomas and Luke opted to sit with Nicole, as did Allison. Nicole's parents sat with Henry and Lynn. She hoped that was the start of a friendship of some kind. Christine had an open seat at the end of the aisle, but stopped to talk with someone. Nicole wasn't sure who the man was and didn't bother to think on it.

The house lights dimmed and the curtains opened. Showtime. Allison took her hand and held it, but didn't dare look away from the stage. A friendly bard with an amiable smile and flashy bells hopped out on stage to set the scene for the audience while pretending to play the lute, which sounded hilariously like a sax. He got laughs when he went to tune it and it now sounded like a drum. One last try produced a sound like a piano and he gave up, deciding to tell the tale without the aid of music.

"I want a guitar like that," Luke remarked.

"So, you can be a one-man band?" Nicole guessed.

"Yeah, and it'd be funny," he answered with a huge grin. Nicole chortled a bit before they focused back on the show.

***

The end of the play was predictable because of the heavy fairytale elements. What wasn't expected was for Samiyah, the violinist, and Lennox, the guitarist, to emerge from the orchestra pit where the audience could see them. They stood on opposite ends of the stage as the hero and villain faced off. Samiyah pointed her violin bow as the hero gripped his sword and Lennox aimed his guitar like a gun as the villain banged his magic staff and it became a blade. Nicole glanced at the kids to see how awed they all were, mouths hanging open and eyes wide.

For the final battle between the hero and the villain, Samiyah and Lennox actually played their instruments in an epic and intense duel. Their posturing against each other was on level with the actors. For the front rows, they could see the fury in each musicians' face to match the sword fight going on between the hero and villain. In the end, when the villain was struck down, Lennox struck a final chord and collapsed as well. Samiyah let off a flurry of notes as the hero posed in victory, finishing with her bow in the air.

The audience stood and cheered, probably for longer than expected. Nicole was on her feet, clapping and whistling. Luke and Thomas screamed. Even Allison had her hands over her head to applaud loudly and hollered. The cheering finally tapered off and the play was able to move on.

The curtains closed on the hero and princess kissing and a light, sweet song from the orchestra. The audience applauded loudly once again. Danny had done a wonderful job on the score and Nicole was certain the crowd appreciated her efforts, even if they didn't realize it. They probably did, considering the love people gave when the hero directed attention to the orchestra. The audience erupted as the orchestra stood and waved. *Maybe the people do realize how much the music helped the show.*

With the show over, Nicole and company flooded back into the lobby to wait for Danny. While waiting, they all talked about their favorite parts and songs. Luke had to air guitar while trying to mimic the sound of the final battle song. Eddie charged over to join him and

Sabrina followed, playing an air violin while she was at it. Thomas challenged Ben to a pretend sword fight. Henry slipped away and bought the boys souvenir foam swords.

"Wow, I'm impressed by what Danny put together," Nicole's father said with his arm around her mother.

Her mother nodded, smiling. "The music was incredible. I honestly didn't know she had that in her."

Lynn stood up a little taller. "I always knew that kid was something special when it came to music."

"Yes, hopefully, she can pursue this. I wish they were selling CDs or something of the music. Quite a few people agreed with me," Henry said, looking around, as if to find those who concurred. The lobby was still packed with people, smiling, talking, enjoying themselves together with the actors trickling out into the crowd.

They all nodded. Nicole hoped Danny could pursue this as a career as well. Before she could voice her opinion, she was hugged from behind and Danny kissed her neck. She laughed.

"I pray this is my girlfriend or you're going to have about twenty people beating the shit out of you," Nicole remarked.

"I could take 'em," Danny joked, and she gave Nicole a squeeze around her middle.

Smiling, Nicole turned to Danny and gave her a small kiss. "You did great, love. We're all impressed."

Danny grinned and then looked out at the crowd here for her. "I didn't expect this many people. Hell, even Elizabeth came." She motioned over to Elizabeth, who had taken pictures and was showing them to Nicole's grandparents.

"She likes you and wanted to be a part of your big break. I'm sure she's happy she came because this show was amazing. What made you think to have Samiyah and Lennox actually show themselves for the final showdown? That was incredible. It added to the tension rather than taking away from the story. Somehow, I felt more invited into the play's world when seeing the musicians."

Danny chuckled. "I wasn't supposed to do that. I know Andrew's pissed, but I thought it would add to the music and the scene."

"It did." The music heightened the battle, but seeing the musicians made it seem like the instruments themselves were fighting, like the battle was so epic even inanimate objects had chosen sides. Seeing the musicians' movement made the music that much more powerful.

"Look, I've got to go make sure the orchestra is okay and check in with Andrew and Calvin. Is there something going on I should know about?" Danny asked, knowing they had plans to go out. This was too huge to not celebrate.

Nicole turned around to face Danny. "I want to take you somewhere. My treat. Is that okay?" Her eyes searched Danny's face, waiting for any sign of distress with the idea of Nicole treating her.

Danny glanced over at their families and smiled. "With them?"

"They'll definitely be there. Is it all right?"

"It's not some place fancy, right?" Danny was dressed fairly well. Not as well as everyone else, but she looked at opening night as coming to work while they looked at it as a special occasion. She had on tan slacks with an argyle sweater vest on top of a white oxford shirt.

"I managed to talk them out of it. That will be tomorrow because of the time," Nicole said. It was almost ten. No one had been sure they'd be able to make those reservations, especially those with children, but they had a better idea of how things would work now. Reservations were made, and their whole party would be in some insanely expensive restaurant that would undoubtedly embarrass Danny tomorrow night.

Danny groaned. "No way out of it?"

"I dunno." Nicole motioned to their families with one hand. "Can you in all honesty beat my father, mother, Lynn, Henry, Mina, Clara, my grandparents, aunts, and uncles in a verbal fight?"

Danny laughed. "I can't even beat you in an argument."

"Then, no, there's no way out of it. We're having a huge dinner tomorrow to celebrate. Go handle your business while I start directing everyone where to go. I'm sure by the time you come back, I'll probably have everyone on the way," Nicole said.

Danny chuckled and gave Nicole another kiss before rushing off. Nicole turned her attention to their families and friends. How the hell was she going to get all these people to a diner? Well, time to find out.

***

Dane was barely ten steps away from Nicole when Andrew found her, glowering. His eyes blazed with fury. He definitely didn't like Lennox and Samiyah showing themselves during the final battle. It ruined his precious vision. To be fair, he had a right to be angry. She'd want to strangle someone, too, if they shoved something into her score without her permission. But, the audience ate it up.

"Look, I'm sorry about the musicians stepping out, but I knew you wouldn't go for it and I knew it'd be great. They wanted to, and it didn't distract the actors," Dane said.

Andrew put his finger up. "They could've ruined everything."

Dane tilted her head to the side. "Not really." The actors knew the musicians would come out with them. They liked the idea, too. But, she didn't want to say that and get them into trouble.

Andrew huffed. "You could've messed up my whole show."

"I'll give you the show was better than I thought it'd be and I don't think I had the power to mess it up," Dane said with the hope he'd take the olive branch.

She honestly thought Andrew got this pet project because his daddy was paying for it, but the audience reacted well. They laughed at his jokes, loved the hero, and maybe the villain a little, and were satisfied with the ending. It was definitely better live than on paper or the bits she'd seen at rehearsal. Of course, it was helped by wardrobe doing a fantastic job and the scenery was nothing short of beautiful.

"I'll bet." Andrew sneered at her. "I don't need your validation. My work speaks for itself."

Dane's brow furrowed. "Whatever. Just be aware, the music didn't ruin anything. Have you talked to anyone? They liked when Samiyah and Lennox got up. They cheered for crying out loud, long and loud. The orchestra got a damn standing ovation. Do you hate the fact that someone wanted to enhance your art that you can't see the forest for the trees?"

"You didn't enhance anything," he fumed, throwing his hands out like a wild man. She could almost smell smoke from the way he burned up. "You were out of line. You messed up."

"Then, what are all these pats on my back?" She jabbed her thumb behind her as two guys walked by and patted her on the back. *They're literally patting me on the damn back for the show!*

"They think the music was good because of the play. It's not the other way around!"

"Are you seriously nuts? I didn't say they thought the play was good because of the music," Dane said.

Ryan pushed his way through the crowd and came over to her before Andrew could hit her with another head scratcher. "Dane, you got people over there looking for you."

"Looking for me?" Dane looked over, thinking it might be more family or friends. Turned out, it was her former family and friends. Dane marched over to them. "What the hell are you clowns doing here?" She couldn't believe she was in front of *Destined for Nowhere*.

Fae drew back, putting a hand to her chest, as a crooked grin settled on her tan face. Cinnamon eyes flashed, partly amused, but something else. "Us? What the hell are you doing here? You vanished for four years and pop up writing music for children's plays?"

Dane snorted and tossed her head to the side. "I vanished. You guys seemed fine with letting fucking Bryan try to replace me."

Maro spoke up. "Please. You think we didn't know he's not good enough to fix your guitar strings. You were gone, though." His voice was just as scratchy as she remembered, something that was due to smoking from the time he was fourteen. The cigarettes hadn't hurt the way he played the keyboard when they were a band.

Dane eyed them, trying to figure out why they were here. They seemed like they'd gotten along quite fine without her. "How'd you know to find me here?"

Trill rolled her eyes, holding thick arms that had hit the drums with so much skill across her chest. "Crow. She handed out, maybe a million flyers, at all sorts of clubs, underlining you did the music for this thing. Most people thought she was nuts. Our fans are mostly gone now, but we remembered you. You walked away from us." A hard frown settled on her face, making her thin visage look severe.

Dane shook her head. "I walked away from everything. I walked away from living."

Their faces softened a bit, and Fae watched her with gentle eyes. "Why?"

Dane shrugged. "It's a lot to explain and not even relevant anymore. I've changed. How have you guys been?"

The exchange was short and generic. Dane didn't have the time for more. She made sure she grabbed Nicole, who was still pushing their families out of the door, and introduced them to her former band mates. They took one look at Nicole and judged her like Crow had when she first met Nicole, except maybe worse since Nicole was dressed to the nines today in a creamy evening gown that was off the shoulders with an embroidered design on the bodice. It took all Dane's self-control to not drool over the dress. They didn't even shake her hand when she offered it. Nicole smiled through the awkward introduction.

"It's good to meet you. Love, I've got to go. I already see Mina heading in the wrong direction," Nicole said and she hustled away, undoubtedly not wanting to stick around for frozen glares.

Trill shook her head. "You left the music scene for high society?"

Dane put on a neutral expression. She didn't owe them anything. "Think what you want, but I'm happier now than I've ever been. Before you judge me or my girlfriend, find out what we've been through. Walk a mile in our shoes and see how you come out in the end. It was good to see you guys, but I've got other stuff to do."

Dane walked off, doing her best not to limp, knowing the band watched her leave. She wouldn't be the person they knew ever again. She had no desire to be that person either. This Dane Wolfe had found something their drugged out goddess of rock and roll never would have even known to look for. She found happiness, love, and acceptance for who she was. Screw them if they wanted to judge her for that.

Dane went to check on her orchestra. They were enjoying a lot of attention from people still around. She figured she could go, but before she found Nicole again, she ran into Calvin.

Calvin wasted no time patting Dane on the shoulder and grinning at her like he sold ice to penguins and made a fortune doing it. "Good work, Dane. We'll talk later, okay? Tomorrow, bright and early."

She nodded. "Sure, and thanks."

He was gone before she could totally figure out what that was about. Shaking it off, she found Nicole again, alone and apparently able to get her massive party out of the theater.

"Care to give a moderate success a ride home?" Dane asked with a lopsided grin.

Nicole chuckled. "Maybe later. But, for now, I'm waiting for a huge success because there's a late dinner to be had."

Dane smiled and rubbed her belly. "That's good. I'm really hungry. I haven't been able to eat all day."

Nicole took her hand and led her out. "Nervous about the show?"

"Yeah." And other things, but the show definitely.

For the ride, Nicole gushed about things in the show she liked, mostly the music, but she enjoyed the costumes as well. Dane grinned so widely it hurt her cheeks. She was surprised when they pulled up to the little diner she introduced Nicole to. It was back when Nicole was the first person to celebrate her birthday with her, before they were lovers.

Dane's forehead wrinkled as she eyed the diner. "You remembered this place?"

Nicole chuckled. "Oh, how could I forget? I first met Crow here and she looked at me as if I smelled bad."

Dane shook her head. "At least she's learned to behave."

"Come on. Everyone's waiting for you."

"Waiting for me?" Dane's face scrunched up, but she didn't resist as Nicole tugged her along.

When they entered, a huge cake with the word "congratulations" written across it greeted them along with balloons, streamers, and cheers. Dane almost jumped out of her skin, especially since the kids had noisemakers and weren't afraid to use them. Then, she grinned.

"Thank you, guys," Dane said. "And since I have everyone's attention, I'd like to do something before eating and passing out."

Dane doubted they expected what she was about to do, even as she turned to Nicole. She doubted Nicole knew, even as she looked this amazing, beautiful woman in her sparkling eyes, more precious than the gems they were colored after. *I will never lose her.* She had to take a deep breath.

"Nick, none of this would've been possible without you. I wouldn't be possible without you. Being with you has been the best three years of my life, even when we were just friends. You've become the most important person in my life, but you've brought so many important people into my life." Dane motioned to everyone in the room. Without Nicole, none of them would know her or want anything to do with her or be aware she still existed. Everything good in her life was possible through Nicole.

Nicole blushed. "Baby, it's okay. It's your night."

"No, it's our night, no matter what. More importantly..." Dane reached into her pocket as she tried her best to get down on one knee. From the collective gasp, she figured they knew where she was going with this, even though she couldn't quite make it into the proper position.

"Love, no, no, no. I don't want you to hurt yourself. Get up," Nicole urged, tears gathering in her eyes.

"I want to do this right. You deserve this done right," Dane insisted through gritted teeth.

"I also like to think you deserve to be able to walk after this."

Dane chuckled. "Fine." She probably wouldn't have been able to get up anyway, not without help. Still, she pulled out the jewelry box. "Light of my life, angel on my shoulder, you have brought me joy and delights beyond anything I could've imagined. I never want to be without you. Will you marry me?" She opened the box to reveal a platinum band hugging three gems, a diamond with two emeralds flanking it.

Nicole gawked at the ring, like she couldn't believe what she was looking at. Dane's stomach trembled and her nerves jumped, even though she was certain she knew what Nicole's answer would be. Still, the silence was a killer.

"Nicole." Mina stepped over and nudged Nicole, causing her to blink and possibly rebooting her brain. Still, she stood, quiet as a grave.

Dane couldn't breathe. *What if this wasn't the right move to make?* Yes, they had been in a better space after their argument, but maybe it wasn't the right time to propose. She needed Nicole to know despite the stupid things she said in the argument and the stupid things she did, she wanted to spend the rest of her life with Nicole and only Nicole. *Does Nick feel differently?*

"Oh, wow. You're waiting for an answer, right? Wow," Nicole said, breathing fairly quickly. Tears slid down her cheeks.

"Nikki," Alicia whispered.

"Oh, god." Nicole panted now and fanned herself. A couple more tears slipped free.

"You okay? Damn it. Do you need to sit down?" Dane looked for the nearest chair as her heart splintered and cracked. This was stupid. She should've known better than to propose when they were still working their way toward normal.

"Yes," Nicole muttered.

"Okay, lemme just—" Dane turned to grab a chair and hide for a moment. How long would it take to piece together a shattered heart? Part of her wanted to die.

"No." Nicole took hold of her wrist. "Yes."

Dane's brow wrinkled and did her best to avoid looking at Nicole. She'd die if she looked at Nicole. "Do you want the chair or not?"

Nicole smiled and pressed herself against Dane. She gave Dane a soft kiss and everyone cheered.

"Yes," Nicole said.

That one little word made the night greater than anything ever could. Forget it was a great opening night. Forget people complimented her music. Nicole said yes to her in front of their friends and family. Nicole said yes!

Chapter Eighteen

DANE WOKE UP TO the sweet feel of Nicole placing light kisses on her cheeks, mirroring how she went to sleep last night. It was a great way to end and begin the day. She wrapped her arms around Nicole's waist and pulled Nicole on top of her. Nicole squealed in surprise, which Dane ended up swallowing as she kissed Nicole properly.

A smile settled on Dane's face as she pulled away. "Morning, Chem."

"Good morning, love." Nicole put her hands on either side of Dane's head, using her right hand to comb through soft locks. Her eyes drifted to the engagement ring. She had spent a great deal of last night staring at it, which made Dane feel overwhelming pride.

One day, Dane would tell Nicole she used her very first paycheck to buy that ring. She hadn't known when she'd give it to Nicole, but she knew eventually she'd give it. Even when she screamed those vile things at Nicole and dared to think she'd leave Nicole, she kept the ring close. She bought it on her own and didn't ask anyone's advice on how to propose. The only thing she regretted was never getting Raymond and Kate's permission, but they didn't seem to resent it. They seemed to understand this was something inevitable. She didn't want them to be upset with her, but considering the congratulations they dished out last night, she suspected it was all good.

"You know, I can feel it on my finger, beyond what you'd expect from a ring," Nicole said.

Squinting, Dane studied Nicole and then glanced at the ring. "Like a weight?"

Nicole nodded. "Not in a bad way, like when you hold my hand, like we're connected from a distance."

Dane smiled and pushed up to give Nicole a kiss. It was like the heavens opened for her and delivered her this angel. She cupped the back of Nicole's head as she pulled away.

"I will cherish you always, angel," Dane said.

"I know. We'll get there, baby," Nicole replied and she kissed Dane's jawline.

"For now, I've got to get to work." Dane sighed.

It was Saturday, but Dane still needed to get to the theater by ten for rehearsals. They had an afternoon show today along with the evening show. Things would be like that for a while, she hoped. If the show got canceled, she'd be shit out of luck. Plus, she needed to see Calvin before work. But, a wicked voice in the back of her head told her to let Nicole have her way with her.

"But, you gonna do something while you're up there?" Dane asked.

Nicole smirked and glanced at the clock. She needed to make sure they had time, too. Nicole seemed to deem her worthy of such a gift as she kissed her way down Dane's neck.

Dane sighed as she reveled in the soft feel of Nicole's perfect lips. There was nothing between them. As Nicole got to her breasts, she went right to work. Her lips and tongue swept across the swell of Dane's left breast while her hand cupped the right. Dane whimpered, her legs spread automatically, and Nicole's body dipped into the new space.

Nicole glanced up and smirked before taking Dane's nipple in her mouth. Dane moaned and lost her hand in Nicole's wild, auburn hair as delicious jolts fired through her. The pleasure skimmed over her before digging deeper, hitting her just right. Squirming, she felt Nicole's free hand slide down her abdomen and her stomach fluttered in anticipation. Her hips practically jumped off the bed to meet Nicole's middle finger. She moaned as Nicole stroked her tenderly, owning her down to her soul.

"Love you." Dane sighed happily, feeling bliss dance down every nerve in her body, making her brain foggy as Nicole touched her with just the right amount of pressure. Her body hummed with a beautiful melody in time with Nicole's attention.

"I love you, too, my fiancée." Nicole lightly bit her nipple and Dane groaned, ready to melt through the mattress from both the attention and the title. *We're engaged. She said yes.* The thought intoxicated her, but Nicole had an even stronger buzz to offer.

Nicole nipped and sucked at Dane's flesh while her finger glided through Dane. Her fingers threaded through Nicole's hair as she kissed her way down Dane's body. At the first touch of Nicole's tongue, Dane groaned, which blended into a content purr, her back arching off the bed. Nicole's tongue was magic and light and all things wonderful.

"You take such good care of me, Nick." Dane squirmed against

Nicole, seeking more, needing to feel Nicole in every inch of her.

Nicole didn't respond, slipping another finger into Dane. Dane bucked as bolts of ecstasy blazed through her, giving all of her to Nicole. She keened as Nicole sucked on her clit with tender, loving care. *So perfect. Tongue, lips, and fingers.* It made Dane's head spin and drift away on a warm current of bliss. The heavens moved as Nicole had her, slipped inside of her, touched her. Another moan escaped from deep in Dane's throat, and she held Nicole close as her body gave into the rapture. Her eyes drifted shut, feeling like she floated away. Nicole kissing her chin brought her back to herself.

"Time to get up," Nicole whispered.

"Damn it. I wanna sleep now," Dane replied. She'd like to curl up next to Nicole's body, sleep for a little while, and then wake up to do it all over again. She wanted to hold Nicole and love her forever and always.

"Sorry. Adult stuff calls."

"I think this is plenty adult." Dane ran her hands up and down Nicole's back. Her body tingled, not just from her orgasm, but from the thought of being able to give Nicole one. *I want to feel her surrounding me with love as she begs me to give her what she craves.*

"You've got me there, but there's work adult stuff." Nicole shot a glare at her. "And you better not say this is work."

Dane gave her a lopsided grin and caressed Nicole's breast. "Never."

"Good. Now, take a shower, and I'm going to start breakfast."

Their morning routine went as usual, except somehow feeling lighter, easier. Dane had stopped fussing over meals in general. It was easier to accept now, understanding what she could've lost, but also understanding what her stubborn behavior did to Nicole. It wasn't fair or right to stress Nicole out at home when the rest of the world did it quite well.

"You wanna meet up for lunch?" Dane asked before taking a bite of her egg sandwich.

Nicole nodded. "If I'm not working on my project. Good?"

Dane smiled. "The best." And Nicole would take the best care of her, as long as she allowed it.

Nicole drove her to work and then set off for a couple of hours at the library. She had planned to go back home for Haydn, knowing he needed the attention, and Dane trusted she would. For now, she had work to focus on.

"Come with me," Calvin said, catching her arm when she was barely inside and pulling her toward the nearest free office space.

"Am I being fired? Or killed?" Dane asked as he shut the door. Maybe he didn't like the fact that she brought the musicians out for the audience to see. She glanced around the bare room, hoping for a clue as to what was about to go down.

Calvin shook his head, unable to keep a smile off his face. "Neither. Have you read the reviews?"

Her eyebrows knitted. "The reviews?" Oh, right. Critics reviewed shows. Reviews had been the furthest thing from her mind last night and this morning.

Calvin shook his head. "Of course, you haven't seen the reviews." He turned to the desk and grabbed his tablet. "It's all local stuff."

He didn't let her scroll through anything, instead holding the tablet for both of them to see and highlighting sentences he wanted her to read. Everyone praised the music, calling it original and gripping. One actually said, "the only original thing about this whole play was the music and it's more than worth the price of admission." She wasn't sure if she agreed with that, but it was nice to see in print. There were a few that devoted several sentences to the epic battle between the violin and guitar. They didn't even say the hero and the villain, but the violin and guitar.

"Do you know how many people last night wanted to buy a CD of the score or wanted to know where they could download it?" Calvin asked.

"No." CDs and downloads were also far from her mind at the moment. She had thrown the possibility of CDs out to Calvin before, but they didn't have the budget for recording studio time.

"We've got to get the music up for people to buy ASAP. Do you know how to do that?"

"Someone in the orchestra probably does." Hell, she had only learned how to text a couple of months ago. If it didn't have to do with making music on a computer, her knowledge ended there. *Crow might be able to help. Or Jody. I'm sure Jody knows how to do this stuff.* "Thought we didn't have the money for this."

"We didn't, but we've pulled it together after last night."

"If you want a clean sound, we need a real studio and not the cell we've been practicing in."

He rubbed his chin. "We'll get you some time. It'll happen. We need to make it happen. This is one thing people can walk away from and have a piece of this play with them, beyond the cups and toy swords. This is something they can all enjoy and pass along to friends to get them to the show or buy a CD."

Dane nodded. "What do you want to do in the mean time?"

"Upload whatever you have to the show's website today if you can. If you can't, let me know within two hours and I'll have someone here to do it. You have digital copies of everything, right?"

"Of course." All their final pieces were saved on her computer. The music wasn't the cleanest since it was recorded in the orchestra room, but it was something.

"Okay, it'll have to do for now. I'll try to get you guys into a studio to properly record as soon as possible for clear and crisp sound."

Dane nodded. Calvin was excited, and she could hardly keep up. She had just gotten engaged, after all. It was too much to process. She'd have to talk to Nicole about the CDs and downloads, though. It seemed important. Surely there were royalties or something she was entitled to.

"I want you to work on a real musical for me," Calvin said.

Dane blinked. "What? I'm already working on this." *How many things does he think I can tackle at once? I'm good, but I'm only human.*

"The music is done." He waved it off.

"But, I have to direct the orchestra." Dane couldn't abandon them. She built this thing, whatever the hell it was, and she needed to see it through to the end with them.

Calvin nodded, as if he understood, and his eyes lost a little fire. "Okay. They are a good orchestra. I'm getting a little ahead of myself anyway. I'm still shopping around for the next show, but I want a musical. I'd let you work directly with the writer, who will be much friendlier than Andrew."

"Ah, you know about him."

Calvin chuckled. "He's been throwing tantrums since day one, but I can understand why. This was his big break, just like you, I suppose. I've been doing this for a long time. I know a strong show when I see one. His is all right, at best. He got a lot of positive reviews. Unfortunately, praise for the score came before praise for anything else. The costumes came second, and that was another department where I did most of the hiring."

Dane struggled not to roll her eyes. Yeah, knowing that would make Andrew much lovelier to work with. Of course, he wasn't ready to put up with her, even when she conceded he was right. "Then, you're scooping me up while you can?" She might be able to get better offers if someone with any clout looked at those reviews, but she liked Calvin and could probably negotiate with him. She'd probably have to get Nicole to help her out with proper negotiating.

A grin settled on his face. "Well, I did give you your start."

She laughed. He had no idea how close she'd been to not meeting him at all, to not trying any of this. He took a chance with her, though, and she'd like to be as loyal to him as common sense would allow. Still, she'd talk the offer over with Nicole when she got the chance. Business advice overall might do her well.

"All right. I'll let you get to work. Consider doing a score for a play where you don't have to lead the orchestra." He motioned for the door to let her know it was okay to leave.

"I will." Dane wasn't sure how she felt about that. She was used to being there and leading the charge if she wrote a song. She knew precisely what she wanted to happen and could correct things if necessary to stay true to her vision. No one else would be able to do that or another person would alter things in a manner that didn't work for her. Still, it was something she'd worry about later.

***

"I can't believe Nick didn't want to go to this," Dane said. She stood in the middle of a huge crowd, listening to some important college person make a speech about something. She tuned out, searching through the sea of shimmering caps and gowns ahead of her to see some glimpse of her love. She couldn't wait to see Nicole walk across that stage, highlighted by the bright sun, sparkling.

"Did you have to make her?" Allison asked, tucked under Dane's arm. The Briarmoors had come to Nicole's graduation, continuing to be awesome. Everyone around her was awesome.

Dane laughed. "I didn't have to. Her mommy made her go." She pointed to Kathleen, who had taken so many pictures of Nicole in her robe that it would've been easy to think it was her first graduation. Kathleen was up by Nicole, wherever she sat in the ocean of teal and gold graduates, probably taking more pictures.

"You'd think this whole thing was Kate's idea from the way she's going on about it," Kimber remarked.

"I'm just happy she came around. She's always giving Nicole such a hard time when my sweet pea is a sweetheart," Alicia said. She held her chin up high.

Dane chuckled. She thought they were right, but it was also clear Kathleen loved Nicole. Maybe Kathleen would accept Nicole was an adult, who could figure out what was best for her on her own. Whatever the case, Dane was happy Kathleen showed such support, especially considering how dejected Nicole had seemed that morning.

Nicole had gotten up that morning acting like it was any other day. Dane had been excited until Nicole let her know they weren't going to the graduation. Dane didn't understand why until Nicole grumbled about no one going, and by no one she meant her parents. When her parents knocked on the door, Nicole had been visibly confused, and then Kathleen took over. Next thing they knew, they were in the crowd and Nicole was with her fellow graduates.

Nicole's family and the Briarmoors met them there. Mina and Clara were there as well, and they had stuck close to Nicole until she disappeared among the graduates. They were all giggles and grins.

"How is she?" Dane asked them.

"Not as dazed as when you proposed, but definitely overwhelmed," Mina replied.

Dane nodded. Nicole had been beyond stressed during her final semester, but she stuck it out. Eventually, she fixed whatever was wrong with her thesis project, but still worried over what would happen once she graduated. Dane thought Nicole might stay at the firm, still wanting to be close to her parents' dream despite having her own. Dane didn't begrudge her that. She'd support Nicole in whatever she decided.

"She'll be okay," Dane said.

"I know. I think she's nervous for the simple fact that she can be," Mina replied.

Dane glanced down at Allison. "Did that make sense to you?"

"Do you have a degree?" Allison asked out of the blue.

Dane blinked and then shook her head. "No. Lucky to have a high school diploma."

Allison nodded, and Dane wondered if she disappointed the girl. That'd suck if she did. It felt good to have Allison look up to her. She didn't have a chance to contemplate for long as the graduates were finally being called. When Nicole walked across the stage, their group erupted. Dane almost lost her voice in the ten seconds Nicole was there.

"Do you need a degree to do music like you need for science?" Allison asked once Nicole was out of sight.

"I'm living proof you don't and most musicians I know don't have degrees. You're going to college, though, you know?" Dane would force her if she had to. School was way too important to miss out.

Allison nodded. "I know. But, maybe I'll play music, too."

Dane pulled her into a one-armed hug. "I think you could pull it off."

***

Lunch after graduation wasn't a surprise for Nicole. No, the biggest surprise of the day was still that her parents were there and patting her on the back, like they hadn't told her she was making a mistake when she started her graduate school journey. The last surprise of the day came during lunch. Her mother pulled Nicole aside for a moment. Her father was already waiting in a quiet corner of the restaurant. Nicole's heart jumped into her throat, fearing the worst.

"Nikki, we are very proud of you," her father said for possibly the millionth time today as he grabbed her into yet another hug.

"Thank you, Daddy," Nicole said, returning the embrace.

"And we don't want to lose your brilliant mind or presence for the firm," her mother said.

Nicole's brow furrowed. "I don't know if I'm going to leave the firm yet." But, the lab offer was tempting, beckoning. It wasn't the end of the world to go someplace new and do new things. Life was about evolving, changing, doing new things to see if they fit. Karisa called her a few days ago and sounded like she would be thrilled to have Nicole. Now, Nicole was certain she'd be thrilled to be there.

"Well, our graduation gift to you is a little self-serving in the sense that we want to have an environmental law division and figured you could use your chemistry degree in that section of law. If that's all right with you," her mother explained slowly, as if she was scared to get it all out and then be turned down.

A feather could've knocked her over. "You want to bring this whole new piece into the firm just for me?"

"Nikki, it's always been our dream for you to inherit our firm in some way. You'd become a partner, of course, but carry on after we retired. Hell, sit in one of our offices," her father said.

Nicole smiled a little. "Well, your offices do have better views."

"Think about it," her mother said.

Nicole shook her head. "There's nothing to think about." Her parents' face fell. "I'd like to do that."

While she wouldn't be able to do experiments or work in a lab, she could still use her knowledge. Besides, maybe she wouldn't be bothered if she worked in a different section of law. It should be a lot less soul sucking. She wouldn't have to put up with the handful of assholes. Her parents came in for another hug and Nicole returned it. She felt more at ease now than she had in a long time with her parents.

"But, not full time for right now. I want to try working at Karisa's lab while the offer is on the table," Nicole said. She needed to get it out of her system. Maybe it would never be out of her system. She had to find out. She'd keep a few clients, let them call her, get advice and such, but most of them would be referred to Mina.

"Take your time," her mother said.

Nicole had to fight back tears on that. She grabbed her parents into yet another hug. She felt free. This was the start of something fresh, new, and fulfilling. She was certain of that.

***

Later that afternoon after the festivities were over, Nicole and Danny arrived home, got into some comfortable clothes, and collapsed on the couch. Haydn nosed their hands, wanting to play. Danny waved him away, aware that wouldn't do anything and laughed as he licked her palm. Nicole chuckled, too.

"This was a great day, but I'm happy it's over." Nicole sighed as she leaned against Danny. It felt nice to cuddle. She felt like she had a lot of snuggling to catch up on now that school was over.

Danny put her arm around Nicole's shoulders and pulled her closer. "That's how I felt opening night."

"I was so nervous that my parents would hate me after I walked across that stage."

Danny kissed Nicole's head. Nicole tucked in tighter against her, missing the feel of being against Danny in such a relaxed, carefree way. Danny kissed the top of her head again while Haydn pushed against both of them.

"They love you, Chem. They're always in your corner."

Nicole nodded. She knew that to be true, but this was the first time in her life she truly went against their wishes. Thankfully, they were excellent parents.

"They offered me a new position," Nicole said.

Danny ran her hand through Nicole's hair and flicked the ends with her finger. "They told me they planned on it."

Nicole pulled back to squint at Danny. "They told you?" She didn't expect her parents to include Danny. *Wow. They really are excellent.*

A small smile lingered on Danny's face. "They were scared the idea wouldn't work. I think they were also scared you'd be upset they hadn't thought of that sooner. You could've been doing environmental law since you graduated law school, but they had pushed you into corporate."

Sighing, Nicole let it go. "It's fine. I probably would've gone into corporate anyway. I knew they wanted me to follow in their footsteps, and I wouldn't have had the courage to do otherwise."

Danny nodded and caressed Nicole's side. "Well, it's done now."

Nicole took a deep breath, but didn't respond. It was done now. She'd get to do something better, hopefully. If not, she had her degree now, and she could definitely do something with it if law didn't pan out.

"I'm going to work in Karisa's lab, too," Nicole said.

"You don't think you'll stretch yourself thin?"

"No. I'm going to work at the lab first. I'll do that full time while clients will trickle in for law. The lab will keep me busy and I get to experience it. I want to stay connected to the firm, but I have to try this."

"If that's what you wanna do, you know I'm right with you. I wasn't sure what you were going to do, but I hope it makes you happy." Danny nuzzled her.

Nicole kissed her cheek. "I wasn't sure what I was going to do either, but I find when I have the choice, I don't mind carrying the legacy. I just want to get some me time in also."

"You definitely earned it. I just hope there's some me in your me time."

Nicole chuckled. "Oh, you're at the top of the list." She snuggled in even closer to Danny and glanced at her engagement ring.

"Next big thing, wedding planning. You ready for that?" Nicole asked.

Danny laughed. "I wouldn't know where to begin."

"We'll take it slow. Get some ideas." They certainly had time.

Epilogue

IT WAS FOUR YEARS to the day since Nicole woke up to find Tyler had left her house and hadn't taken his cousin with him. It was a day of new beginnings and better times. It started her on a course that changed her life, led her to a new career and Danny told it was like a rebirth for herself. The perfect day to get married. Besides, Nicole had been celebrating this anniversary for years anyway. Why not have the best day of her life on the best day of her life? Danny concurred.

"Girl, you couldn't plan this before I got this big?" Mina asked with a sigh. She motioned to her belly, swollen with six months worth of baby. She still looked gorgeous as the maid of honor in her purple bridesmaid dress.

"You're hardly big. If anything, you should've planned accordingly. You knew this date for longer than six months," Nicole countered. They were in a spare room in her parents' house. The wedding was in the backyard. Danny hadn't wanted anything fancy, and Nicole wanted something to highlight their family. Her parents jumped at the chance to host. Danny's orchestra offered to do the music, but they were invited and neither bride wanted them to work on the occasion.

Mina curled her lip. "Oh, yes, let me pre-plan my pregnancy."

Nicole scoffed as she brushed her auburn curls from her bare shoulders. "You did."

Nicole's dress was simple, but she fell in love with it the moment she saw it. Plain white with a violet sash around the waist and a gown that fell to her feet. Danny insisted on her having a tiara, proclaiming her a queen as well as an angel. Nicole didn't put up a fight, even though the tiara was expensive. Danny had good control over her spending now and they could splurge for some things at the wedding.

Fighting off a laugh and failing badly, Mina waved that off. "Details, details. Let me go join Clara and we can get this show on the road."

"Oh, yes, run from the argument. This is the only time you can run, after all."

S. L. Kassidy

"Don't even start. When your nephew drops in three months, you're going to have deal with tons of comeuppance."

"Oh, please. He'll be keeping you up at night for months to come."

Mina rolled her eyes and dipped out seconds before her mother came in. Kathleen had cried twice today and looked ready to cry again.

"I don't think I'm ready," her mother admitted in a low voice.

Nicole let loose a sigh, but she smiled. "Mommy."

Kathleen sniffled. "Getting married. Next will be having babies. What am I supposed to do as a grandmother?"

"Scream at officials when they don't make the right calls at little league games? Ask what the dance instructor is doing when the kid lands wrong on a jump? Make sure everyone comes to the piano recital?" Her mother would do all of that and more. But, that wouldn't be for a while.

Kathleen laughed, even though she was crying again. "I'm so proud of you, Nikki, for everything you've accomplished."

"I know, Mommy. Now, let's get me down the aisle before Danny thinks you talked me out of it." She wiggled her eyebrows.

Kathleen chuckled more. "She's come a long way, Nikki, and I'm happy she's in your life."

"I know, Mommy." It had taken a lot of work to get here, but Nicole knew. That mark was another reason the day was significant. Danny had changed even her parents, opened her mother up to whole new viewpoints. Danny was the real angel, and she'd tell her that when they said their vows to each other.

Kathleen took her arm and led her out of the room. Her father met her and took her arm. The wedding began. Crow and Terri escorted Mina and Clara down the aisle. They were dressed in tuxedos with violet vests and ties to match the bridesmaids' gowns. Nicole had to consciously breathe in and out when it was her turn and she saw Danny at the end, waiting for her.

Danny looked like a miracle wrapped in a white tuxedo with a purple vest and tie. She wasn't sure how she got to Danny, but it felt like she floated. Her father patted Danny on the bicep and kissed Nicole on the cheek before he sat down. Her mother hugged them both.

"Take care of each other," her mother said.

They nodded and turned to the priest. He was her grandparents' priest and had no problem with officiating over a same sex marriage. While he spoke, Nicole lost herself in Danny's eyes. Familiar slate misted over, foggy with affection. Then came the vows. They had written their own and wanted to surprise each other.

Nicole would go first. She feared she wouldn't be able to talk after Danny went. Or, knowing Danny, she'd grab her guitar and be an impossible act to follow. Nicole wouldn't mind, but she needed to get her words out first.

"Danny, you always call me 'angel,' not realizing you were heaven sent to me. You've changed my world for the better, and I will spend the rest of my life endeavoring to do the same for you. I will support you through everything, in sickness and health, 'til death do we part. You make each day worth more than anything I can think of. You're all the world and more to me, my love, and you always will be. I want to spend more days with you, building on this lovely life we have," Nicole said.

Danny sniffled as tears ran down her cheeks. She didn't bother to wipe them away. "You stole my words, angel. The only thing I can tell you for you to understand how much you mean to me is that you've taken music's place as the most important thing for me. Not the first spot or the third spot, but all the spots. You're beyond music. You've given me things beyond measure, beyond words, and I'll do my best to return that. You're everything to me, and I'll spend the rest of my life making sure you know it."

There were rings, kissing, and tears after that, from the brides and the audience. Yes, it was the best day of Nicole's life. She looked at Danny.

"I love you, and I'm going to keep on loving you," Nicole promised.

Danny smiled. "Me, too. Love you so much. Thank you for making this the best day of my life, twice."

Nicole laughed. "Oh, no. We're sharing a brain now."

"Why not? We're sharing a life. Let's get going. I want to do our first dance."

Nicole arched an eyebrow. It had to be a good sign, Danny wanting to dance in front of people. They'd show off their love and then get on with their lives, which was now a life. They had evolved and come out better for it. They were wed, they were one, and they'd stay that way.

The End

ABOUT THE AUTHOR

What is there to know about me? Not much. I was bred, born, and raised in New York and I have no desire to live anywhere else. One day, I would like to travel to a few places, but for now I am content where I am.

I started out writing poetry in junior high and continued to do so for ten years. I wrote short stories, usually fantasy and romance stories, for my own entertainment throughout high school and college. Back then, I wrote strictly for me and those stories remain locked in the back of my closet in little notebooks, written in my almost unreadable, tiny handwriting. In between writing those stories and poetry, I managed to get a college degree in history.

After graduating college, I had a semester off before graduate school and I didn't really have anything to do with my time. So, I took a chance and wrote a fan-fic and dared to upload it to the Internet. I was surprised that other people enjoyed my work and I've been posting ever since. I had quite a bit of fun with fan fiction and eventually decided to try my hand in original fiction. I suppose it was sort of like coming back around to what I had been doing in high school and college, except this time the stories were for whoever wanted to read them. I uploaded my first original story a few years ago and haven't looked back. I plan to continue writing as long as I continue getting ideas for stories and it continues to be fun.

Connect With S.L. Kassidy Online

E-Mail slkassidy@gmail.com

Facebook SL Kassidy

Other Books by S. L. Kassidy

Please Baby
ISBN: 9781311485137

Jayce Newton's life is going downhill after she rescues her little niece from an awful situation. She plans to hold onto her niece and gain custody of her, but there are some factors against her. Her girlfriend doesn't want the baby around. Her mother wants to take the baby from her, and her brother has disappeared. Things only seem to get worse when Gus Tucker comes into her life.

Gus Tucker's life isn't going much better. She recently divorced her wife and moved into a new home. She's looking forward to a new start and spending time with her sister. Before she can do that, though, she ends up causing trouble for Jayce Newton, getting her fired from her job and kicked out of her home. She tries to make it up to Jayce by taking her in during her time of need. Now, it's just a struggle to see if they're able to coexist in the same house with a baby between them.

Scarred Series

Scarred for Life
ISBN: 9781310171352

Dane Wolfe is a loner. Forsaken by her family and betrayed by people close to her, she has lost all faith in people and spends her days wandering the streets with no direction or meaning. She drifts through life, existing and nothing more. Nicole Cardell is a successful attorney. She has too much faith in people and is being taken advantage of by her boyfriend, Tyler, Dane's cousin. She's tired of his selfish ways and tosses him out. The bad relationship leaves her questioning her judgment. Circumstances bring Dane and Nicole together and a friendship brings them closer. They're able to heal each other and bring balance to each other's lives. Their peace is shattered when family causes trouble and tears them apart. Will they find their path back to each other and to the love that was slowly growing?

New Cuts, Old Wounds

ISBN: 9781310217289

In this sequel to *Scarred for Life*, Nicole Cardell and Dane Wolfe have been together for a year. They are doing their best to move forward with their relationship and open up to each other. It's time to meet family members. Dane's nervous about meeting Nicole's family, but she's even more nervous about Nicole meeting her family. Nicole is eager for both. Nicole thinks Dane should bond with her family while Dane thinks she needs to get as far away from them as possible. The Wolfe family seems to agree with Dane, but keep inviting her to things and Nicole keeps accepting the invites. Will family make or break Dane and Nicole?

Bandages

ISBN: 9781942976103

Nicole and Dane return in the third installment of the *Scarred* series. Life is good. The musician gave the lawyer a ring, a not-engagement ring, a promise; this is forever. But, they both still had some growing and healing to work through.

Healing is strange. There are those days when the bandage falls off on its own and you think you're good to go. Days when laughter comes easy and you forget the past. And there are days when the past doesn't want to be forgotten; you still need a stitch or a cast to hold yourself together. There are even relapses when the poisonous past needs release.

Share their journey through eighteen short stories of play, passion, and a deepening partnership. You'll enjoy the journey as much as where it leads.

First Degree Burns

ISBN (epub): 9781942976257

Dane and Nicole are back in this sequel to Bandages. Nicole arranges a camping trip for Dane to meet her father's side of her family. Nicole is trying to move their relationship forward, but things do not go the way that she planned. Dane has a lot more excitement on her first camping trip than either of them thought. Hopefully, it doesn't ruin what they have already.

Desert Palm Press

Note to Readers:

Thank you for reading a book from Desert Palm Press. We have made every effort to edit this book. However, typos do slip in. If you find an error in the text, please email lee@desertpalmpress.com so the issue can be corrected.

We appreciate you as a reader and want to ensure you enjoy the reading process. We would like you to consider posting a review on your preferred media sites such as Amazon, Smashwords, Bella Books, Goodreads, Tumblr, Twitter, Facebook, and/or your blog or website.

For more information on upcoming releases, author interviews, contest, giveaways and more, please sign up for our newsletter and visit us as at Desert Palm Press: www.desertpalmpress.com and "Like" us on Facebook: Desert Palm Press.

Bright Blessings